MODERN HUMANITIES RESEARCH ASSOCIATION
NEW TRANSLATIONS
VOLUME 6

GENERAL EDITOR
ANDREW COUNTER

FRENCH EDITOR
MALCOLM COOK

INGÉNUE SAXANCOUR

OR

THE WIFE SEPARATED FROM HER HUSBAND

NICOLAS-EDME RÉTIF DE LA BRETONNE

Translation, introduction, and notes

by

Mary S. Trouille

INGÉNUE SAXANCOUR

OR

THE WIFE SEPARATED FROM HER HUSBAND

by

Nicolas-Edme Rétif de La Bretonne

Translation, introduction, and notes

by

Mary S. Trouille

Modern Humanities Research Association

2017

Published by

The Modern Humanities Research Association,
Salisbury House
Station Road
Cambridge CB1 2LA
United Kingdom

First published 2017

ISBN 978-1-78188-182-8

www.translations.mhra.org.uk

CONTENTS

LIST OF ILLUSTRATIONS

ACKNOWLEDGEMENTS

The idea for a critical French edition of *Ingénue Saxancour* and an accompanying English translation first came to me in the fall of 1999 when I taught this text for the first time in a graduate course on marriage and domestic violence in eighteenth-century France. Because the French version of the novel was out of print, we had to use photocopies taken from Gilbert Lely's 1979 abridged edition published by Lattès in the series *Classiques interdits*. Lely's edition had long been out of print, and series title reflected the obscurity into which the novel had fallen. In 2002, Daniel Baruch published a fine critical edition of eight of Rétif's key auto-biographical texts together in a single volume, including *Ingénue Saxancour* — an edition now unfortunately out of print, as is its companion volume edited by Pierre Testud. And Rétif's novel had never been translated into English.

Thanks to the work of Testud, Baruch, Lely, David Coward, and a few other scholars, Rétif's importance as a late Enlightenment thinker has in recent years become more widely recognized among eighteenth-century specialists. However, the texts themselves are still not as well known to the general public or as readily available as they deserve to be, particularly among readers in the English-speaking world. Given the intrinsic value of *Ingénue Saxancour* and the novel's appeal from both a literary and sociohistorical perspective, I felt that critical editions in French and in English translation should be made available at an affordable price to a broader audience.

This project would not have been possible without the encouragement of Malcolm Cook, who directs MHRA's Critical Texts series, and who encouraged me to publish a French edition of Rétif's novel in that series in 2014 and then to prepare an English translation of the novel for MHRA's New Translations Series. I also wish to thank Illinois State University for a research grant that enabled me to work on this project at the Bibliothèque Nationale in Paris during the summer of 2012. I am also grateful to the American Society for Eighteenth-Century Studies for granting me the Theodore Braun Research Travel Fellowship that enabled me to return to Paris the following summer to complete work on the French edition of the novel. In addition, I wish to express my sincere thanks to the staffs at the Bibliothèque Nationale, Northwestern University Library, and Illinois State University Library for their research assistance and for their help in finding illustrations for this edition, as well as to Pierre Lescault for allowing me to use his two splendid portraits of Rétif in both the French and English editions of the novel.

Special thanks go out to David Coward for his helpful comments on the first article I published on *Ingénue Saxancour* in *Studies on Voltaire and the*

Eighteenth Century. Above all, I wish to thank Françoise Le Borgne of the Université Blaise Pascal for including me in the memorable two-day colloquium she organized in Clermont-Ferrand in June 2012 on 'Le Drame conjugal dans l'œuvre de Rétif de La Bretonne.' For at this conference, I was able to meet and exchange ideas with a wonderful group of Rétif scholars, including Pierre Testud, whose work I had so long admired. It is to him that I dedicate this translation, in deep gratitude for his many contributions to our understanding of Rétif's life and works and for his encouragement of my work.

Ꜫ/₂₀ Rétif de La Bretonne.   Pierre Lescault

FIGURE 1.   Pierre Lescault's 1985 portrait of Rétif de La Bretonne.
By permission of the artist.

Lescault's portrait of Rétif figures prominently in his *Hommage à Rétif* (see Fig. 4). It was inspired by the 1787 oil painting on wood discovered in a Paris flea market in the 1960s by the writer Claude Seignolle, who later recalled: 'In the jumble of items on display was a small oil painting dating back to the late eighteenth century. Painted on an octagonal piece of wood, it showed the profile of a man's face with a sardonic expression — a face strangely familiar. After scraping away the thick coating of dust on the back, I was deeply moved to read: *Rétif de La Bretonne 1787*. It's the only portrait of its kind we have from this period in the chaotic and ardent life of the author of the *Nuits de Paris*' (Claude Seignolle, *Intégrale des romans et nouvelles III. La Nuit des Halles*, Paris, Phébus libretto, 2002, p. 186).

According to Pierre Lescault, this oil painting of Rétif at age 53 (pictured on the front cover of this edition) offers the best likeness of the writer: 'I saw this portrait in the home of writer Claude Seignolle. He kept it in his powder room from fear it would be stolen, and I think that's what finally happened. It's the only good likeness we have of Rétif' (e-mail from Pierre Lescault to Mary Trouille, 14 January 2013).

INTRODUCTION

Nicolas-Edme Rétif de La Bretonne's novel *Ingénue Saxancour ou La Femme séparée* is a thinly veiled account of his daughter's disastrous marriage to an abusive husband. From the time of her marriage in May, 1781, until she left her husband in July, 1785, Agnès Rétif suffered continually from severe physical, sexual, and emotional abuse. Published in 1788, Rétif's novel scandalized the public with its graphic descriptions of his son-in-law's sexual perversity and brutal violence. Rétif's novel remains shocking even two centuries later and continues to raise disturbing questions concerning power relations in abusive marriages and childhood experiences that foster such abuse.

Unsettling questions are also raised by the form of the novel, which is told in first-person narrative from Agnès's point of view and in her voice. Rétif's narrative ventriloquism is so convincing that editors, critics, and readers alike assumed that the novel was written by his daughter. It was not until the publication in 1889 of the first third of Rétif's diary outlining the initial stages of the novel's composition that the question of its authorship seemed to be resolved.[1] Yet knowledge that Rétif was the principal author gives the novel a peculiar voyeuristic cast that becomes all the more unsettling in light of accusations by his estranged wife and son-in-law that he had engaged in incestuous relations with his daughter — accusations borne out by explicit entries in his diary.

Perhaps most disturbing of all are the accusations leveled against Rétif concerning his motives for writing and publishing this account: Was he, as some charged, a shameless exhibitionist willing to reveal his family's darkest secrets in order to attract attention and broaden his readership? An unscrupulous opportunist hoping to capitalize on his daughter's misfortunes and risk her reputation simply to sell more books and pay his debts? Or was he, as he himself claimed, trying to warn young women about the dangers of marrying men of dubious backgrounds against their father's wishes? In my view, Rétif was all this and more: a pioneer far in advance of his time with his stark portrayal of spousal

---

[1] See the diary entry for 22 April 1788, in Rétif de La Bretonne, *Mes inscripcions, 1779–1785; Journal, 1785–1789*, edited and annotated by Pierre Testud (Paris: Editions Manucius, 2006), ¶1410, p. 562 . Unless indicated otherwise, subsequent references to Rétif's diary are to Testud's two-volume critical edition: *Mes Inscripcions (1779–1785); Journal (1785–1789)* published in 2006 and *Journal: Volume II, 1790–1796* (Paris: Editions Manucius, 2010). See Appendix D in the French edition of *Ingénue Saxancour* (published by MHRA in 2014) for key passages in Rétif's diary dealing with Agnès's marriage, her relationship with her father, and the composition of the novel (referred to in his diary as *Femme séparée*).

abuse and his call for liberal divorce laws that would allow women to escape from abusive relationships and to remarry.

A Tragic Chain of Events

In an episode of *Les Nuits de Paris* titled 'Les Deux Sœurs,' Rétif paints the following verbal portrait of his elder daughter:

> Agnès had a noble appearance, as imposing as it was beautiful. Her character reflected her person. She was proud, direct, and rather brusque, but also good-natured, kind-hearted, and supremely generous. Her frank, honest nature sometimes caused problems for her; for such people are easily duped as a result of their natural integrity.[2]

Written in 1788, the same year Rétif was finishing *Ingénue Saxancour,* this description mirrors the image he presents of Agnès in the novel and foreshadows the terrible events that would befall her.

In March, 1780, when she was nineteen and living in Paris with her paternal aunt Bizet, Agnès caught the attention of Charles-Marie Augé, a thirty-five-year-old childless widower living in the neighborhood[3] (whom Rétif calls Moresquin in the novel). Madame Bizet had long been acquainted with his family, and so when he expressed eagerness to meet Agnès with an eye toward marriage, she readily agreed to introduce them. Although Agnès found her suitor physically repulsive, stupid, and pretentious, her aunt stressed the advantages of the match:

> My dear niece, you're aware of your father's financial situation and of your mother's extravagance. It's a penniless household from which you can expect little support. A very good match has been proposed for you […]. The parents are well off […]. Their son is an only child; he'll inherit it all, and these people have an annual income of at least a thousand *écus,* in addition to the father's salary. The son is a widower; but it's common knowledge that he made his wife very happy during their ten years together! He himself has a job and hopes to succeed his father when he retires. I doubt that a better match could ever be found.

We later learn that most of this is false: that the suitor is in fact nearly destitute, having lost his job due to his professional incompetence and lack of integrity, that his first wife had died of grief after ten years of terrible mistreatment, and

---

[2] 'Les Deux Sœurs', Episode 363, in *Les Nuits de Paris, ou Le Spectateur nocturne* [1788–94], vol. 7, Part 14, in *Œuvres complètes,* 113 vols (Geneva: Slatkine Reprints, 1987–88), vol. 85, pp. 3349–54 (p. 3349). Unless indicated otherwise, subsequent references to Rétif's works (other than *Ingénue Saxancour*) will be to the Slatkine reprint edition, referred to as *OC.* All translations are mine.

[3] Augé lived on the rue de la Mortellerie (present-day rue de l'Hôtel de Ville), not far from the quai de Gesvres where Rétif's widowed half-sister Bizet lived.

that his parents' reputation and financial situation had been seriously compromised by their son's misconduct.

Madame Bizet was so eager to promote the marriage that she invited her brother to dine with the Augés at her home. But like his daughter, Rétif took an immediate dislike to her suitor and made it clear that the match was out of the question. Why then did Agnès marry Augé? This is a question that clearly haunts Rétif. In the dozen or so versions of the story he presents in different works, he assigns blame in varying degrees to the people involved. In *Ingénue Saxancour*, Rétif presents his sister as an innocent, but gullible victim of Augé's machinations. However, in *La Femme infidelle*, he claims that she was well aware of Augé's lack of fortune and failed career and that she nevertheless promoted Agnès's marriage in order to free herself from responsibility of providing for her niece, with whom relations had soured: 'For more than eighteen months, things went smoothly for Ingénue at her aunt's. But then an unfortunate circumstance arose that ruined everything. My sister disapproved of my daughter's elegant attire. Frequent quarrels soured their relations, and she wanted to see her niece married.'[4] In his autobiography *Monsieur Nicolas*, Rétif goes a step further and accuses his sister of lying to them: 'Margot wanted to marry off my daughter in order to be rid of her because, being pious and very stupid, she found that her niece dressed in too worldly a fashion. This was the sole reason that led her to lie and deceive us and to ruin my daughter's life.'[5] And in a subsequent passage of his autobiography, Rétif claims that his sister succeeded in convincing him to accept the marriage by falsely claiming — in league with Augé and Agnès's mother — that Agnès was pregnant: 'Should I be blamed for consenting to my daughter's first marriage? But her mother, her aunt, and L'Echiné all told lies about her; they accused her of being pregnant by that man.' He speculates that his sister might have even have urged Agnès to become pregnant in order to force him to accept the marriage: 'Perhaps her aunt even advised her to follow that despicable course of action.'[6]

Rétif was even more critical of his wife's role in promoting the match. His anger stemmed from long-standing tensions in their marriage caused by financial problems and by mutual infidelities that neither sought to hide. He claims that, despite her knowledge that Augé was a good-for-nothing, she encouraged the match to spare herself the expense of providing for Agnès, to punish her for her preference for her father, to alienate them from each other, and to punish him

---

[4] *La Femme infidelle*, *OC*, vol. 45, p. 789. Key passages, letters, and documents from *La Femme infidelle* are presented in Appendix F in MHRA's French edition of *Ingénue Saxancour*.

[5] *Monsieur Nicolas, ou le cœur humain dévoilé*, 'Huitième Epoque', *OC*, vol. 69, p. 3025.

[6] *Monsieur Nicolas*, 'Huitième Epoque', *OC*, vol. 69, p. 3048. Rétif repeats this assertion in *La Femme infidelle*: 'They claim that L'Echiné boasted that he had forced us to consent to their marriage' (*OC*, vol. 45, p. 793). All translations from the French are mine unless indicated otherwise. L'Echiné is the name Rétif gave to Augé in *La Femme infidelle*.

for his affair with a much younger woman. This was neither the first nor last time Agnès found herself caught in the cross-fire in the bitter war between her parents.

However, it was above all Augé whom Rétif blamed. He insists that Augé was so blinded by his passion for Agnès that financial concerns — even Rétif's refusal to give her a dowry — made no impression. Rétif's biographer Ned Rival maintains that Augé *was* in fact motivated by financial considerations: the dowry of 1200 *livres* promised by her aunt Bizet.[7] Rétif himself suggests that Augé hoped to profit by marrying into the family of a well-known author, with friends in high places who could advance his career.

In *Ingénue Saxancour*, Rétif presents both his daughter and himself as tragic — and largely innocent — victims of the machinations of those around them. In her narration of events, Ingénue underscores her naiveté and the trust she placed in her aunt's and mother's advice. But in his autobiography *Monsieur Nicolas*, Rétif suggests that Agnès was not entirely blameless: that she was motivated by a desire for financial security and by fear of being unable to find another match for lack of a dowry, as well as by the urge to leave the oppressive atmosphere of her aunt's house and to be independent of her mother, whom she 'abhorred.'

Agnès and Augé were married on May 1, 1781. Neither of her parents attended the ceremony and her aunt left immediately afterward. In his description of the wedding in the novel, Rétif points to the stark differences in social class and upbringing between Ingénue and her husband and presents the first detailed portrait of Moresquin:

> Moresquin […] is a short, dark-haired man with a swarthy complexion.[8] His eyes are deceitful, his face repulsive, his mouth disgusting. As for his moral qualities, he's a monster! He's cowardly, trite, brutal, groveling, and full of insolence. Utterly lacking in ability and integrity, he's the most impudent and inept liar, the most garrulous gossiper and malicious slanderer imaginable.

---

[7] After examining the marriage contracts from Augé's three marriages, Ned Rival concludes: 'This foray into the archives, where I also found the certificate for Augé's third marriage in January 1795 […] (which brought a more modest dowry than the previous two marriages) clearly gives the impression of a dowry-hunter cunning enough to curry favor with sanctimonious childless old ladies raising pretty nieces and ready to provide a dowry for them. It's the same scenario in two out of the three cases' [Ned Rival, *Les Amours perverties: Une biographie de Nicolas-Edme Rétif de La Bretonne* (Paris: Librairie Académique Perrin, 1982), pp. 170–71].

[8] Rétif's biographer Adolphe Tabarant draws the connection between the pseudonym Rétif chose for Augé in *Ingénue Saxancour* and his dark complexion: 'simply replacing the nickname L'Echiné [used in *La Femme infidelle*] with the nickname Moresquin, suggested by his swarthy complexion' [Adolphe Tabarant, *Le Vrai Visage de Restif de La Bretonne* (Paris: Eds. Montaigne, 1936), p. 329]. Reflecting on the connections traditionally made between physical traits and moral character, Rétif writes: 'as with all monsters, his dark complexion was the outward expression of his vile soul' [*Supplément à la Femme séparée* (1788), vol. 27 of *Les Contemporaines* (2nd edn), repr. in *OC*, vol. 25, pp. 304–39 (p. 32)].

> The darkness of his soul surpasses that of his body […]. He commits the
> cruelest, most odious, most villainous acts secretly in the dark of night simply
> for the pleasure of causing pain.

Rétif underlines the radical difference in moral character between the spouses
and in so doing anticipates the horrors, sexual and otherwise, awaiting the chaste
and inexperienced bride. Once they are alone, Moresquin tears off Ingénue's
clothes and sodomizes her.

Rétif makes it clear that the marriage was doomed from the start, not only
because of his son-in-law's vicious character, financial irresponsibility, and
professional ineptitude, but also because both spouses had been raised in troubled
families in circumstances that predisposed them to marital problems. Both were
spoiled as children, Agnès by her paternal grandparents (who raised her in her
early years) and Augé by his mother, who refused to discipline her turbulent son
to vex her husband. Both suspected they were born of an adulterous liaison; both
as a result scorned their mothers, which clearly contributed to Augé's intense
misogyny and probably to Agnès's low self-esteem. In the novel, Ingénue is
shocked by the contempt her husband openly expresses toward his mother,
rightly anticipating that a man who shows so little respect for his mother was
unlikely to respect his wife: 'Oh, God! If he speaks this way to his mother, what
kind of treatment can I expect?' Ingénue exclaims. 'No,' he replies. 'You're an
honorable woman, but that bitch over there fooled around before her marriage,
and she continued to do so afterwards. That's why I'm so unlike my father, who's
a good man […]. It's she who's the source of all my vices!' This analysis reflects
Rétif's insight into the psychodynamics of dysfunctional families and shows the
way he shapes the reader's judgment of Moresquin.

Moresquin soon reveals the brutality, cruelty, and sexual perversion that
characterize his true nature. When they had been married less than a month, he
tells the story of his past crimes and of the mistreatment inflicted on his first wife
in order to frighten Ingénue into submission: 'You need to know right away that
it's very dangerous to anger […] or defy me. Since you're now my wife and there's
no escape, no refuge for you anywhere, the simplest course for you is to do
everything I tell you. Otherwise, you can be sure that no enslaved negress
anywhere in the New World will be as miserable as you.' Moresquin's first
violence toward Ingénue occurs only a few weeks later. Angry to find the bread
at dinner hard, he throws it in her face so violently that it draws blood. Even
Moresquin is frightened by his rage and asks for forgiveness, but as Ingénue
points out, 'once he began mistreating me, his forced politeness gradually gave
way to the abusive behavior that came to him naturally.' Familiarity breeds
contempt in men of Moresquin's sort:

> As his brutal passion for me waned, his respect for me diminished with every
> day that passed; he grew used to living with a woman whom he had cut off

FIGURE 2.   *Ursule aux crampons*, illustration by Louis Binet, engraved by Jacques Le Roy, in *La Paysanne pervertie* (1784), vol. 4, p. 18. (BnF). Violence against women had been a central theme in Rétif's works well before he began writing *Ingénue Saxancour*.

from her family by marrying her and who no longer had anyone's support. For another man, this would have been a source of tenderness and devotion. For Moresquin, it was an inducement to oppress me and to reduce me to the harshest servitude.

The novel recounts in excruciating detail Moresquin's metamorphosis into an increasingly abusive husband and the transformation of Ingénue's life into a living hell. He mistreats her on a daily basis and takes pleasure in humiliating her in front of others. He loses one job after another and then gambles or drinks away what little money his wife can earn as a dressmaker working at home. Ordering her about like a servant, he has Ingénue stand at dinner and serve him and his friends while the maid eats with them at the table; he then forces her to eat leftovers from their plates. He regularly returns home late at night, often drunk, flies into a rage for no reason, shouts obscenities at her, beats her, and then forces her to have sex with him in increasingly brutal, perverse fashions. Moreover, he shows a marked predilection for forced oral and anal intercourse, which Gilbert Lely views as a manifestation of his sadism and latent homosexual tendencies: 'In anal intercourse [...], the sex act takes on a more violent character than in ordinary relations,' remarks Lely. 'In many passages of her narrative, Ingénue's euphemisms and ellipses only thinly veil her husband's sodomidical demands and his penchant for irrumation. When imposed in a tyrannical spirit, oral sex of that kind becomes a degrading act for the woman who submits to it.'[9] Similarly, in a pamphlet titled *Dom Bougre aux Etats-Généraux* attributed to Rétif, sodomy is described as 'an act of despotism and tyranny imposed by the husband.'[10]

When Moresquin learns that Ingénue is pregnant, he becomes even more abusive and violent toward her, as if to punish her for the temporary loss of her charms and for the extra mouth they will soon have to feed, but also because she is less able to defend herself. The increased abuse suffered by pregnant women has been noted by psychologists and social historians for these same reasons,[11] which attests to the realism of Rétif's account. As Ingénue's figure grows less

---

[9] Gilbert Lely, 'Introduction', *Ingénue Saxancour, ou La Femme séparée* (Paris: Lattès, 1979), pp. 5–26 (p. 16).

[10] Rétif, *Dom Bougre aux Etats-Généraux* (Paris, 1789), p. 10.

[11] See, for example, Roderick Phillips, *Family breakdown in late eighteenth-century France: Divorce in Rouen, 1792–1803* (Oxford: Oxford University Press, 1980), pp. 118–20. Phillips's findings are echoed in two articles published in the March 21, 2001 issue of *JAMA*, which found homicide the leading cause of death among pregnant or recently pregnant women. See Isabelle Horon and Diana Cheng, 'Enhanced Surveillance for Pregnancy-Associated Mortality — Maryland, 1993–1998', pp. 1455–59; and Victoria Frye, 'Examining Homicide's Contribution to Pregnancy-Associated Deaths', pp. 1510–11. Also see Marie Desurmont, 'Violences pendant la grossesse, violences après la naissance', in Anne Bretonnière-Fraysse and others, *De la Violence conjugale à la violence parentale: Femmes en détresse, enfants en souffrance* (Toulouse: Erès, 2001), pp. 51–66.

appealing, Moresquin forces her to dress in dirty, shapeless clothes, with rags tied around her waist as a further humiliation: 'Languid and ill, I was nothing more than an object of loathing in that monster's eyes. Reduced to the harshest servitude, I became his servant, and the maid was my mistress!' When she is six months pregnant, Moresquin kicks her so violently in the back that she suffers continually through the rest of her pregnancy. As a result of this mistreatment, their son is born a month premature and Ingénue falls dangerously ill following the delivery.

Once Ingénue's health and beauty are restored, Moresquin's lust for her returns, and she soon finds herself pregnant again. He is once more out of work and tries to force her to become the mistress of an important official who could advance his faltering career. Deaf to her tears and her moral arguments, he threatens to beat her severely if she fails to secure a job for him. This is only the first in a series of schemes Moresquin devises to prostitute his wife, either for money or to advance his career, but Ingénue manages to resist each time. He succeeds nevertheless in prostituting her in spite of herself by introducing several debauched companions into their bed early one morning when she is overcome with lassitude and mistakes — or claims to mistake — the intruders for her husband.

During this same period, Moresquin befriends a handsome young clerk named Fromentel, whom he openly encourages to woo his wife. After leaving Ingénue alone with him for several hours during an afternoon stroll, Moresquin furiously inspects her body for traces of their lovemaking and beats her severely for her alleged infidelity. Yet he forces her to see Fromentel again, inviting him repeatedly to their home. Entries in Rétif's diary and six letters addressed to Agnès found among Rétif's papers clearly suggest that she was indeed romantically involved with her husband's friend, whose real name was Blérie de Sérivillé, a munitions clerk at the Arsenal.[12] Moresquin seems to relish the idea of being cuckolded by

---

[12] In his diary entry for 30 October 1785, Rétif notes that he had discovered letters from Blérie to Agnès, addressed to her using the pseudonym Madame Dulis at the Berthets' apartment where she had been staying: 'I happened to find Blerie's letters to Agnès, but didn't mention them to her. We must be tolerant of involuntary faults; the cruel passion of love calls for a father's indulgence' (*Journal*, ¶548, vol. 1, p. 204). But in his diary entry for 20 November of that year, Rétif notes: 'Spoke [with Agnès] about Blerie's letters. [...] How unhappy must be any woman whose heart has been taken in by these vile robots' (*Journal*, ¶567, vol. 1, pp. 217–18). In that same entry, he refers to six letters that Agnès received from Blérie in the summer and fall of that year. Regarding these letters, Paul Cottin writes: 'They leave no doubt at all about the tender feelings that Agnès and Blérie felt for each other' [*Mes Inscripcions: Journal Intime de Restif de La Bretonne*, ed. by Paul Cottin (Paris: Plon, 1889), n. 1 to p. 134]. For extended excerpts from these letters, see Appendix C, Excerpts 6–11, in the MHRA's French edition of *Ingénue Saxancour* and Appendix D, Excerpts 18 and 21, for Rétif's comments on them in his diary.

this man, yet appears intensely jealous of him. Ingénue claims that Moresquin is merely *pretending* to be jealous in order to have another pretext to mistreat her.[13] But Lely argues convincingly that Moresquin's jealousy is very real and that it reflects a masochistic desire to be cuckolded, much like Sacher-Masoch, the prototypical sadomasochist who took out advertisements in newspapers to arrange sexual encounters for his wife with strangers. According to Lely, 'Moresquin's masochism [...] was, by its very nature, inextricably linked to his sadism, given that these two tendencies always coexist in the same individual, despite the dominance of one tendency or the other at different times.'[14] Similarly, Charles Porter remarks that 'Moresquin's very act of bringing Fromentel to Ingénue is a clear indication of masochism; this is a secondary but real motivating force in his personality.'[15]

Lely suggests that Moresquin's repeated attempts to prostitute his wife, his introduction of companions into her bed, his encouragement of her liaison with Fromentel, and his intense jealousy can be seen as expressions of latent homosexual desires: 'Jealous men of this sort identify unconsciously with their unfaithful wife and, if they could read clearly in their heart of hearts, they would explain their delirium this way: The woman I adore must give herself each day to new lovers so that I, who identify with her so completely, can revel in my utter ignominy.'[16] So intensely does Moresquin identify with his wife that he derives a keen voyeuristic, homoerotic pleasure from her lovemaking (real or imagined) with others. It is hardly surprising then that Moresquin should take pleasure in training his wife to perform sexual services he would have her offer prospective 'clients'. Nor is it surprising that he encourages Fromentel to woo Ingénue and then urges her in bed to pretend she is having sex with their friend. Indeed, one of the rare times Moresquin has intercourse with Ingénue 'without defilement' (*sans profanation*), he asks her about her lovemaking with Fromentel. According to Lely, this suggests that his masochistic desires prevailed that night over his usual sadistic impulses.

On numerous occasions, Moresquin forces Ingénue to have intercourse under the mocking gaze of their maid or, worse still, within earshot of drunken companions. Some laugh uncomfortably at her humiliation and try to stop him, but others become sexually aroused and propose to share her favors with her husband. The most humiliating incident occurs during a visit to the country home of Fromentel's brother. Knowing that their friend is asleep in the room next to

---

[13] Rétif offers this explanation both in *Ingénue Saxancour* and in *La Femme infidelle*. See Appendix F, Excerpts 2 and 4, in the MHRA's French edition of *Ingénue Saxancour*.

[14] Lely, p. 19.

[15] Charles Porter, *Rétif's Novels, or, An Autobiography in Search of an Author* (New Haven, CT: Yale University Press, 1967), p. 314.

[16] Lely, p. 22.

theirs, Moresquin makes love as noisily as possible, shouting obscenities, excited at the thought that his friend will hear them. Linked to Moresquin's exhibitionism is his voyeurism, its reverse. In a later episode, hidden in a closet, he watches — and forces Ingénue to watch — Fromentel having intercourse with a prostitute.

Rétif's Realism

In *Ingénue Saxancour*, Rétif depicts the plight of battered wives with a stark realism unprecedented in the literature of the period, revealing in painstaking detail both the material and psychological obstacles they needed to overcome in order to break free from their tormentors. Given Augé's monstrous mistreatment of Agnès on a daily basis during their four years together, one wonders why she stayed with him so long. (They were married on 1 May 1781, and she did not leave him definitively until 21 July 1785.) Speculating why Agnès waited so long before seeking a legal separation that would have secured protection from her husband, Daniel Baruch points to Agnès's lack of financial resources, the social stigma attached to women who left their husbands, the weakness of their legal position, and the lack of support available to battered wives (the absence of women's shelters and other social services for women): 'Augé had the law and public support on his side; a woman who abandoned her home and child was hardly an object of pity. [...] Rejected by everyone, with no women's organization to support her and without much backbone of her own, Agnès [...] was like a sheep led to slaughter.'[17] As Ingénue herself remarks: 'leaving one's home and child is a truly scandalous and risky move!'

These social and material barriers clearly played an important role in delaying Agnès's separation from Augé. However, it was the psychological barriers she faced that proved most difficult to overcome. As Leonore Walker points out in her study of battered women, passivity and masochism are learned behaviors in response to abuse. Her insights are echoed by other feminist psychologists and historians, particularly by Lucy Gilbert and Paula Webster, who present a compelling analysis of how parents traditionally taught their daughters submission to paternal and marital authority, which led to complicity with abuse.[18]

---

[17] Daniel Baruch, *Restif de La Bretonne* (Paris: Fayard, 1996), p. 211. Regarding the social stigma attached to wives separated from their husbands in eighteenth-century French society, see Nadine Bérenguier, 'Victorious Victims: Women and Publicity in *Mémoires Judiciaires*', in *Going Public: Women and Publishing in Early Modern France*, ed. by Elizabeth C. Goldsmith and Dena Goodman (Ithaca: Cornell University Press, 1995), pp. 62–78. Also see Julie Hardwick, 'Seeking Separations: Gender, Marriages, and Household Economies in Early Modern France', *French Historical Studies* 21.1 (Winter, 1998), 157–80; and Roderick Phillips, 'Women's Emancipation, the Family, and Social Change in Eighteenth-Century France', *Journal of Social History* 12, 4 (Summer, 1979), 553–68.

[18] See Leonore Walker, 'Battered Women and Learned Helplessness', *Victimology* 2 (1977–78), pp. 525–34; and Lucy Gilbert and Paula Webster, *Bound by Love: The Sweet Trap of*

However, Michelle Massé suggests that masochism can also serve a positive function as a survival mechanism for dealing with the social and psychological constraints imposed on women by eighteenth-century society.[19] Similarly, Jessica Benjamin argues that submission and masochism are basic coping mechanisms internalized by battered women and other oppressed groups: 'The individual tries to achieve freedom through slavery, release through submission to control.'[20]

Agnès's passive submission to her husband's abuse stemmed above all from a sense of helplessness due to the circumstances surrounding her marriage: the strained relations between her parents, her estrangement from them, and the feeling of being abandoned by her entire family. Even her aunt — the only member of her family with whom she remained in contact and who had played such a determining role in arranging the marriage — was of little help to her: 'What could I do? There was no one to help or support me. My aunt was a spineless woman, who hardly dared to keep me even for a day when I fled to her house.' Her father had cut off all ties with her when she persisted in marrying Augé. Only in the fall of 1783, after she had endured two and a half years of living hell, did Agnès finally find the courage — or become desperate enough — to write to her father to ask him to visit her. When the visit finally did take place, Agnès was too ashamed and her father too self-absorbed for either of them to reach out to the other, which tragically prolonged her suffering.

Agnès was rendered more helpless and vulnerable by her three pregnancies. As Rétif explains in the novel, she did not dare resist her husband when he mistreated her then, for fear of hurting her unborn child. Regarding the very real dangers physical abuse represented for pregnant women, Alain Lottin remarks: 'During these episodes of violence, how could any woman not feel intense fear for her life and that of her child, given that any miscarriage — indeed any childbirth, whether full term or not — was a perilous time during which death was always lurking in the shadows.'[21] Agnès's fears seem well justified, since her first two pregnancies resulted in premature births to sickly children, the second of whom died. A third pregnancy ended in a miscarriage, which Agnès ascribes (like the premature births of her first two children) to her husband's

---

Daughterhood (Boston: Beacon Press, 1982). However, Elizabeth Waites argues that labeling as masochistic the result of socially imposed or conditioned restrictions 'is at best an evasion of determining factors and at worst a naive excuse for cruelty'. See 'Female Masochism and the Enforced Restriction of Choices', *Victimology* 2 (1977–78), pp. 535–44 (p. 539).

   [19] See Michelle Massé, *In the Name of Love: Women, Masochism, and the Gothic* (Ithaca, NY: Cornell University Press, 1992), p. 42. Also see my discussion of the Gothic heroine's tendency toward masochism in *Wife-Abuse in Eighteenth-Century France* (Oxford, UK: Voltaire Foundation, 2009), pp. 172–73 and 261–65.

   [20] Jessica Benjamin, *The Bonds of Love: Psychoanalysis, Feminism, and the Problem of Domination* (New York, NY: Pantheon Books, 1988), p. 52.

   [21] Alain Lottin, 'Le Couple et sa désagrégation', in *La Désunion du couple sous l'Ancien Régime: L'Exemple du Nord* (Lille: Université de Lille III, 1975), 149–80 (p. 155). See also note 11 above.

mistreatment. Yet once their first — and only surviving — child was born, she viewed him as the strongest chain binding her to her husband: 'I thought of my son, who bound me to Moresquin more strongly than any vow at the altar.'

Moresquin continually reminds Ingénue of her lack of family support in an effort to increase her sense of isolation and break her spirit: 'Bitch, I aim to make you the lowliest of servants groveling at my feet. [...] Your stingy scoundrel of a father abandoned you to me, so don't expect any help from him. If he didn't want me to mistreat you, he would have given you a dowry.' He views her as a slave — as a mere extension of himself, a piece of property to use and abuse as he pleases: 'You exist for me and for me alone, do you understand? Your family [...] sold you to me like a negress, so I'll do with you as I please. Who can you turn to for help? Obey me!'

It's not long before Ingénue has internalized this abject view of herself. After only a few months of living with Moresquin, she is so stripped of self-esteem, so lacking in a will and identity of her own, that her husband's monstrous behavior soon appears normal to her. She describes herself as a slave to explain her passivity and lack of resistance to her tormentor: 'In his hands, I was a passive being that he used and abused according to his whims and passions more despotically than the cruelest slaveholder of the New World ever treated his female slaves.' Indeed, the description Ingénue gives of herself in this passage corresponds exactly to what Moresquin — at the beginning of their marriage — warned her she would become if she dared oppose his wishes: 'Since you're now my wife and there's no escape, no refuge for you anywhere, the simplest course for you is to do everything I tell you. Otherwise, you can be sure that no enslaved negress anywhere in the New World will be as miserable as you.' The cruel irony here is that, by *not* resisting him, by *not* seeking to escape from him early in the marriage, by *not* heeding this chilling warning, Ingénue became exactly what Moresquin warned her she would become.

While it may be unfair to blame the victim, one cannot help but deplore Ingénue's weakness of character and lack of resourcefulness in dealing with her husband. She seems as much a victim of her own spinelessness as she is of her husband's monstrous abuse. In any case, that is how she is perceived by other women — both within the novel and among Rétif's female readers. For example, in a letter to Rétif, his close friend Grimod de La Reynière conveyed the criticism of the novel expressed by his aunt, Madame de Beausset:

> In her view, the moment Ingénue allowed herself to be debased, she no longer seemed worthy of compassion. [...] At her husband's first attempt to degrade her, [...] she should have fled from him and sought refuge with the first person she encountered. I tried to defend the author by insisting that he had merely recounted what actually happened. This angered my aunt even more; she thought it was shameful that you should dishonor your wife and children this way in the eyes of the public. Indeed, a book of this kind can only cause

irreparable harm to the reputation of Madame Auger, who is debased in a truly abhorrent manner and plays a pathetic, contemptible role throughout the entire work. [...] There's every indication that she was treated like the most abject slave, and that she endured this treatment with an indolence that comes from weakness.[22]

In *Monsieur Nicolas*, Rétif recalls that the Countess of Boufflers-Rouvrel had also reacted to his novel with great indignation for similar reasons.[23]

FIGURE 3.   1806 Portrait by Louis-Léopold Boilly of Rétif's close friend Alexandre-Balthazar-Laurent Grimod de La Reynière (1758–1838). (BnF)

---

[22] La Reynière conveyed his aunt's objections to the novel in a letter to Rétif dated 29 May 1791, which Rétif reprinted in *Le Drame de la vie*, vol. 5, *OC*, vol. 38, p. 1317. For further excerpts from this letter, see Appendix C, Excerpt 29, in the MHRA's French edition of *Ingénue Saxancour*. Madame de Beausset's criticisms of *Ingénue Saxancour* echo those La Reynière himself made in 1786 of *La Femme infidelle*, which included an earlier version of Agnès's story.
[23] Rétif, *Monsieur Nicolas*, 'Neuvième Epoque', *OC*, vol. 69, p. 3144.

Ingénue's working-class neighbors (presumably modeled after Agnès's neighbors in Paris) react to her passive acceptance of oppression and degradation in much the same way as the aristocratic de Beausset and de Boufflers. When Ingénue's maid boasts in the neighborhood of whipping her mistress at her master's bidding, the neighbors are outraged. Five of the women burst into the apartment in Moresquin's absence, beat the maid soundly, order her to pack her bags, and then depart without speaking a word to Ingénue, who watches the scene dumbfounded. 'They barely looked at me,' she remarks.

> Based on what they said, I realized they took me for a woman with no feelings, no heart, who stayed with a monster like Moresquin out of sheer stupidity.[24] Alas! They didn't know that that I was utterly lacking in resources and support! [...] Yet what they said gave me a new idea that might prove helpful and that I was able to put to use that very same evening.

While this passage seems to confirm Ingénue's spinelessness, it also illustrates quite strikingly how a battered woman's sense of helplessness can be transformed by the solidarity and intervention of other women. The 'new idea' that Ingénue's neighbors inspired in her was the need for witnesses to her mistreatment. When she flees to her aunt's house that same night after Moresquin threatens to kill her for firing their maid, she refuses to return home when her husband comes to claim her unless her aunt's maid accompanies them. The servant witnesses Moresquin's verbal abuse first-hand and reports it to her mistress. Not until she had a witness to her husband's abuse does her aunt finally believe her.

The positive effects of female solidarity are illustrated even more strikingly in the episode discussed earlier concerning the Moresquins' weekend visit to the Fromentels' country house. After Moresquin awakens the entire household with his violent lovemaking and obscene language, Fromentel's sister-in-law is so outraged that she sternly chastises him for his behavior and demands an apology, which he sheepishly gives. Before the Moresquins leave, Madame Fromentel takes Ingénue aside and urges her to be firmer with her husband and no longer tolerate his mistreatment: 'Bare your teeth to that cowardly brute, resist him, and you'll see the results!' Although she seems more sympathetic to her plight than Ingénue's neighbors, Madame Fromentel suggests here that by *not* resisting her husband's abusive behavior, Ingénue is partly responsible for her own oppression.

---

[24] Like Ingénue's neighbors, Mary Wollstonecraft expresses scorn for women who passively submit to mistreatment. To Rousseau's claim that it is woman's lot to obey even a tyrannical husband, she retorts: 'Of what materials can that heart be composed, which can melt when insulted, and instead of revolting at injustice, kiss the rod? [...] Let the husband beware of trusting too implicitly to this servile obedience, for if his wife can with winning sweetness caress him when angry, [...] she may do the same after parting with a lover'. See *A Vindication of the Rights of Woman with Strictures on Political and Moral Subjects* [1792] (New York: Source Book Press, 1971), p. 106.

Following her advice, Ingénue resolves to stand up to her husband and to respond to any threat of violence with violence of her own. When he raises his arm to strike her during the trip home, she cries: 'If you dare strike me, you monster, I'll kill you, unless you kill me first!' When he threatens her again, she pulls out a knife, ready to defend herself. Like most bullies, Moresquin is really a coward at heart; he backs down and hides behind Fromentel in fear. For the first time in her marriage, Ingénue is able to speak her mind and to denounce her husband's mistreatment:

> I reproached him for his scandalous, cruel, and despicable behavior. I was like a madwoman, a fury. 'Monster! My mind is made up. [...] I'm resolved to kill you or to die, but to die avenged!' [...] Moresquin remained silent. As for me, I was trembling all over, but deep down inside, I was feeling only the courage I had just shown through my words.

In this episode, Rétif offers a penetrating analysis of the psychology of the battered wife. He shows that it is not enough to urge a woman to resist abuse; one must explain to her *how* and *why* to resist. The positive effects of Madame Fromentel's counsel show the importance of offering solidarity and firm advice to the victims of domestic abuse. Astonished by the immediate improvement in Moresquin's behavior once she shows firm resistance to him, Ingénue was deeply grateful to Madame Fromentel for her help, 'for she was not the first to have given me this advice, but she was the only one who had spoken to me forcefully enough to persuade me to take it seriously.' Yet at the same time, Rétif shows the dangers of violent resistance, since Ingénue is prepared to kill Moresquin if he abuses her further or be killed by him defending herself. As heroic as her resistance may seem, it is a sober reminder of the multitudes of women condemned to death for murdering abusive husbands or killed trying to fight back. A second, even more tragic consequence of responding to violence with violence is that it can lead to child-abuse by abused spouses — or, at the very least, to an increasingly violent home environment that has a negative impact on children. This is, in fact, what occurs in Ingénue's own marriage:

> At the slightest murmur from his son, Moresquin pushed me out of bed to tend to him, even though he needed nothing. [...] I finally rebelled against this and, to punish the child for his capriciousness, I whipped him. Furious, Moresquin rushed toward me in the darkness with his dagger. I threw open the windows and called to the night watchman for help [...]. What a life!

Ingénue found that this violent resistance gradually lost its effectiveness and proved too draining for her, both physically and emotionally. If she relaxed her vigilance even slightly, Moresquin immediately took advantage. She also sensed that outsiders, unaware of the abuse she had suffered, disapproved of her behavior. In any case, Moresquin soon realized that Ingénue was no match for him physically and that her father was unable — or unwilling — to back up her threats of reprisals if he mistreated her: 'Seeing that nothing happened if he mistreated me, Moresquin [...] gradually became as brutal as before.'

Although Ingénue fled her husband on numerous occasions,[25] she always returned to him within a day or two under pressure from her family, who at first did not seem to take her complaints of abuse seriously and, later, when they did, feared the domestic turmoil, scandal, and expense a separation would entail:

> My mother shuddered at the thought that she and my father would have to provide for me. She arranged things in a way that led my father to insist that I return to Moresquin. He took me there himself and even stooped so low as to speak in a cordial manner to that wretch, thereby worsening my situation. Moresquin believed that my father was taking his side against me, as my mother later assured him. Seeing that I no longer had any support, he started to persecute me again.

When Ingénue's situation became even more desperate in the third year of her marriage, forcing her to flee to her parents' house with increasing frequency, her father was sympathetic to her plight, but insisted each time that she return to her husband. After weeks of escalating violence and nightly threats to smother her in bed, Moresquin pursued her one night with his sword, which he thrust at her through the floorboards of the attic where she took refuge before escaping to her parents' home. When her parents again sent her back to her husband, Ingénue was in such despair that she resolved to kill herself in such a way that Moresquin would be charged with murder and then executed. The tension was defused by the arrival of her mother, but this near-death experience gave Ingénue the courage to reveal at last the full horror of her situation to her father and to ask for his help in securing a permanent separation. Thus it was not until after four years of marriage, when her situation became utterly unbearable, that Ingénue overcame her shame and disclosed the full extent of the abuse she had suffered. Even then, she claims that there were certain details she could not bring herself to recount.

Given Ingénue's utter lack of resources, leaving her husband was out of the question without her family's moral, financial, and legal support. It was not until

---

[25] Ingénue flees from her husband seven times in the novel: to her aunt's home in mid-December 1782 and January 1783, to her parents' home in late January 1785 and late February of that year, and twice again before leaving him definitively in July 1785. Several of these dates match Rétif's accounts in *Monsieur Nicolas* ('Neuvième Epoque', *OC*, vol. 69, pp. 3100–01) and in his diary (¶479, vol. 1, p. 172; ¶491, vol. 1, p. 177; ¶521, vol. 1, p. 189). A key difference is that, according to these accounts, when Agnès fled in January 1785, she went to Blérie's apartment, not to a neighbor's (as Rétif claims in the novel). Dismayed to learn that Blérie was not married and fearing that Agnès's reputation might be compromised, Rétif took her to his apartment for the night and back to Augé the following day. For Rétif's account of this incident in *Monsieur Nicolas*, see Appendix B, Excerpt 4, in MHRA's French edition of *Ingénue Saxancour*.

her father was fully convinced that her life was in danger that he agreed to help her obtain a legal separation. But even then, her father left the decision up to her and pointed out the negative consequences of leaving her husband: the social stigma attached, the expense and complications of the legal proceedings, the risk of retaliation from her husband, and, above all, the fact that she would have to leave her young son with Moresquin until the hearing and perhaps even definitively. Prior to the 1789 Revolution, French custody laws were strongly biased in favor of fathers' rights, particularly when male children were involved — especially if charges of adultery had been brought against the mother.[26] Since Moresquin (like Augé) had publicly accused his wife of adultery, it would have been difficult for her to secure custody of her son without a bitter court battle, which she risked losing. Not surprisingly, the child remained with his father and Ingénue (like Agnès) never sought custody of him.

After finally escaping from her waking nightmare, Ingénue's joy is clouded by feelings of guilt and anguish from having to leave her young son with Moresquin, who clearly was unfit to raise him:

> For the first time in four years, I went to bed in peace, feeling a deep tranquility that nothing could disturb. Oh, what a delicious pleasure it was to be mistress of myself after such a long servitude! [...] I nevertheless felt a cruel torment to have left our four-year-old son in Moresquin's care [...]. I didn't want to leave my doves with him because he once amused himself by twisting their necks. I didn't want to leave my little dog with him, and yet I left my son behind! But I had no choice!

When Augé finally tracks down Ingénue where she is hiding, her despair is intensified by the fact that he has turned their son against her in retaliation for leaving him: 'When I tried to kiss the child, he pulled away and tried to scratch me. I left in tears, filled with even greater loathing for the wretch who was robbing me of everything he could!'

It was not until February 1786 that Agnès finally filed for a legal separation, in order to give herself legal protection from Augé's stalking and continued violence against her. The court eventually granted her a separation and permission to live with her father and ordered Augé to leave her alone, an order he did not always obey. Although divorce became legal in France in September 1792, Agnès did not actually file for a divorce until July 1793 on the grounds of incompatibility, rather than physical abuse. By then, she had begun a liaison with Louis-Claude Vignon,

---

[26] Even under the liberal divorce law of 1792, children seven years or older were entrusted to their father's care in cases of divorce by mutual consent or for reasons of incompatibility, and mothers accused of adultery by their husbands were routinely deprived of custody of younger children as well. Regarding French custody laws of the period, see Phillips, *Family Breakdown*, pp. 171–75.

an office clerk ten years her junior. A few days after her divorce was granted in February 1794, Agnès left her father's home to live with Vignon, to whom she bore a son that August. However, the couple did not marry until 1798. Perhaps Agnès's experience with Augé made her wary of marriage as an institution.

Motives for Writing and Publishing the Novel

Rétif claims that his primary aim in writing *Ingénue Saxancour* was didactic and moralistic: the desire to warn young women of the dangerous consequences of disobeying their parents in the choice of a husband and of failing to inquire into the financial situation, morals, and background of a suitor before agreeing to marry him. The novel's subtitle reflects its ostensibly didactic purpose: *Histoire propre à démontrer combien il est dangereux pour les filles de se marier par entêtement et avec précipitation, malgré leurs parents: Ecrite par elle-même.* [Story illustrating how dangerous it is for young women to marry obstinately and hastily against their parents' wishes: Written by herself.] 'If this is Rétif's main motive in writing the novel,' asserts Porter, 'it implies [...] a certain pride in the infallibility of his own judgment.'[27] In a preface to the novel, the fictional editor[28] insists on the need to reinforce paternal authority to counteract romantic notions spread by the popular literature of the period that encouraged women to follow their own heart instead of their fathers' wishes in choosing a husband. Rétif reiterates this didactic message at several key turning points of the novel, such as when Ingénue finally has the courage to leave her husband:

> I have recounted all this for the sole purpose of showing young women the terrible consequences of my transgression and the dangers of failing to make careful inquiries into the character and morals of one's suitor. Alas! For in taking a husband, we give ourselves a master [...] who has control over our body, our soul, even our chastity, indeed over the happiness or sorrow of every moment of our life!

In a postscript to the novel, Rétif insists on the need to communicate this lesson to his readers as forcefully as possible by giving a frank, unvarnished account of

---

[27] Porter, p. 320, n. 56.

[28] *La Femme infidelle* was first published under the pen name Maribert-Courtenay. In a second postscript appended to the unabridged edition of *Ingénue Saxancour*, Marivert is again presented as a close friend of the narrator's family and as 'editor' of this equally controversial text, which the family was supposedly reluctant to publish: 'It is I, *Marivert*, who now takes up the pen to complete this text that I'm publishing, without the consent either of my friend Mr. Saxancour, nor of Madame Ingénue his daughter' (*OC*, vol. 55, p. 257). A footnote found at the end of the preface to *La Femme infidelle* explains the discrepancy in spelling: 'The name is pronounced Marivert; it's an ancient Celtic name [...]'. He then goes on to trace the fictional editor's lineage back to the bastard son of the 'illustrious house of Courtenay' in the Loiret region of north central France

what happened — in all its complexity and horror — in order to best serve the public interest: 'It's the great, indeed immeasurable public good served by this work — that of edifying young women — that has compelled me to publish it.'[29] In *Monsieur Nicolas*, reflecting on his reasons for writing *Ingénue Saxancour*, Rétif underscores his 'boldness to tell the whole truth, jeopardizing my reputation and that of others, sacrificing them with me to the public good.'[30] Commenting on Rétif's writings on marriage, which together constitute a kind of *'manuel de morale conjugale'* [guide to moral behavior in marriage'], Testud observes that his didacticism tends to be rather shallow and self-serving and that *Ingénue Saxancour* was written much more as a personal vendetta against Augé than as a useful moral lesson for the public.[31]

At the beginning of her tale of marital misery, Ingénue puts forth a Rousseauistic pact of truth and sincerity: 'My intention is to omit no element of the story. All the details are important, and those that may seem the most trivial often have a strong connection to what happened later.' And later she adds: 'I wish to tell only the naked truth, pure and simple.'[32] In Baruch's view, Rétif's fierce adherence to what he considers the truth — regardless of who might be hurt by these revelations — constitutes 'the seed of all the narcissistic literature of the twentieth century, a kind of writing that stems neither from Montaigne nor Rousseau, characterized by a violence, a bitterness, and a display of private life that are without precedent.'[33]

Despite Rétif's claims that the desire to serve the public good was his chief motive in writing *Ingénue Saxancour*, most of his biographers agree that he published the novel above all to denounce his son-in-law's mistreatment of his daughter and his wife's role in promoting the marriage. In *Les Nuits de Paris*, Rétif admits that this was his chief motivation in writing both *La Femme infidelle* and *Ingénue Saxancour*: 'These two works are not novels, but *factums* —

---

[29] This passage, attributed to the fictional editor Marivert-Courtenay, appears in the second of two postscripts at the end of the novel. For a discussion of the role attributed to Marivert-Courtenay (sometimes spelled Maribert) in Rétif's works, see the section titled 'About the Text'.

[30] *Monsieur Nicolas*, *OC*, vol. 68, p. 2916.

[31] Pierre Testud, *Restif de La Bretonne et la création littéraire* (Geneva: Droz, 1977), pp. 250–51.

[32] In a text titled 'Memento' appended to Paul Cottin's edition of the diary, Rétif defends his commitment to presenting the truth, however disturbing it might be to some readers: I beg to inform fair-minded readers that my approach is completely different from that of other novelists who alter and distort their story to suit their needs: for I present only true facts and follow them wherever they lead. I will never lie or mislead. Too bad for me if the truth has become monstrous and if people prefer what's plausible to what's true' ('Memento', fol. 121, Cottin, p. 325). According to Cottin, this text was found by Funck-Brentano in the Archives de la Bastille, along with a few other short manuscripts in Rétif's handwriting. The text is not dated, but might well refer to *Ingénue Saxancour*.

[33] Baruch, *Restif de La Bretonne* (1996), p. 184.

statements of fact and a settling of scores.'[34] In the fictional editor's preface to the novel, Rétif summarizes his grievances against his son-in-law. 'What will readers find in this work?' he asks.

> A reckless girl who, against her father's wishes, marries a despicable, deceitful man, who before their marriage had lied about his character and financial situation; [...] a man who, after the wedding, reveals his true self and subjects his unhappy wife to all the vile caprices of a debauched libertine, [...] to all the torture that an executioner can inflict; a man who compels her to flee and then pursues her in a rage after she has escaped his fury.

In *Monsieur Nicolas*, Rétif expresses the intense pain and desire for vengeance he still felt years later over his daughter's marriage: 'That scoundrel, that monster brought her nothing but misery! I call down the wrath of heaven upon his head! May he bear the full burden of the suffering he has inflicted on her, the memory of which still rains down on my wretched heart like drops of boiling oil!'[35]

In writing and publishing *Ingénue Saxancour*, Rétif was also strongly motivated by a desire to clear himself of blame for his daughter's disastrous marriage and for not acting sooner to free her from her tormentor. He underscores his firm opposition to the match in order to minimize his responsibility and to justify his refusal to give Agnès a dowry or to visit her during the early years of her marriage. And once he learned of the problems in his daughter's marriage, he claimed, somewhat hypocritically, that he was too upset by her situation to intervene, as in *La Femme infidelle*, where we read: 'My Papa came to see me twice: once at the end of 178* and a second time early last year. He did not come back for a long time due to the pain my situation caused him.'[36] As we have seen, Rétif spills a great deal of ink blaming others for what happened — especially his wife and Augé, but also his sister and Agnès herself. He expresses regret for not helping his daughter sooner, but insists that his wife and sister hid the truth from him and that, when he finally learned the truth, he was too sick to intervene as quickly or as forcefully as he would have liked.

---

[34] Rétif, *Nuits de Paris, ou le Spectateur nocturne*, 7 vols in 14 parts (London, 1788–1789), vol. 7 (Part 14), Episode 168, p. 3146. To this claim, Rétif's friend Grimod de la Reynière responded: 'The arguments you invoke to justify the publication of *Ingénue Saxancour* are more specious than solid. If it's a factum, why publish it as a novel?' Letter of 7 July 1791 to Rétif reprinted at the end of vol. 5 of *Le Drame de la vie*, *OC*, vol. 38, p. 1321. For extended excerpts from this letter, see Appendix C, Excerpt 31, in MHRA's French edition of *Ingénue Saxancour*.

[35] 'Mes Ouvrages', appendix to *Monsieur Nicolas*, *OC*, vol. 71, p. 4579.

[36] *La Femme infidelle*, *OC*, vol. 45, p. 811. In *Ingénue Saxancour*, Rétif gives the date of this first visit as 25 November 1783, which corresponds to the date given in his diary. In the novel, Ingénue receives a second visit from her father in late June or early July 1784 — eight months after his first visit. However, there is no mention of this second visit in Rétif's diary, in which he normally recorded such events. The diary, like the novel, records more frequent visits between father and daughter in the months leading up to her separation from Augé in July 1785.

In an episode of *Les Nuits de Paris* titled 'Les Deux Sœurs' (1788), Rétif summarizes his daughter's conjugal misfortunes and then concludes: 'Agnès was supremely unhappy, but her father was unaware of her situation for a long time; and when he finally learned of it, already ailing and weakened by age, he was unable to make full use of his paternal authority to punish the man responsible for her misery. He simply petitioned the local magistrate to allow his ill-treated daughter to take up residence in his home.'[37]

Rétif's use of third-person narration may reflect a desire to distance himself from events that were still extremely painful to him, but also from accepting responsibility for what happened. The closest Rétif ever came to an admission of responsibility was in *Monsieur Nicolas*, where he expressed bitter regret for entrusting his daughter to his sister's care: 'Woe is me! Knowing how narrow-minded she was, why did I ever let my daughter go live with her! But despite my misgivings, everything was arranged, much against my better judgment.'[38]

In an intriguing article concerning Rétif's secret activities as a police spy in the 1770s, Baruch suggests another reason why he may have hesitated to intervene in his daughter's marital problems: Augé, who had worked as an informant for the Paris police's vice squad during that period, knew of Rétif's activities and might use that information against him:

> Restif's secret activities provide new insight into his relations with Augé. [...] He demonstrated a curious spinelessness in his dealings with him. It's clear that he was intimidated by Augé, as if his son-in-law had way of blackmailing him in order to silence him [...]. It was in fact because Augé knew about his father-in-law's secret past that Restif refrained from opposing Agnès's marriage as well as the abuse that followed and that he only responded in a restrained and prudent manner (petitioning the magistrate for permission for his daughter to live with him).

Noting that police commissioner Sartine had served as a witness at Augé's wedding to his first wife, Baruch adds: 'In addition, it would have been difficult for Restif to directly attack Sartine's protégé.'[39] Indeed, on 14 July 1789, Augé did in fact succeed in having his father-in-law arrested and briefly detained as *un espion du roi* [spy for the king].[40] A striking example of Rétif's deference toward

---

[37] *Nuits de Paris*, vol. 7 (Part 14), Episode 363, *OC*, vol. 85, p. 3350.

[38] *Monsieur Nicolas*, *OC*, vol. 69, p. 3027. For extended excerpts from the passage from which this excerpt is taken, see Appendix B, Excerpt 1, in MHRA's French edition of *Ingénue Saxancour*.

[39] See Baruch, 'L'Indagateur et la marquise: Enquête sur l'activité policière de Restif', *Etudes rétiviennes* 6 (Sept., 1987), pp. 84–85.

[40] There was in fact a secret network of spies called the *Secret du Roi*, employed by King Louis XV without the knowledge of the government. It sometimes promoted policies that contradicted official policies and treaties. It is unclear, however, whether Rétif was ever part of that particular network in his work as a police informant.

his son-in-law is found in *La Femme infidelle*, when Ingénue is persuaded by her parents to return to her husband after fleeing from him for the third time (in late January 1785): 'My father spoke to him with a calmness and restraint that surprised me, taking his hand and speaking to him politely, despite the quarrel they had had together.'

Porter argues that Rétif's failure to help his daughter in the time of her greatest need reflects a serious lack of character and 'moral fiber.' Despite his claims to be a wonderful father, he emerges as weak, ineffectual, even indifferent most of the time, according to Porter, who points out that Rétif is so busy blaming everyone else for Agnès's marriage that he 'forgets how much the fault is his.'[41] While Porter considers Rétif's self-portrait in *Ingénue* self-flattering as well as self-deceiving, Lely finds this 'virtuously conventional self-portrait' both hypocritical and dull: 'Mr. Saxancour is Rétif himself beneath the dullest of masks that he naively considered flattering.'[42] Instead, I would argue that the feeble excuses Rétif invokes to justify his inaction — that he had been misled by appearances and rumors or too busy, too ill, too trusting of other people's opinions to intervene — reflect above all a deep sense of guilt over what happened.

An even less altruistic motive that prompted Rétif to publish *Ingénue Saxancour* was a pressing need for money. Faced with a personal financial crisis heightened by the economic and political instability that gripped France in the 1780s, Rétif was under intense pressure to publish. His desperate search for material that would sell led him to write increasingly sensationalist material drawn from his stormy family life. The irony is that these works were so tasteless and — with the exception of *Ingénue Saxancour* — so devoid of literary value, that they attracted few readers. These financial pressures also explain why Rétif pillaged and recycled material with increasing frequency during this period. 'The need for material compelled this writer to view his work as a vast quarry that he could mine on a regular basis,' Béchir Garbouij observes. 'What's more, Rétif's interminable volumes gather together [...] all sorts of useless things: apothecary receipts, minor news events, petty settling of scores, court records [...]. Underlying the entire corpus of his writings is the assumption that nothing is off limits.'[43]

---

[41] Porter, p. 308.

[42] Lely, p. 12.

[43] Béchir Garbouij, 'Rétif conteur: l'utopie, l'inceste, l'histoire', in *Frontières du conte* (Paris: Editions du C.N.R.S., 1982), p. 103.

Reader Response

Even Rétif's closest friends and greatest admirers were outraged by the publication of *Ingénue Saxancour*. They accused him of being a shameless exhibitionist willing to reveal his family's darkest secrets merely to attract attention, an unscrupulous opportunist hoping to capitalize on his daughter's misfortunes and risk her reputation simply to increase his book sales and pay his debts. 'One understands why Rétif's friends voiced their disapproval,' remarks Tabarant. 'They wondered whatever had possessed a father to publicly reveal his daughter's secret shame. They were outraged by this sequel to the *Femme infidelle* that they considered even more offensive than its predecessor.'[44] Michel de Cubières-Palmézeaux, Rétif's friend and first biographer, declared: 'Only a madman would willingly dishonor himself by publicly dishonoring his family in this way.'[45] In a letter to Rétif on 19 May 1791, Grimod de La Reynière dismissed Rétif's attempts to justify the novel's publication: 'However well justified, your desire for revenge against her husband has blurred your judgment. For in slinging mud at him [...], much of it sullied your daughter as well [...]. If she ever becomes a widow, who would want to marry a woman whose reputation has been tarnished in this way?' Rétif's response, which has been lost, prompted another angry missive from La Reynière on 7 July, in which he alluded to the scandal caused by the novel. He predicted that it would bring only grief to him and his family:

> The public revelation of such unspeakable acts has provoked a great scandal! [...] If you knew what people in Paris have written to me about it, you would shudder in horror! [...] Had I been called upon to judge this work's suitability for publication, it never would have seen the light of day! Not only will it hurt your reputation as a writer, but it will haunt you in your old age.[46]

---

[44] Tabarant, p. 332.

[45] Commenting on *La Femme infidelle* in the same passage, Cubières-Palmézeaux adds: 'These two novels [...] seem to have been written in a fit of madness. [...] Let us draw the curtain on all this depravity and pity its author, who could not have published these works except in a state of delirium or frenzied agitation' [Michel de Cubières-Palmézeaux, 'Notice historique et critique sur la vie et les ouvrages de Nicolas-Edme Restif de La Bretonne', repr. in Paul Lacroix, *Bibliographie et iconographie de tous les ouvrages de Restif de La Bretonne* (Paris: Fontaine, 1875), p. 44].

Cubières's criticisms are echoed by Charles Monselet, another of Rétif's early biographers, who writes: '*Ingénue Saxancour* is the story of Rétif de La Bretonne's older daughter, a distressing story that has no doubt been exaggerated on purpose. It is difficult to comprehend how Rétif could have dared expose his family's dirty laundry in this way. Self-destruction has its limits; and in *Ingénue*, as in *La Femme infidelle*, he has crossed the line without any real interest or benefit to the reader' [Charles Monselet, *Rétif de La Bretonne, sa vie et ses amours: documents inédits, ses malheurs, sa vieillesse et sa vie* (Paris: Aubry, 1858), p. 158].

[46] La Reynière, letters to Rétif of 19 May and 7 July 1791, repr. in *Le Drame de la vie*, 5 vols (Paris, 1793), vol. 5 (*OC*, vol. 38), pp. 1317 and 1321). For extended excerpts from these two letters, see Appendix C, Excerpts 30 and 31, in MHRA's French edition of *Ingénue Saxancour*.

The reaction of Rétif's friends to the publication of *Ingénue Saxancour* echoes their reaction to *La Femme infidelle* two years earlier. This earlier novel had been roundly criticized by several of Rétif's closest friends. François Marlin was so incensed by the novel's publication that he broke off his friendship with Rétif: 'I'm reading your *Femme infidelle*: I despise you. You're spewing out lies: I despise you [...]. You're attacking the defenseless, misrepresenting or slandering those closest to you: I despise you.'[47]

Rétif ignored the warnings of friends and critics alike and went on to publish even more scandalously self-revealing works in the decade following the publication of *Ingénue*. As David Coward points out, 'few would think it wise to write books quite so personal as *La Femme infidelle* or *Ingénue Saxancour*, and fewer still would be capable of the *Anti-Justine*, in which most members of his family play shameful parts.'[48] Peter Wagstaff condemns Rétif's *Anti-Justine* in even stronger language: 'The role of the father [...] consists in subjecting his daughter to the widest possible variety of sexual assaults, for their mutual gratification. All in all, the book is a barren and tedious work, exemplifying the futility and inadequacy of Rétif's response to the need for an articulation of his sexual contradictions.'[49] Rétif himself recognizes his exhibitionist tendencies in the opening lines of his autobiography *Monsieur Nicolas*, but insists (as he had in *Ingénue Saxancour*) that he is writing the truth in the service of the public good: 'Compelled to tell the truth, and sacrificing myself, in order to be useful to my contemporaries and to posterity, I have presented nothing but accurate accounts. I show the workings of the heart, not in terms of plausibility, which is often so misleading, but according to reality.' And a few pages later he adds, defiantly: 'I will be faithful to the truth, even when the truth exposes me to scorn.'[50]

Not surprisingly, the most vehement denunciations of *Ingénue Saxancour* came from Rétif's son-in-law. In a letter to the government censor who had approved its publication, Augé denounced the novel as defamatory, not only toward himself, but also toward his wife and mother-in-law. He asked the censor to stop its publication.[51] When this failed, he accused his father-in-law of libel and of subversive writings and had him arrested. Rétif denied the charges and

---

[47] François Marlin, letter to Rétif reprinted in the second edition of *Les Contemporaines*, 2nd edn, *OC*, vol. 27, pp. 340–41. See Appendix C, Excerpt 21, in MHRA's French edition of *Ingénue Saxancour*.

[48] David Coward, *The Philosophy of Restif de La Bretonne* (Oxford: Voltaire Foundation, 1991), p. 810.

[49] Peter Wagstaff, *Memory and Desire: Rétif de La Bretonne, Autobiography and Utopia* (Amsterdam and Atlanta: Rodopi, 1996), p. 151.

[50] *Monsieur Nicolas*, *OC*, vol. 64, pp. i, 4.

[51] 'I don't understand why this man is publishing such grievous insults against my wife and his own' [Charles-Marie Augé, letter of 16 September 1789 to Toustain-Richebourg, repr. by Rétif in *Le Thesmographe* (*OC*, vol. 110), pp. 489–92].

was released. In the days that followed, he wrote and published a rebuttal of
Augé's charges titled 'Dénonciation d'un beau-père par son gendre calomniateur'
[Denunciation of a father-in-law by his slanderous son-in-law].[52] Unable to block
the novel's publication, Augé destroyed any copies he could find.[53]

Rétif remained unperturbed by the storm of criticism unleashed by his novel.
He insisted that the expressions of gratitude from his daughter and from Madame
Laruelle for having denounced their tormentors and avenged their suffering far
outweighed any censure he faced. In *Monsieur Nicolas*, he claims that it was at
Madame Laruelle's request that he published *Ingénue Saxancour* and that she was
profoundly grateful to him for the sense of vindication and closure it gave to her:

> It was at Madame Laruelle's request that I published *Ingénue Saxancour*,
> which so outraged Madame de Boufflers. This book comforted her deeply
> wounded soul. She died at thirty-two in my daughter's arms, exclaiming 'My
> sister! [...], I am now avenged, because the book has been published, and its
> readers are horrified by the descriptions in it of my husband. I die content,
> and I owe this satisfaction to my friend your father.'[54]

There is no way of verifying whether these words were actually uttered by
Madame Laruelle on her deathbed. Rétif is known to have invented or
fictionalized other episodes in *Monsieur Nicolas*. We do know that Madame
Laruelle did exist, that she was close friends with Agnès, and that she died in her
early thirties of tuberculosis.[55]

A Close Collaboration?

In his 1875 bibliography of Rétif's works, Paul Lacroix suggests that Agnès may
have been the principal author of *Ingénue Saxancour*: 'It's very possible indeed
that this book was written by Agnès, who knew how to write and who, like her

---

[52] 'Dénonciation d'un beau-père par son gendre calomniateur', repr. by Rétif in *Nuits de Paris*, *OC*, vol. 86, pp. 199–200, 202. Augé's text is preceded by Rétif's summary of his son-in-law's life and crimes (pp. 193–98) and followed by his denial of Augé's accusations (pp. 201, 203–237). For excerpts from Augé's denunciation and from Rétif's denial and counter-attack, see Appendix C, Excerpts 27 and 28, in MHRA's French edition of *Ingénue Saxancour*.

[53] Augé and his allies may well have succeeded in limiting the distribution of the novel. In his bibliography of Rétif's works published in 1875, Paul Lacroix noted: '*Ingénue Saxancour* is nearly impossible to find today. It was only after an exhaustive search that Solar was able to track down a copy' (Lacroix, p. 316).

[54] *Monsieur Nicolas*, 'Neuvième Epoque', *OC*, vol. 69, pp. 3144–45. For extended excerpts from the passage from which this is taken, see Appendix B, Excerpt 6, in MHRA's French edition of *Ingénue Saxancour*.

[55] In his diary entry for 23 February 1790, Rétif writes: 'Laruelle died yesterday 22'. This corresponds to the date of her death found by Philippe Havard de La Montagne in the parish records of Villabé (Essonne), as Testud notes in his two-volume edition of *Monsieur Nicolas, ou le cœur humain dévoilé* (Paris: Gallimard, Bibliothèque de la Pléiade, 1989), vol. 2, p. 1376.

mother, wrote poetry and theater plays.'[56] This theory is dismissed by Bachelin and Lely, two of the novel's past editors, who point to Rétif's diary entries concerning the work's composition as irrefutable proof that he was the sole author. In the notes to his 1931 edition of the novel, Bachelin insists that Agnès was simply too young, too close to her experience, and insufficiently practised as a writer to recount what had happened with the necessary detachment and literary skill: 'It is indeed possible that Agnès knew how to write, but let us agree on the meaning of that verb,' he asserts, 'and I cannot believe that a young Agnès could have been capable of capturing the monstrous figure of Augé-Moresquin in so accurate and powerful a manner.'[57] However, Tabarant argues — convincingly, in my opinion — that Agnès must have been an active collaborator in the novel's composition. For, in his view, the character portrayals and descriptions of abuse are too realistic, detailed, and intimate not to have been supplied — at least in part — by Agnès herself: 'The book's tone never ceases to be that of a female autobiography,' Tabarant maintains. 'I will even venture to say that, even if she did not write a single line of *Ingénue Saxancour*, Agnès closely followed its preparation and that she was probably the first to read through the pages. [...] As he wrote, she was reading over his shoulder — and did not object.'[58] Tabarant suggests a close collaboration — indeed a strange complicity — between father and daughter in recording the intimate details of the Augés' sadomasochistic sexual relations. It is also possible, but unlikely in my view, that Rétif used Agnès's story without her consent or knowledge. In any case, to support her petition for separation from her husband, Agnès would have revealed enough of her experiences to Rétif to enable him to write the 'Mémoire contre Augé' — the details of which closely parallel the descriptions of abuse in the novel.

If Agnès did, as seems likely, collaborate in the composition of the novel,[59] one wonders why she was willing to help write a book that could humiliate her publicly and further damage a reputation already sullied by Augé's public accusations of adultery and incest. Perhaps she felt compelled to defend and vindicate herself by telling her side of the story. Yet the acquiescence Tabarant

---

[56] Lacroix, p. 315.

[57] Henri Bachelin, 'Notes', in *Le Ménage parisien, suivi de [...] Ingénue Saxancour*. In *Œuvres de Rétif de La Bretonne* (Paris: Editions du Trianon, 1931), vol. 5, pp. 485, 487.

[58] Tabarant, pp. 329–30.

[59] At the colloquium on 'Le Drame conjugal dans l'œuvre de Rétif de La Bretonne' held in Clermont-Ferrand in June 2012, Pierre Testud pointed out that, before writing *Ingénue Saxancour*, Rétif had already described violence against women in a number of texts — notably in the episode in which Ursule is whipped and brutally beaten in *La Paysanne pervertie*. According to Testud, 'Rétif had a very fertile imagination in this respect and so had no need of his daughter's help to describe the abuse inflicted by Moresquin in *Ingénue Saxancour*'. However, this question is certainly open to debate.

attributes to Agnès may also reflect her extreme dependence on her father, both emotionally and financially, which would have made it difficult for her to refuse.

By agreeing to reveal such intimate details and private humiliations to Rétif, Agnès unwittingly may have laid the ground for the incestuous relations that began less than a week after the novel was completed. Rétif's diary indicates that the final version of *Ingénue Saxancour* was completed on 22 April 1788 and that full-blown incestuous relations with Agnès began on April 28.[60] The closeness in dates suggests a causal connection between composition of the novel and the father-daughter incest. Expressions of Rétif's incestuous inclinations toward Agnès are found much earlier in his writings; allusions to far from innocent caresses between them are found in his diary as early as January 1785.[61] Like her passive submission to her husband's abuse, Agnès's incestuous relationship with her father may have resulted from weakness of character and a sense of helplessness, perhaps even from a twisted sense of duty. Madame de Beausset's apt remark cited earlier that 'Agnès plays a pathetic, contemptible role throughout the entire work' also applies to her life, which the novel tragically mirrors.

For a long time — perhaps even from the beginning of his marriage — Augé had suspected Rétif of less than innocent father-daughter relations with Agnès. This was a chief source of his jealousy and fierce hatred of his father-in-law. On numerous occasions, Augé publicly railed against his father-in-law, accusing him of incest and various other crimes. His attacks intensified in the spring and summer of 1788, after his suspicions were perhaps confirmed by gossip from servants or neighbors in the apartment building where Rétif lived with his

---

[60] In his diary entry for 28 April 1788, Rétif wrote: 'matin: cares[sé] Senga [...]. le soir [...] persuadé Senga.' [In the morning, caressed Senga [...]. That evening [...] persuaded Senga.'] Concerning this entry, Testud comments: 'La fin du numéro suivant éclaire l'enjeu de cette persuasion.' [The end of the following entry explains the nature of this persuasion.'] Indeed, the entry for 29 April could not have been clearer: 'foutu Senga' [fucked Senga]. See *Journal*, ¶1416 & ¶1417, vol. 1, p. 564–65 (cited in Appendix D, Excerpts 38 and 39, in MHRA's French edition of *Ingénue Saxancour*).

[61] See, for example, the entry for 22 January 1785: '[...] le soir, *A. pat.*' (*Journal*, ¶477, vol. 1, p. 171). Commenting on this entry, Testud writes: 'Lire: *Agnès patiens* (Agnès tolérant mes caresses, ou mes attouchements), ou bien *Agnès patinée* (caressée). Suivent quelques lettres raturées et illisibles' (p. 171, n. 2). [Read: *Agnès patiens* (Agnès allowing my caresses, or my fondling), or instead *Agnès patinée* (Agnès caressed). This is followed by several words that are crossed out and illegible.] See also Testud's commentary regarding the abbreviated Latin entry for 28 January 1785 (¶478): 'L'interprétation de ces abbréviations latines reste douteuse. On peut lire hypothétiquement: *Agneti dedi subsidia* (le soir, j'ai donné des secours à Agnès), mais le latin, ici comme ailleurs quand il s'agit d'Agnès, doit cacher un sens érotique' (*Journal*, vol. 1, p. 171, n. 4). [These Latin abbreviations remain difficult to interpret. Hypothetically the words *Agneti dedi subsidia* can be interpreted to mean: in the evening, I came to Agnès's rescue; but the Latin, here as elsewhere, when referring to Agnès, tends to hide an erotic meaning.]

daughters.[62] David Coward notes that the timing and intensity of Augé's outbursts against his father-in-law seemed to coincide with changes in the father-daughter relationship: 'His "insane" outbursts tend to follow the course of his wife's incestuous adulteries. [...] Augé's attempts to bring Restif to justice in the autumn of 1789 coincided exactly with one of Agnès's reappearances in Paris. After 1791, when sexual relations between father and daughter ceased, Augé became calm.'[63] In *Ingénue Saxancour*, Rétif alludes several times to Augé's accusations, no doubt in an effort to lessen their impact. Indeed, the publication of *Ingénue* and Rétif's countless other attacks on Augé reflect an obsessive desire to discredit him and his accusations. As Testud remarks, 'With this in mind, it's easier to understand the fierce hatred that pitted Rétif against his son-in-law: Augé, who accused his father-in-law of incest, knew the truth, and so Rétif did everything in his power to discredit him.'[64]

The scandalous details of Rétif's incestuous affair with Agnès were recounted by Alexandre Dumas père in a second-rate novel titled *Ingénue: Un Amour interdit de Restif de La Bretonne* published in serial form in 1853–54. Dumas wrote the novel in collaboration with Paul Lacroix, an archivist and librarian at the Bibliothèque de l'Arsenal who later published the first bibliography of Rétif's works. In doing research for the novel, Lacroix may well have drawn on the collection of Rétif's manuscripts housed at the Arsenal, including his diary entries through August 1787, which document the early stages of his incestuous relations with Agnès. The novel so outraged Agnès's two sons that they sued Dumas and Lacroix for libel.

According to Baruch, 'Agnès must have been grateful to a father who had already done so much to help her, and who now sought to restore her dignity by exposing her sufferings to the public.'[65] While Rétif no doubt saw the novel's publication as a victory over Augé, there is no evidence that Agnès shared his jubilation. Rétif's friends suggest that, quite to the contrary, it was humiliating for her to have her degradation exposed in such graphic detail. It is likely that Agnès viewed the novel and its publication with great ambivalence, in much the

---

[62] Recounting Rétif's bitter dispute with his landlord that eventually caused him to move out, Baruch speculates about the role that servants' gossip might have played in the conflict: 'Auger's accusations of pimping and incest did not perhaps fall on deaf ears. Women working as servants in the same building see, hear, and understand many things'. Baruch, *Restif de La Bretonne* (1996), p. 215.

[63] Coward, p. 757, n. 36. Contrary to Coward's assertion, entries in Rétif's diary suggest that his sexual relations with Agnès continued after 1791, albeit with less frequency, until she left her father's home to live with Vignon in February 1794, shortly after her divorce was finalized. In his study of Rétif's diary, Testud writes: 'The *Journal* confirms without a doubt that Rétif had incestuous relations with both his daughters. Until 1793, he primarily had relations with Agnès, who lived with him after separating from her husband.' See Testud, 'Le *Journal* inédit de Restif de La Bretonne', *SVEC* 90 (1972), 1578.

[64] Testud, 'Le *Journal* inédit de Restif, p. 1578.

[65] Baruch, *Restif de La Bretonne* (1996), p. 210.

same way as she seems to have viewed Rétif himself. She appears to have had lingering doubts (encouraged perhaps by her mother) whether Rétif was really her father — doubts he claims to have shared. In both *Monsieur Nicolas* and *La Femme infidelle*, Rétif maintains that Agnès was not his daughter and that she was conceived by his wife in a liaison with another man.[66] Testud dismisses these claims as a mere ploy to counter public accusations of incest made against him by his wife and son-in-law: 'Rétif no doubt considered this the best way to appear innocent,' writes Testud. 'The texts we have at our disposal suggest that Rétif never doubted for a single moment that he was her father.'[67] Baruch insists that Agnès and Marion were Rétif's real daughters because of the intensity of his feeling for them — a debatable interpretation since Baruch alludes to this same intensity of feeling as proof of Rétif's incestuous inclinations toward them.[68] The question of whether or not Agnès was Rétif's biological daughter is clearly a controversial one that is open to debate. Rétif may never have known for sure himself. My own view is that, even if they were not biologically related, their sexual relationship can still be considered incestuous, since Rétif had raised Agnès and since they had always viewed each other as father and daughter. Rétif may well have claimed that Agnès was not his daughter to counter his wife's and son-in-law's accusations of incest (as Testud suggests), but also to assuage his own feelings of guilt for having seduced her.

Beginning in late 1787, Rétif's cryptic and often crude entries in his diary suggest a tense, highly sexualized love-hate relationship with Agnès, whom he refers to sometimes by the anagram *Senga*: 'no luck with Senga,' 'failed with A[gnè]s, quarrel, tears,' 'persuaded Senga,' 'quarrel, Senga badly fucked,' 'Senga rebuffed me,' 'Senga in the evening, against her will,' 'Senga vigorously fucked,' 'quarrel, Agnès left in a huff,' and 'huge quarrel with Agnès'.[69] The diary traces

---

[66] See *La Femme infidelle*, *OC*, vol. 45, pp. 558–59, and *Monsieur Nicolas*, *OC*, vol. 69, pp. 3028–29.

[67] Testud, *Création littéraire*, pp. 640, 644, n. 187.

[68] Baruch, *Restif de La Bretonne* (1996), pp. 175–76.

[69] The original French reads: 'Non réussi avec Senga', 'râté A[gnè]s, querelle, pleurs', 'persuade Senga', 'querelle, mal foutu Senga', 'Senga m'a refusé', 'le soir Senga malgré elle', 'Senga foutue sévèrement', 'querelle Agnès coup tête', and 'grande querelle d'Agnès'. Diary entries ¶1285 and 1296 (for 19 and 31 December 1787), ¶1416 (28 April 1788), ¶1375 (16 June 1788), ¶1390 and 1395 (3 and 8 July 1788), ¶1867 (10 November 1789), ¶2562 (9 November 1791), and ¶2706 (2 April 1792).

Iwan Bloch maintains that there was a 'shocking increase' in the incidence of incest in eighteenth-century France and a peculiar fascination with it among writers of the period. He cites numerous examples of well-known figures who are rumored to have engaged in incestuous relations: the regent Philippe d'Orléans, the Maréchal de Richelieu, Cardinal de Tencin, Cardinal de Fleury, Duc de Choiseul, Sade, and Rétif de La Bretonne. See Bloch, *Rétif de La Bretonne: Der Mensch, der Schriftsteller, der Reformator* (Berlin 1906), pp. 165–68, 381; cited by Otto Rank in *The Incest Theme in Literature and Legend* (1912; Baltimore: Johns Hopkins University Press, 1992), p. 356.

the course of their incestuous relations over several years: Agnès's wavering resistance to Rétif's increasingly frequent and insistent sexual advances, her reluctant capitulation, quarrels followed by tearful reconciliations, Agnès's abrupt departures to stay with friends for progressively longer periods until she left home definitively in February 1794. From beginning to end, the affair seems to have been fraught with tension and unhappiness.

A Confusion in Narrative Voice

The collaboration between Rétif and Agnès in writing *Ingénue Saxancour* led to a confusion in narrative voice that surfaces at various key turning points in the novel. The intrusion of Rétif's point of view into Ingénue's narrative is especially apparent in the following passage:

> I was afraid of missing out on a good match. I agreed to let others pester my father [...] and lead him to believe I was in love. I didn't realize that a busy man with frail health and many preoccupations is easily provoked. Nor did I realize that a dangerous seductress was trying to rob me of his heart. [...] My father gradually became estranged from me; he saw me as an ungrateful, rebellious daughter. [...] But all that would not have been enough to alienate the heart of a father such as mine. It was the vile, odious Moresquin who finally drove him away.

Rétif seems so intent on exculpating himself that he intrudes into the narrative, creating fissures and discontinuities in Ingénue's voice. Instead of criticizing her father for his coldness toward her in her time of need and his failure to intervene sooner, Ingénue awkwardly enumerates multiple excuses for his behavior. A similar confusion in narrative voice is found in a number of other passages. For example, when Moresquin pressures Ingénue to ask her father for money to pay his gambling debts, Mr. Saxancour refuses for reasons that Ingénue awkwardly defends, even though Moresquin has threatened to beat her severely if she fails.

This confusion in narrative voice led in turn to uncertainty among critics and scholars over the novel's authorship. Rétif's narrative ventriloquism is so convincing that many readers — misled by the subtitle 'histoire écrite par elle-même' [story written by herself] — assumed that the novel was written by his daughter. It was not until 1889 that the question of its authorship seemed to be resolved by Paul Cottin's publication of portions of Rétif's diary outlining various stages of the novel's composition. Crucial new insights have been gained thanks to the recent publication of Pierre Testud's far more complete and more accurately transcribed critical edition of Rétif's diary, which includes nine years of subsequent entries apparently unknown to Cottin. Yet knowledge that Rétif was the principal author gives the novel a peculiar voyeuristic cast that becomes all the more unsettling in light of accusations by his estranged wife and son-in-law that Rétif had engaged in incestuous relations with his daughter — accusations borne out by explicit entries in Rétif's diary.

The confusion in narrative voice in *Ingénue Saxancour* stems not only from the tension between Rétif's and Agnès's very different perspectives concerning the events recounted in the novel, but even more from the contradictions between the heroine's self-portrayal as an ingénue and the degradation inflicted on her by Moresquin. She establishes her persona as an ingénue in the opening sentence of the novel: 'I don't need to write a preface to explain the moral purpose of these memoirs. I'll simply tell my story in an artless, ingenuous manner, and the lesson will be clear through the example I present.' Similarly, in the 'Avis de l'Editeur,' the fictional editor writes: 'I shuddered as I read in these memoirs such a truthful account written so artlessly [...] by a young woman who describes what she has felt and suffered to the point of despair.' This persona is reinforced by the name Rétif chose for her and by the heroine's self-presentation throughout the novel as naive, innocent, and chaste. Yet this self-portrayal is undermined by Ingénue's detailed account of her degrading experiences with her husband. Neither her protestations of innocence, nor her frequent recourse to ellipses and euphemisms to hint at the sexual abuse and other forms of degradation she suffered for four years can hide the fact that she is anything but an ingénue. Indeed, the fact that she repeatedly underlines her artlessness is an artifice in itself.[70]

The tension between Ingénue's persona of chaste innocence and the pernicious influence of her husband first appears in the description of her wedding night:

> Moresquin, a vile and despicable man, [...] found himself alone at last with a modest, innocent, timid, and inexperienced young woman. [...] It seemed that pleasure had purified his sordid soul or perhaps that, finding me pretty, he wanted to begin with a delicate pleasure. [...] But I later learned that some of his caresses constituted liberties of a most sinful nature, even between a husband and wife ....[71]

---

[70] A similar contradiction is found in the self-portrayal of Suzanne Simonin, heroine of Diderot's novel *La Religieuse*, particularly in the seduction scenes with the mother superior of Sainte-Eutrope.

[71] The ellipsis at the end of this quotation is found in the original French text. Commenting on this scene, Christine Roulston remarks: 'This shift to a moral register distances Ingénue from the present moment, absolving her from having to respond directly to Moresquin's advances. By redirecting the narrative in this way, Ingénue retains her status as moral agent and avoids the question of any sexual complicity. The ellipsis, which critics agree signals anal penetration, is potentially also an elision of Ingénue's own response to these illicit "caresses," which her future knowledge further safeguards.' See Christine M. Roulston, 'Marriage, Sexuality, and the Meaning of the Wedding Night in Eighteenth-Century France', in *Heteronormativity in Eighteenth-Century Literature and Culture*, ed. Ana de Freitas Boe and Abby Coykendall (Burlington, VT: Ashgate, 2015), pp. 59–76 (75).

It turns out that the 'delicate pleasure' to which Rétif alluded here was neither delicate nor pleasurable for Agnès, since (according to Gilbert Lely) it refers to forced anal intercourse,[72] in which Moresquin indulged for three nights before deflowering his bride.

The fissures in the heroine's self-presentation as an ingénue are particularly apparent in the episode where Moresquin introduces several companions into their bed, whom she claims to mistake for her husband:

> I was so exhausted that I soon fell into a deep sleep. I don't know how long I slept. But when I awoke, I found myself in complete darkness, with Moresquin caressing me in a more tender, more decent fashion than usual. I even thought I heard him sigh. I was truly astonished!

Ingénue claims she did not realize what had happened until a neighbor told her about a violent argument in the courtyard involving her husband, in which others reproached him for his reprehensible behavior toward his wife. 'I answered that I hadn't heard anything. But I shuddered, thinking about all that had happened to me! With horror, I realized that there must have been three men, at least ....'[73] The sentence breaks off, but Ingénue suggests here that at least three men *not* her husband had intercourse with her without her realizing it — an implausible claim. Since she claims to have been awake enough to hear her bedfellow sigh and to realize he was behaving in a way atypical for Moresquin (that is, with gentleness), she should also have realized that this man was *not* in fact her husband — any more than the two or more men who followed. Her claim that she was unaware at the time of what was happening to her masks her failure to resist — indeed her complicity in — what amounted to prostitution, even to a kind of *tournante*.[74] These discontinuities undermine her credibility and her self-presentation as a naive, artless narrator.

The confusion in narrative voice in *Ingénue Saxancour* also reflects tensions and contradictions in the motives that may have led Rétif to write and publish the novel. Was he motivated by a desire to reveal the truth or mask it, to enlighten or titillate his readers, to vindicate his daughter or exploit her suffering in order to advance his career? I would argue that all these motives, contradictory as they may be, might well have played a role in the writing and publishing of Rétif's novel. The use of first-person narrative presented in the naive voice of a victimized

---

[72] Gilbert Lely, 'Introduction', *Ingénue Saxancour, ou La Femme séparée* (Paris: Lattès, 1979), pp. 5–26 (p. 16).

[73] The ellipsis is found in the original text.

[74] A *tournante* is sexual intercourse with a group of men imposed on a woman by her partner, who makes her sexually available to his friends or associates. (The term is also applied more generally to gang rapes.) For a chilling account of this practice in the low-income *banlieues* of contemporary France, see Samira Bellil's memoir *Dans l'enfer des tournantes* (Paris: Gallimard, 2003), translated as *To Hell and Back: The Life of Samira Bellil* (Bison Books, 2008).

female narrator serves to titillate readers, while at the same time moving them to pity, then to indignation, and ultimately to a realization of the need for changes in attitudes and laws regarding spousal abuse. There is a tension between the pornographic aspects of the novel on one hand and the didactic and reformist aspects on the other. Yet both reflect a sensationalist approach designed to win a larger audience for Rétif's works in order to fulfill both monetary and polemical aims. In the end, it is difficult to separate these different aspects of the novel, so closely are they intertwined.

Fact or Fiction?

In examining *Ingénue Saxancour*, one inevitably confronts the problems of fictionalized (auto)biography posed by Rétif's writings. If the work is a novel, or at least to some extent fictionalized, to what extent are we justified in accepting the events it portrays as having really happened? In *Mes Ouvrages*, Rétif refers to *Ingénue Saxancour* as a novel. However, the work's self-presentation is as an autobiography — or, to be more precise, as an *histoire* (a history or 'real-life' story) presented in the first person. Yet, as we have seen, the work was viewed by contemporary readers — and notably by Rétif's friends and family — *not* as an autobiography, but as a scandalous biography. We have also seen that certain nineteenth-century scholars (such as the bibliographer Lacroix), taking the work's self-presentation at face value, viewed the work as Agnès Rétif's autobiography, but that later scholars rejected this theory on the basis of entries in Rétif's diary that 'proved' he was the work's sole author. These same scholars point out that many of the events recounted in *Ingénue Saxancour* are corroborated by entries in Rétif's journals, thereby substantiating the novel's 'truth value.' One could argue that the diary offers no concrete proof of the 'reality' of the events portrayed in the novel, on the grounds that journal-writers sometimes indulge in high levels of deception and self-deception, particularly when writing about abusive or troubled relationships, and that their account of events should therefore be regarded as unreliable, even suspect. (This ties into the larger question — often raised by historians and literary theorists — concerning the accessibility of the 'real.' According to this view, any account whatsoever of the past is inevitably filtered through the prejudices and desires of the observer and thus can never be regarded as objective 'proof.')

Although I agree that Rétif's diary entries should be read with a certain degree of circumspection, I feel they provide useful information, more reliable than that typically found in diaries. Scholars generally agree that Rétif's journals — *Mes Inscripcions* and its untitled sequel (referred to simply as the *Journal*) — were never intended for publication, based on the fact that they are written in an unpolished, cryptic style, often in an abbreviated Latin code that even specialists sometimes find difficult to decipher. Moreover, the diary consists largely of brief

FIGURE 4.   Pierre Lescault, *Hommage à Rétif* (1985). By permission of the artist, who notes at the bottom of the lithograph that this engraving was displayed 'in conjunction with a symposium on Rétif de La Bretonne held in Auxerre in June 1986.' In the background to the right is a farmyard scene recalling Rétif's childhood home in northwestern Burgundy. Floating above is Victorin, one of the figures from his *Découverte australe par un homme volant* (1781). To the left is a surreal collection of figures evoking the wide array of female characters in his works.

Describing this portrait, Lescault explained: 'It's a dry-point engraving that represents the La Bretonne family farm, with Rétif and his mother in the courtyard and Victorin hovering in the sky above. In the center foreground is a head-and-shoulder portrait of Rétif and, on the side, are the women he possessed (or dreamed of possessing) and their shadows, with shoes and lingerie strewn at their feet' (Lescault, e-mail to M. Trouille, 2 January 2013).

entries that merely record daily events (birthdays, anniversaries, manuscripts begun or completed, people seen, events attended), with little commentary or introspective reflection. In my view, therefore, Rétif's diary provides valuable corroboration for a number of the events described in *Ingénue*.

These questions concerning the truth value of *Ingénue Saxancour* are compounded by the fact that many of Rétif's editors and biographers — even a few recent biographers, such as Baruch — have tended to take his autobiographical writings at face value as authentic memoirs. Yet one must distinguish carefully between the events of Rétif's life and the fictionalized presentation of certain events in *Ingénue*, which is not so much an authentic memoir/*histoire* (history) as he claims in the work itself, as a complex blend of fact and fiction that he describes elsewhere as a *roman à clé*.[75] As Testud and Coward both point out, the mediations between fiction and reality in *Ingénue Saxancour* are complex and problematic. These problematic interconnections are further complicated by Rétif's underlying aims, both personal and polemical, discussed earlier. For example, he describes in detail — and no doubt exaggerates — the various ploys and deceptions used by his son-in-law Augé and his allies to persuade Agnès to marry him. The episodes leading up to their wedding serve to establish Augé's unscrupulous character and Agnès's naiveté with the dual function of foreshadowing the failure of their marriage and blaming her husband and mother for it, while exculpating both Rétif and his daughter. These episodes — like the chapters describing Ingénue's strained relations with her parents, Moresquin's attempts to prostitute her, and her repeated denials of having an affair with her husband's friend — illustrate the complex mediations between fiction and reality in Rétif's writing and must be read with a certain critical distance.

Yet the descriptions of mistreatment in the formal police complaints filed by Agnès against Augé in December 1785, and in her petition for separation in February 1786, do closely parallel descriptions of abuse in the novel. For example, in response to Augé's formal complaint to local magistrates that his father-in-law had unlawfully taken his wife from him and refused to give her back,[76] Agnès and Rétif countered with battery charges against him and with a detailed account of the abusive treatment that had forced her to flee their home. The parallels between this 'Mémoire contre Augé' and *Ingénue Saxancour* are quite striking, as the following excerpt from the 'Mémoire' illustrates:

---

[75] See, for example, *Monsieur Nicolas, OC*, vol. 69, pp. 3144–45; and 'Mes Ouvrages', Appendix to *Monsieur Nicolas, OC*, vol. 71, p. 4729.

[76] Under French law of the period, a woman could not move out of her husband's residence without his permission — or that of a magistrate — unless she could demonstrate that her life was in immediate danger.

Before long, she feels the full effects of his villainy: stale bread thrown in her face, kicks to the abdomen and a punch to her swollen cheek when she is six months pregnant; threats to stab her with a sword two weeks after she had given birth, forcing her to flee to her aunt's, dressed only in her nightgown; […] cruel pinches on her arms to make her wriggle when performing her conjugal duty […]; disgusting talk about her to his friends in her presence, including obscene details about her private parts and crude descriptions of how he had sex with her in the most brutal, unnatural manner; despair of the unhappy woman who wished to drown herself […]. This, your honor, has been my daughter Agnès's fate. [77]

Similarly, the episode in which Moresquin tracks down Ingénue after she leaves him and has her arrested as a common prostitute — a final indignity that led her to file for a separation — corresponds to events that took place in February 1786 and that are recorded in Rétif's diary.[78] That same month, while the events of his daughter's ordeal were still fresh in his mind, Rétif began the first version of *Ingénue Saxancour* (titled 'L'Epouse séparée'), which he completed a few weeks later. The longer final version was given to the censor in late summer 1788. This second stage of the novel's composition might well have provided an opportunity to add or invent new horrors and new self-justifications. In other texts written in the late 1780s, we see that when Rétif returned to earlier texts, he often revised and embellished them extensively.

Beyond the question of the novel's relation to actual events in Agnès's marriage, there is the larger question of its documentary value and the extent to which we are justified in reading larger cultural and historical significance into *Ingénue Saxancour*. Was the type of abuse Ingénue suffered in her marriage typical or excessive for the period? What can the relationship between Ingénue and Moresquin tell us about the psychology of wife-batterers and battered wives? Finally, how does the novel tie in with eighteenth-century debates concerning spousal abuse, separation, and divorce? These are questions I examine in the final section of this introduction.

Rétif's Reformist Impulses: A Pioneer against Spousal Abuse?

Despite the dark sides of *Ingénue Saxancour* (its pornographic and sensationalist aspects and the less than altruistic motives that may have pushed Rétif to write it), despite the sexism and anti-feminism of some of his other works,[79] and even

---

[77] *Journal*, ¶586, vol. 1, pp. 230–34. The composition of Rétif's 'Mémoire contre Augé' is discussed in the section titled 'About the Text'. Extended excerpts are presented in Appendix D, Excerpt 25, in MHRA's French edition of the novel.

[78] See the journal entries for 21 and 24 February 1786 in Appendix D, Excerpts 29 and 31, in MHRA's French edition of the novel.

[79] The most stridently anti-feminist of Rétif's works are probably *Les Gynographes* (1777) and *L'Andrographe* (1782). Regarding Rétif's views on women, see Rori Bloom, 'Privacy, Publicity,

despite his problematic relationships with his wife and daughters, many commentators argue that the novel reflects strong reformist, even feminist impulses. For in this work, Rétif showed himself to be a reform-minded pioneer far in advance of his time through his graphic depictions of spousal abuse, his call for greater public awareness of this perennial problem, and his crusade for liberal divorce laws that would allow women to escape from abusive relationships and to remarry. 'Even though by the end of *La Femme infidelle*, Rétif had shown himself to be a reactionary male chauvinist,' declares Baruch, 'women will forgive him out of gratitude for this other book [*Ingénue Saxancour*], a passionate plea for subjugated wives and battered women humiliated and sexually abused by brutal, drunken husbands who gamble away the couple's money.'[80] Similarly, Coward maintains that Rétif used Augé's conduct 'to promote a new social charter which [...] sought to protect wives and children against brutal husbands.'[81]

Through the depth and forcefulness of his analysis of abusive relationships, Rétif goes well beyond a personal vendetta in *Ingénue*. His denunciation of his son-in-law leads to a much broader call for public exposure of abusive husbands and for the passage of laws to prosecute them and to protect their wives. After describing how Moresquin humiliates and sexually assaults Ingénue in front of his drunken companions, Rétif indignantly exclaims: 'There should be laws against such cruelties; it should not be permitted for a husband to treat his wife in such an insulting, indecent manner!' Similarly, in *La Femme infidelle*, after recounting Ingénue's flight from her husband, Rétif calls for fairer treatment of abused wives forced to flee from their husbands and for more equitable property settlements in their favor: 'After four years of drudgery and three children, one of whom died because of the mistreatment I endured during my pregnancy, I deserve a far better salary than a few towels, a few handkerchiefs, and two pairs of sheets.'[82] Rétif makes it clear that Moresquin's behavior was a monstrous aberration that violated every norm of acceptable behavior within marriage; yet his graphic presentation of such an extreme case of spousal abuse called those same norms into question and made clear the need for better laws and institutions to protect women against abusive husbands.

Pornography: Restif de La Bretonne's *Ingénue Saxancour*', *Eighteenth-Century Fiction* 17.2 (January, 2005), 231–52; Dennis Fletcher, 'Rétif de La Bretonne and woman's estate', in *Woman and society in eighteenth-century France*, ed. by Eva Jacobs and others (London: Athlone Press, 1979), pp. 96–109; Denise Brahimi, 'Rétif féministe? Etude de quelques *Contemporaines*', *Etudes sur le XVIIIe siècle* 3 (1976), 77–91; and Guy Bruit, 'Rétif de La Bretonne et les femmes', *La Pensée* 131 (1967), 125–37.

[80] Baruch, *Restif de La Bretonne* (1996), pp. 184–85.

[81] Coward, p. 755.

[82] Rétif, *La Femme infidelle*, OC, vol. 45, p. 831. For the full text of the passage from which this passage is taken, see Appendix F, Excerpt 4, in MHRA's French edition of *Ingénue Saxancour*.

Because of Agnès's disastrous marriage, as well as his own conjugal misfortunes, Rétif was a fervent advocate for the legalization of divorce. He was jubilant when a divorce law was finally passed in September 1792: 'O wise law of divorce! Bless you!' he wrote in 'Mon Calendrier,' adding that he would celebrate it again every year on 9 August, date of his wife's birth, to thank her for divorcing him.[83] Above all, he praised the divorce law as a liberation for abused wives like his daughter: 'Ingénue, thanks to the wise and sacred law of divorce, finally divorced the vile L'Echiné in 1794 and married citizen Vignon, with whom she lives in peace.'[84]

In the 'Supplément à la *Femme séparée*' written in July 1788, Rétif bitterly lamented his lack of legal recourse against Augé: 'What is one to make of the laws of a country that offer no way for a father to punish the atrocities of a despicable and demented son-in-law like Moresquin? [...] When will there be protective laws that will prevent the wrongs done to law-abiding citizens or make up for them?'[85] He fantasized about taking the law into his own hands: 'I should be able to go to Moresquin's home, [...] have him taken and held by two thugs, while I, in accordance with the laws and my paternal authority, beat him a hundred times with a club.'[86]

Frustrated by the lack of laws to punish his son-in-law for his abuse, Rétif used his fiction to settle scores with him and to give closure to this painful episode of his life. Obsessed with hatred for Augé and haunted by feelings of guilt over what happened to Agnès, Rétif wrote a dozen different versions of her story over a fifteen-year period, each with a different dénouement and a new punishment meted out to his villainous son-in-law: death by hanging after murdering his wife in one version, death by gunfire after murdering his mother-in-law in another;[87] a slower, more painful end from syphilis in a third version; life imprisonment in a penal colony in a fourth, and so on.[88] 'Given the recurrence of this theme,' remarks Testud, 'one realizes both the obsessive nature of this drama for Rétif

---

[83] Rétif and his wife were divorced in January 1794, a few weeks before their daughter's divorce was finalized; neither remarried.

[84] See Rétif, 'Mes Ouvrages', appendix to *Monsieur Nicolas*, *OC*, vol. 71, p. 4729.

[85] 'Supplément à *La Femme séparée*', in *Les Contemporaines*, 2nd edn, *OC*, vol. 27, pp. 322–24. Extended excerpts are presented in Appendix E, Excerpt 3, in MHRA's French edition of *Ingénue Saxancour*.

[86] 'Supplément à *La Femme séparée*', *OC*, vol. 27, p. 323.

[87] See 'La Fillette reconnue', in *Le Drame de la vie*, *OC*, vol. 37, pp. 968–70.

[88] Regarding Rétif's sequels and supplements to *Ingénue Saxancour* and the obsessive nature of his writing, see Testud, *Création littéraire*, pp. 496–98 and 503–06, and his notes to *Monsieur Nicolas*, vol. 2, pp. 1283–84. Extended excerpts from these sequels are presented in Appendix E in MHRA's French edition of *Ingénue Saxancour*. Also see Appendix C, Excerpts 25 and 26, for the open letter to Augé that Rétif published at the end of *Le Thesmographe* (*OC*, vol. 110, pp. 499–501) to denounce his mistreatment of Agnès and his continued harrassment of her and her family after she left him.

and his belief in the power of literary creation, capable in his eyes of subduing the monster Augé, if not to crush him, and its power to finally exorcise the demon of gloom. He feels his existence reaffirmed and strengthened by writing.'[89] Through his fiction, Rétif was able to exact punishment against Augé in ways denied by the judicial system of the period. And of all these works, *Ingénue Saxancour* remains the strongest indictment of his son-in-law. Indeed, two centuries later, Rétif's novel is still one of the most powerful depictions of spousal abuse ever written and among the most probing analyses yet made of the twisted psychology of the abuser and the abused.

---

[89] Testud, *Création littéraire*, p. 516. Similarly, Coward observes, 'Rétif's method of dealing with Augé was simple: in life, he walked in dread of him, but his fictions deal with him fearlessly' (Coward, p. 755).

FIGURE 5. Portrait of Rétif in his early forties (c. 1776), artist unknown. This portrait, originally in color, was given by Agnès Rétif's second husband Louis-Claude-Victor Vignon to Charles Monselet, one of Rétif's early biographers. In 1971, the painting was acquired by Raymond Clavreuil, bookseller and art collector in Paris. It appeared in the catalogue published in conjunction with the bicentenary celebration of Rétif's birth: *Je suis né auteur, pour ainsi dire. Rétif de La Bretonne* (Auxerre: Bibliothèque de la ville d'Auxerre, 2006), p. 4. (BnF)

Contrasting this early portrayal of Rétif with the portrait done in 1785 by Binet and Berthet (Fig. 6), Claude Jaëcklé-Plunian remarks: 'This portrait may have been done around the time that Rétif's novel *Le Paysan perverti* became a bestseller. The representation of Rétif as a prosperous-looking bourgeois is atypical, but reflects perhaps his hope at the time that his writings might enable him to enter the ranks of the bourgeoisie. He wears an elegant jacket, lace jabot, and stylish wig [...]. The haughty expression seems at odds with the timid smile, but the keen look in his eyes, animated by his lively imagination, is also clearly recognizable in the later portrait engraved by Berthet.' Claude Jaëcklé-Plunian, 'L'Image de Rétif de La Bretonne, hier et aujourd'hui: Variations autour de quelques portraits de Rétif (http://retifdelabretonne.net/wp-content/uploads/2014/04/L'image-de-Rétif.pdf).

ABOUT THE AUTHOR

Born in 1734 in Sacy in the northwest corner of Burgundy, Nicolas-Edme Rétif (or Restif) was the eldest of nine children born to Edme Rétif, a prosperous farmer, and his second wife Barbe Ferlet. His father also had eight children by his first wife, including Marguerite-Anne (Margot), who would later serve as matchmaker in Agnès Rétif's disastrous marriage. In 1740, Edme Rétif bought an estate near Sacy called La Bretonne, the childhood home that Nicolas idealized and recalled nostalgically in his autobiography *Monsieur Nicolas* (1794–97) and in *La Vie de mon père* (1779), a biography of his father in which he painted an idyllic tableau of rural life in in pre-Revolutionary France. Years later, when he launched his literary career, Rétif adopted the nobiliary particle de La Bretonne in memory of his childhood home and no doubt to add a touch of distinction to his name; but after the Revolution, when aristocratic surnames became suspect, he changed the spelling to Labretonne.

After receiving an education in parish schools, Nicolas was apprenticed at the age of sixteen to a printer in Auxerre. His parents had originally destined him for the priesthood because of his fragile health, but that plan was abandoned due to the boy's marked interest in the fair sex, which only intensified with the passing of time. At the end of his four-year apprenticeship, Rétif found employment in Paris as a typesetter and worked in various print shops before returning to Auxerre to work as foreman in the print shop where he had been apprenticed. It was in Auxerre that he met and married Agnès Lebègne, daughter of a local apothecary, in April 1760. Their daughter Agnès was born the following March. The couple would have three more daughters, but only the youngest Marie-Anne (whom they called Marion) survived into adulthood, along with the eldest Agnès. The marriage, which ended in divorce in 1794, was stormy from the start and marked by frequent, often prolonged separations.

Soon after Agnès's birth, the couple moved to Paris, where Rétif continued to work as a typesetter. In 1767, after publishing his first novel *La Famille vertueuse*, Rétif left his job as foreman in Quillau's print shop to devote himself full-time to his literary career. In his autobiography, he would later marvel at his self-confidence: 'I left my job in the print shop before knowing what success, if any, my book would have; I'm amazed today at the self-assurance I showed back then!'[90] Over the following four decades, Rétif would go on to publish over 200 works, many of them produced in his own print shop, on a dizzying array of subjects in a wide range of genres — novel, biography, autobiography, short story,

---

[90] Rétif, *Monsieur Nicolas*, in *Œuvres complètes*, vol. 68, p. 2673.

theater, moral treatise, political pamphlet, and science fiction.[91] The variety of styles and tones is equally remarkable, ranging from pornographic to smugly moralistic didacticism, from crudely graphic and sexist to lyrical, idealistic, even utopian at times. Indeed, the range, unevenness, and sheer volume of his writing have tended to discourage comprehensive scholarly study of Rétif's life and literary career, which makes the work of Daniel Baruch, David Coward, and especially Pierre Testud all the more admirable.

Among Rétif's more unconventional works (of which there are many), perhaps most notable is *Le Pornographe ou la Prostitution réformée* (1769), a plan for regulating prostitution said to have been implemented by the Emperor Joseph II of Austria and to have caught the attention of other rulers as well. This was the first of his *Idées singulières*, a series of reform-minded texts Rétif penned over the next two decades: *Le Mimographe ou le Théâtre réformé* (1770), *Les Gynographes ou la Femme réformée* (1777), its sequel *L'Andrographe ou l'Homme réformé* (1782), *Le Thesmographe ou les Lois réformées* (1789), and *Le Glossografe ou la Langue réformée* (a plan for the reform of spelling and word usage never actually written, but put into practice in his own writing). Utopian in tone, these texts were often traditionalist in intent, especially when it came to women, as the title of a section of *Les Gynographes* makes clear: 'Projet de règlement proposé à toute l'Europe pour mettre les femmes à leur place et opérer le bonheur des deux sexes' [Draft legislation proposed to all of Europe to put women in their place and foster the happiness of both sexes]. In keeping with the encyclopedic ideal of the Enlightenment, Rétif was interested in all facets of society, and he did not hesitate to push beyond the limitations of his knowledge and experience in elaborating bold and at times outlandish theories.

In his own day, Rétif was best known for his short-story collection *Les Contemporaines* (1780), as well as for *Le Paysan perverti* (1775) and its sequel *La Paysanne pervertie* (1784), epistolary novels depicting the corruption of rural innocence by the seductive vices of the city. All three works were lavishly illustrated, which increased their popularity and discouraged pirated editions. Today, Rétif's best-known works are his voluminous autobiography *Monsieur Nicolas, ou le Cœur humain dévoilé*, which scholars compare favorably to Rousseau's *Confessions*, and the eight-volume *Nuits de Paris, ou le Spectateur nocturne* (1788–1794), vivid vignettes of everyday life in Paris drawn from his work as a police spy roaming the streets at night in the years leading up to and during the French Revolution.[92]

---

[91] The Slatkine reprint edition of Rétif's complete works (published in 1987–88) comprises 117 volumes. The entire collection is now available on-line through the Bibliothèque Nationale's catalogue, which lists the series title as *Oeuvres complètes* (instead of using the more common spelling *Œuvres*).

[92] Regarding Rétif's activities as a police spy in the 1770s, see Baruch, 'L'Indagateur et la marquise', pp. 73–87.

In addition to his prodigious output of published works, Rétif kept a secret diary in which he wrote brief entries each morning about his work and experiences the previous day: people encountered, places visited, anniversaries celebrated or mourned, manuscripts begun, continued, or completed. Begun in 1770 as stone inscriptions carved into the stone embankment of the Ile Saint-Louis during Rétif's daily strolls there, the diary was then continued on paper until at least 1796, based on the notebooks found among his papers. Given Rétif's compulsion to record his daily activities, Pierre Testud speculates that he probably continued his diary until his death in 1806[93] and that this final portion of his diary may be lost forever. Or perhaps it still exists hidden away in an attic or archive somewhere — an intriguing thought indeed.

Although not nearly as well known today as Rousseau (whom he admired) or Sade (whom he despised), Rétif was quite well known in his own lifetime and much admired by some readers, especially by a group of fellow writers who became his close friends — notably Mercier, Beaumarchais, and Grimod de La Reynière. Lavater called him 'le Richardson français,' and his works were praised by other writers both in France and abroad, including Benjamin Constant, Gabriel Sénac de Meilhan, and Friedrich von Schiller, who, in a letter to Goethe in 1798, encouraged him to read *Monsieur Nicolas*. Half a century later, Gérard de Nerval devoted one of the six biographies in *Les Illuminés* to Rétif, in which he praised his narrative gifts and keen observation of manners.[94] And, in the early twentieth century, he was rediscovered by the surrealist poets, who admired his prophetic visions and science fiction writing in works such as *La Découverte australe par un homme volant* (1781).

Rétif was nonetheless much criticized by some of his contemporaries for his moral platitudes, exhibitionist tendencies, and sensationalism and by others for his uneven style, neologisms, frequent digressions, and at times shameless padding of his works. The prominent eighteenth-century literary critic La Harpe dismissed his writing as vulgar and second rate, dubbing him scornfully 'le

---

[93] In 2006 and 2010, Pierre Testud published a two-volume critical edition of Rétif's journal that is far more complete and accurate than the partial edition published by Paul Cottin in 1889. In his introduction to volume 1, Testud writes: 'It is certain that Rétif continued to keep a diary, even if no trace of later entries have yet been found. He died on 3 February 1806 and, as long as he had the strength to hold a pen, he must have continued to keep a record of his daily life' (*Journal*, vol. 1, p. 13). For further discussion of Rétif's diary and extensive excerpts from Testud's edition, see Appendix D in MHRA's French edition of *Ingénue Saxancour*.

[94] See Gérard de Nerval, 'Les Confidences de Nicolas', in *Les Illuminés: Récits et portraits* (Paris: V. Lecou, 1852), pp. 77–242. While praising Rétif's gifts as a writer, Nerval did not hesitate to call attention to his personal failings and sloppiness of his style, which he attributed to the haste with which he wrote and to his eccentric spelling and typographic practices.

Voltaire des femmes de chambre' and 'le Rousseau des Halles'[95] [the Voltaire of chambermaids and the Rousseau of the fishmongers]. Similarly, writing to his wife in 1783 from the prison of Vincennes, Sade exclaimed: 'Above all, for God's sake, don't buy anything by Rétif! He's nothing but a trashy pop fiction writer, and I can't imagine why you ever thought of sending me anything of his.'[96] There is no doubt that Rétif's reputation suffered in his later years when, faced with bankruptcy and under intense pressure to publish, he churned out increasingly sensationalist material drawn from his stormy family life. He was roundly condemned, even by his friends, for airing his family's dirty laundry in *La Femme infidelle* (1786) and *Ingénue Saxancour* (1789), which many rightly saw as personal vendettas against his wife and son-in-law. Even more controversial was Rétif's salacious novel *L'Anti-Justine, ou les Délices de l'amour* (1793), in which he appeared to extol the pleasures of father-daughter incest. But these criticisms cannot take away from the value of Rétif's œuvre as a whole, which stands out as unique in late eighteenth-century French literature for its imaginativeness, flamboyance, and vivid, often moving portrayals of the everyday lives of ordinary people against a backdrop of social change and political upheaval.

Rétif's final years were marked by failing health and increasingly dire financial circumstances, made more difficult still by the hard economic times following the Revolution that made bookselling a perilous business. Toward the end of the preface to his autobiography, Rétif mournfully confided to his readers: 'I'm entrusting my spirit to you in order to survive a few days longer, like the Englishman condemned to death who sold his body. [...] Even though I've redoubled my efforts over the past seven years, all my hard work has not sufficed to pay my debts. It's becoming a worthless enterprise.'[97] A poignant epitaph for a lifetime of arduous labor and frustrated ambition.

[95] Les Halles were the vast central food market in Paris, which moved to Rungis outside the capital in the 1970s. When used pejoratively, as it is here, the term refers to the working-class tone and content that characterizes much of Rétif's fiction.

[96] The original French, difficult to translate, reads: 'Surtout n'achetez rien de ce Restif, au nom de Dieu! C'est un auteur de Pont-Neuf et de Bibliothèque bleue, dont il est inouï que vous ayez imaginé de m'envoyer quelque chose'.

[97] 'Je vous livre mon moral pour subsister quelques jours de plus, comme l'Anglais condamné qui vend son corps. [...] Tout mon travail, quoique redoublé, ne suffit pas depuis sept ans à payer mes dettes. C'est qu'il devient nul pour le produit'.

FIGURE 6.   1785 portrait of Rétif de La Bretonne by Louis Binet. Engraving by Louis-Sébastien Berthet (BnF). Used as frontispiece in *Le Drame de la vie*, vol. 1. Marandon's tribute to the author below reads: 'Son esprit libre et fier, sans guide, sans modèle,/Même alors qu'il s'égare étonne ses rivaux.//Amant de la nature, il lui dut ses pinceaux/Et fut simple, inégal et sublime comme elle.' [His mind, free and proud, with no guide or model to follow,/Impresses his rivals even when it rambles or goes astray.//A lover of nature, he owed his art to her/And was as simple, inconsistent, and sublime as she.]

Regarding the iconography of the portrait, Claude Jaëcklé-Plunian observes: 'The four corners of the illustration are decorated with symbols that evoke the "natural" characteristics identified with the author and his rural origins: [...] Beehive and bees, models of organization, order, and prosperity, are paired with hens and chicks, farm animals useful to man. Symbol of gentleness, innocence, and purity, the lamb represents rebirth. The sheaf of wheat completes this representation of life, since grain signifies the promise of regeneration. Each of these four images exemplifies man's relation to nature; through his labors, man is the hero who tamed nature, the defender of civilization' (Claude Jaëcklé Plunian, 'L'Image de Rétif de La Bretonne, hier et aujourd'hui' (http://retifdelabretonne.net/wp-content/uploads/2014/04/L'image-de-Rétif.pdf).

ABOUT THE TEXT

Sources of the Novel

In *Le Thesmographe*, Rétif explains that *Ingénue Saxancour* is a continuation and amplification of the story of his daughter's marriage presented in the last section of *La Femme infidelle*,[98] a bitter novel about his wife and their stormy marriage published two years earlier in 1786. In this earlier novel, in a series of letters to a friend, the narrator Jeandevert describes the circumstances of his daughter Ingénue's disastrous marriage. But to heighten the novel's dramatic effect, Rétif inserts a forty-page account of Ingénue Jeandevert's marital woes written in her own voice titled 'Causes de ma fuite et de ma séparation' [Reasons for my escape and my separation] — much of which reappears word for word in *Ingénue Saxancour*. This first-person narrative is then followed by a series of letters exchanged among the principal characters (drawn in part from actual letters and court documents) dealing with problems in the marriage.

In 'Mes Ouvrages' [My Works], Rétif reveals that *Ingénue Saxancour* is not based solely on his daughter's experiences, but also on those of his daughter's close friend Catherine Laruelle: 'It is already well known, as I acknowledged in my story [*Monsieur Nicolas*], that not all these loathsome deeds were the doing of L'Echiné [Augé], but are a mixture of the abuses inflicted on my elder daughter and on a tall, beautiful woman named Madame Moresquin. That lady (who went by the name Laruelle and not Moresquin) had been sold and prostituted in a house of ill-repute, etc.'[99] In *Monsieur Nicolas*, Rétif recalls a walk he took with Madame Laruelle in 1786, during which she told him the story of her nightmarish marriage to an abusive husband whom her parents had forced her to marry and from whom she had finally separated fourteen years later:

> 'Supremely unhappy with the most abominable of husbands — a brutal, cruel, and dissolute man who debased and prostituted me — I endured this all

---

[98] In *La Femme infidelle*, Rétif presents the story of Agnès's marriage primarily in Part III, letter 188, and Part IV, letter 227. See *Œuvres complètes*, 113 vols (Geneva: Slatkine Reprints, 1987–88), vol. 45, pp. 614–22, 787, 942. Unless indicated otherwise, subsequent references to Rétif's works (other than *Ingénue Saxancour*) will be to the Slatkine reprint edition, referred to as *OC*. Key passages, letters, and documents from *La Femme Infidelle* are presented in Appendix F.

[99] Rétif de La Bretonne, *Monsieur Nicolas, ou Le Cœur humain dévoilé*, 'Neuvième Epoque', in *Œuvres complètes* (Geneva: Slatkine Reprints, 1988), vol. 69, pp. 3143–44. Rétif's friendship with Madame Laruelle continued until her death from tuberculosis in 1790, mentioned in his diary entry for 23 February 1790.

before reaching a drastic decision. [...] If you only knew all the horrors Mr. Moresquin inflicted on me! [...] No words can express these horrors. Suffice it to say that not a single part of my body was treated with respect; he debased me more than the lowliest whore; he prostituted me without my knowledge. I'll stop now: such abominations would sully your imagination.'

Always in search of new material, Rétif urged Madame Laruelle to tell him her story: 'She did so, and I wrote the book I just mentioned, blending her story with that of my older daughter.'[100]

Pierre Testud points to a third possible source for Rétif's novel. In a letter to Rétif written in September 1785, a draftsman from Chartres named Sergent recounted the story of another abused wife, which Testud describes as very similar to *Ingénue Saxancour* and which he summarizes as follows: 'This correspondent presents a nine-page account in which he tells the story of a respectable and virtuous young woman married to a monster whose chief occupation is to debase her; he humiliates her, using the crudest expressions, and "yielding to his taste for libertinism, turns his home into perpetual orgy that his wife is forced to witness."' As Testud remarks, 'this account shares a number of features with *Ingénue Saxancour.*'[101]

Comparison of *Ingénue Saxancour* with Madame Laruelle's story in *Monsieur Nicolas* and with accounts of Agnès's marriage in *La Femme infidelle* and in Rétif's diary suggests that a few of the most shocking incidents of sexual abuse described in *Ingénue* — such as Moresquin's introduction of other men into Ingénue's bed and his other attempts to prostitute her — may have been drawn *not* from Agnès's own experiences, but from those of Madame Laruelle. Similarly, the orgy scenes in Rétif's novel (in which Moresquin humiliates and sexually assaults his wife in front of drunken companions) may have been inspired in part by Sergent's letter summarized earlier.

Yet despite the possible incorporation into the novel of a few incidents involving other abused wives, most commentators — as well as Rétif himself — maintain that the novel is based above all on the experiences of his older daughter Agnès. In a parenthetical note inserted in the middle of Madame Laruelle's story, Rétif explains: 'In *Ingénue Saxancour*, I recounted some of these horrors and

---

[100] Rétif, *Monsieur Nicolas*, OC, vol. 69, p. 3144. Madame Laruelle (whose husband's real name was Léonard Hucher) is mentioned several times in Rétif's diary. The first reference is found in the entry for 30 May 1786; other references are found in entries for June and July 1786, and for 24 April 1787. This is significant because it was during this same period that Rétif completed *La Femme infidelle* and began writing the definitive version of *Ingénue Saxancour* (begun on 8 June 1786). In his entry for 6 November 1786, he notes that he gave Madame Laruelle the proofs of *La Femme infidelle* to read.

[101] Testud, *Rétif de La Bretonne et la création littéraire* (Geneva: Droz, 1977), p. 504. Also see Testud's notes to *Monsieur Nicolas* (Paris: Gallimard, Bibliothèque de la Pléiade, 1989), vol. 2, p. 1376 (note 6 to p. 402).

named that man [Moresquin] as the perpetrator; and the strange thing about it is that another man, who shall remain unnamed, denounced this book everywhere as a story about him.' This unnamed man was of course his son-in-law Augé. Later in the same passage, Rétif reiterates this claim in a tribute to his novel that Madame Laruelle is said to have pronounced on her deathbed, with Agnès at her side: 'My sister! (for we are now sisters, brought together in the same book by your father and having had so many of the same experiences that your husband thought he recognized himself in the portrait presented of my husband), I am now avenged [...].'[102] The fact that Rétif's son-in-law recognized himself in Moresquin — so clearly that he had Rétif arrested for libel — suggests that Augé was indeed the chief prototype for Moresquin.

Rétif's biographer Adolphe Tabarant dismisses the Laruelle story as a decoy used by Rétif to divert the public's attention away from his daughter. 'This is just a specious argument. Ingénue Saxancour is Agnès and only her,' he insists. 'Everything scandalous in this book concerns Agnès's married life; Rétif's son-in-law Augé, the 'monster,' has simply exchanged the nickname L'Echiné for that of Moresquin, based on his swarthy, "Moorish" complexion.'[103] According to Daniel Baruch, a more recent Rétif biographer, the incorporation of Madame Laruelle's experiences into *Ingénue Saxancour* merely serves to heighten the tragic tone of the novel, but without significantly changing Agnès's story, given the strong parallels between the two women's experiences. 'Thanks to the narratives presented earlier in *La Femme infidelle* and *Mes Inscripcions*, it's now possible to tell what's what,' he writes. 'The addition of Madame Laruelle's story did not change much, except to intensify Auger's portrait, transforming it into an archetype of sorts of an abusive husband, the only portrait of its kind in the literature of the period.'[104] Similarly, Pierre Testud views *Ingénue Saxancour* as an amplification of the story of Agnès's marriage presented in *La Femme infidelle* — a dramatization in which the tragic aspects of her narrative are intensified and rendered more horrific by incorporating elements from Madame Laruelle's story: 'In this case, Rétif's imagination elaborates on the initial facts and intensifies the appalling aspects of the situation [...]. There is absolutely no doubt that this work is a literary elaboration of a personal drama that Rétif experienced through his daughter, but in a way so intense that only this dramatic amplification could do justice to its representation.'[105]

---

[102] *Monsieur Nicolas*, 'Neuvième Epoque', *OC*, vol. 69, p. 3145.

[103] Adolphe Tabarant, *Le Vrai Visage de Restif de La Bretonne* (Paris: Eds. Montaigne, 1936), p. 329. Reflecting on the parallels traditionally drawn between outward appearance and moral character, Rétif writes: 'tous les monstres étaient ainsi, que leur couleur était l'expression de leur vilaine âme' [Rétif, *Supplément à la Femme séparée* [1788], vol. 27 of *Les Contemporaines* (2nd edn), repr. in *OC*, vol. 25, p. 325].

[104] Baruch, *Restif de La Bretonne* (Paris: Fayard, 1996), p. 210.

[105] Testud, *Création littéraire*, pp. 503–4.

The strongest evidence that *Ingénue Saxancour* is based above all on Agnès Rétif's experiences is found in Rétif's diary, which corroborates certain key dates and events mentioned in the novel, such as when Ingénue flees from her husband's violence and where she stayed after she separated from him. Of particular interest are the entries concerning the police complaints and legal proceedings against Augé and the 'Mémoire contre Augé' that Rétif began writing in early August 1785, shortly after Agnès left Augé definitively. The parallels in the descriptions of abuse in the 'Mémoire contre Augé' and the novel (parallels discussed in the Introduction) are quite striking. Repeated references to the *mémoire* in Rétif's diary in late summer and fall of that year show that he devoted many hours to this document, a first version of which was completed in early December and inserted into his diary entry for December 4.[106] This first version was given to Agnès's lawyer Cavagnac to counter the legal action Augé took on December 2 in a failed attempt to force his wife to return to him. In the months of court proceedings leading up to the final separation hearing in March 1787, Rétif continued to revise and expand his judicial memoir to include accounts of further incidents involving Augé (also described in the novel) and additional complaints against him. A final reference to the drafting of the *mémoire* is found in Rétif's diary entry for 25 February 1787: 'Went to Madame Bleret's home to talk about the Monster, then worked on the addition to the accusations against him […]; finished the report.[107]

Composition of the Novel and Its Publication History

Rétif's diary indicates that he completed the account of his daughter's marriage in *La Femme infidelle* in early February 1786,[108] and that on March 18, he began writing a first version of *Ingénue Saxancour*, a 28-page short story titled 'L'Epouse séparée' [The wife who separated from her husband]. This first version was completed a few weeks later and published in November of that year in *Les Françaises*, along with two other short stories describing Agnès's marriage.[109]

---

[106] *Journal*, ¶586, vol. 1, pp. 230–34. For the full text of this journal entry, see Appendix D, Excerpt 25, in MHRA's French edition of *Ingénue Saxancour*.

[107] *Journal*, ¶990, vol. 1, p. 426. The 'Madame Bleret' referred to here is no doubt Blérie's sister-in-law, in whose home Augé had behaved so outrageously during a holiday visit.

[108] In his diary entry for 10 February 1786, Rétif writes 'A l'imprimerie, deux pages de liaison de l'Infid. pour finir l'art. de ma fille'. [Sent two pages to serve as the link between *La Femme infidelle* and the story about my daughter.] (*Journal*, ¶647, vol. 1, p. 262.)

[109] The two other stories concerning Agnès's marriage are titled 'L'Epouse aimant un autre homme' [The wife who loved another man] (XIXe Exemple) and 'L'Epouse d'un homme veuf' [The widower's wife] (XXVIe Exemple), which like 'L'Epouse séparée' (XXIe Exemple) are found in vol. 3 of the 1786 edition of *Les Françaises* (vol. 50 in the Slatkine reprint edition).

Composition of the novel was interrupted for two years, perhaps because Rétif found the events of Agnès's marriage too painful to write about or simply because he was preoccupied with the legal proceedings against Augé and busy with other writings. He may also have wanted to wait until the legal issues had been resolved and a degree of closure had been reached before finishing the novel. Rétif's diary indicates that *Ingénue Saxancour* was finally completed on 22 April 1788 and that the final version was given to the censor in late summer of that year. Printing began on June 27 and was concluded on September 21. The novel was approved by the censor Toustain-Richebourg on November 18 and went on sale shortly afterwards. However, the date that appears on the copyright page of the original Paris edition published by Maradan is 1789.

A second edition of the novel did not appear until 1922. Published by the Paris-based Bibliothèque des curieux in the collection 'Les Maîtres de l'amour,' it reproduced the entire original text of 1789. In 1931, Henri Bachelin published a third edition in volume 5 of a nine-volume collection of selected works by Rétif. Bachelin shortened the novel nearly by half by omitting all material extraneous to the story of Ingénue's marriage: theater plays, poetry, and background stories of minor characters inserted by Rétif to increase the number of pages and potential revenue from sale of the book. In the original version of the novel, Rétif had tried to justify these long digressions in the novel as a necessary diversion from the painful events of Ingénue's marriage.[110]

In a fourth edition published in 1948 (and then reissued by Pauvert in 1960 and by Lattès in 1979), Gilbert Lely chose to omit the story of Ingénue's mother's infidelities at the beginning of the novel, in addition to all the material cut by Bachelin. He convincingly argued that these episodes, like those concerning Ingénue's childhood friends, 'are, strictly speaking, extraneous to the main plot and give a slow start to a novel that otherwise is truly unique in the writings of Rétif de La Bretonne through its relentless cruelty.'[111]

In 1978, as part of the '10–18 Collection' published by the Union générale d'éditions, Daniel Baruch brought out a more complete edition of the novel (minus the plays and poetry), followed by various ancillary materials. This same

---

[110] For example, in the unabridged 1789 edition, Ingénue's narrative is interrupted by insertion of a one-act play to which Moresquin takes his wife in the hope of attracting the attention of a important official who might advance his faltering career in exchange for her favors. In a rather lame attempt to justify this digression, she explains: 'I inserted this play to provide a respite from the horrors I'm recounting. Indeed, people must have noticed that I had delayed relating this episode by all possible means. I'm interrupting it whenever the occasion arises to give my imagination a rest. It's an art in this sad undertaking to add these incidental episodes, and what would be a grave defect in any other work is, in this case, the highest degree of perfection!' (*Ingénue Saxancour, OC*, vol. 54, Part 2, p. 180.)

[111] Gilbert Lely, 'Introduction', *Ingénue Saxancour, ou La Femme séparée* (Paris: Lattès, 1979), p. 10.

version of the novel reappears in Baruch's fine critical edition of eight of Rétif's key autobiographical texts published in 2002 by R. Laffont and now unfortunately out of print, as is its companion volume edited by Pierre Testud.

The Present Edition

In the present edition, I have chosen to omit all the material cut by Bachelin, as well as the episode at the beginning of the novel concerning Ingénue's mother's infidelities that Lely omitted from his edition. I agree with Lely's argument that, like the incidental plays and poetry, these episodes are extraneous to the story of Ingénue's marriage, distracting from the narrative and diminishing its impact on the reader. Similar criticisms were expressed by Grimod de la Reynière in a letter he wrote to Rétif after first reading the novel in 1791:

> Once I finally succeeded in getting a copy of *Ingénue Saxancour*, I read it very attentively and with great interest. My only criticism is that the book's appeal is diminished by the addition of some parts that are quite unrelated to the story, one of which was even published separately, and that — regardless of what you may say — were only added as padding. It would have been better to include only two of these additions, instead of creating this hodgepodge that spoils the overall effect of the novel as well as the impact of these separate pieces that we'd enjoy much better if they didn't keep interrupting your story this way.[112]

In defending the cuts he chose to make in his abridged edition of the novel, Lely convincingly argued: 'It seemed to me that *Ingénue Saxancour* could only benefit from this pruning and that the statue of the infernal couple, freed of the brambles surrounding it, will emerge more clearly in its naked perversity.'[113]

A thornier question arose concerning how best to end the novel. In the original 1789 edition, Ingénue's story seems to end on an upbeat note with her departure in 1787 for a peaceful three and a half-month stay in the country with her friend Félicité after the court finally grants her a separation from her husband. This conclusion parallels actual events in Agnès Rétif's life. But rather than end here, Rétif then inserted a full-length three-act comedy titled *Epiménide*, which Agnès supposedly gave Félicité to read. The play is followed by Ingénue's account of her sister Marion's thwarted marriage prospects, based loosely on real-life events.

---

[112] Letter from Grimod de La Reynière of 29 May 1791, repr. in *Le Drame de la vie*, *OC*, vol. 38, p. 1316. For extended excerpts from this letter, see Appendix C, Excerpt 30, in MHRA's French edition of *Ingénue Saxancour*.

[113] Lely, 'Introduction', pp. 11–12.

The original 1789 edition concludes with two postscripts[114] written in the voice of Marivert-Courtenay, under whose name Rétif first published *La Femme infidelle* and who is presented here as a family friend and editor of *Ingénue Saxancour*. In the first postscript, the fictional editor recounts how Moresquin falsely accused Marion of stealing a neighbor's watch, which prompted an angry exchange of letters between Saxancour and his son-in-law. This is followed by Saxancour's death and Moresquin's murder of Ingénue, for which he is sentenced to hard labor for life.[115]

In the second postscript, Marivert-Courtenay explains his reasons for publishing the account of Ingénue's disastrous marriage: 'It is I, *Marivert*, who now take up the pen to complete this work that I'm publishing without the authorization either of my friend Mr. Saxancour or of his daughter Madame Ingénue.' Alluding to the continuing threat to the family posed by the monstrous son-in-law, he adds:

> It's my duty as a friend. I shudder sometimes when I think that if Mr. Saxancour were to die, then two lovely and timid young women would be exposed to all the rage, wickedness, and zeal that villainy can produce. That's the reason for the publication of these memoirs, for this pilfering of sorts [...]. Moreover, as I explain in the preface, what also compels me to publish this work is the great, indeed immeasurable public service it offers by opening the eyes of young women.

These prefatory remarks are then followed, rather incongruously, by a somewhat different version of the events from that related in the preceding two sections (the

---

[114] In vol. 55 of the Slatkine reprint edition of the complete works, Ingénue's narrative ends on p. 134, followed by the play *Epiménide* (134–241) and Ingénue's account of her sister's failed marriage prospects (241–49), which are followed in turn by the first postscript (249–56) and second postscript (256–60).

[115] In the introduction to his edition of the novel, Lely explains: 'The post-scriptum [...] are totally fictional and serve only to elude the reader's curiosity, since in fact Ingénue (Agnès Rétif) did not die until 1854 and Moresquin (Augé) was not sent to prison in the Antilles, but was condemned to death and executed on the Place de la Grève' (p. 11). Although Lely is correct in pointing to the fictional nature of the events recounted in the two postscripts, he is quite mistaken in the alternate facts he presents: Agnès Rétif actually died in 1812 at age 51, *not* in 1854. And, contrary to the legend spawned by Paul Lacroix that Augé was executed in 1793 (supposedly for murdering his mother-in-law), Rétif's ex-son-in-law went on to marry a third time in 1795 and to continue his career as a tax-collector until 1810, as Baruch points out in the introduction to his edition of Rétif's novel. In Baruch's opinion, the fact that Augé was still employed as a civil servant in 1810 in Savoie, where he received positive reviews for his work, suggests that Rétif's charges of professional incompetence were exaggerated, perhaps even unjust: 'It's unlikely that he could have remained a civil servant for forty years if he had drawn attention for debauched or reprehensible behavior or for the incompetence and laziness Rétif accused him of on many occasions' [*Restif de La Bretonne*, 2 vols (Paris: R. Laffont, 2002), vol. 2, p. 468.]

false accusations of theft against Marion, the murder of Ingénue by her husband, and his subsequent punishment).

In order to maintain the coherence of the narrative, I chose (like Lely) to end the novel with the conclusion of Ingénue's story and her departure for Félicité's house in Normandy — an ending that (as noted earlier) mirrors actual events in Agnès Rétif's life. This ending is also more in keeping with the unconventional — and indeed transformative — arc of the narrative: the fact that Ingénue, like Agnès, managed to escape her marriage and to expose the abuse her husband inflicted on her. As Christine Roulston observes:

> *Ingénue Saxancour* is one of the few novels in which the wife successfully separates from her husband without being punished or dying at the close of the narrative. The relative autonomy she eventually achieves signals a transformation in the perception of conjugal sexuality. Ingénue is the given the right to function as an individual by being able to leave her marriage behind and to expose its violence.[116]

The fact that Rétif considered such radically different endings to his novel no doubt reflects a certain ambivalence to its publication and a very real ambivalence to the outcome of his daughter's marriage. To give a more complete picture of the creative process behind the novel's composition, the two postscripts Rétif appended to the original 1789 edition are included in English translation in the present edition.[117]

---

[116] Roulston, 'Marriage, Sexuality, and the Meaning of the Wedding Night in Eighteenth-Century France', p. 76.

[117] For the original French text of the two postscripts appended to the original 1789 edition of the novel, see Appendix E in MHRA's French edition of *Ingénue Saxancour*, pp. 243–46. Also presented in Appendix E (pp. 246–51) are excerpts from the 'Supplément à *La Femme séparée*', completed on 29 September 1788, published soon thereafter in vol. 27 of the second edition of *Les Contemporaines*, and reprinted in *OC*, vol. 25, pp. 304–52. This 'Supplement' to *Ingénue Saxancour* presents a much longer alternative ending to the novel that combines various elements of the accounts given in the two postscripts.

To make the text more readable for modern audiences, several additional changes have been made to the formatting and punctuation found in the original French edition. In the late eighteenth century, quotation marks were a relatively new form of punctuation; dashes or italics were generally used instead to indicate dialogue. For this edition, following modern usage, all dialogue has been set in quotation marks, with paragraph breaks added each time there is a change in speaker. Overly long paragraphs in the 1789 edition have been divided into shorter ones where paragraph breaks are warranted. Similarly, overly long sentences connected by commas, colons, or semi-colons have been divided into shorter sentences for greater clarity. As was often the practice in eighteenth-century novels, Rétif makes frequent use of ellipses. Because they tend to distract from the story rather than to enhance it, the ellipses have been removed, except in cases where they serve a clear stylistic purpose, such as creating suspense or reflecting confusion or hesitation on the part of the characters.

Contrary to the lavishly illustrated original editions of *Les Contemporaines* or *Le Paysan et la paysane pervertis*, the original 1789 edition of *Ingénue Saxancour* contained no illustrations at all. In the turbulent months leading up to the French Revolution, Rétif's finances were in disarray, as were those of the country as a whole, so neither the author nor his readers were in a position to pay for an expensive illustrated edition. To remedy this lack, illustrations from other works by Rétif have been chosen to illustrate the present edition, along with portraits of the author, his two daughters, and various friends mentioned in the novel (Mercier, Grimod de La Reynière, and Fanny de Beauharnais). Most of the illustrations have been taken from original editions of Rétif's works, including *Les Françaises, Le Paysan perverti, La Paysanne pervertie, La Dernière Avanture d'un homme de quarante-cinq ans, Les Nuits de Paris,* and *Aline et Valcourt*. Many of these illustrations were drawn to Rétif's specifications by Louis Binet and engraved by his close friend Louis Berthet, in whose home Agnès took refuge after leaving her husband in 1786. Also included are two engravings by Carlo Farnetti from Henri Bachelin's 1931 edition of *Ingénue Saxancour*, as well as eighteenth-century prints by Charles-Melchior Descourtis and Pierre-Gabriel Berthault picturing views along the Seine in Paris mentioned in the novel.

FIGURE 7.   Portrait of Agnès Rétif. Artist and date unknown. Published in *Monsieur Nicolas, ou Le Cœur humain dévoilé*. Preface by Marc Chadourne. (Paris: Au Cercle du livre précieux, 1959), vol. 6, opposite p. 560. (BnF)

In a short story titled 'Les Deux Sœurs', Rétif paints the following verbal portrait of his daughter: 'Agnès had a noble appearance, as imposing as it was beautiful. Her character reflected her person. She was proud, direct, and rather brusque, but also good-natured, kind-hearted, and supremely generous. Her frank, honest nature sometimes caused problems for her; for such people are easily duped as a result of their natural integrity' ('Les Deux Sœurs', Episode 363, in *Les Nuits de Paris, OC*, vol. 85, p. 3349).

Ingénue Saxancour

or

The Wife Separated from Her Husband

Story illustrating how dangerous it is for young women to marry
obstinately and hastily against their parents' wishes

Written by herself

EDITOR'S PREFACE

∽

I know of no works as useful as those depicting the causes of misfortune in stories drawn from real-life events. We should repeatedly warn young women: *You must not marry against your parents' wishes on a whim or for a passing fancy!* But girls are so tired of hearing these platitudes that their truth no longer makes any impression. So it is a kind of heroism when a courageous writer, scorning the trivial niceties of today's insipid publications, takes it upon himself to publish a story that is as true as it is horrible, exposing himself to its inevitable failure among all our superficial readers and squeamish ladies of fashion. What will people find in this work? An imprudent girl who, against her father's wishes, marries a despicable, deceitful man who, before the wedding, lied about his character and financial situation, but who never was able to lie about his mind, given that intelligence is the only mask that a dim-witted hypocrite is unable to put on; a man who, after the wedding, reveals all his vices and subjects his unfortunate wife to all the whims and turpitudes of a debauched libertine, all the vile abuse of a corrupt scoundrel, all the torture that a torturer can inflict; a man who compels his wife to flee and who pursues her relentlessly after she escapes his fury.

This work contains what polite French society would call *horreurs*. I agree, but I feel that these horrors must be included so the book can be of use to girls who are inclined to marry against their parents' wishes, especially those who defy the sacred authority of an enlightened father. I recall that when *La Femme infidelle*[118]

---

[118] *La Femme infidelle* was first published by Rétif in May 1786 under the penname Maribert-Courtenay — the same pseudonym he used when he published *Ingénue Saxancour* three years later (using the alternate spelling Marivert). This bitter novel details Rétif's stormy marriage to Agnès Lebegue. In the fourth and final section, Rétif (alias Jeandevert) describes his daughter Ingénue's even more disastrous marriage in a series of letters to a friend. To heighten the dramatic effect, Rétif inserts a forty-page account of Ingénue Jeandevert's marital woes written in her own voice titled 'Causes de ma fuite et de ma séparation' (much of which reappears word for word in *Ingénue Saxancour*). This first-person narrative is followed by a series of letters exchanged among the principal characters (drawn in part from actual letters) dealing with problems in the marriage.

La Femme infidelle is available in Slatkine's two-volume reprint edition of Rétif's complete works: *Œuvres complètes* (Geneva, 1988), vols 44–45. Unless specified otherwise, all references to Rétif's *Œuvres complètes* are to the Slatkine reprint edition (referred to henceforth as *OC*). The entire 113-volume set is available through the Bibliothèque Nationale's on-line catalogue (http://catalogue.bnf.fr). Key passages from *La Femme infidelle* are presented in Appendices C and F in MHRA's French edition of *Ingénue Saxancour*.

first appeared, a great lady complained that such dreadful things should not be published![119] But what's truly dreadful is for a girl to marry, against her father's wishes, a vile man whose villainy he has unmasked. In any case, that great lady is under no obligation to read *Ingénue Saxancour*, in which these terrible events are recounted with artless naïveté. These events were veiled in the fourth part of *La Femme infidelle*. Here, they are laid bare, and the monster appears as hideous in the narrative as he is in real life.[120] But such works are only useful insofar as they inspire horror. Yet, I admit that I shuddered in reading these memoirs, where I found such realistic descriptions, written artlessly, without being weakened, enlivened, and prettied up — *dehorribilized* (as the English would say) — by a young woman who depicts what she has felt and suffered to the brink of despair.

In today's society, marriages like Ingénue Saxancour's, contracted against the father's wishes, are common occurrences, made more common still by the false morality of certain plays in the theater. But, in her case, the consequences were truly horrific! To what dire straits the wretched Saxancour is constantly reduced! And if she was indeed guilty, how terrible the punishment! Read her story, young ladies, and tremble!

---

[119] This is probably an allusion to the strong criticisms of *La Femme infidelle* expressed by Madame de Beausset, Grimod de La Reynière's aunt, whose comments are discussed in the introduction. La Reynière conveyed his aunt's objections in a letter to Rétif dated 29 May 1791 and expressed equally strong criticisms of his own in a letter dated 7 July of that year. For excerpts from these letters, see Appendix C, Excerpts 30 and 31, in MHRA's French edition of *Ingénue Saxancour*.

[120] The relation between the narratives presented *La Femme infidelle* and *Ingénue Saxancour* is underscored in a footnote on the title page of the later novel that claims that Ingénue Saxancour's real name is 'Jean-de-Vert' (alternate spelling of Jeandevert, the heroine's last name in the earlier novel).

INGÉNUE SAXANCOUR

~

You no longer speak to me of those lovely lands
Where women idolized by a gallant people
Receive the praise owed to their beauty,
Companions to their husbands and queens wherever they go.[121]

I have no need to write a preface to explain the moral aim of these memoirs. I will tell my tale simply and candidly, and the moral will emerge from the example I'll provide. How fortunate my female readers will be if they learn this lesson at my expense!

* * *

In her youth, my aunt had been apprenticed as a seamstress to Madame Brocard, who had since been widowed and left in difficult financial circumstances. That woman had a pretty, rather frail daughter whom my aunt Bitez[122] had known as a young child and to whom she had grown very attached. Evicted from their apartment for failing to pay their rent, they arrived penniless at my aunt's to ask

---

[121] Drawn from Voltaire's play *Zaïre*, the original French reads: 'Vous ne me parlez plus de ces belles contrées, / Où d'un peuple poli les femmes adorées / Reçoivent cet encens que l'on doit à leurs yeux, / Compagnes d'un époux et reines en tous lieux' (Act I, Scene 1, lines 9–12). The lines that follow are even more relevant to Rétif's novel: 'Libres sans déshonneur, et sages sans contrainte, / Et ne devant jamais leurs vertus à la crainte! / Ne soupirez-vous plus pour cette liberté? / Le sérail d'un soudan [sultan], sa triste austérité, / Ce nom d'esclave enfin, n'ont-ils rien qui vous gêne?' [Free without dishonor and chaste without constraint,/And never owing their virtues to fear! / Do you no longer yearn for this liberty? / A sultan's harem, its grim austerity, / This status as a slave, do not these disturb you in any way?] Zaïre, heroine of Voltaire's tragedy, is a slave and favorite concubine in the Sultan of Jerusalem's harem. Like Ingénue, Zaïre is a captive; but unlike Ingénue, she is in love with her captor.

[122] Bitez is an anagram of the married name of Rétif's half sister Marguerite-Anne (Margot) Bizet (1727–1808), with whom Agnès was living before her marriage. It was at Madame Bizet's home on the quai de Gesvres that Augé met Agnès and began courting her. Madame Bizet, whom Rétif calls Madame Betzi in *La Femme infidelle*, was the childless widow of a jeweler (*marchand bijoutier*) in Paris. She served as matchmaker in her niece's marriage and provided her with a generous dowry of 12,000 *livres*, along with some furniture and linens. In the 1780s when these events took place, the French *livre tournois* was roughly equivalent to 10 € (or about $11) in today's purchasing power. [Source: Giacomo Casanova, *Histoire de ma vie*, éd. Jean-Christophe Igalens et Érik Leborgne (Paris: Robert Laffont, Coll. Bouquins, 2013), t. I, pp. 1543–44.] If this information is correct, 12,000 livres would have been worth approximately €120,000 or $134,000.

her for lodgings in the building she managed. Although certain of never being paid, my aunt could hardly refuse to give them shelter. She welcomed them with tender compassion and provided them with basic furnishings and other necessities, since all their belongings had been confiscated when they were evicted.

When the two women were settled, my aunt said to me: 'My niece, I would not advise you to visit our neighbors if Madame Brocard and her daughter were well off. Our time should not be wasted, and such visits always entail a certain danger; but these women are destitute. Let not a day go by without one of us paying them a visit. Poverty deserves respect.' I promised my aunt that I would follow her wishes. Every other day, I went up to see Madame Brocard, and I gradually became friends with her daughter, even though she was fifteen years older than I.

One day, six months after my aunt's former mistress moved into the building, I found them both very excited when I arrived. I did not ask why; but since they kept whispering into each other's ear, I cut short my visit. I had started to leave when they stopped me: 'Are you at all reluctant to marry?' asked the mother.

'I don't know, Madam; it all depends on the person in question. In any case, if you have something to say to me on the subject, speak first to my aunt about it.'

'Very well!' replied Madame Brocard, who was raised in a respectable family. 'Mademoiselle is right; it's Madame Bitez who should hear about this first.' With that, I went back downstairs.

The next day, as it was my aunt's turn to visit Madame Brocard, they could speak to her freely. They no doubt spoke to her at length, for that night at dinner, Madame Bitez spoke the following words to me, which I'll never forget:

'My dear niece, you're aware of your father's financial situation and of your mother's extravagance. It's a penniless household from which you can expect little support. A very good match has been proposed for you involving a suitor who has spoken to Madame Brocard and with whom I am myself acquainted since his parents resided in the flat below Madame Brocard when he was a child. The parents are well off, both still living. Their son is an only child; he'll inherit it all, and these people have an annual income of at least a thousand *écus*, in addition to the father's salary. The son is a widower; but it's common knowledge that he made his wife very happy during their ten years together! He himself has a job and hopes to succeed his father when he retires. I doubt that a better match could ever be found. Think about it carefully. The man is thirty-five years old; you're only nineteen. But one risks everything with a young husband! He's a mature man, not good-looking; but what good is a handsome man who cares more for himself and is vainer than a woman! Looks are unimportant! However, it's entirely up to you.'

Such were the words my aunt spoke to me. What she said was perfectly reasonable, or so it seemed, and I let myself be taken in, as she had been taken in

Ah! qu'il est laid !

FIGURE 8. 'It was at Madame Brocard's that I saw him for the first time. I was repelled by his ugly, vulgar appearance. I thought to myself: "I will never have anything to do with that man."' Illustration by Louis Binet, engraved by Louis Papin, in *Les Contemporaines* (1780–82), vol. 6, Nouvelle 40, p. 523. The original caption (visible below the image) reads 'Ah! qu'il est laid!' [Oh! How ugly he is!] (BnF)

herself.[123] Fooled by appearances, Madame Brocard had won over my aunt. No one was at fault here but the monster who sought to satisfy his brutal passion by all possible means, inept deceptions that could easily have been exposed, but at the same time so outrageous that it never entered our minds that they were entirely without foundation.

It's at this point in the story that Moresquin — deceitful, brutal, deranged, vile, cowardly — appeared on the scene. I hadn't yet seen him, although he had noticed me and had already condemned me in his own mind to the misfortune of becoming his wife! Alas! Can we ever escape our fate? It was at Madame Brocard's that I saw him for the first time. I was repelled by his ugly, vulgar appearance. I thought to myself: 'I'll never have anything to do with that man.' It was my guardian angel that inspired these thoughts. I replied coldly to his convoluted compliments which struck me as muddled and absurd; it was clear to me that this man had no idea what he was saying. That night, I told my aunt: 'The match you're proposing doesn't suit me.'

'Oh! You young women are all alike! When a man isn't a dandy, a pretentious young beau with pretty curls, they don't care for him! Come, come, my niece, a man is always handsome enough when he's respectable and is able to provide all the essentials to his wife, with a degree of comfort to boot.' These arguments made a certain impression on me, and the truth is that my aunt, who now denies having contributed to my marriage, was responsible for it more than anyone else.

After further discussions, my resistance gradually weakened. Madame Brocard harangued me at length as well, and I found myself far more confused than persuaded by these endless debates. I didn't know how to defend myself. Alas! I know today what I should have done: to question everything and to demand proof of the benefits that people were making so much of to me. The whole illusion would then have shattered on its own, and I would have escaped my misfortune! But there were no doubts in my mind. For here were two wise old women, one of whom was my aunt, who had known Moresquin and his family for thirty years, who assured me of his fine character, good conduct, and sound financial situation.

---

[123] In *La Femme infidelle*, Rétif suggests that his sister urged Agnès to marry Augé in order to free herself from the responsibility of providing for her niece, with whom her relations had soured: 'For more than eighteen months, things went smoothly for Ingénue at her aunt's. But then an unfortunate circumstance arose that ruined everything. My sister disapproved of my daughter's elegant attire. Frequent quarrels soured their relations, and she wanted to see her niece married' (*La Femme infidelle*, OC, vol. 45, p. 789). In *Monsieur Nicolas*, Rétif goes a step further and accuses his sister of lying to them: 'Margot wanted to marry off my daughter in order to be rid of her because, being pious and very stupid, she found that her niece dressed in too worldly a fashion. This was the sole reason that led her to lie and deceive us and to ruin my daughter's life' (*Monsieur Nicolas*, OC, vol. 69, p. 3025). For the full account in *Monsieur Nicolas* concerning Agnès's stay with her aunt and Rétif's accusations against his sister, see Appendix B, Excerpts 1 and 3, in MHRA's French edition of *Ingénue Saxancour*.

I suspected nothing; how could I? So I gradually softened my resistance and finally agreed to let them introduce Moresquin to my father.

My aunt went all out in support of Moresquin. She invited him to dine with my father at her home. It was against all the rules and simply shouldn't have been done. My father said as much. But as the dinner wasn't at his home and, as he had taken no part in these arrangements and had no wish to embarrass my aunt, he agreed to come. Moresquin made an unfavorable first impression on him, as one might expect. But he still wanted to reserve judgment. During dinner, he was listened to him politely and, since his father's presence stopped him from trying to impress, the stupidity of his remarks was tolerable. As for Moresquin senior, he was a good, decent man, whose only fault in my eyes was to have fathered such a despicable character. Monsieur Saxancour quite liked the father, but remained undecided regarding the son. As we were leaving the table, Moresquin went so far as to ask for my hand in marriage.

'Not so fast, sir! I hardly know you.'

'But monsieur, Madame Bitez, who is a respectable woman, knows me as does Madame Brocard.'

'It's because my sister knows you that I dined with you. But I need to know you personally in order to even consider giving you my daughter's hand.' Moresquin wanted to say something further, but was intimidated by my father's look of impatience. My aunt in turn asked for his opinion.

'I don't yet have a feeling about him; but I'm waiting to make up my mind.'

'For that to happen, you need to allow him to visit us and to come here yourself from time to time.'

'I forbid my daughter to receive male visitors. As for you, you're free to receive visits from whomever you like without my permission.'

'I see you don't like him!'

'I'm telling you, sister, that I don't yet have an opinion on the matter. That man hardly makes a good first impression; but I'll need more time to form a positive or negative opinion of him.' Such was my father's response.

Monsieur Saxancour was extremely busy at the time. He refused to meet with Moresquin when he asked, which is why Moresquin decided to write to him. His letter is a masterpiece of absurdity. (We won't include his letter, which is published in *La Femme infidelle*.)[124]

---

[124] See Appendix C, Excerpt 1, in MHRA's French edition of *Ingénue Saxancour*. Describing Moresquin's letter in the unabridged edition of *Ingénue Saxancour*, the narrator remarks: 'His letter is a masterpiece of absurdity. We must reprint it without changing a single word, without adding a single punctuation mark'. However, the letter is omitted from the original 1789 edition of *Ingénue Saxancour*, where Rétif simply refers the reader to the letter in *La Femme infidelle*. (See the Slatkine reprint edition of *Ingénue Saxancour*, *OC*, vol. 55, pp. 22–23.) Introducing the letter in *La Femme infidelle*, the narrator remarks: 'His ridiculous style and idiotic turns of phrase made my mind up for me. I told my sister that I didn't want a stupid robot, an

This letter made up my father's mind definitively. He resolved to turn Moresquin down politely, but firmly. He didn't know that man. Nor did he realize to what extent, despite his lack of intelligence and good sense, Moresquin had managed to captivate my aunt and how successfully Madame Brocard had argued his suit to me. They believed they were promoting my happiness, and everyone joined together to deceive my father. Alas! I was above all the one they were deceiving!

When Mr. Saxancour showed Moresquin's letter to my aunt, she was embarrassed by it, but did not take long to respond: 'Indeed!' she exclaimed. 'You, you're smart and witty; does that make you any richer? Come now! It's not intelligence that brings success in business; and, in that respect, fools succeed better than witty people.' Unfortunately, what she said was only too true! My father sensed this and, although his resolution did not waver, he decided to soften his refusal somewhat. Yet, on one occasion, he did lose patience.

When his letter went unanswered, Moresquin dared come seek a response himself at my father's residence. At the time, Mr. Saxancour was living was in the home of Madame Leeman, mother of the young woman who for a time had been my companion during our apprenticeship together with Madame Claire. My father had a way of seeing who came to his door; he recognized Moresquin and did not respond. Moresquin finally lost patience and left. A moment later, I arrived, not knowing that Moresquin had been there. I knocked, but my father did not answer. I knocked several times again and called out: 'Papa, I know you're home. Open the door for me!'

Mr. Saxancour can be quite short-tempered and brusque; believing I had come on account of Moresquin, he was outraged. He opened the door, but only to treat me most harshly. I threw myself at his feet and asked for his forgiveness. I promised to submit entirely to his will, and he forgave me on that condition. He forbid me from seeing Moresquin or from having anything to do with him. I feel obligated tell the whole story, since the detestable husband given to me by fate criticized my father for not opposing his marriage suit. My father hit me for the first and last time. I wanted to escape, but he called me back in a fearsome tone. When a big strong neighbor boy stepped forward to ask what was going on, my father pushed him away so violently that he nearly knocked him over. The young man smiled and left. He later told me that he had been very angry to be treated so badly, but fearing to further irritate my father against me, he had simply smiled in an effort to defuse the tension.

---

automaton, as a son-in-law' (*OC*, vol. 45, pp. 791–92). Rétif quotes Moresquin's letter verbatim in *Les Contemporaines*, where he adds the following comment: 'This crazy, verbose, incomprehensible letter was the first reason that led me to oppose my elder daughter's unfortunate marriage' (*Les Contemporaines*, 2nd edn [1784], *OC*, vol. 19, letter 45, n. p.). In the original edition of *La Femme infidelle*, this letter — like all those from L'Echiné — are filled with errors in spelling and grammar, presumably reproducing those in Augé's correspondence.

Following this incident, my aunt was very annoyed with my father. She no longer dared speak to him of Moresquin. But she received Moresquin in her home. He also visited Madame Brocard's apartment, where I was sometimes sent under various pretenses. When I found him there, I wanted to leave, but they showed me different things that forced me to stay. The situation remained the same all winter until the month of February. But I almost forgot to mention that in January 1781, I received a love letter from Moresquin that should have had the same effect on me as the one written to my father. (That letter, worthy of its author, can be found in *La Femme infidelle*.)[125]

The affectation with which Moresquin speaks in the postscript of a château and its surroundings shows that he wanted to be seen as a man with influential connections. The truth is that, contrary to his suggestion in the letter, he was acquainted neither with Mr. Lebègue, the estate's owner, nor even with the estate manager. From his first wife, Moresquin had inherited a small property worth about a thousand *écus*[126] in les Andelys.[127] He had played up this modest fortune, speaking about it as if it were an estate; and, by giving its location, his aim was to make people think that he was on friendly terms with the local nobleman. This was the impression made on my aunt, a good but dim-witted woman, who easily convinced me of it, given my lack of experience. However, I should point out that she never agreed to let me show this letter to my father. It's not that she didn't find it admirable; after reading it five or six times, she said to me: 'Your father claims that Moresquin lacks intelligence! But in my view, the fact that he sent such a well-written letter shows how smart he is.' I smiled, for I clearly sensed the flaws of his convoluted style and of the muddled ideas he was incapable of expressing. But I was deluding myself. I even hoped — dare I admit it? — I was hoping to dominate a fool. I didn't realize that a pretentious fool is the most self-assured, self-righteous of men.

---

[125] See Appendix C, Excerpt 2, in MHRA's French edition of *Ingénue Saxancour*.

[126] In the years leading up to the French Revolution, the silver *écu* was equivalent to 3 *livres*. If one *livre* was roughly equivalent to €10 in today's currency (according the the source cited in n. 122 above), one silver *écu* would have been worth about €30 or $33. If this information is correct, Moresquin's farm would have been worth about €30,000 ($33,000).

[127] Les Andelys is a commune on the Seine, northeast of Evreux in Normandy. Commenting on this postscript, Baruch notes that Augé had indeed inherited a farm worth 1,000 *écus* in the commune of Muyds (Muids) from his first wife, as part of her dowry. [Baruch, *Restif de La Bretonne* (2002), p. 446, n. 1.]

While all this was happening, my mother was away taking care of her mother's meager estate; for just as she couldn't leave when she had business to attend to, she couldn't return once she had left. It took her six months to settle an estate in which her share was only 750 livres. But she finally arrived on January 21. My father felt obligated to tell her about the match that had been proposed for me, although he knew that she didn't love me. It was the third or fourth marriage proposal he had received for me. I haven't mentioned them, since I didn't know these men and since their proposals had no effect on my life. My mother listened very carefully to what my father told her. She said she would look into the matter herself.

My aunt could not stand my mother, and as soon as she heard that her sister-in-law was aware of the situation, she exclaimed: 'Oh, well! The marriage will not take place, now that my sister-in-law is meddling in the affair.' After hearing these words and what some other people said, I began to look upon Moresquin's proposal in a more favorable light. It never occurred to me that this man was deceiving us; that he had no money, no job, no means of support; that he had been cut out of his father's will, given how undeserving he was. These thoughts never entered my mind, nor my aunt's. In short, I was afraid of missing out on a good match. I agreed to let people hound my father, to exasperate him, and to let him believe I was in love. I didn't realize that such a busy man, in frail health, would be easily annoyed. Nor did I know that a dangerous seductress[128] was trying to close his heart to me, that this young, attractive girl was taking advantage of his complaints against me to gain his trust and friendship.

At the time, my sister was out of favor with the entire family because of all the slanderous things my mother had said against her; I too hated this sweet, innocent sister. In these circumstances, the seduction of my father was almost inevitable; for, in addition to Elise Leeman's striking beauty, this young woman was aided by a shrewd and unscrupulous mother. Such was the situation when my mother, after gathering all the facts and carefully considering them, decided that I had to be married to Moresquin to punish me for all the wrongs she claimed I had done to her.

It's impossible to fully describe how cleverly my mother was able to mount this odious plot! To gain my father's trust, she pretended to share his opinion of Moresquin; she criticized my aunt and falsely portrayed me as headstrong. And what made her truly culpable toward me was that she abused her maternal authority by dictating letters to me to send to my father — letters that were bound

---

[128] Sara (Elise Debée-Leeman) was the daughter of Rétif's landlady at the time. Rétif had a brief but passionate sexual liaison with this young woman, whom he viewed as his adoptive daughter, but who left him for a younger aristocratic lover. He describes his affair in several of his works, including *La Dernière Avanture d'un homme de quarante-cinq ans* (1783), *La Femme infidelle* (1786), and the 'Huitième Epoque' of *Monsieur Nicolas* (1795).

FIGURE 9.   'Tall and shapely, Mademoiselle Leeman had the provocative charm of pretty blondes. "You are displeased with your wife and children," she told him. "Place your affection and trust in an adoptive daughter who will love and cherish you and be the delight of your golden years."' Illustration by Louis Binet, engraved by Antoine-Cosme Giraud (known as Giraud l'aîné), in *La Dernière Avanture d'un homme de quarante-cinq ans* (Genève: Regnault, 1783), frontispiece to Part I titled *Le Quarantecinquenaire assis, tenant dans ses bras la belle Sara* [The 45-year-old man seated and holding the lovely Sara in his arms]. The original caption reads: 'Qu'a mon cher Papa? Que sa fille chérie connaisse toutes ses peines' [What is troubling my dear Papa? Let his beloved daughter know all his troubles]. (BnF)

to irritate him because they were really quite brazen. I was very uncomfortable writing them and, although I was doing this without my aunt's knowledge, I sensed that everything my mother was doing furthered my aunt's schemes. My father gradually became estranged from me. He saw me as an ungrateful and rebellious daughter whose desire to marry had made her disrespectful and disobedient. And at the same time, the lovely Leeman girl, who was tall and shapely with the provocative charm of beautiful blonds, was telling him: 'You are displeased with your wife and children. Place your affection and trust in an adoptive daughter who will love and cherish you and be the delight of your golden years.' But all that would not have been enough to alienate the heart of a father like mine. It was the vile, the odious Moresquin who finally set his heart against me.

My mother, who had set all the gears in motion, carefully observed my father to know when the best time would be to pull out all the stops. With a crazy man like Moresquin, the opportunity was bound to arise before long. He came to the house one evening when my father was having dinner. Mr. Saxancour received him coldly and didn't even offer him a chair. Nevertheless, he stayed during the entire meal that lasted a quarter hour. My father repeated his refusal, assuring him that he did not wish for me to marry and that when he did, he would give me a dowry. Moresquin insisted he was not interested in a dowry. My father replied: 'It may suit you to marry a girl without a dowry. But it does not suit me at all to marry her off with nothing and, in my current situation, I cannot do otherwise. Therefore, Sir, I am rejecting all your offers.' That was the whole conversation. My father got up from the table and left the room.

As soon as he was outside, Moresquin railed against my father in the most outrageous manner. He dared to say that my father's behavior toward him had been deceitful, even though he had always refused his offers in the clearest, most precise, strongest, and most humiliating manner. He claimed he had been played for a fool and that my father deserved a good beating for treating him this way. I dare not go on. My father was told that these outrageous statements had been made in my presence. My mother went to far as to claim that I had replied in a most shocking fashion when asked if I would send Moresquin packing for what he had just said to my father, that I was so depraved as to respond: 'I won't reject him because of anything he'll do to others, but for what he would do to me.' My father was beside himself with anger, but more against me than against Moresquin himself — against me, who was innocent and not even there when Moresquin had spoken and unaware of what he had said. In his righteous anger, my father cursed me and declared that he didn't wish to see me anymore. And, indeed, we didn't see each other again until the day of my ill-fated wedding.

People will wonder why I didn't go see my father, why didn't I banish Moresquin from my presence? Alas! I was hounded by my mother and by my aunt. Although they hated each other, they agreed on that one point. I didn't believe that my aunt could be so sadly, so grossly mistaken; nor did I believe that a mother could wish for her daughter's endless misery and ruin her life intentionally! I did write to my father, but they intercepted my letters and destroyed them. My mother, who since has become such a fierce enemy to Elise Leeman, conspired with the girl's mother to make sure nothing reached my father that might thwart their very different aims, but aims that coincided in one respect: to make my wedding happen despite my father's opposition, taking advantage of his ill health.

So that fateful knot was tied! My father gave his written consent to the notary, calling down curses upon us in a thundering voice. He did not attend the mass, nor did he sign the marriage certificate; he did not wish to see me afterwards, just as he had refused to see me beforehand.[129] My mother had held out false hopes to Moresquin to bring my father around before long, but she did not succeed in this.

I've now arrived at the time of my misfortunes. Everything I've recounted until now has only been the prologue to what follows. May I find the strength to continue! My intention is not to omit a single element of the story. All the details are important, and those that may seem the most trivial often have a strong connection to what happened later.

---

[129] Agnès married Augé on 1 May 1781. Rétif did not attend his daughter's wedding, nor did he even record the date in his diary. He may have tried to blot out the event from his memory, either because it was too painful or because he was so caught up in his affair with Sara/Elise Debée — or perhaps for both reasons. In his diary entry for 18 February 1781, he writes: 'Sara told me horrible things about her mother that I recounted in *La Dernière Avanture d'un homme de 45 ans*. I comforted her; I promised to serve as her father and, since my real daughter had married against my wishes, that she would take her place in my heart' (*Journal*, ¶31, vol. 1, pp. 51–52). Rétif did not mention Agnès again in his diary until his first visit to her more than three years later in November, 1783. Yet his entry for 1 January 1785 reflects the intense pain her marriage caused him and his obsessive hatred of Augé. Unless indicated otherwise, references to Rétif's diary are to Pierre Testud's two-volume critical edition: *Mes inscripcions, 1779–1785; Journal, 1785–1789* (Paris: Editions Manucius, 2006) and *Journal: Volume II, 1790–1796* (Paris: Editions Manucius, 2010). For relevant excerpts from Rétif's diary and for discussion of its publication history, see Appendix D in MHRA's French edition of *Ingénue Saxancour*.

My mother did not accompany me to the altar. This deceitful behavior seemed to me a bad omen. As for my aunt, that aunt who had arranged the match, she did attend the ceremony, but only reluctantly and went home as soon as the blessing was given.

I remained alone with the Moresquin family — that is to say his father, the only respectable person present; his mother, a nasty, scheming, vulgar woman; his aunt; and two or three other relatives. Accustomed to keeping better company, I was stunned! I was seized with a kind of panic and asked myself several times: 'Where am I? What am I doing here?' The words, the manners, everything seemed strange to me. Moresquin and his father were the only ones I knew. His father was continually kind and polite toward me. The son no longer forced himself to be polite. But I feel I must now describe the entire family so that my readers can have a clearer idea of what they were like.

Moresquin senior was a fifty-five-year-old man, gentle by nature, not very smart or witty, but with good sense. His manners, although lacking in refinement, were straightforward and civil, as were his conversation and appearance.

Madame Moresquin was a little old woman, with a dark and wrinkled face and eyes that glowered malevolently. She was impatient, haughty, garrulous, and as malicious as the fairy godmother Carabosse,[130] whom she resembled. The following incident at the wedding dinner shows what she was like. A dish of fresh peas was being served. After she had served a small helping to each guest, she called out to her cook: 'Marie! Marie!' But the girl was too busy and didn't hear her. So when someone took another serving and gave me a second helping, Madame Moresquin cried out indignantly: 'Marie! Marie! Hurry up and take away these peas! Otherwise there won't be enough left for my dinner tomorrow!' Blushing with embarrassment, Moresquin chided his mother very disrespectfully. And so, even at this first dinner, people were arguing; for the father took his wife's side against his son, and I sensed that they were about to blame me for being served a helping of peas I hadn't asked for. Fortunately, the family friend who had served me scolded the whole family for this petty squabble. They fell silent, ashamed, and the cook took away the controversial dish.

Moresquin, star of the celebration, is a short, dark-haired man with a swarthy complexion.[131] His eyes are deceitful, his face repulsive, his mouth disgusting. As

---

[130] Carabosse was the evil fairy godmother in the classic fairy tale *Sleeping Beauty*.

[131] Rétif's biographer Adolphe Tabarant draws the connection between the pseudonym Rétif chose for Augé in *Ingénue Saxancour* and his dark complexion: 'simply replacing the nickname L'Echiné [used in *La Femme infidelle*] with the nickname Moresquin, suggested by his swarthy complexion' [Adolphe Tabarant, *Le Vrai Visage de Restif de La Bretonne* (Paris: Eds. Montaigne, 1936), p. 329]. Reflecting on the connections traditionally made between physical traits and moral character, Rétif writes: 'as with all monsters, his swarthy complexion was the outward expression of his vile soul' ['Supplément à la *Femme séparée*' (1788), vol. 27 of *Les Contemporaines* (2nd edn), repr. in *OC*, vol. 25, pp. 304–39 (p. 32)].

FIGURE 10. 'As soon as we were alone, he knelt down at my feet and spouted a stream of overblown gibberish that he tried to phrase in a polite, even tender manner. I was so taken aback that I didn't notice how ridiculous he sounded. He tried to undress me; but I pushed him away without thinking or really knowing what I was doing.' Illustration titled *Première déclaration d'Edmond à Madame Parangon* by Louis Binet, engraved by Sébastien Le Roy, in *Le Paysan perverti* (Paris: Esprit, 1776), vol. 2, lettre 87, p. 137. (BnF)

for his moral qualities, he's a monster! He's cowardly, trite, brutal, groveling, and full of insolence. Utterly lacking in ability and integrity, he's the most impudent and inept liar, the most garrulous gossiper and malicious slanderer imaginable. The darkness of his soul surpasses that of his body; he commits the cruelest, most odious, most villainous acts secretly in the dark of night simply for the pleasure of causing pain. Rotten son, rotten husband, rotten father, he's the type of person the law in its wisdom should suppress, for he resembles those poor wretches that the most terrible of accidents have plunged into an incurable rage.

Moresquin's aunt, partially blind, had been given a menial job at the parish church.[132] She had been a kept woman who, after passing from bed to bed, ended up marrying an old widower who had been her first lover. Once pretty, she became a scheming and rather vulgar courtesan. Today, she is a little old woman — wrinkled, nasty, and jealous, like all women of her kind.

Such were the main characters at the wedding. It was with people of this ilk that Ingénue found herself — a young woman used to to well-mannered companions and accustomed to living with a man of distinguished merit and with a pious, courteous aunt. A feeling of fear, disgust, even horror welled up in her soul, and she said to herself softly: 'I'm lost!' She looked around her: alone, isolated, without any support, she saw only odious people. Moresquin's father was the only one who inspired in her a certain measure of confidence on account of his kind air, polite conversation, and moderate behavior.

This gloomy day passed by quickly, although entirely without amusement. An evening more unpleasant still was about to follow.

Moresquin — a vile and despicable man, the most corrupt of low-level clerks (who are more corrupt than other men) — found himself alone at last with a modest, innocent, timid, and inexperienced young woman. One imagines that he was going to indulge in the usual brutality of his tastes, manners, and character. But no, I will not slander him; I wish only to tell the pure, simple, naked truth. Moresquin was drunk with joy, proving the maxim I once read in Shakespeare: 'Pleasure is the balm of life; 'tis virtue under a sweeter name.' It seemed that pleasure had purified his sordid soul or perhaps, finding me pretty, he wanted to begin with a delicate pleasure. As soon as we were alone, he knelt down at my feet and spouted a stream of overblown gibberish that he tried to phrase in a polite, even tender manner. I was so taken aback that I didn't notice how ridiculous he sounded.

He tried to undress me, but I pushed him away without thinking or really knowing what I was doing. Becoming more aggressive, he ripped off my cuffs, as well as my lace collar. I began to cry. He apologized, but continued until he had finished undressing me. He then carried me over to the bed and threw himself

---

[132] *Tronchière*: woman in charge of the collection box (*le tronc*) at the entrance of a church.

on top of me. I cried out involuntarily, begging him to spare me and to take pity on me. Smiling, he said: 'I don't mean to kill you.' It was the first time he had addressed me using the familiar *tu* form.[133] I was startled, as would be any self-respecting young woman who had never been exposed to aggressive behavior thanks to her austere air and manners when faced with the brazen advances of libertines. I defended myself. Instead of becoming angry, Moresquin tried to overcome my resistance through gentleness and caresses. But I later learned that some of his caresses constituted liberties of a most sinful nature, even between a husband and wife....[134] Natural impediments that he boastfully described at the time (and even since then) as a jewel, delayed for three days what he called his triumph. It also marked the end of his decency.

After Moresquin had succeeded in deflowering me and had indulged in his pleasures to the point of satiety, his brutality was nearly fully revealed to me. Until then, he had hid his financial distress from me. But the fourth day after our wedding, he admitted to me that he was obligated to sell the few remaining belongings left by his first wife. I tried to stop him. But he bluntly replied: 'How else do you expect to eat tonight?' These words struck me like a stake in my heart, and I sunk into my chair, unable to get up. Moresquin left the apartment.

As soon I was alone, I began to cry. But hearing Moresquin return, I tried to hide my tears, which were only too visible for him not to notice. He tossed four coins toward me, saying: 'I could only get this much, even though what I pawned was worth at least six *louis*.'

'It's true,' I said, 'and that's what bothered me. I know how much we're losing! It would have been better to find a different solution or to cut down on expenses in the meantime.'

'Waiting for what? The death of my parents? For that's my only hope.'

'But you have your salary?' Moresquin shook his head sideways.

I asked him: 'Did you receive advances on your salary?' He did not answer and left the apartment.

The maid he had at the time, said to me: 'Madame, I don't understand Monsieur at all. He must have been crazy to marry you. He has no way to support

---

[133] Among the upper ranks of eighteenth-century society, as well as the educated middle classes, it was customary for married couples to address each other using the formal *vous* form. The fact that Moresquin *tutoyed* his new bride would have seemed surprising, even insulting, to a young woman like Ingénue.

[134] It turns out that the 'delicate pleasure' to which Rétif alluded here was neither delicate nor pleasurable for Agnès, since (according to Gilbert Lely) it refers to forced anal intercourse, in which Moresquin indulged for three nights before deflowering his bride. See Lely, 'Introduction', *Ingénue Saxancour, ou La Femme séparée* (Paris: Lattès, 1979), pp. 5–26 (p. 16). Regarding Rétif's use of ellipses in this scene and elsewhere in the novel, see Christine M. Roulston, 'Marriage, Sexuality, and the Meaning of the Wedding Night in Eighteenth-Century France', p. 75.

you, no job. Bit by bit, he has sold everything remaining from his wife's business and even some of his own belongings.'

I listened in total shock, then cried: 'He's out of work?'

'Yes, Madame, he lost his post three months ago. And when I said to him: "But, sir, you want to marry this young lady against her father's wishes? How will you support her?"

'He replied: "It's better for her to be unhappy than for me to go crazy over her, as I'm doing now. I'm going to throw myself in the river if I can't have her."

"Well!" I answered. "It would be better to drown yourself now rather than later; for that's what you'll wind up doing after you've made her miserable and had children with her, if she stays with you long enough for that!"'

I was in despair! I saw the situation as hopeless; I felt lost, with no means of support. I ran over to my aunt's to tell her everything. She couldn't believe it and ended by saying: 'Take heed, my niece! This servant is furious that her master has married! She's nasty, as he told me more than once. She's inventing all this to amuse herself and to upset you. Perhaps she's even in league with him to test you.'

'That would be a strange way to test me,' I replied.

'You know that he's no genius,' my aunt responded. 'In any case, you should be reassured by the fact that he made his first wife happy.'

I found my aunt's words reassuring. The only thing that still bothered me was the humiliation of having been tested by my husband and his servant. I returned home with a calm and proud demeanor that clearly perplexed Catherine the maid, to whom I did not speak the rest of the day.

Moresquin came home around ten o'clock. During supper, he talked about having spent the evening at a café. I didn't doubt that he had come from work, but I kept this idea to myself, suspecting that his words were only meant to test me further. I was lost in thought, and Moresquin asked me what was wrong. 'Nothing,' I replied. 'At any rate, you could have refrained from asking Catherine to tell me such a lot of nonsense.'

'But you needed to know the truth.'

'I know the truth. Let's not talk about it anymore. Since you have no money or job, I'll need to work as a seamstress. Catherine will bring work to me, deliver the finished work to my clients, and do the cooking.' Moresquin replied that he wasn't in such dire financial straits, that his parents were rich, and that he couldn't stand the thought of me working. This answer seemed to confirm my aunt's suspicions, and I felt reassured.

Yet the very next day, to allay my concerns, I sent Catherine to the homes of various people I knew to find sewing work for me. When she returned, I set to work and had her help me. 'Madame,' she declared, 'I'm warning you that, if this keeps up, I won't stay here. It will be too hard. In any case, no matter how hard you work, Monsieur will behave just as he did with his first wife; he'll spend the money as fast as you earn it.'

'What do you mean? I know that his first wife was quite happy with him.'

'Happy! She died of grief because of him!'

'Be quiet, Catherine! You're going too far in what you're saying, and if Mr. Moresquin is in league with you to test me, that's really disgusting!'

'Oh, Madame! Don't go repeating to him what I've been telling you simply to be helpful! Besides, you'll get to know him soon enough at your own expense. But I won't be here to see it, because I'm quitting today. I'm leaving. I don't want to stay here any longer.'

'Won't you wait at least until Mr. Moresquin hires another girl?'

'And why should I? Come now, Madame, do can do without a maid.'

I didn't know what to think about all I was hearing. I often saw Moresquin grow impatient over a moment's delay. He didn't yet blame me, but complained in general terms, using plural forms of address in order to include me. I saw that he was incapable of doing anything useful around the house. When he had had enough of me in bed, he went to sleep, or else he scolded Catherine in the plural or played stupidly with his dog that he enjoyed teasing. He was so completely useless that he often interrupted my sewing when it was only half done and forced me to accompany him for a walk. I asked him how his work at the office was going. After awhile, he sullenly replied that he was going to change jobs because his salary was only six hundred livres, which wasn't enough. I pointed out to him that he should have put off getting married. He squeezed my hand and ground his teeth, without answering me. Six weeks passed this way.

Before recounting the first incident that concerns me, I need to tell you about another one that frightened me by revealing Moresquin's true character to me. A few weeks after our wedding, around the third, we went to have dinner at his parents' house. The maid who worked for his father was rather sullen and often tipsy. As she was carrying a platter, Moresquin's mother, an impatient and cantankerous woman, cried out to me: 'Good heavens! Take that platter away from her; she's about to drop it!' I ran over to her, but the girl refused my help and shouted insults at me that made me laugh, seeing that she was drunk. At that very instant, Moresquin entered the room, heard the maid shouting at me, and flew into a fury. It was natural, I agree, that he should have her leave the room where we were, but he grabbed hold of her and beat her senseless before we could intervene. He then threw her over the railing of the staircase. Moresquin's father arrived right at that moment and angrily rebuked his son, whom he knew only too well. He placed all the blame on him for what had happened, disregarding anything his wife or I could say to excuse him. The maid filed a complaint the next day, and Moresquin's father gave her a settlement that he himself proposed. I must admit that I wasn't surprised to see Moresquin reprimand a girl who had insulted me. But I was frightened by his extreme mistreatment of her and by the flair he showed for hurting people and causing them pain. This incident proved costly to the family. It's common knowledge that this affair forced his parents to sell their last silver platter. It was also the reason behind their decision to leave Paris to go live in the provinces.

One day when Catherine went to deliver some sewing, she made a point of not returning in time to prepare the evening meal. I set the table. The bread was hard, because we had eaten at my in-laws' home the night before. When Moresquin came home, he sat down at the table and asked for Catherine. I told him that she should have returned more than an hour earlier. After finishing his soup, he picked up the bread, looked at it, and flew into a rage. Throwing it in my face, he cried: 'That's a fine loaf of bread!' Trembling, with a bleeding face, I nearly fainted from the distress and pain I felt and from all the other painful emotions a woman would feel finding herself, for the rest of her life, bound to a brutal man who, for no reason, behaves in the most extreme, revolting manner. Moresquin was himself alarmed by what he had just done. He kneeled down at my feet and asked me to forgive him.

'I see that the situation is hopeless,' I replied. 'You're too hot-tempered; the slightest little thing sends you into a rage. I already saw the most alarming example of this in your treatment of that unfortunate girl who worked for your parents and who's now suing you in court. You're unable to control your temper, and that's a great misfortune both for you and for me!'

Moresquin showed signs of impatience as I spoke, yet took it upon himself not to become angry, and I said nothing further. But he had begun, and once he began mistreating me, his forced politeness gradually gave way to the abusive behavior that came to him naturally. As his brutal passion for me waned, his respect for me diminished with every day that passed; he grew used to living with a woman whom he had cut off from her family by marrying her and who no longer had anyone's support. For another man, this would have been a source of tenderness and devotion. For Moresquin, it was an inducement to oppress me and to reduce me to the harshest servitude.

To achieve his ends, he gradually increased his bad behavior. He ordered the maid around harshly. Addressing Catherine and me together, he included me in his tirades. He soon went farther, making me the sole target of his insults. The most obscene harangues were addressed to me and accompanied his brutal caresses. I was mistreated in a way that made Catherine's lot seem far preferable to my own, since her contemptible master would not have dared treat her as he did me, simply because I was his wife. Seeing the way he treated me, one would have thought I was a vile prostitute, compelled to put up with all his whims, to bear any liberties that this depraved man wished to take, even in the presence of the maid who snickered or left the room. Any resistance on my part only caused him to treat me more roughly, not with beatings, strictly speaking, but he would bend me over and, holding me down, pull up my skirts and expose me in that position when the maid came back into the room, or — what was even more horrible — as his friends were arriving at his invitation! He then took pleasure in my shame and embarrassment and in the ill humor that would inevitably follow. He joked about it in his usual way in the most obscene and crude manner, saying: 'She's in a bad mood because she only got two, three, or four, instead of six,' etc.

His vile friends usually asked him to spare me. They often sought to protect me from him, especially one evening after supper when, having drunk far too much, he wanted to enjoy his marital rights in front of them. There should be laws against such excesses; it is simply not permissible for a husband to commit such an indecent assault on his wife! People will no doubt feel that I should have defended myself on these occasions. But I was already pregnant, and I could have been hurt. That evening, I was forced by means of threats and violence to go into an alcove with French doors where Moresquin took his pleasure with me, with his friends only two feet away sitting at the table. He then forced me back among them. I shudder when I recall what nearly happened. These were all unscrupulous men drunk with wine. What had just taken place, almost right in front of them, had inflamed their desire. My disheveled appearance when Moresquin forced me back into the room excited them even more. One of them even dared suggest to Moresquin to follow the custom of Sparta.[135] I heard this expression without becoming alarmed. Moresquin asked for an explanation, because he is very ignorant. Fortunately, he took it badly and became quite angry; for I heard him say: 'She's my wife, and you're scoundrels to propose such a thing to me!' They pointed out that he had behaved in a way that made them doubt whether I really was his wife. And if that was indeed the truth, then he truly was a contemptible wretch! The men grew angry and nearly came to blows. They all left, saying: 'Madame, your husband is a real scoundrel, and we'll never set foot in here again. If you stay with him much longer, you're bound to be miserable!'

My heart sank; my situation seemed even more hopeless than before. I spent the night bemoaning my fate. The next morning, the brute spoke most harshly

---

[135] This is an allusion to the custom of wife-sharing in Ancient Sparta. Citing Polybius, a Greek historian of the Hellenistic Period, Paul Cartledge notes that 'when a man had produced enough children, it was both both honourable and customary for him to pass his wife on to a friend'. See Paul Cartledge, *Spartan Reflections* (University of California Press, 2003), pp. 123–24.

to me, seeing the dire straits his expenses and ineptitude had put him in and the fact that, unlike his first wife, I had no business with which to support him. I shed bitter tears. His mother arrived at that very moment and asked me what was wrong. I repeated what her son had said to me, the abuse he had heaped on me, and I added that I was upset that he had just lost his job working for the tax collector.[136] Moresquin came at me like a madman and, in front of his mother, beat me so brutally that, for three weeks, my face was all black and blue.

Trembling, his mother appeared stunned, but simply said: 'This wife will be like the other one.' She asked Moresquin to leave us alone. As soon as he had left, I told my mother-in-law everything. I gave her a detailed and truthful account, not only of what had happened the day before, but also on all the other days, beginning with the incident when he threw stale bread in my face. As I was recounting that event, Moresquin came home again. Standing behind the door, he had heard part of what I had said and, fuming with rage as usual, he entered the room as I was finishing my story. He began by hitting my hand so violently that it was numb for two hours. Taking me onto her lap, his mother exclaimed: 'Monster, dare to hit her in my arms!' It was the only time she ever defended me. Exploding in invectives against her as he had against me, Moresquin hurled a stream of humiliating insults at her.

'Oh God!' I cried. 'If he speaks this way to his mother, what kind of treatment can I expect?'

'No,' he replied, 'I won't speak ill of your morals. It took me three days to take your maidenhead. You were chaste as a girl, and you're an honorable woman. But that bitch over there (speaking of his mother) fooled around before her marriage and she continued to do so afterwards. That's why I'm so unlike my father, who's a good man. How dare she criticize me, when she's the source of all my vices!'

I shuddered with horror at these words. Moresquin gradually calmed down. He came to ask our forgiveness and promised to show better behavior in the future. His mother refused to forgive him, however. She told me privately that she would never forgive him and that she would change her will to leave what she could to me and to any children we might have at the time of her death.

---

[136] *Le receveur de la capitation: La capitation* was a poll tax established toward the end of Louis XIV's reign to pay for his foreign wars. In principle, it was to be paid by all Frenchmen, including the aristocracy. However, by 1789, the *capitation* — and those who collected it — had become extremely unpopular among the middle classes, who paid 9% of their income for this tax, in contrast to the nobility (who were taxed only about 1% of their income) and the clergy (who paid virtually nothing). The *capitation* was replaced by the revolutionary government with an income tax (*la contribution*) calculated on an individual's declared income and thus designed to be more equitable.

Figure 11.   'Moresquin came at me like a madman and, in front of his mother, beat me so brutally that, for three weeks, my face was all black and blue.' Illustration by Louis Binet, engraved by Pouquet, in *La Dernière Avanture d'un homme de quarante-cinq ans* (Genève: Regnault, 1783), frontispiece to Part II titled *Le Quarantecinquenaire en fureur levant la main sur la perfide Sara, qui pousse un cri* [Enraged, the 45-year-old raises his hand ready to strike the perfidious Sara, who cries out in fear]. The original caption reads: 'Ne me frappez pas!' [Don't hit me!] (BnF)

To mark the peace, Moresquin and I walked his mother home and stayed for supper. We didn't leave his parents' house until ten that evening. On the way home and after we had arrived, Moresquin spoke the following words to me:

'You don't really know me yet. I recounted several incidents from my childhood to your aunt Bitez that should have disgusted her and closed her door to me. But she's an old fool who understands nothing once she's been won over. You need to know right away that it's very dangerous to anger me. I'm known as *Frappe-d'abord*,[137] and when I worked as a tax-collector,[138] I used to hit people in a way that injured them or at least made them suffer on the spot. So you'd be taking serious risks by defying me. Since you're now my wife and there's no escape, no refuge for you anywhere, the simplest course for you is to do everything I tell you. Otherwise, you can be sure that no enslaved negress anywhere in the New World will be as miserable as you.

'People told you that I made my first wife very happy. That may be true, but only because she had loved me from the time we were children. I intimidated her, and she did everything she could to please me. It's in this sense that she was happy. She was hardly well treated for her trouble, and I had been her husband even less time than I've been yours when I'd already given her a good beating. But she kept quiet about it and told everyone how happy she was. Because of this,

---

[137] Moresquin's nickname *Frappe-d'abord* literally means 'Hit First' and reflects his short temper and violent nature.

[138] Like Augé, Moresquin worked as a *commis aux Aides*. The *Aides* were excise taxes levied on the sale of a variety of items, including wine, liquors, candles, tobacco, soap, and leather. The *commis aux Aides* visited farms, cellars, and shops to compute and collect the taxes due on these items. The *commis aux Aides* occupied the lowest rung of the tax-collecting bureaucracy of the ancien régime known as *la Ferme générale*, an outsourced customs and excise operation that collected taxes on goods on behalf of the French king under six-year contracts. The major tax collectors in that system were known as the *fermiers généraux*. With their colossal fortunes, corrupt bureaucracy, and army of heavy-handed *commis* like Moresquin, the *fermiers généraux* had, by the end of the eighteenth century, become a hated symbol of the inequalities and injustices of the ancien régime. Known for their heavy-handed methods and boorish behavior, the *commis* were especially reviled by the common people, as Nicolas Boileau suggests in a line from one of his poems: 'Un commis engraissé des malheurs de la France' [A clerk enriched by France's misfortunes] (*Épître* V). Moresquin was clearly in his element working as a *commis*.

she was honored and respected. As for me, I showed so little restraint that on the day she died, I gave her another slap. I regretted this, since the effort she made not to cry when people entered the room stopped her breathing. I didn't want her to die, but only stop her from complaining, because it irritated me. I had warned her three or four times about this before hitting her. But that isn't what I meant to tell you to warn you how dangerous my blows can be.

'As my mother told you, I behaved very badly as a child. My mother, who is a spiteful woman, spoiled me simply for the pleasure of frustrating her husband and my nanny. I remained scrawny until the age of seven, when I finally began to grow, which delighted my mother. I was never a handsome child. One day, a philosopher came to our house, looked at me, and said to my parents: "Is that your son over there? ... Surely he is, because he looks a bit like Madam, but in an ugly sort of way. He won't be handsome. And I don't think he's either honest or good-natured; for his kind of ugliness is always the sign of wickedness. If you take my advice, you'll send this child away into the care of prudent guardians who will watch over him carefully until his character has been fully reformed. I can see in his eyes and features that he has a dark, deeply malicious soul." He looked at me intently as he spoke.

'My father remained silent. My mother was incensed, but dared not speak, because they needed the help of this man who had judged me so severely. I was nearly eight years old at the time. After hearing what the man said, I gave him a dirty look, crept up behind him, and kicked him in the shin. He quickly turned around and said, rubbing his leg: "He's just proved what I told you: he hurt me! Watch out! This child will cause you a great deal of trouble!" He left right after saying this, and my mother never allowed me to be punished for what I had done. She insisted to my father that I was right not to let people speak that way about me. My father acquiesced; and, from that moment, he took a violent dislike to me. I felt exactly the same way about him!

'As I grew older, everyone saw how vicious and unruly I was becoming. To annoy my father, my mother took pleasure in seeing me disrespect him and in letting me beat the servants. Had he dared touch me, she would have looked at him disapprovingly; so he didn't dare. And thus, I arrived at the age of twelve — fighting, biting, pricking servant girls with knives, scissors, or pins, which often caused them to give me a good thrashing. But as soon as my mother learned what had happened, they were fired.

'When I turned twelve, a dance instructor was hired to teach me proper bearing and manners. As you can imagine, I wasn't easy to handle and the instructor, unwilling to put up with me, treated me like a rebellious troublemaker. One day, he took the liberty of kicking me because I was mocking him and preventing him from teaching the other pupils, who took lessons along with me at his home. A swift kick in the shins was my response. The instructor chased after me, but I escaped.

'The next day, I went to the teacher's house and rang his bell. He opened the door and, seizing a big stick, cried: "Ah! There you are!" I ran quickly down the stairs, but I came back an hour later, armed with a rope that I strung a foot above the stairs across the darkest part of the staircase. I rang the bell loudly. Certain that it was me, the dance teacher rushed out with a big stick in his hand and tripped on the rope as he went down the stairs. His head hit a cornice, cracking his skull open and causing his death. Although there was no evidence against me, my parents gave money to the widow in order to avoid a scandal. There was even talk of sending me to a penal colony.[139] Despite what my enemy the philosopher said, my mother resisted the idea, insisting that it was just a childish prank, that I had no way of knowing it could cause the teacher's death, and other arguments of that kind. My father acquiesced to keep the peace.

'At the time, I was learning to read and write with a tutor who came to our house. After each lesson, he complained to my mother that I was fooling around during class and not doing any of the homework he assigned to me. One day, I warned him that he'd better stop complaining or he'd have me to deal with. The first thing he did when he found my parents both at home was to inform them of my threat and of the reason behind it. My father called me a monster, a bad apple. Even my mother was displeased. She criticized me for the money we were wasting on my tutor and for perhaps giving him an excuse for his incompetence. She shrewdly urged me to apply myself to show that, if I wasn't learning anything, it was the tutor's fault and not mine. While saying this, she gestured to the tutor to make him understand that she was on his side. He understood what she meant, but was incensed at her poor judgment. He nevertheless hid his feelings and left the room with my father. I don't know what was decided between them; but that evening, my father told me that I would henceforth take lessons at my tutor's house. I didn't mind this at all, hoping to take advantage of the freedom I'd have to come and go. But I was accompanied by an older pupil who came to get me and brought me home.

'I worked well the first few days, doing as the other pupils did. Since I didn't know anyone yet, I wasn't sure which boys would be willing to make mischief with me. But, by the end of the week, having figured out which boys were the troublemakers, I endeavored to instill a spirit of revolt in them so I could take revenge against the tutor. I stopped applying myself; I no longer studied and did messy work. The teacher seemed to be waiting for an occasion to make an example of me, and he seized it eagerly, as if fearing he might miss his chance. While I was talking to one of the oldest pupils, he grabbed ahold of me, crying: "Ah, I caught you disturbing the others!" And on the spot, he whipped me five or six times with a leather strap, adding: "That's what it takes to deal with a troublemaker like you." I was furious, but hid my anger.

---

[139] Later in the story, we learn that Moresquin was in fact sent to a penal colony for other misdeeds.

'After class that day, I gathered together the strongest and meanest of my classmates. I pointed out that the way I had just been treated was an affront to them all and that their turn could come any time at the whim of a tyrant who had just tested how far he could go at my father's urging. My speech made quite an impression. The boys cried out in rage, especially one named Chabert, whom you no doubt have heard of because of his tragic demise. He swore that if his father caused him to be treated that way, he never would have forgiven him; he urged me to seek revenge against mine. I was of a similar mind, but explained that my desire for vengeance was entirely directed at our teacher. Together, Chabert and I came up with a plan to convince our classmates to tie him up, give him a sound thrashing, leave him that way, and then desert his classroom for good. The two of us spent three days working out our plan alone. We noticed that, after our lessons were over, the teacher, who was a bachelor, remained alone in the classroom quietly noting our progress and preparing reprimands or encouragements for the following day. We decided that was the best moment to act.

'When our plan was all set, the occasion to carry it out arose, not on its own, but contrived by Chabert, who persuaded one of the best pupils to do the worst possible job on his writing assignment. After class was over, the teacher was busy grading our papers. Four of us hid to keep watch: Chabert, the young pupil he had maliciously led astray, myself, and a fourth boy, son of a tollgate controller who was a real troublemaker. We saw the teacher take up the star pupil's paper, put it down angrily with a look of indignation, and then record a grade for it in his grade book, which he normally kept under lock and key. Setting it down at one end of the table, he continued grading papers. While his back was turned, one of us snuck in to take the grade book.

'We quickly withdrew without a sound. When we were in a safe place, the first thing we did was to read the note concerning the culprit, which read as follows: "*Colson, for outrageously bad writing and inexcusable negligence, whipping, June 23; no recess for three days and negative report to his father.*"

'"My friends," I exclaimed, "see how persecuted we are by a tyrant. We must avenge ourselves!" I suggested that the four of us return to the teacher's house, grab ahold of him when he opened the door, tie him up, give him a good whipping, and then leave him tied up like that on his bed.

'"He'll cry for help," said the star pupil.

'"We'll gag him!" replied Chabert. And as he spoke, he pulled out a small horse bit from his pocket.

'We went back to the teacher's house and knocked at the door. He let us in, not suspecting any trouble. Catching him unawares, we grabbed ahold of him. He tried to cry out, but Chabert gagged him with the bridle bit. We then tied him up, pulled down his pants, and gave him a sound whipping as he lay face down on his bed with legs and arms bound. We whipped him as long and hard as we could; the leather straps of the whips were completely frayed. We left him there nearly motionless with scarcely the strength to beg us for mercy. We then left, double-locked his door, and threw the key into the urinals.

'The next morning, we went to school like the other pupils. The teacher's door was locked and we couldn't hear him answer because he was in the second room with the inner door shut. We all went home and told our parents that the teacher was absent. It wasn't until noon that his neighbors had a locksmith open his door. They found the poor teacher in the same position we had left him, covered in bruises. They untied him and removed the gag; all the words he had been forced to hold back came pouring out. He accused my three classmates and me, and our parents were quickly alerted. When confronted by our parents, three of us brazenly denied having anything to do with what had happened. And if the star pupil hadn't revealed the whole plot, the teacher might have been seen as a madman. It became a serious matter. Chabert was given the whipping of his life by his father, and the fourth boy was sent to the prison at Bicêtre.[140]

'As for me, I was sent to a penal colony in the Caribbean,[141] where I acquired a certain stature among my comrades, who called me the lieutenant. I regularly took them to task, and in this way curried favor with our superior. I gained his trust, but also the hatred of my fellow prisoners, who plotted to kill me. Fortunately, I was warned of their plot and, taking advantage my greater freedom, I escaped. A negro woman saw me escape and promised to keep my secret. However, knowing how untrustworthy her kind are, I forced her to accompany me into a forest to serve as my guide. As an extra precaution, I killed her with a knife blow to the back when we reached the edge of the woods.

'I was lucky to find a ship that was about to leave for France. I offered my services as a cabin boy. Since I was short with a swarthy complexion, as I still am today, they took me for a sailor's son. And, as they were extremely short-handed, they didn't ask too many questions.

'When I arrived in Bordeaux, I wrote a letter to my parents in which I invented a story about what had happened, telling them that there had been a shipwreck.

---

[140] *Bicêtre*: Founded in 1634 on the southern outskirts of Paris, Bicêtre was originally designed as a military hospital, but with the help of Vincent de Paul, it was finally opened as an orphanage in 1642. Over its long history, Bicêtre was used as an orphanage, a prison, a lunatic asylum, and a hospital. Its most notorious resident was the Marquis de Sade, who (like Moresquin's accomplice) was sent to the prison wing of Bicêtre.

[141] Iles de Salud, an archipelago of three small islands in the Caribbean off the coast of French Guiana — Ile Royale, Ile Saint-Joseph, and Ile du Diable — site of an infamous colony where French prisoners (*les bagnards*) were sent until 1953 and often subjected to abysmal treatment. In a footnote following a particularly violent scene in *La Femme infidelle*, Rétif comments: 'Quel sort pouvait attendre une femme honnête d'un meurtier, d'un homme exilé dans sa jeunesse pour ses violences?' [What fate could a good woman expect if married to a murderer, a man exiled in his youth for his violent behavior?] (*OC*, vol. 45, p. 820).

They sent me money. I deserted my ship and arrived home one evening in a dreadful state. They immediately sent me away from Paris into the provinces, where they found me a low-ranking post as a tax-collector.[142]

'People will tell you that I was sent to the penal colony because I stole ten *louis d'or*[143] from the desk of one of my father's friends; but that's not true. When I stole things, it was from my parents or occasionally from their servant. As for the ten *louis*, it's not my fault if they were never recovered. I'd boast about it if I had stolen the money, because I would have had reasons to do so — such as, for example, to humiliate my father, who always insisted that he was a respectable man. I found that irritating, even nauseating.

'These little thefts at my parents' house often fueled rumors about me and were the only occasions in which my mother didn't support me. For some time, I had been looking for an opportunity to prove to my parents that they could be robbed by others besides me. I kept close watch on the maids in particular. I would have loved to get one of them fired to prove myself right. An opportunity eventually arose. One of our young servants gave into temptation and stole something, and I accused her of stealing it. My parents didn't believe me and were certain that I had stolen what was missing. They spoke to me harshly, and I became very angry. The girl was in despair and came to see me in my room one day when my parents were away.

---

[142] See note 138 above.

[143] The *louis d'or* was a gold coin issued in France from 1640 to 1795. The name derives from the depiction of the portrait of King Louis on one side of the coin; the French royal coat of arms is on the reverse. According to Shepard Pond, the gold *louis* was worth 24 *livres* in the 1770s when the events recounted in the novel would have taken place. See Shepard Pond, 'The Louis d'Or', *Bulletin of the Business Historical Society* (Harvard University), vol. 14, no. 5 (Nov. 1940), pp. 77–80 (p. 79). If one *livre* was roughly equivalent to €10 in today's currency (according the the source cited in n. 122 above), one gold *louis* would be equivalent to €240 (about $260). If this information is accurate, ten *louis d'or* would have been roughly equivalent to €2,400 (or about $2,600) in purchasing value today.

'"Why do you want to be the ruin of me?" she said to me. "What did I ever do to you, Monsieur?"

'"You're a scamp, and I know you're guilty."

'"I'm not, really, believe me."

'"Yes, you are!"

'"No, truly, sir, I didn't take anything."

'"If you want me to believe you …, you're pretty…. You'll have to …." The girl tried to resist. I gave her a slap that knocked her over, and I told her that if she didn't give in, I was going to cry out and tell everyone that I had caught her in the act of stealing from me. She was so frightened that she gave in.

'As I was having my way with her, my parents returned home. My mother grabbed ahold of me. I said to her: "What can I say! She offered herself to me so I would hide her thefts, and I gave in." My mother believed me and wanted to have the girl arrested. My father was against the idea. He took the girl aside with my mother and questioned her. She told the truth; yet they still weren't sure. But as my bad luck would have it, I had been overheard with the maid by two neighbors; when they saw me leaving angrily, they realized I had been caught in the act. They came to tell my parents everything. My father was furious; my mother was persuaded by what they said and didn't know how to defend me. They fired the girl, after paying her well, and then hired an old, ugly maid to replace her.

I was furious at the failure of my plan. One of the two neighbors who had denounced me (for my mother gave their names to me) had an elderly father who lived three leagues from Paris — a half-day's journey.[144] One day, he came to see her. I was at the barber's shop when he passed by. One of the barbers said: "Ah! That's Mademoiselle Rosette's father. He must be coming to see his daughter." I left the shop and went up the stairs after the man who was coming to see his daughter for the first time since she had rented an apartment in our building. He entered our apartment by mistake and, as he looked around to see if he recognized his daughter's furniture, I grabbed ahold of him shouting: "Thief!" Knocking him over with a punch of my fist, I pushed him to the ground and continued shouting for help. My parents, who were visiting a neighbor, rushed home. They found me pinning down the poor man, who couldn't speak and whom no one recognized. He was taken to the hospital, and it was only the following day that he was able to speak, revealing he was the father of Mademoiselle Rosette, the florist. I thought I had finally proven myself right to my mother, declaring: "You see that you really were robbed in the past, and that I was unfairly accused because my father detests me. Yet, if it weren't for me, you would have been robbed just now!" My mother agreed with me. But it was a different story when the man's identity was revealed.

---

[144] Before the Revolution, the *lieue de Paris* was equivalent to about 3.9 km or 2.4 miles. So the neighbor's father lived approximately 11.7 km or 7.2 miles from Paris.

My parents had to hush up the affair by giving money to Rosette for her father's medical care and to keep her quiet about what had happened. But the man died three days later, and I was avenged.

'After this, my father declared that he no longer wanted me at home; he even wanted to have me sent to prison. But with the help of a relative, my mother secured a post for me as a low-level tax-collector in the provinces. That's where I really found my calling. It's a charming situation for a young man to do that kind of work! He can do anything he likes with complete impunity — forge documents, beat people up, spy on them, even murder them, so long as he demonstrates zeal for his work. He has a free hand, even in matters beyond his superiors' interests. He's an invaluable fellow, and they'll do anything to keep him on, as was clearly proven to me on more than one occasion.

'From the beginning of my posting, I had made a name for myself through my relentless pursuit of tax-evaders among the local farmers. I spent entire nights spying on them, on the lookout for fraud. I caught them in the act, reported them, and obtained convictions. News of my success spread through my director all the way up the ladder to the *Fermiers généraux*.[145] I received a bonus and a promotion, and my salary was raised from six hundred *livres* to a thousand per year.[146]

'It was during this period that I had a run-in with the mailman in the town of A*** where I was working at the time. I asked him if he had any letters for me or my colleagues. "My letters are organized by district," he replied. "When I'm in your neighborhood, I'll find your mail if there is any, and I'll leave it at your address." I wanted to make him search for my mail in his pouch, but he refused. We argued about it and, since he was a loud-mouthed boor, he hurled insults at me. I ran my sword through him and was forced to flee. But since I was so valuable to my superiors, they backed me up and my case was settled. It's true that the man didn't die of his wounds, but the affair still cost my family two thousand *écus*.[147]

'I was then sent to work in the town of S***, where I continued to serve my employers with great zeal. But I wasn't as fortunate there as in my earlier posting in A***. One night, I was ambushed and beaten nearly to death. I was transported to my landlady's, who took very good care of me, along with her daughter, a rather pretty young lady named Madelon Destroches. My convalescence was long! But after awhile, I had regained enough strength to become aware of

---

[145] *Fermiers généraux*: Heads of tax collection in France prior to the 1789 revolution. See note 138 above.

[146] In the 1770s when the events of this episode took place, the *livre tournois* was worth approximately 10 € in today's currency, so Moresquin's annual salary would have been equivalent to roughly 6,000 € in today's currency (about $6,500) initially and, after his promotion, to around 10,000 € (about $11,000).

[147] Two thousand silver *écus* was roughly equivalent to 60,000 € ($65,000) in today's currency, a small fortune for Moresquin's parents, especially given what their son had already cost them for his past misdeeds.

Madelon's charms, and I began to court her. She at first mocked me. I became bolder in my pursuit of her, and she grew angry at me. Her resistance made me suspicious, so I spied on her and discovered that she had a sweetheart. By then, I had fully recovered and began to go out again. I spread rumors that Madelon was a woman of easy virtue and that I had slept with her, but that I no longer wanted anything to do with her because I had found her in flagrante delicto with her sweetheart. When these rumors reached the mother and daughter, they were both furious with me, especially the elder Destroches, who resolved to punish me and to avenge her daughter.

'With this in mind, she came into my room one morning when I was still in bed. Without warning, she threw off the blanket and the sheets. Then seizing a handful of birch branches, began to whip me with all her might. I was still half asleep and totally disoriented. All I heard was the old lady shouting at me: "Vicious slanderer! Villain! Ungrateful wretch whom I nursed back to health, how dare you spread dirty lies about my daughter!" I finally realized what was happening and, springing out of bed, I grabbed hold of the old woman and disarmed her. I was about to give her a good whipping in return when her daughter, who was probably listening at the door, rushed in armed with a broom handle. She hit me with it on the shoulders, but not very hard. I let go of the mother and taking hold of the girl, pushed her over onto the bed. The mother ran out to get help. Seeing that the girl was choked with rage, I seized the opportunity to take from her what she had refused me earlier. Her mother heard her cries and rushed back in. I found myself attacked by both women at the same time. Although hardly very big or strong, I managed to push them out of my room. The mother came at me with the broom handle. I grabbed ahold of it and knocked the daughter over with such force that she hit her head against the corner of the stairs and opened a deep wound. Taking advantage of the turmoil, I escaped.

'When word got out that the daughter would not pull through, I was sent to T***. My superiors were afraid of losing a valuable collaborator.

'About three months after I arrived in T***, I fell in love with the daughter of a local carpenter. She was pretty, but had no dowry. A wigmaker's assistant had been courting her. But when her parents heard that I was the only child of well-off parents, they pushed her to choose me over him. The girl and her suitor wanted to know my intentions. They had even secretly agreed between the two of them that if I was inclined to marry and if marriage were possible, he would withdraw his proposal. One day when I was out for a walk, the young man approached me politely: "Monsieur," he said, "I see that you're paying regular visits to Mademoiselle Julien."

"Yes, what of it?"

"Nothing, sir, except that I was courting her before you arrived here. But since I'm a reasonable person and you're a better match than I am, I'll yield to you if your intentions are the same as mine."

"And what *are* your intentions?"

"But to marry Mademoiselle Julien, of course."

"Then you mustn't alter your plans at all, my friend. I'll have some fun with her and then, when I'm tired of her, you can marry her."

'The fellow didn't take kindly to what I said to him. He made a move toward me, and I drew my sword, dealing him a blow that cut a nerve or a tendon, I'm not sure what exactly. As a result, his head remained turned sideways toward his shoulder. I can't help laughing when I think about it now. But at the time, I was forced to flee, and my parents had to pay an indemnity. Nevertheless, my superiors found another position for me at Château S*** S***, but with only a salary of five hundred *livres* this time.

'It was in that town that I delivered the best slap ever dealt by a human hand. In South America, I had learned a special way to fight that often came in handy when dealing with tax-evading country folk. Although no wounds ever appeared, several had died from the blows I gave them by using my thumb to penetrate between their ribs and wound their inner organs. I found this technique very useful in my fistfights in South America and later in my work as a cellar rat,[148] when I often found myself confronted with ruffians much stronger than I was.

'Getting back to the story of my famous slap, I was in church one day in a village where there was often fraud and rebellion. Some of the villagers had given me a good beating, but I had managed to send *ad Patres*[149] the most infamous tax-evader in the town, thanks to my talent at fist-fighting. The vicar was especially angry with me because the dead man had been his friend. During mass that week, I was standing in an area hidden behind the altar where some young men were flirting with the young women in charge of taking the collection. Thinking it would be alright to join in the fun, I tried to take some holy water from the font held by the prettiest of the girls, who slapped me and ran off to complain about me. The matter should have ended there, but the priest sent someone to tell me to leave the church, which I ignored. When mass was over, I encountered the vicar at the door still wearing his priestly garment. I made no attempt to avoid him, and when I passed by him, he slapped me hard, saying: "If Jesus Christ used a whip to drive out the merchants who profaned the Temple, how should we deal with someone like you who insults religion in the most outrageous fashion!" I walked up to the priest and dealt him a blow so powerful that it knocked him over and sent him flying down ten steps. He didn't recover, and he was the fifth or sixth person who bit the dust by my handiwork. I had to leave town quickly and escaped to Paris. By an incredible stroke of good luck, I wasn't known in the village by my real name, and the director hid my identity

---

[148] Clerks like Moresquin were referred to pejoratively as 'cellar rats' because their duties included the inspection of wines and other alcoholic beverages in people's cellars in order to collect excise taxes on these items.

[149] To send *ad Patres*: To send people to their death.

because he still wanted my services. My parents again paid compensation to bury the scandal. But this last affair exhausted their finances and cost them half their fortune. But thanks to them, my identity was never discovered.

'After my return to Paris, I finally felt at peace. My thoughts were calmer and I felt drawn to a quiet life. Realizing how much my rash behavior had cost my father and the difficult financial straits he now was in because of me, I promised I would behave myself in the future. They found a job for me in an office similar to the one headed by my father. At first I seemed to be meeting my parents' expectations, and they were pleased with me. I should add that I had fallen in love and, when that happens, I'm capable of the greatest self-control. It was like that when I fell in love with you. There's nothing I wouldn't have done to make a good impression on your father if he had agreed to meet and hear me out. It's true that I wouldn't have cared less what he thought of me afterwards, but what of it? I would still have fooled him.

'In the apartment building where I'm living today[150] lived a woman who had been friends with my parents and who had lovely niece. When we were children, people called us the husband and wife and, as she grew to adulthood, young Manette had lost neither the memory of these amusements from our childhood, nor her fondness for me. This feeling remained deep in her heart. My father and especially my mother were thrilled at the apparent change in my conduct. Speaking to Manette's aunt, they described me as a young man who was on the path to reform: "We want very much to take advantage of this change to arrange his marriage," explained my mother. "A good wife who loves him would assure his complete reform."

'The aunt knew how her niece felt about me and agreed to my mother's plan: "That's not all," my mother added. "Our piece of mind depends on the two of you, Madame. I'm sure that, more than any other woman, your niece would have the greatest influence over my son. He loves her!"

'"And doesn't dislike him!" the aunt replied.

---

[150] Augé's apartment was located on the rue de la Mortellerie (now rue de l'Hôtel de Ville), which runs parallel to the Quai de l'Hôtel de Ville on the right bank of the Seine, opposite the Ile Saint-Louis.

"'Ah! This is truly a great joy!" exclaimed my mother. "Please God that we can accomplish such a worthy goal within a week!"

"'That would be a bit too soon," the aunt replied. "But if the truth be told, I don't foresee any objections either from my niece or from me. So let's not rush into anything and let the young couple court for a while and get to know each other better."

'My mother didn't care for this delay, nor for this extended courtship. Not that she foresaw what would happen, quite to the contrary. But she was afraid that once Manette got to know me better, her opinion of me would change, or that I would do something reckless, or perhaps that people concerned for Manette's welfare would tell her things about me that would raise alarms about my conduct and character. Nothing like that actually happened. Manette loved me and, as soon as I was sure of it, I adopted the tone that suited me best: that of master. The more I treated her that way, the happier she appeared. She happily yielded to all my wishes, so I thought I could ask her for anything, including her favors before marriage. When she refused, I warned her that if she didn't consent and give me the right to criticize her later on, I'd conclude that she didn't really love me and I would break off our engagement. This threat made her give in. And as soon as she did so, I controlled her completely. I even made her beg me to marry her and would not agree to it until her aunt bequeathed to me, in my name, a property she owned in Les Andelys in Normandy. She had to give in to my demands, because I said her niece was pregnant and warned her that I would run away to England if things didn't go my way. It's for that reason that she bequeathed everything to me and that I gained sole control of my wife's dowry both before and after her death to do with as I pleased.

'People have told you that my first wife[151] was happy in our marriage. You can judge for yourself based on what I'm about to tell you. She had a small business selling household linen that her aunt gave her as part of her dowry. Her work covered our household expenses. What I earned served only to satisfy my own amusement, and my wife often gave me extra money for my own use. I made sure to maintain tight control over her. At the slightest sign of resistance or disrespect, I slapped her, which kept her in her place. In truth, Manette became melancholy, but she was submissive and smiled whenever I ordered her to do something. Only her aunt dared speak up from time to time. Yet I reacted to her comments in a way that forced her to tone them down; for when she criticized me too sharply, a pair of slaps to her niece's face made the aunt kowtow to me.

'So you see that I was the happiest of men. I had a wife that kept the household going; I was the undisputed master; everyone lived in fear of me. But my wife's health was fragile, and she fell ill. I wasn't convinced it was a serious illness. One

---

[151] Augé's first wife, Marie-Françoise Quenet, died in April 1780, only a few months before he asked for Agnès's hand in marriage (in August of that same year).

morning when she complained of feeling worse than usual, I gave her two slaps to see if a bit of rigor would quiet her down. She fell silent. After that, I went out, more or less sure to find her up and about when I came back. I returned that evening to find her on her deathbed. She passed away after kissing my hands.

'This stroke of bad luck took me completely by surprise! I was furious at my wife's aunt and gave her a hard time, accusing her of not taking proper care of Manette. My mother criticized her as well. The aunt replied quite haughtily to us both. I was so outraged that when I arrived at my office, I made a solemn promise to my colleagues that I would treat them to a good dinner the day she went to join her niece. I had to wait only two weeks for my wish to come true and paid for the dinner quite willingly. But not knowing my reasons, the head boss disapproved of what I had done and fired me. This caused me a great deal of harm, given that I've been without a job since then. The menial work given to me by a family friend doesn't really count; he did it only to deceive your father in case he wanted to check if I had a job.

'From everything I've just told you, you can see that I'm not a fellow that can be pushed around. So my advice to you is to do what you're told; for I'm used to being the boss, never to be contradicted, and to be waited on hand and foot by my wife. Think too about how you can make yourself useful and bring money into the household, no matter how. That's all I have to say to you. It's three in the morning! My story took a long time to tell. I'm going to sleep now, so get out the warming pan and warm my bed.'

Such was the story told me by Moresquin. I can't guarantee that everything he told me was true! All I can say is that he took great pleasure in boasting about having committed the most atrocious crimes and that his subsequent behavior will prove that he was indeed capable of carrying them out.

The vile scene in front of Moresquin's friends was often acted out again with minor variations. The same sort of disgusting words and descriptions were repeated daily in front of the libertines Moresquin brought home with him. And on a daily basis, I was slapped or punched or had my arm twisted. Had I not heard Moresquin's tale of his youthful exploits, I would have been deeply shocked! But given how despicable I knew him to be, his behavior seemed completely natural to me. I was nevertheless in despair to be the victim of his villainy.

FIGURE 12. 'I returned that evening to find her on her deathbed. She passed aways after kissing my hands.' Original copper engraving by Carlo Farneti. In *Le Ménage parisien, suivi de la Femme infidèle. Ingénue Saxancour*. In *L'Œuvre de Restif de La Bretonne*, ed. by Henri Bachelin (Dijon & Paris: Éditions du Trianon, 1931), vol. 5, p. 391. (Northwestern University Library, Charles Deering McCormick Library of Special Collections)

Moresquin wanted me to earn money, but often kept me from doing my work, which was hardly surprising, given how irrational he was. When he grew bored, because he had nothing to do, he would say to me: 'Get dressed, we're going out.' I reminded him that I had one thing or another to finish, but he remained deaf to any such sensible remarks. It wasn't out of kindness that he took me out, but so that people in the neighborhood would say that he made me happy and, even more, from an ostentatious desire to show me off. For this monster was stupidly conceited enough to take pride in my few remaining charms. When we crossed paths with one of his friends or acquaintances, he would puff up with pride and say: 'This is my wife,' as if to say: 'You see! Admire this beauty and consider what finesse it took for me to win her hand, despite her father's opposition! Aren't I clever!' He'd recount all the obstacles he'd had to overcome to marry me. After that he'd name my father, first showing pompous pride in his talents, but then criticizing him in every way possible, as if he were both honored and ashamed to be his son-in-law. I suffered cruelly through these conversations, but I was beginning to learn from experience to keep silent. Had there been any doubt in my mind about this, I was soon to be fully persuaded in the cruelest way of the need to keep quiet!

For five months, I had been the most miserable of wives and pregnant for four, when I experienced the most outrageous treatment! Moresquin was having his wig adjusted in front of the fireplace where a pot was cooking on the fire. I asked him to move back a bit from the fire to avoid interfering with the cooking. He chose to ignore my request and instead moved closer to the fire, preventing me from keeping an eye on the pot. A bit annoyed, I left the room and went to have some cooked pears for lunch. A minute later, not surprisingly, the pot boiled over. Moresquin, who was sitting right next to the fire, flew into a fury. Leaving the pot as it was, he launched into a tirade against me, railing against the gourmandise I showed in eating cooked pears, calling me a gluttonous bitch who had all the vices of a whore (but using more foul language than that). And, after a long string of insults, he ordered me to remove the pot from the fireplace. Without uttering a word, I slipped by him as best I could and, as I was obeying him, he kicked me in the back. Then, not finding me mistreated enough, he kicked me again so violently that, from that moment until the premature end of my pregnancy, I suffered from constant pain. The wigmaker's assistant rescued me from further violence, for Moresquin would otherwise have continued to give in to his rage. But I suffered the humiliation of seeing myself demeaned in front of a man of that sort who, because of his position, could spread rumors about my misfortune in fifty different households.

Three weeks after this terrible scene, as I was suffering a great deal from the injury Moresquin inflicted on me, he grew annoyed with me for being listless and gloomy. He spoke to me so harshly that I began to cry. He twisted my arms and pretended to laugh. I tried to get away, but he held on to me and hit me on the

FIGURE 13.   'As I was obeying him, he kicked me in the back. Then, not finding me mistreated enough, he kicked me again so violently that, from that moment until the premature end of my pregnancy, I suffered from constant pain.' Illustration titled *Ursule foulée aux pieds* by Louis Binet, in *La Paysanne pervertie* (1784), vol. 3, p. 318 (Estampe 25). (BnF)

neck with the side of his hand, causing excruciating pain. He assured me that he had broken a man's neck that way back when he was working as a tax-collector, and to tell the truth, I felt as though he might have broken mine. But he didn't give me time to think about it much because a flood of insults followed. I recall only one thing he said, as it was so revolting and reflects his character so clearly. Using the vilest language again, he told me that I was even worse than a whore, since at least a woman of that sort supports her lover, whereas I was ruining him. I continued to cry, hoping he would be moved by my distress. This only seemed to harden his heart against me. Still sobbing, I finally cried out to him: 'You want to make me die of grief, just like your first wife!' At these words, he flew into a rage and pinched me hard on my hands and punched me on my face so violently that an inflammation I had in my mouth at the time grew into an abscess that eventually had to be drained through my cheek after I gave birth. Imagine how much I suffered! I was in pain for more than three years. In fact, I'm still not entirely recovered from the injury, which will affect me for the rest of my life!

Languid and sickly, I was nothing more than an object of loathing in that monster's eyes. Reduced to the harshest servitude, I became his servant, and the maid became my mistress. Such were the extremes to which I was reduced that I could be seen scraping the mud from the master's and servant's shoes, while Moresquin stood over me brandishing his cane. He forced me to carry out this lowly task, rubbing my nose with the filthy brush if the work wasn't as perfect as he expected. My face smeared with muck, I became an object of derision for both master and servant! And don't forget that I was pregnant, barely able to move, grimacing in pain on account of my injured back and swollen cheek, plunged into the deepest misery, utterly lacking in support, estranged from my father and betrayed by my mother! Even now, I shudder to think of the anguish I suffered and the horrors I endured.

Yet this was not the most extreme cruelty I suffered! Among Moresquin's acquaintances were two men as vile and nasty as he; both were sworn enemies of my father. One was a dissolute drunkard, but not without talent — a bachelor

---

[152] Like Paul Cottin, Daniel Baruch identifies Criher as 'Richer, un plumatif voué aux compilations historiques (1720–1798)' [Richer, a scribbler who compiled collections of historical anecdotes and essays]. See Baruch, *Restif de La Bretonne* (1996), p. 443. They are referring to historian and biographer Adrien Richer, who published works such as *Vies des hommes illustres* and *Essai sur les grands événements par les petites causes*. However, when the anagram Criher appears in the diary (entry ¶566 for 19 November 1785), Testud challenges this identification (*Journal*, vol. 1, p. 217, n. 3).

[153] Another pseudonym, alluding no doubt to Jean de Nivelle, a fifteenth-century French baron who sided with the Duke of Burgundy against the French king and who, as a result, became an object of scorn and a symbol of disloyalty. His name is the origin of the expression 'être comme ce chien de Jean de Nivelle qui s'enfuit quand on l'appelle' [to be like that dog Jean de Nivelle who runs away when he's called].

named Criher.[152] The other was Jean de Nivelle,[153] who at the time was married to a woman he treated miserably and whom he had forced by beatings to give herself to a man who had courted her before their marriage. It was these two men Moresquin invited home to witness the humiliation of their enemy's daughter. I served dinner to these three monsters, while the servant sat with them at the table. I was forced to remain standing and wasn't allowed to eat until after they were finished. The vile Criher and even viler Jean de Nivelle jeered scornfully at my sorry state. Moresquin had them address me using the familiar *tu*-form, as if I were their servant or mistress. I refused to put up with other indignities, except for one that Moresquin sprang on me by surprise and that was extremely humiliating and unpleasant …. There was yet another humiliation that I refused to tolerate, despite a whipping, which was to hold the chamber pot for these swine …. I dare not speak of it. Suffice it to say that, after the three of them had produced as much filth as they had uttered, I was forced to clean up after them. Never have I witnessed such a horrible scene, and I'd prefer to die rather than live through it again. Just the thought of it made me ill for several days, especially since at every meal, Moresquin jokingly recalled the vile treatment I had endured, encouraging his servant and libertine guests, his worthy friends, to laugh about it. I still shudder to think of it!

I gave birth prematurely. I thought I would die from the string of cruel abuses I suffered. Fate, which robs tender husbands of beloved wives and happy marriages, spared me only to endure endless days filled with grief. I languished and suffered, and my suffering was intensified by the milk fever that infected my swollen cheek. But I didn't die. Annoyed at seeing me so listless and at having to support me in that state, Moresquin considered sending me to the charity hospital Hôtel Dieu,[154] where he said I wouldn't last long. But realizing that I was more likely to die if he kept me at home, he had second thoughts and changed his plans. No sooner had he made this decision that he began to hurl insults at me, calling me a scumbag and accusing me of being infected with a shameful venereal disease. As he made these outrageous accusations against me, he became so enraged, so carried away, that he hit me savagely and twisted my arms when I dared to complain.

'I wish you'd die!' he cried. 'I don't intend going broke on account of a bitch who brought me nothing!' (I had brought him only my father's curse, a dowry worthy of Moresquin!) The nurse who cared for me after the birth is still alive; she can attest to the state she found me in when she returned to my bedside; for whenever she left the room to carry out Moresquin's orders, he took a perverse

---

[154] *Hôtel-Dieu*: Charity hospital for the poor and indigent, where crowded and unsafe conditions often led to epidemics and a high mortality rate well into the eighteenth century. The hospital, the oldest in Paris, is still located next to Notre-Dame on the Île de la Cité and is still in operation.

pleasure in mistreating me. The doctor who delivered the baby can affirm this as well.[155]

It's hard to believe, but I recovered! The care I received from my nurse, who befriended me, restored my health. As I regained my strength and the color returned to my cheeks, Moresquin's brutal passion for me was rekindled. He expressed his lust for me in the most obscene manner. He forced me to dress up and receive guests. One evening, I experienced especially cruel mistreatment toward the end of a dinner he hosted for three friends to 'live it up and have a wild time,' as he put it. While they were eating, Moresquin dominated the conversation with the most licentious and disgusting remarks. His vile friends smirked, but replied with a certain decency and self-restraint. After they had emptied a few bottles and were about to have dessert, Moresquin took advantage of the moment when I left the table to change plates. He followed me quietly to the kitchen, which was next to the alcove containing my bed. As soon as I had put down what I was carrying, he grabbed ahold of me in the most obscene manner and bent me over so brutally that I felt like my back was breaking. He wanted to satisfy his lust, and when I resisted, he pulled a hairpin out of my hair and thrust it into my arm. I had no choice but to give in to this savage attack. It's impossible to relate everything that happened — Moresquin's vulgar comments, the crude replies and laughter of his friends! After an entire quarter hour of humiliations, I was forced to finish serving dessert and to listen to that monster's revolting account of his exploits!

---

[155] This is one of several instances where Ingénue invokes the testimony of potential witnesses who could support her accusations of abuse against her husband. In addition to the doctor who delivered her son and the nurse who took care of her afterwards mentioned here, Ingénue later invokes the testimony of her aunt, as well as her aunt's maid, who accompanied her home one night after she fled from her husband's violence. As Rori Bloom has argued, Ingénue's narrative can be read as a judicial memoire in which she builds her case against her husband: 'Despite her self-characterization as an innocent victim, she constructs her case with the skills of a practiced prosecutor'. See Bloom's article 'Privacy, Publicity, Pornography: Restif de La Bretonne's *Ingénue Saxancour, ou La Femme séparée*', *Eighteenth-Century Fiction*, 17.2 (January, 2005), 231–52 (239–40).

A few months after this vile abuse, I realized that I was pregnant for a second time. I shuddered in fear and horror. As soon as Moresquin learned of my pregnancy, he pressured me in the most despicable manner to go speak on his behalf to the head of an office where he hoped to work. Using obscene words I refuse to repeat (he never expressed himself like a gentleman), he added that, since he wouldn't be risking anything, I shouldn't act like a prude and that he didn't care what I'd need to do, provided that the director gave him a job.

Moresquin hired a clever hairdresser who did a magnificent job on my hair; everyone said so when they saw me. But all I felt was a heavy heart. I wasn't ready until four o'clock in the afternoon. Thinking we would go by carriage to the director's home, I was quite surprised when Moresquin ordered me to leave on foot with him. He took my arm and, after parading me all through the neighborhood, told me that he was taking me to a light comedy that the director would be attending.

'When he sees you,' Moresquin remarked, 'there's no doubt that he'll be drawn to you. And here's what you'll say to him when you see him.' (He dictated what I should say.) 'And if you don't secure a job for me, you're the one I'll hold responsible.'

I felt more dead than alive. Moresquin noticed this and was pleased, since, in his view, it made me all the more appealing. Squeezing my wrists so hard I thought they would break, he warned me: 'That's a little foretaste of what awaits you if I don't get that job. I expect to have food on the table; my children will be mine, but you'll be a whore when I tell you to be, chaste when I choose. You exist for me and for me alone, do you understand? Your family abandoned you and sold you to me like a negress, so I'll do with you as I please. Who can you turn to for help? Obey me, and if you do right by me, you'll be more gently [   ].'[156] I shuddered and continued onward like a criminal being led to the gallows.

When we arrived, the play had already begun. We were escorted to the box seats Moresquin had taken, where he seated me noisily. All eyes turned toward us, and the monster was pleased to see that my pitiful charms had caused quite a stir. During the performance, people had pointed me out to the director, who was eyeing me with great interest. But when he heard that I was Moresquin's wife, he declared: 'Oh, poor woman!' The monster overheard him and quickly changed his mind. He was worried that since this man was attracted to me, he might have him locked up instead of giving him a job. Given all the crimes in his past, he admitted that this was a real possibility and he decided to take me home. But that was only the beginning of the distress I was to experience that day.

---

[156] The last word of the sentence is missing in the original 1789 edition. The sentence ends with 'doucement — ?' [gently]. Perhaps Rétif meant to write 'traitée' [treated]. Or, what is more likely, he intentionally omitted a crude term for sexual intercourse, as was often his practice, in order to avoid problems with government censors.

On the way home, Moresquin thought of another office director who didn't know either of us. He told me to present myself as the wife of a colleague whom he named and to go to the man's home that very evening to ask for a job for him. He led me to the door and forced me to enter after showing where he would wait. I was extremely uncomfortable! Above all, I didn't know how such a lie could possibly succeed. But not daring to hesitate, I asked to see the master of the house who, unfortunately for me, was at home having dinner with his family. When he heard that a young lady had asked for him, he left the dining room and went to his office where a servant had shown me in.

'How can I help you, lovely lady?'

'Monsieur, although I don't have the honor of your acquaintance, I've heard that you are generous and compassionate. My husband lost his position as a clerk, and we are in desperate straits.'

'I'll be generous if you are, my darling. If you know about me, you must have heard that I like pretty women.' As he said this, he touched my cheek and chin.

Throwing myself at his feet, I begged him: 'Have pity on me, sir, and let my husband have a job, or else he'll beat me to death.'

'The devil take him! What a downright brute! But will you be kind to me?' I must admit that I didn't understand what he meant. I replied that I felt it was my duty to be kind, when I could be. 'Then we're agreed. Send your husband to me tomorrow. As for you, my lovely, when he's here, I'll have word sent to you where I can meet with you alone.' As he finished speaking, he gave me a kiss and, after showing me the way out, he left the room.

I went to find Moresquin, who was overjoyed. On the way home, he had me describe in detail what the director had dared say and do. He didn't seem to mind much and had expected worse. When we arrived home, he gave me strict instructions how I should act when the director summoned me, expressing himself in the most revolting manner, ordering me to do the vilest things, describing them in detail, and forcing me to practice with him in ways I found shameful and humiliating. He went so far as to give me several slaps on my infected cheek when I failed to do what he wanted quickly enough. That evening was undoubtedly one of the cruelest of my life, second only to the dinner with my father's two enemies. The hatred, repugnance, nausea, and sheer disgust I felt are beyond description. But I had to obey or be beaten, have my arms twisted, or worse.

The following day, the hairdresser returned to our flat. I was decked out even more magnificently than the day before with all new clothes and accessories. Moresquin paid for everything on credit. He then went to the office for his interview. I was in the carriage that took him there and was to appear if needed. As expected, Moresquin was given a job right away. But his new colleagues having recognized him, he was about to be let go when he was able to send word to me to join him. I entered the office of the director who, when he saw me, changed

FIGURE 14.   'Throwing myself at his feet, I begged him: "Have pity on me, sir, and let my husband have a job, or else he'll beat me to death."' Illustration by Louis Binet, engraving by Jacques Le Roy, in *Le Paysan perverti* (Paris: Esprit, 1776), vol. 1, lettre 32, p. 164. (BnF)

his mind and insisted that my husband be hired, whether he was a good or bad fellow, capable or not.

At this order, the head clerk bowed and asked Moresquin to follow him. As soon as I was alone with the director, I felt I must speak clearly to him. I told him all about Moresquin's monstrous behavior, the demands that brooked no reply, and the revolting instructions he had given to me. The director was moved by my plight. He offered to rescue me from that monster, to love and take care of me. I asked nothing better than protection from Moresquin, but did not want to dishonor myself. I spoke of my father, a highly respected man. Hearing his name, the director exclaimed:

'Ah! He's the brother of one of my friends, a venerable and saintly priest whom I honor, in spite of all my faults! Come, come now! If you sin a little with me, your saintly uncle's prayers will wipe the slate clean. You absolutely have to become my mistress! And you'll have nothing more to fear from Moresquin.'

Surprised by the director's tone and no longer trusting him, I tried to leave, but he stopped me: 'You are truly virtuous. I'll give your vile husband a job after all, without expecting anything from you, out of consideration for your father and your uncle. I'll hire him immediately at an annual salary of 1,800 *livres*.' I was delighted; it was the first moment of joy I had experienced since I was married.

I returned to our flat without seeing anyone else at the office. I waited impatiently for Moresquin to return to tell him the news. He didn't come home until around eight in the evening, nearly an hour after leaving the office. I thought it strange that he hadn't returned right away out of curiosity. But instead, he had invited one of the director's flunkies for drinks in order to find out all he could about his new boss. He didn't learn much, except that everyone was against him and that he wouldn't keep his job. He entered the room, with a worried look.

As he remained silent, I spoke first, which I rarely did: 'I have good news for you. Your salary will be 1,800 livres a year, and you'll certainly be given preferential treatment.'

'What? What?' he replied. I began to explain what had happened, but he cut me off. 'Don't try to persuade me that Monsieur Le T***[157] is giving me all that simply out of consideration for your uncle or your father. It's because you've been his whore. Come on, you can't fool me! So remember now that everything depends on you and that I expect more!'

Nothing I could say made any impression on this despicable man. Whether he was pretending or really believed it, he insisted that I had given in to the director; this idea led him to ask me a thousand vile questions that I can't repeat and tried to forget. 'What a scoundrel!' I thought to myself. 'No matter what I do, he turns everything into a poison that he forces me to swallow!' I began to

---

[157] In a footnote to his 2002 edition of Rétif's works, Baruch identifies Monsieur Le T*** as Le Tellier. [*Restif de La Bretonne* (2002), vol. 2, p. 550, n. 1.]

cry. Moresquin saw my tears as a confirmation of his conjectures and, to console me, he repeated his detestable morality. I denied having slept with the director, and he commended me for denying this. In the end, he seemed almost reasonable, in his own strange way.

The next day, Moresquin returned to the office. Convinced that he could do whatever he pleased, he was haughty toward his colleagues and received the news of his sudden promotion with an insolent air. In short, from his very first day on the job, Moresquin disgusted Monsieur Le T*** so completely that he came close to firing him then and there.

The second day was worse still. Moresquin behaved even more haughtily and outrageously. People were so taken aback that they didn't say anything. He proposed having lunch together; his colleagues accepted. After a few rounds of drinks, Moresquin couldn't hold his tongue, imprudent as ever. He clearly insinuated that I was the director's mistress and that he was his protégé. His colleagues were dumbstruck with astonishment. But as soon as lunch was over, Monsieur Le T***'s right-hand man told him what had just happened. The director at first found it difficult to believe, but was finally convinced and gave orders to deal with Moresquin accordingly. They left him alone that afternoon and let him leave at dinnertime, but gave orders to the doorman to keep him from returning. Without a care in the world, Moresquin dined at home, repeating what he had said to me the night before. The following morning, he left for the office in high spirits.

About an hour later, I saw him arrive home, fuming with anger. He began by breaking a chair. He was so enraged that I was trembling with fear and dared not ask a single question. He hadn't yet looked at me, but finally turned his eyes toward me. 'You bitch!' he cried. 'You spoke against me behind my back!' I thought I was done for and threw myself at his feet, swearing that I hadn't said anything against him. He was no doubt about to mistreat me cruelly when a wine merchant's assistant came to our door. This man didn't know that Moresquin had been fired.

'I've come to tell you that there's a plot afoot against you,' he warned. 'I was making deliveries in your neighborhood and, since you seem like a good fellow, I decided to warn you. People want to turn the director against you because you unwisely claimed that your wife was on friendly terms with him and many other things that were misinterpreted. That's why I came to advise you to make the first move to avoid being fired. Your colleagues are planning to speak against you today, so there's no time to lose. You still have time to defend yourself.'

Moresquin listened intently to what the deliveryman had to say. Afterwards, he turned to me: 'I was going to beat you,' he admitted. 'But this isn't your fault, it's mine. You must return to speak on my behalf.' I was loathe to return, but since Moresquin's job was on the line, I didn't hesitate. And although I was dying of shame, I left right away.

When I arrived at the home of Monsieur Le T***, I was told that he was out. I waited for him there until evening. Then I saw him leaving and understood that he hadn't wanted to see me. I ran to his carriage and cried: 'Dear sir, for the love of God and humanity, please listen to me!'

'No, I won't listen to you. But tomorrow, I'll send someone to speak with you.'

Since the carriage was leaving, I withdrew and went to tell Moresquin what the director had said. He seemed deeply disheartened, but hadn't given up hope. He spoke to me in a calm and gentle manner the rest of the evening. The next morning, he left the apartment to leave the coast clear, he said, for the person who was to come speak with me. And indeed, hardly had he been gone a quarter of an hour before a beardless Capuchin friar entered the room. Greeting me with a kindly air, the friar asked if I was alone. Reassured by my insistence that I was indeed by myself, he sat down next to me and asked me to listen carefully to what he was about to say:

'My dear young lady, it's impossible for Monsieur Le T*** to help you, however much he wishes to oblige you. Yesterday during lunch, your husband spoke boastfully of dishonorable relations between you and the director, who for the sake of his reputation can no longer see you or take any interest in you. That is what I was sent to tell you.'

'Oh, Monsieur! What will become of me? Please help me, Father! I can confide in you,' I cried. 'I'm the unhappiest of women, the most miserable for all possible reasons! I'm married to a cruel and evil man, whom I wed against the wishes of my father, whose heart I broke.'

'Very well! I know a way to help you out of your predicament. Let yourself be guided wholly by me.'

'Father, I'll do everything you tell me to.'

'Excellent! You must leave your home, enter a convent where I'll take you, and stay there as a resident, but incognito. You'll have the liberty to go out whenever you wish.' (At that moment, I heard a rustling in the alcove that served as our kitchen, but didn't pay much attention to it. I stayed on my guard, however.) The friar continued: 'There are situations, like the one you find yourself in, for example, that release us from our scruples. Your husband is a scoundrel who would sell you willingly. That would be an abomination, and you must refuse to have anything to do with his schemes.'

'Certainly, Father, if that was his intention, I would never agree to take part in any criminal acts!'

'That *was* his intention, you can be sure of that; and what I've just told you proves it only too clearly. But, you're still in a difficult predicament, Madam. Monsieur Le T*** holds you in high esteem. You can accept his help. As for your monster of a husband, we'll know how to keep him quiet. What answer should I give to Monsieur Le T***? And when will you leave here?'

FIGURE 15. 'I shuddered when I heard these words, fairly certain that Moresquin was hiding in the kitchen listening to our conversation.' Illustration by Louis Binet, engraved by Louis-Sébastien Berthet, in *Les Contemporaines* (1780), v. 1, Nouvelle 6, p. 231. The original caption reads 'Il est là! …. Il revient! …. Il revient!' [He's over there! … He's coming! … He's coming back!]

'But, Sir, leaving one's home and child is a truly scandalous and risky move! I'll consent to it only on two conditions: that my husband be given a job that can support him and that you can assure me that I'll be able to live respectably in a convent.'

'There's no need to hide from you any longer the fact that I've come here to calm your scruples and that I'm speaking on behalf of Monsieur Le T***, whose advice you can trust without any qualms, given your situation. As for your monster, there are ways to deal with him, and we'll have him locked up if you agree to bestow your favors on Monsieur Le T***. There you have it.'

'I'll never consent to become anyone's mistress, Father.'

'But you can, in all good conscience!'

'No, that will never happen.'

'Let yourself be persuaded!'

'No, no, Sir! How can a man of the cloth like you get involved in such a scurrilous business? How can you violate in this way the principles you were taught!'

'Principles must yield to necessity. You're lost if you don't accept.'

'I'll appeal directly to Monsieur Le T***,' I replied, 'and he won't remain deaf to the pleas of an unfortunate and helpless woman.'

'No, nothing you can say will change his mind. He wants you to give in and, on that condition, he'll provide for you. As for your husband, imprisonment at Bicêtre[158] will be his fate. Monsieur Le T***'s mind is made up, and what he's proposing is the only reasonable solution. We know more about your husband than you do. His tongue is even more dangerous than his hands, despite the fact that he has killed several people, as he himself has claimed.'

'I still hope to move Monsieur Le T***.'

'No, as I've already said, you won't change his mind. You must understand that, however much he wishes to help you, he remains firm in his principles! It's Monsieur Le T*** himself who is telling you this!'

I shuddered when I heard these words, fairly certain that Moresquin was hiding in the kitchen listening to our conversation. Clutching Monsieur Le T***'s hand, I warned him: 'This disguise is dangerous, Sir! You should leave here as quickly as possible!' This warning was accompanied by an expressive glance toward the kitchen.

Monsieur Le T*** stood up and was heading out the front door when Moresquin appeared. (He had left the kitchen through the door to the hallway outside.) 'Father,' he said chuckling, 'I see you're leaving! I'd be delighted to have a few words with you. So let's go back inside!' Pushing the director back inside the door, Moresquin continued: 'I heard everything, Father, and I know who you

---

[158] *Bicêtre*: Prison on the outskirts of Paris. See note 140 above.

are. Give me a job, or I'll have you arrested and taken to the convent. You're in my power now, and I'm not about to take pity on you. Come, come, Father Le T***, don't put on airs with me! What I need is a job, a written guarantee of our agreement, and a hundred *louis* in cash or as a bill of exchange.'

Feeling trapped and well aware of the kind of man he was dealing with, Monsieur Le T*** agreed to sign the bill of exchange for a hundred *louis*. But he was able to worm his way out of Moresquin's other two conditions with various promises and equivocations. Moresquin let him leave, but not after telling him he was wrong to have asked me directly for my favors, because he alone could grant them. He added that if the director wished to make suitable arrangements, he would leave fully satisfied. Monsieur Le T*** seemed alarmed by this brazen offer. He left hurriedly saying that he wasn't refusing, but that he was too flustered at that moment to take advantage of the offer.

After Monsieur Le T*** had left, Moresquin burst out laughing in a sinister manner. He told me not to bother preparing dinner and to get dressed for an outing, since we were going to Quai de la Rapée[159] to enjoy some fish stew. Although still shaking from what had just happened, I had no choice but to obey. Not knowing whether Monsieur Le T*** would accept or refuse Moresquin's vile proposition, I was extremely attentive and apprehensive, but tried my best to hide my feelings. Moresquin invited two of his colleagues to join us and was in the best of spirits during our outing. He ordered me to be merry, and I did as children do who laugh through their tears because they see the whip in hand. It's impossible to repeat what he said during lunch. It was a stream of obscenities and self-interested schemes of the vilest nature that left our two guests in a state of stupefaction and disgust!

The following day, Moresquin waited for word from Monsieur Le T***, but it never came and never would, aside from expressions of indignation and scorn. I was forced to return to his home, but his door remained closed to me. Moresquin was too dangerous a man, and on this occasion, it was his excessive villainy that saved me.

---

[159] In the eighteenth century, Quai de la Rapée (also known as Quai de Bercy) was a major port on the Seine where cargo (especially wine) was unloaded for delivery to the warehouses nearby. Contiguous to the Paris city limits of the time, Bercy was the thriving center of the Paris wine trade, as well as a popular gathering place for dining, street theater, band concerts, and fireworks.

The hundred *louis* lasted less than three months. Out of work, Moresquin gambled and lost. He treated his friends to lavish dinners so they would think I was Monsieur Le T***'s mistress and kept by him. He managed to defame me, without causing any damage to Monsieur Le T***'s reputation. People thought instead that I had become someone else's mistress. The day the money ran out, I endured another cruel scene. You'll recall that I was pregnant at the time with my second child, a daughter who was born sickly and who died in infancy. Moresquin wanted to go to the theater and for me to go with him. I reminded him that we had no money and that it would be better for him to go by himself and stand in the parterre than to pay for seats for the two of us. He ordered me to go anyway. But my objections had annoyed him and, on the way to the theater, he treated me like a slave, or rather, as a prostitute that a libertine forced to walk in front of him. Everyone was staring at us, and I felt I would die of shame.

We became momentarily separated in the crowd and I took advantage of the confusion to return home. I figured that he would continue on to the theater and was preparing to leave for my aunt's when he arrived soon after. I fled through one of the two doors, but Moresquin caught me by my skirt and punched me so hard that I fell down unconscious. Thinking he had killed me, he left me lying there in the cold, dark hallway outside our door. He locked me out and went to bed. I came to, I'm not sure when, but it was nighttime and all was quiet. Fearing I would die of the cold, I dared to knock at our door, but Moresquin refused to open. A neighbor heard me and came to my rescue. Although she was a nasty woman, she took pity on me. She helped me to her apartment where she let me warm myself by the fire, thereby saving me from death. But the frailty and death of the poor babe I was carrying resulted from the mistreatment I suffered at the hands of the child's abominable father. In the morning, the woman brought me back to the monster. I must admit that I expected him to kill me. But instead, he chose to hurl insults at me, insults so horrifying that it made our hair stand on end and that prompted our neighbor to declare:

'Beat her, kill her, and you'll be hung. Force her to sleep outside your door; even if it kills her, it's none of my business. But let me make one thing quite clear: I'm a respectable woman. But what kind of a person are you? And if your wife is as terrible as you say, what kind of a couple are you?' And, as she was leaving, she added: 'If the ceiling collapses and crushes you, it would be good riddance! People like you are better off dead than alive.'

This latest violent ordeal left me weak and listless again. As I neared the end of my pregnancy and was no longer presentable, I was treated like a dog. Moresquin had recently taken in his sixteen-year-old goddaughter, an ugly, low-class, and thoroughly despicable character. He took pleasure in giving her authority over me. When he returned home, he always asked for a full report of my behavior in order to punish me. That monster, who was so like her godfather, made my life hell. I was slapped in her presence and forced to eat sitting on the floor while she

FIGURE 16.   'Raising his cane, ready to beat me, he shouted: "Slut, poison, vermin, I want
you dead!"' Artist and engraver unknown. Illustration from *Aline et Valcourt* (Paris: Veuve
Girouard, 1795), Letter 16, vol. 1, Part I, p. 112. (BnF)

ate at the table. I endured other indignities as well, such as having my skirt pulled up and being whipped by her, with her vile godfather behind her counting the blows, often crying: 'Harder! Harder!'

These indignities, which I was too ashamed of to speak of to others, became known to our neighbors due to the indiscretion of the goddaughter, who boasted in the neighborhood about their treatment of me. But she then became the victim of her own indiscretion. The woman to whom she recounted the whipping incident cut her off abruptly and immediately went to tell three or four neighbors what she had just learned. These working-class women were all indignant. They came straight to our apartment and arrived just as the goddaughter was mistreating me again quite badly. I rebelled at this treatment and was threatening to slap her. She came up to me, saying 'So go ahead and slap me!' But I didn't have the nerve.

'You're right not to touch me,' the girl replied, 'for you'd be sorry! You'd be kicked and punched more times than you could count.'

Just as she finished this sentence, she received a slap so powerful that it knocked her over onto her chair. She stood up, shouting: 'Ah, you slapped me, you bitch!' But, at the same time, the five women surrounded her, crying:

'What this little devil needs is to be taught a good lesson!' And they continued slapping her until their strength gave out. Utterly exhausted, the girl dropped to her knees. Yet the women were so enraged that they started beating her again. They finally stopped and helped her to her feet, but only to say: 'Go pack your bag and beat it, bitch! Don't stand there gaping like a ninny! Get moving!' Seeing their hands raised, ready to beat her some more, the girl summoned the strength to get up and pack her bags. As she left, they gave her a swift parting kick, accompanied by suitable epithets.

I was dumbfounded by this confrontation, which had taken place in my home, carried out by strangers! They barely looked at me and, talking among themselves, said almost nothing to me. Based on what they said, I realized they took me for a woman with no feelings, no heart, who stayed with a monster like Moresquin out of sheer stupidity. Alas! They didn't know that that I was utterly lacking in resources and support! Nor did they know that my mother, my cruelest enemy, would have done everything in her power to stop me had I sought refuge with my father! Yet what they said gave me a new idea that might prove helpful and that I was able to put to use that very same evening.

Moresquin did not return until midnight. I had just gone to bed, overcome by my miseries and by the turbulent events of that day. When he asked for his goddaughter, I recounted in detail all that had happened. It's impossible to describe how enraged he became; he was seething with anger. Raising his cane, ready to beat me, he shouted: 'Slut, poison, vermin, I want you dead! But first, get up and make my dinner.' As he stood there grinding his teeth and foaming with rage, I became so terrified that I fled to the home of my aunt Bitez, the one responsible for my misfortune. I arrived there at one in the morning. Moresquin came to get me almost immediately after, but I refused to return home with him unless accompanied by Mme Bitez's servant. Her presence helped restrain the bully a bit. But more importantly, the servant reported to her mistress the dreadful things that Moresquin said to me that night, which finally convinced my aunt of the truth of what I had been telling her before, but that she had trouble believing. He was unmasked at last.

Not long after these events, I gave birth to my daughter. Moresquin found her pretty and bragged about her in the most revolting manner. He hired a wet nurse, following his twisted logic that my charms, which he treated with so little care, could be a useful resource for him. Yet despite his stupidity, there was a certain logic behind his mistreatment of me that was perfectly in keeping with his vile character: he had understood that by degrading and terrorizing me to the breaking point, I would have less strength of character to resist his criminal schemes. So anything that might have led him to make things easier for me never occurred to him. In any case, he was such a brute that he couldn't have treated me with kindness even if he were reasonable enough to want to. And here's the proof, for the incident that I'm about to describe could not have been premeditated; it was a outburst of sheer brutality that took me completely by surprise.

It was New Year's Day 178[3],[160] four days after the birth of my daughter.[161] That morning, the wigmaker had come to groom Moresquin, who asked for biscuits for him and his hairdresser. I hadn't been mistreated since I gave birth, and so I laughed and said as I served them that men normally didn't eat biscuits. It was wrong, I admit, for me to play with fire in this way. I never imagined that,

---

[160] Ingénue's daughter was born in late December 1782, so the incident described here would have taken place on New Year's Day 1783 (not 1782 as written in the original text).

[161] Concerning the birth of a second child, Baruch writes: 'There is no documentary evidence of the birth of this second child, nor is it mentioned in Rétif's diary' [Baruch, *Restif de La Bretonne* (2002), vol. 2, p. 406, n. 1]. In *La Femme infidelle*, Ingénue claims to have borne *three* children, including a daughter who died in infancy: 'After four years of drudgery and three children, one of whom died because of the mistreatment I endured during my pregnancy, I deserve a far better salary than a few towels, a few handkerchiefs, and two pairs of sheets' [*OC*, vol. 45, p. 831). A second surviving child is mentioned in a letter sent by Ingénue to her husband in *La Femme infidelle*: 'I realize that you aren't able to support a wife and two children [...]. I know that you would like to keep the older child with you, so I'll take the younger one [...]' (*OC*, vol. 45, pp. 860–61). See the full text of this letter in Appendix C, Excerpt 14, in MHRA's French edition of *Ingénue*. Given the fact that Rétif and his daughter remained estranged until November 1783, it would hardly be surprising that no mention of these births is found in his diary. Nor would three pregnancies three years in a row be surprising given Augé's sexual proclivities and the lack of reliable birth control during that period. Rétif claims that the letters included in *La Femme infidelle* and his other works are authentic; whether they actually are is an open question.

by joking this way, I had just unleashed a terrible storm! Knocking the biscuits out of my hands, Moresquin grabbed ahold of me like a madman and might have killed me if it hadn't been for the wigmaker and my nurse. As they restrained him, he launched into a furious stream of insults against me and my family. Pale and trembling, I felt a deathly shudder run through me, followed by a cold sweat all over my body. The pitiful state I was in only seemed to increase his brutality. As soon as the wigmaker had left, the monster knocked over the table along with everything on it. He then seized a drawer containing all my sewing things, emptied it onto the fire, and smashed the drawer to pieces. After that, he locked and bolted the door and, taking up his sword, screamed that he was going to kill me and then himself. The nurse managed to restrain him long enough for me to escape. He was making so much noise that he didn't hear me open the door. Although it was only six in the morning, I fled in my nightgown through the cold to my aunt's. She quickly put me to bed and, thanks to her care, saved my life. She nearly died of shock at seeing the state I was in when I arrived.

Moresquin has since claimed that he was glad to hear of the condition I was in when I escaped and of the shock it caused my aunt, hoping to get rid of us both for good at the same time. It's true that this wretch was accustomed to cause the death both of strangers and of people closer to him. If his own parents hadn't made the wise decision to move away after his father's retirement, he would have caused them to die of grief. It's certain that the only reason they left Paris was to avoid being continually exposed to his abusive behavior and its consequences.

It's time now to describe Moresquin's reputation among his colleagues and to explain why he wasn't chosen to replace his father when he retired.

Weakened by the passing years and almost unable to fulfill his duties any longer, Moresquin's father nevertheless postponed his retirement in the hope that his son would succeed him. But Moresquin had alienated his superiors by his misconduct since his marriage, as well as by his brutal behavior in his younger days. And he was now looked upon as even more despicable after his recent dealings with Monsieur Le T***, news of which had spread through the offices of the capital. There was no longer any hope to salvage his career. Despite all this, Moresquin's father dared speak up for him. He was interrupted as soon as he mentioned his son. However, to show their appreciation for his long years of service, his superiors increased his annual retirement pension of 1,200 *livres* by 400 *livres*. 'You should use this supplement to make your son respect you,' they told him. The old man accepted, but was heartsick to have fathered a monster who had dishonored the family name.

Moresquin was enraged to learn that he had nothing to hope for, not even the lowliest position in his father's office. He tried to pick a quarrel with his father, accusing him of working against his interests. Night after night, he went to his parents' home to insult them and to hound them into giving him money. They soon realized that they would never have enough to satisfy him and resolved to put twelve leagues[162] between themselves and their son. They made all the necessary arrangements without telling him, and Moresquin didn't learn about their move until the day of their departure, so carefully had they kept their plans secret. When he realized what was happening, Moresquin flew into a rage that knew no bounds. But he was forced to leave after their neighbors intervened and threatened to have him arrested if he didn't leave his parents alone. It didn't take him long to pester them again in their new home. But there, as in other places outside Paris, people aren't isolated as they are in the capital, where people are only interested in their own affairs. Moresquin's father had alerted his new neighbors about the problems with his son, as well as the local magistrate, who made it his duty to help him. The effectiveness of these arrangements was proved to Moresquin as soon as he visited his parents for the first time after their move. He was severely reprimanded and returned to Paris full of rage. He had a victim waiting for him there, and she would suffer all the abuse he hadn't been able to inflict on his parents.

I was weak and listless after giving birth and after the scene that had followed a few days later. Seeing that I was of no use for his vile schemes in my wretched condition, Moresquin indulged in the full measure of his vicious character and endeavored to make my life unbearable by tormenting me on a daily basis. He called me dreadful names and hurled the vilest insults at me. If I dared utter a single word of complaint, I was pinched and beaten and my arms twisted. It's impossible to describe the extent of the abuse I suffered. He became possessed by a kind of lascivious frenzy, that was in no way amorous. It seemed as though my condition drove him to torment me. He spoke to me using crude expressions used by libertines with prostitutes and forced me to commit acts that were disgusting and against the laws of God and nature.

One night when I was experiencing a great deal of pain from my infected cheek and from a bad case of diarrhea, Moresquin took pleasure in my suffering and crudely remarked that I was of much better use to him sick than healthy. Another time when I was deathly ill and totally exhausted, he pinched me so hard in the

---

[162] Before the Revolution, twelve leagues (the *lieue de Paris*) was roughly equivalent to 30 miles or 50 km. See note 144 above.

midst of his brutal lovemaking that it caused me to cry out in pain and to make a sudden violent movement. Pleased with the effect, the monster pinched me again several times until he reached orgasm, while I fainted from the pain. In his hands, I was a passive being that he used and abused according to his whims and passions more despotically than the cruelest slaveholder of the New World ever treated his female slaves. What could I do? There was no one to help or support me. My aunt was a spineless woman, who hardly dared to keep me even for a day when I fled to her house.

Despite all this suffering, what I've described wasn't yet the full extent of my misery. For the monster was about to become jealous! This vile and criminal man, who would gladly have sold me to the most odious of libertines for the right price, was about to ..., well, *pretend* to be jealous to make me more submissive and more likely to go along with his detestable schemes in order to dishonor me.

Autumn had arrived, and it was the feast day of St. Denis.[163] The weather was nice, and I was feeling better. A beloved wife would have died from what I had endured! As for me, I was on the mend thanks only to a reprieve of sorts. Seeing how nice the weather was when he woke up, Moresquin ordered: 'Get dressed. Today is the last chance for the whores of Paris to strut their stuff; if you're not yet there among them, you will be soon, so hurry up. You won't return home without turning a trick or two.' Accustomed to even cruder language I haven't dared repeat, I went ahead and dressed for our outing.

We left at eleven that morning for the Arsenal,[164] where Moresquin ran into one of his colleagues, a tall young man that some might find attractive, but whose looks I found rather insipid. Moresquin addressed him familiarly and, inviting him to take my arm, asked him to stroll with us along the boulevards. The young man politely offered me his hand. When I hesitated, a menacing look from Moresquin forced me to accept. From then on, the monster made a point of walking ten steps ahead of us. From time to time, he stopped to wait for us and to spout obscenities at us that Fromentel[165] did not seem to find at all amusing. Indeed, he confided that Moresquin was not his friend and that they had little in common. Apologizing for his bluntness, he added that he in fact despised him. I felt I could trust this young man, who seemed decent and well-mannered to me. I didn't realize that, when it came to clerks, there wasn't a single honest man among them and that they were all immoral scoundrels — some openly so and

---

[163] *Le jour de Saint-Denis*: 9 October (1783).

[164] Reference to the Jardin de l'Arsenal, a public garden in front of the munitions warehouse located at that time on the right bank of the Seine between the Bastille and quai de la Rapée.

[165] The character of Fromentel is based on an acquaintance of Augé, Blérie de Sériville, a munitions clerk ('commis des poudres et salpêtres') at the Arsenal, with whom Agnès is thought to have had an extramarital affair. Rétif calls him Rizblé in *La Femme infidelle* and Timori in *L'Anti-Justine*. See notes 12 and 187.

FIGURE 17.   'We left at eleven that morning for the Arsenal, where Moresquin ran into one of his colleagues, a tall young man that some might find attractive, but whose looks I found rather insipid. He addressed him familiarly and, inviting him to take my arm, asked him to walk with us along the boulevards. The young man politely offered me his hand.' Illustration by Louis Binet, engraving by Jacques Le Roy, in *Le Paysan perverti* (Paris: Esprit, 1776), vol. 1, lettre 65, p. 286. (BnF)

others seemingly more respectable and, hence, more dangerous. Fromentel was in this second category.

Fromentel spent the whole afternoon with us, after which we went with him to a vaudeville theater to see a show and then dined together at our house. We didn't part until midnight. What was both extraordinary and strange was that Moresquin remained calm throughout dinner, conversing in a reasonable and courteous manner, not always in good taste, but sociable at least.

After the young man left, Moresquin asked me what I thought of him. I replied that he was very nice. The monster didn't respond; but scarcely had we gone to bed that, indulging in his usual brutality, he told me that I had only to imagine that I was holding Fromentel in my arms in order to respond to his passion. I dared not say a word. But since I wasn't following the brute's orders, he twisted my arms and poked me hard in my ribs, spurring me on as if I were a donkey or a mule. He fell asleep afterwards and left me alone the rest of the night. The next morning, I was up before him.

The following two days passed peacefully enough, until Sunday came. I wasn't even harassed by Moresquin, who indulged, as he often had during my illnesses, in a private vice,[166] which I found extremely repugnant because of the things the monster uttered aloud as he engaged in this depravity. Sunday eventually arrived, a terrible day that I can't recall without shuddering again. For Moresquin is not only a despicable scoundrel; he's also unhinged. As you'll see, there's madness in what you're about to read. However, I need first to explain that this wretched man, who had been unemployed for quite some time, had just found a job filling orders for firewood, a lowly line of employment filled only by the most incapable types. Here's how that came about.

During a fireworks display at Place de la Grève,[167] we had crossed paths with a marquise who was acquainted with my father. Shameless as ever, Moresquin spoke to her of his dire financial straits and pressed her to help find work for him. The lady spoke of firewood delivery, and Moresquin accepted the position, which paid only six hundred *livres* per year. He started work, but it didn't last long. These types of clerks are sometimes responsible for collecting money owed for large deliveries made to well-known figures. That particular Sunday, Moresquin had gone to collect money at the home of one such person, whose staff had offered him lunch. He had overindulged and came home drunk.

---

[166] *Private vice*: masturbation.

[167] *Place de la Grève*: Large public square (now called Place de l'Hôtel de Ville) in front of Paris city hall, where public celebrations — as well as public protests, worker strikes, and public executions — were held and where day laborers used to go in the hope of finding work. This square is not far from where Augé's apartment was located on rue de la Mortellerie (now rue de l'Hôtel de Ville).

FIGURE 18.   *Quai Saint-Bernard c.* 1780, engraving by Charles-Melchior Descourtis after
the color painting by Pierre-Antoine de Machy. (BnF)

Let's return now to the incident I alluded to earlier.

Fromentel came to see us, following the pressing invitation he had received. Moresquin was overjoyed to see him, which suggested to me that dreadful scenes hold a peculiar charm for this monster. We dined merrily. Moresquin, whose mind was already clouded from all he had imbibed at lunch, drank a great deal more, no doubt to get completely drunk. Afterwards, he proposed a stroll over to the Jardin du Roi.[168] He told his friend to walk ahead with me, because he had to collect some money to take to the firewood supplier. Moresquin was to join us later with our son, whom he liked to carry around on his shoulders. It was agreed that Fromentel and I would walk along the right bank of the Seine and then meet up with Moresquin at quai de la Rapée,[169] where we would take the ferry across the river together to the Jardin du Roi. But he had no intention of meeting us there, in light of the horrid scheme he had devised. Instead, he crossed over the Pont Marie and then walked along the quai Saint-Bernard to the park. We waited in vain for him at the ferry landing. We finally took the ferry across, assuming part of what had actually happened: that Moresquin, half drunk, had forgotten the path he himself had laid out and that he had gone the other way and had already arrived.

And we did in fact find him at the Jardin du Roi. He was furious! Gnashing his teeth in anger, he came up to me and hissed in my ear: 'You bitch, you whore, you went up to Fromentel's apartment and … in his room! I can tell by your blushing and how red your ears are. If we were at home, I'd find other proof as

---

[168] The Jardin du Roi was renamed the Jardin des Plantes after the 1789 Revolution.

[169] In the 1780s, there were no bridges linking the quai de la Rapée to the left bank of the Seine where the Jardin du Roi was located; the first Pont d'Austerlitz was not built until 1805. Moresquin proposed to his wife and their guest to walk along the right bank of the Seine from their apartment near the l'Hôtel de Ville to the quai de la Rapée, where they were to meet him and then take a ferry together across the river to the Jardin du Roi. But instead, Moresquin crossed over the Seine on the Pont Marie (the bridge linking the quai de l'Hôtel de Ville to the Île Saint-Louis), walked across the island and the Pont de la Tournelle to the left bank, and then followed the quai Saint-Bernard to the park, where his wife and Fromentel eventually found him.

Figure 19. 'Grabbing ahold of me, he kicked and punched me. "This doesn't feel as good as what Fromentel did to you, bitch, does it! But after the sunshine comes the rain and, after pleasure, comes pain."' Illustration titled *La fille séduite* by Louis Binet, engraved by Louis-Sébastien Berthet, in *Les Contemporaines* (1780), vol. 3, Nouvelle 19, p. 201. (BnF)

well. But tonight you'll be shafted with a different rod than the one that gave you so much pleasure!' Hearing these foul words, I asked him how he could even imagine such a thing since it was only the second time I had seen this young man. I insisted that, even if it had been a hundred times, I had too much self-respect to behave in such a manner, that Fromentel had not said anything improper to me, and that if he had, I would certainly have put him in his place. I added that I detested his class of men in general, that I refused to ever see him again, and that I would ask him to refrain from visiting us in the future.

'If you utter a single word, I'll beat you to a pulp, right here in this park.'

Moresquin was not really jealous. But he had somehow gotten into his head a monstrous delusion that was still hazy in his mind and unclear to me, but that had prompted his outburst against me. This delusion (or was it instead a deliberate scheme?) would become clear soon enough. Laughing, Moresquin then went up to Fromentel, who was holding our son, and spoke to him in a friendly tone. That evening, he invited him to stay for dinner, during which he stupidly took pleasure in playing the role of the cuckold Arnolphe in Molière's play *L'Ecole des femmes*. He told Fromentel that I loved him and, pretending to be joking, said: 'If I'm to be …,'[170] it's better that it happens because of a handsome lad like you than by another' and a thousand other similar statements made with the crudeness, tactlessness, and stupidity of a man utterly lacking in good breeding. I blanched, while the young man blushed and departed as quickly as he could.

After Fromentel left, Moresquin asked if I remembered what he had promised. 'I can't believe that you'd be so unjust as to punish me for a mere figment of your imagination,' I replied. He answered me with a slap, and I cried out in indignation. Grabbing ahold of me, he kicked and punched me. 'This doesn't feel as good as what Fromentel did to you, bitch, does it!' he yelled. 'But after the sunshine comes the rain and, after pleasure, comes pain. Tell me now, slut, how does this feel?' And he went on hitting me. I was screaming with pain, unable to break free. He then wanted to inspect me to find proof. What he did to me then caused such pain that I felt nauseous. He claimed to have found proof. It felt like a terrible nightmare. But it was nothing like what was to follow.

Moresquin declared me guilty and insisted that there was only one way I could earn his forgiveness. I understood that to mean that he was planning to sell me to some libertine. But I was too numb to respond. He forced me to tidy up my

---

[170] The missing word is probably 'cuckolded' (*cocu*). By comparing himself to Arnolphe (Agnès's guardian and would-be husband in Molière's *Ecole des femmes*), what Moresquin means here is: 'If I'm to be cuckolded, it's better that it be by a handsome fellow like you.' In *La Femme infidelle*, Rétif offers a more nuanced explanation of Augé's peculiar, seemingly contradictory attitude toward Blérie de Sérivillé (see Appendix F, Excerpts 2 and 4, in MHRA's French edition of *Ingénue Saxancour*). For further discussion of this aspect of Augé's character, see the introduction.

Figure 20. *Vue intérieure de Paris représentant le Port-au-Blé depuis l'extrémité de l'ancien marché aux Veaux jusqu'au Pont Notre-Dame* [View of central Paris showing the Port-au-Blé river port from the end of the old livestock market to the Notre-Dame Bridge] by Pierre-Antoine de Machy (1785). Engraving by Pierre-Gabriel Berthault. (BnF)

hair and, opening the door, said we would take a walk to clear his head of gloomy thoughts. It was useless to resist, and I followed him out the door. It was close to midnight, but Moresquin often walked around outside, with me or with others, until two in the morning. He took me along the Seine to the Port-au-blé[171] and then led me into an apartment building on a dark and narrow street nearby. When we reached the fourth floor, Moresquin knocked at the door, which was opened by a petite woman. Although neatly dressed, she had a brazen look about her. I didn't recognize her at first, but her bearing and Moresquin's overly familiar manner with her made me realize that she was a prostitute I had often seen in our neighborhood. I shuddered at the thought of being in the home of a street-walker! After taking a few liberties with her, Moresquin whispered in her ear. She looked at me closely as she listened to him. When he was finished talking, she replied out loud that what he had proposed was out of the question because if word got out, she would be locked up for the rest of her life. Moresquin assured her that no one would ever know and that he'd make sure that I acted in a way that would not expose her involvement.

'Since you're an old friend, I'd like to help you out,' she said. 'But you'll need to rent a room on your own, because she can't work here. If she chooses freely to form a partnership with me, that's fine, and we'll share like sisters. But I'll never agree to what you asked.'

'All right then, leave us for a moment,' Moresquin replied. 'When you return, she'll have agreed to everything.' The woman left us alone.

As soon as she had gone, Moresquin said to me: 'I told you that there's only one way to win my forgiveness. This whore earns a good living. She's a good-hearted girl and has a solid clientele. Since you don't go out much, people don't know you. All we have left is six hundred *livres*; we're broke. You're not clever enough to get yourself set up as a kept woman. This girl here earns at least two *louis* a week; I need you to bring in money. Last night, I offered you to her as a partner, and she asked to see you. But she doesn't want to do anything without your consent. If you agree, you'll earn more than she does; she said so herself. You'll never have to go out on the street; she'll bring men to you. I promise that I'll treat you with a gentleness that will astonish you and will love you a hundred times more than if you were mine alone. I have a taste for women of that sort, and if you become one to please me and to help me out, I'll be crazy for you. You'll see that I'll be as good a pimp as I am a bad husband. Your fate is now in your hands. What do you say?'

---

[171] The Port-au-blé was located not far from the Augés' apartment near the Hôtel de Ville on the right bank of the Seine opposite l'Ile de la Cité. Wheat and other cargo was unloaded there from boats and taken to the Halles nearby.

Falling to my knees, I begged him: 'My dear husband, you can't be serious! What about your parents, not to mention mine? And what about the people you know and the rest of society?'

'No one will know.'

'I'm not so sure! I'd be mortified if anyone found out.'

'No one will! I'll cover for you. The perception that we're happily married will keep everyone quiet. In any case, from this hidden alcove, you'll be able to see anyone who enters the building and, if you don't come out, Zaïre won't mention you.'[172]

What could I possibly say to such a man? I couldn't speak to him either of religion or honor, so instead I insisted on the fact that I would soon be known as a prostitute and dishonored. Contrary to my expectation, the monster did not become angry with me; for I could have made noise, cried for help, and unmasked him! Poor wretch that I was, I didn't realize that had I made a scene, the monster would have ruined my reputation, saying that he had just found me in this house of ill repute. He would have had the police take me to the Saint-Martin hospital and had me interned there.[173] It was from Moresquin himself that I learned the horrible details of what he had planned to do.

Instead of becoming angry, Moresquin spoke to me gently, pointing out that we were penniless and that if I obliged him in this way, he would worship me as his benefactress. What was I to do? I thought of asking him to open a window and then for a glass of water and, when he had his back turned, of throwing myself out the window down to the pavement below.[174] As I was turning this idea over in my head, we heard someone come up the stairs and open the outer door. Moresquin had me hide with him in the secret alcove mentioned earlier. And it's a good thing he did. For it was Fromentel that Zaïre had brought back with her.

---

[172] The arrangement proposed here seems to have been that Ingénue would be concealed in a small room adjacent to Zaïre's boudoir and that, if she did not like the looks of a particular client that Zaïre brought her, she could make that known simply by refusing to come out.

[173] The hôpital Saint-Martin was a public hospital founded in 1607 by Henri IV on the northern edge of Paris (in what is now the quartier Saint-Denis) to treat victims of the plague and other infectious diseases. In the eighteenth century, this hospital specialized in treatment of skin ailments (such as scabies and scrofula) and various chronic illnesses, including cancer and venereal diseases — afflictions that all inspired dread and revulsion. Moresquin seems to imply here that he would have accused his wife of engaging in prostitution and of suffering from venereal disease in order to have her interned in the hôpital Saint-Martin as a way of bringing shame and humiliation to her and her family.

[174] The dénouement Ingénue imagines here resembles the suicide of Suzanne Simonin, heroine of the 1966 film Jacques Rivette drew from Diderot's 1760 novel *La Religieuse* about a nun who tried unsuccessfully to revoke her vows. In Rivette's film, the nun escapes from the convent, but later throws herself out a window to her death, rather than prostitute herself in order to survive.

The pair sat down and began to carry on in a vile manner, during which Fromentel murmured my name two or three times. When Zaïre asked him why, he told her everything that had happened that day, admitting that could kick himself for not doing what he had heard my husband accuse me of and that he hoped to take advantage of the situation another time. He added that the husband was surely mocking him by speaking as he had, since he should have realized that one wouldn't dare act so brazenly on a first outing with a respectable woman like me. Zaïre, who had completely understood that Fromentel was talking about me, urged him to take advantage of the first chance he got, assuring him that he'd be doing me a favor. The young clerk answered Zaïre that I was so alluring that he was still burning with desire and wanted to spend the whole night with her. She agreed and, when she left the room to make arrangements, she deftly helped us slip away.

It was nearly one in the morning when we got home. Moresquin was in a pensive mood. After awhile, he said: 'I see that you were telling the truth. And since you're not guilty, my dear wife, your generosity will be all the greater if you do what I'm asking of you. If you do that for me and give me the pleasure of counting you among the class of women that I place above all others, you'll see how I'll honor and respect you! I'm very keen on this idea, and I wish to use gentle persuasion to gain this favor from you.' I had nearly finished undressing as he was speaking to me. I didn't answer. He came over to kiss me, imploring: 'Say you will, say you'll consent!' I began to cry. 'You're crying. Ah, you're going to agree!' I didn't dare say no. Moresquin kneeled down and kissed my feet, calling me his goddess, his mistress, his adorable little whore.

Hesitating, I finally said to him timidly, 'My friend ….' He didn't let me finish and covered me with kisses, carried away by what he had just said. I felt nauseous; he filled me with revulsion and loathing.

'My friend,' I continued when he stopped, 'you can't be serious! You would certainly regret it if I did what you're asking me today.' Seeing him gnash his teeth, I was filled with trepidation, so I added: 'But since you are unfortunately destined to be poor, wouldn't there be some way for me to become a kept woman, secretly and without causing any scandal? (I protest that I loathed what I was proposing. But I feared being beaten, perhaps to death. I was alone, in the middle of the night, with a vile, homicidal man.) 'It seems to me that if I were given time to fully recover in peace, I might become appealing enough to attract a respectable man. That way, I wouldn't have to risk dishonoring you in the most shameful manner.'

I said nothing further, waiting for Moresquin's reply, which was that he would be jealous of a respectable man who kept me, but not of the public in general. And since everything had been arranged, he expected to be obeyed: 'It's your choice: beatings or good treatment. In any case, even with beatings, you won't be able to avoid what's been decided. My mind is made up, so there's nothing more to say.'

FIGURE 21. 'I had trouble getting to my feet and was still stumbling about when Moresquin got out of bed and, in a fit of anger, knocked me to the ground.' Original copper engraving by Carlo Farneti from Bachelin's 1931 edition of *Ingénue Saxancour* in *L'Œuvre de Restif de La Bretonne*, vol. 5, p. 419. (Northwestern University Library, Charles Deering McCormick Library of Special Collections)

Indeed, there was nothing I *could* say, so I choked back my tears. The monster grabbed ahold of me and, as he put it, gave me lessons of …. I can't possibly repeat what he said. Suffice it to say that he sullied every part of my body, and that I thought that I'd die from the revulsion I felt. After one especially disgusting act, he finally left me alone and fell asleep.

I was so exhausted that I soon fell into a deep sleep. I don't know how long I slept. But when I awoke, I found myself in complete darkness, with Moresquin caressing me in a more tender, more decent fashion than usual. I even thought I heard him sigh. I was truly astonished! The hours passed; I was in a state of utter exhaustion. After awhile, the curtains were opened, and I realized that it was broad daylight, even though the shutters were still closed. Moresquin came back to bed and fell asleep, and I did as well. When I awoke again, he pushed me out of bed onto the floor. I had trouble getting to my feet and was still stumbling about when he got out of bed and, in a fit of anger, knocked me to the ground. I begged for mercy.

'Bitch, I aim to make you the lowliest of servants groveling at my feet. You no longer have either a father or a mother. Your stingy scoundrel of a father abandoned you to me, so don't expect any help from him. If he didn't want me to mistreat you, he would have given you a dowry. Think about that, scumbag!' And, with that, he left the room.

I could never understand Moresquin's behavior that day, nor what had happened during the night or, rather, earlier that morning; for after he left, as I lay there motionless, I heard the clock strike twelve noon. He hadn't opened the shutters, so I called over to a neighbor, who opened them for me. She asked what had been going on at our apartment. Earlier that morning around ten o'clock, she had heard people in the courtyard threatening my husband and calling him a miserable scoundrel. They were talking about me and warned that they'd be keeping an eye on him in the future. I answered that I hadn't heard anything. But I shuddered, thinking about all that had happened to me! Horrified, I realized that there must have been three men, at least ….[175]

---

[175] The ellipses are in the original text. Most Rétif scholars agree that the episodes in which Moresquin urges his wife to prostitute herself and then succeeds in introducing several men into her bed are based *not* on his daughter's experience, but on those of her friend Catherine Laruelle. Rétif suggests this himself in 'Mes Ouvrages': "It is already well known, as I acknowledged in my story [*Monsieur Nicolas*], that not all these loathsome deeds were the doing of L'Echiné [Augé], but are a mixture of the abuses inflicted on my elder daughter and on a tall, beautiful woman named Madame Moresquin. That lady (who went by the name Laruelle and not Moresquin) had been sold and prostituted in a house of ill-repute, etc.' ['Mes Ouvrages', Appendix to *Monsieur Nicolas*, OC, vol. 71, p. 4729.] See the introductory section 'About the Text' in this edition for further discussion of the sources for Rétif's novel. For the full text from 'Mes Ouvrages', see Appendix B, Excerpt 8, in MHRA's French edition of *Ingénue Saxancour*.

I was in despair. Overcoming my shame, I finally wrote to my father. But either he didn't receive my letter, or else he didn't consider me worthy of an answer. Or perhaps this letter was the reason for the visit he later paid me the following month on November 25.[176]

Although no help arrived in the meantime, my situation became a bit easier to bear. I was nevertheless reduced to the harshest servitude, cleaning the monster's boots, grooming him, doing piecework as a seamstress for the working-class women of the neighborhood, laundering silk stockings and articles of silk lace, and delivering the work myself. In short, I had joined the ranks of the working poor. I did my best to earn a living serving a harsh master, who often interrupted my work to make me clean his boots. I looked after our son who, capricious and spoiled by his father, pestered me constantly. Every night, I was up taking care of this child, who often cried for no reason. I was frequently sick with colds and bronchitis because at the slightest murmur from his son, Moresquin pushed me out of bed to tend to him, without letting me put on anything to keep warm. But at least he no longer spoke to me of his loathsome schemes. Quite to the contrary, he pretended to scorn prostitutes in conversations with his friends. In short, he played the role of hypocrite. He no longer allowed me to tend to my appearance and forced me to wear a dirty negligee around the house. One day, he soiled a white negligee I was wearing with his muddy boots. Another time, he smeared grease all over a silk robe I had made out of one of my old dresses and forced me to wear it like that, with a bundle of rags wrapped around me. I put up with all that, but couldn't get used to the beatings. Moresquin had a way of hitting people that caused intense pain for several days. I couldn't understand what made him act that way.

---

[176] There is no mention of this letter in Rétif's diary, in which he generally recorded important correspondence (such as a first letter from Agnès would certainly have been after nearly four years of estrangement). However, in *La Femme infidelle*, Rétif refers to a letter that Ingénue sends to her father in a moment of despair and that led to his visit the following month (on 25 November 1783). (See *OC*, vol. 45, p. 811.) At the end of *La Femme infidelle*, he includes a copy of this letter, as well as a letter from Ingénue similar to the one described here purportedly sent to him on his birthday when she is seven months pregnant with her first child (23 October 1781). See Appendix C, Excerpts 3 and 4, in MHRA's French edition of *Ingénue Saxancour*. This would hardly be the first time that Rétif transposed or conflated real-life events in his writings.

That's how things were when my father came for a visit on November 25, the day peace was declared with Britain.[177] He was startled at my unkempt appearance. But I was too ashamed to tell him of my troubles and simply pressed him to come see me again. I hoped that the next time, I would be able to speak openly to him of my suffering. Alas! Eight months passed without a visit from him. He had no idea of the dire straits I was in.

What happened during those long eight months? Less horrible incidents than what had occurred until then, but unbearable just the same. I'll mention just a few. Among Moresquin's friends was a clerk named Champdépines,[178] badly scarred on his neck and face from scrofula. He was the ugliest, nastiest, and vilest of men, second only to Moresquin in the repulsion he inspired in me. He was in the habit of coming to our apartment, sometimes with Fromentel. Moresquin took a malicious pleasure in making me perform the dirtiest, most menial tasks in front of these two men. For example, if he came home muddy from the street, he would prop his legs on a stool and, without saying a word, had me kneel in front of him to clean all the mud off his shoes and leggings. And, once I had finished, he often knocked me over with his foot, laughing at my embarrassment and at the disarray in my appearance. And if Champdépines came home with him, he often had me clean his boots as well. But Fromentel refused. This humiliating treatment led Champdépines to treat me quite brazenly, while at the same time cooling the other man's passion for me.

One day when I was busy doing housework, Champdépines arrived alone. During their vile orgies, Moresquin encouraged him to speak to me using the familiar *tu* form of address. So, as he walked in, he said unceremoniously 'How are you?' and tried to take my chin in his hand. I ducked and didn't respond. A moment later, while I was bending over to tend to the fire, he had the insolence to take a liberty with me that was … decidedly brazen. I responded with the mightiest slap I could muster. Champdépines declared that I deserved to be kicked, but that he would refrain. In any case, I had no right to turn my nose up at him, he insisted, since he had held me closer than that. These words were the only inkling I ever had into what had happened the morning after the dreadful visit to the prostitute.

---

[177] In his diary, Rétif notes that his meeting with Agnès (on which this episode in the novel is based) took place on 25 November 1783, proclaimed a day of celebration by Louis XVI for the signing of the Treaty of Versailles between France and Britain that ended hostilities between those two countries following the American Revolutionary War. The diary entry for that date reads: '*Pax. Agnetem.* Publication de la paix. Je vais voir Agnès' [Proclamation of the peace treaty. I go to visit Agnès] (*Journal*, ¶309, vol. 1, p. 130). The treaty, which formally recognized the independence of the United States, had actually been signed on 3 September.

[178] In *La Femme infidelle*, Rétif calls this character Lépinaie and identifies him as a *contrôleur des Bois à brûler* (person who collects money for the bulk sale of firewood to regular customers) — a low-paying post that Moresquin had himself occupied for a short time.

'What do you mean?' I cried.

'Stop acting so high and mighty! I won't tell you,' he answered, still using the familiar *tu* form of address. He then fell silent, but I shuddered at the horrible thought that had crossed my mind.

Moresquin arrived home soon afterwards. Champdépines didn't tell him what I had done, but I overheard him urging him to humiliate me, which the monster was always ready and willing to do. After having me clean his boots, he pushed me over, exposing me indecently and blackening my white shawl with his freshly polished shoe. He then told me to bring his …[179] in front of the fire, where he relieved himself while chatting with his friend. After he was done, he stood up and, with a wave of his hand, ordered me to clear everything away. I was used to doing this for him, and so appeared unaffected by this task. But Champdépines wasn't satisfied. I brought dinner to the table, and the two men sat down. My chair was in its place, but as I was about to sit down, Moresquin pushed it away and ordered me to remain standing behind him. The two men held up their glasses, which I filled. After several glasses of wine, Moresquin asked for water. I filled his glass, which he emptied in my face so that the whole front of my blouse was soaked to the skin. I didn't say a word, but I was shivering with the cold. After the two monsters had finished gorging themselves on food and drink, Moresquin made me kneel down with my chin touching the table and forced me to eat leftovers from the three plates, including that of my son, who had mixed water into his food. I felt nauseous, especially at the thought of eating Champdépines's leftovers. Moresquin noticed this and proceeded to …[180] in my plate. This disgusting mess was followed by a slap. In a drunken rage, he was about to kick me onto the floor. Champdépines restrained him and, satisfied at my humiliation, took the dirty plate away, seated me at the table, and served a tasty morsel to me on a clean plate. But I had lost my appetite and couldn't eat a bite.

Three days after this incident, Moresquin was fired from his job collecting payment for firewood deliveries. As a result, he found himself in desperate financial straits and reduced to depending on his father's generosity. Here's an account of the villainy that deprived him of that job.

Moral corruption has reached new heights nowadays. The man who gave Moresquin his job had taken the wife of one of his clerks as his mistress. This clerk, named Lemore, was a fellow as mediocre as Moresquin, but far less despicable. For convenience, the boss had hired Madame Lemore as his wife's lady's maid. People think that little arrangements of this kind will remain a secret, but word always gets out. A local porcelain-maker needed firewood and

---

[179] The word missing here (also missing in the original unabridged version of the novel) is probably *chaise percée* (portable toilet).

[180] The word missing here (also missing in the original unabridged version of the novel) could be *cracher* (spit) or — more likely, given Moresquin's cruel vulgarity — *uriner* (urinate).

Moresquin happened to be in charge of his account. To thank him for good service, the client invited Moresquin and me to dine with him the following Sunday. During the meal, our host, mistakenly believing he could count on Moresquin's discretion, entertained us with the story of Madame Lemore's relations with her employer. Moresquin derided his boss even further, perhaps because he already suspected the affair or simply because the pleasure of maligning people made him pretend to know more than he did. The next day, Moresquin — who despite his modest salary, often treated himself and others to expensive meals — invited several colleagues to lunch with him, during which he repeated everything he had learned about their colleague. He couldn't have chosen a worse audience, since one of his guests, a clerk named Marsouin, was his sworn enemy and repeated everything to Lemore the following morning. The two of them relayed the whole story to their boss who, in a fit of rage, fired Moresquin in the most humiliating way possible.

Moresquin had the effrontery to ask to confront the porcelain-maker, who brazenly denied being the source of the story. To express his scorn for Moresquin, he spit in his face and said: 'That's all I have to say to a lying scoundrel like you!'

Fired and penniless, Moresquin demanded that I appeal to his boss to take him back. The director replied that he would have liked to help me, but that my husband was a rascal and a rogue, a bad lot of the worst kind, who didn't even refrain from slandering his own wife. This proves that Moresquin had already begun defaming the wretched woman whom he had tried to prostitute. Declaring that he would oppose any attempt to rehire Moresquin, the director added:

'If, by chance, Moresquin goes over my head to be reinstated, I would prefer to resign than to have him working under me.' Sensing what his refusal would cost me at home, I fainted. The director seemed moved by my plight and expressed sympathy for me, but was unwilling to sacrifice himself to help me.

The marquise who had recommended Moresquin for his last job learned of his firing from his boss. She wrote the culprit an angry and threatening letter in which she said, among other things, that his parents were unfortunate indeed to have such a dishonorable son. When I brought him the news of his boss's absolute refusal to rehire him, I tried to calm his fury by promising that I would do all I could to enlist my father's help in finding a position for him. Although this calmed him down at first, he was penniless in the meantime. He pawned some things at the pawnshop and borrowed some money on interest. He grew impatient with me and began pressuring me again with his shameful propositions. He went so far as to say that, since we were doomed anyway, he'd rather make me do what he wanted beforehand. In the morning, he sometimes said to me as he was leaving:

'Vixen, scumbag, whore, there better be money waiting for me when I come home, or you'll be sorry!'

On those days, you can imagine how I trembled when evening came. Once or twice, I sold some of my old clothes; but the third time, there wasn't anything left to sell. But what good did it do to sell my things the first two times? None at all! When I gave him the money, he asked me how many clients I had needed to …. I began to cry, so first he believed that I had prostituted myself and, later, that my father had given me this money. It was only on the third occasion, when I had nothing to give him, that he knew the truth. He flew into a rage, and I thought he was going to kill me.

'What!' I cried. 'You actually thought … ? What would your son say if his mother had become a despicable streetwalker, prostituting herself to the dregs of society?' These words seemed to make an impression on him, but not for long.

Such was my painful situation when my father finally visited me again.[181] He had heard that Moresquin had lost his job and sensed how much I must be suffering. I begged him to try to help my husband find a job. He reluctantly agreed, but suggested that it would be best for me if Moresquin sent me back to live with my parents. I was of another opinion, especially once I learned whom my father planned to ask for help: a powerful and influential man, well positioned to serve as my protector.[182]

I hadn't seen my mother for a long time. Alas! Without realizing it, I added a new mark against me to all my earlier mistakes. When I saw her, I begged her to

---

[181] In the novel, Ingénue receives a second visit from her father in late June or early July 1784 — eight months after his first visit. However, there is no mention of this second visit in Rétif's diary, in which he normally recorded such events. And what is more curious still is the fact that Rétif describes this episode as Saxancour's third (not second) visit to his daughter. The diary, like the novel, records more frequent visits between father and daughter in the months leading up to her separation from Augé in July 1785.

[182] The protector in question is Louis Le Pelletier de Morfontaine (1730–1799), prévôt des marchands in Paris from 1784 to 1789, whom Rétif later calls Olaüs Magnus in the novel. Rétif became acquainted with him in 1784 and asked for his help in dealing with Augé. The *prévôt des marchands* was director of Paris's municipal administration and hence one of the city's most influential men. Entries in Rétif's diary indicate that he was occasionally a dinner guest in Le Pelletier's home. As for Legrand, Cottin identifies him as 'avocat au Parlement, troisième secrétaire du prévôt des marchands' [lawyer in Paris's high court, third secretary to Le Pelletier]. See *Mes Inscripcions* (1889), p. 144, n. 2.

urge my father to help find a job for Moresquin, convinced that if he owed his position to my father and to my father's friend, my husband would be forced to treat me gently and fairly. My mother — a devious schemer by nature who had ulterior motives — sensed that by placing Moresquin in the office of my father's most influential friend, she could spoil their friendship. During this period, she had used her charms to alienate as many of my father's friends as possible; but the high office of this particular friend put him beyond her reach. She seized on the idea that I could give her a way to dishonor my father through his connection to Moresquin. But she was careful not to speak of helping Moresquin directly to Mr. Saxancour, who would have sensed the trap she was laying for him. She decided instead to contact a friend my father had in the provinces who was close friends with the high-placed official. She told him about the dire financial circumstances confronting her elder daughter, whose husband had just lost his job. Monsieur d'Oiseaumont[183] was touched by my plight. To surprise my father, following my mother's suggestion, he wrote to their mutual friend and secured a position for Moresquin before mentioning anything about it to Mr. Saxancour. It was only after everything was settled that he wrote to his friend:

'A meeting has been arranged for you with Mr. Olaüs-Magnus[184] on such and such a day. He's expecting you, and your son-in-law will be given a job. This worthy gentleman will be delighted to help you out, etc.'

Mr. Saxancour didn't suspect the trap that was being laid for him. Despite his usual caution, he was flattered by this unexpected mark of esteem. He came to show me Abbé d'Oiseaumont's letter. But his visit got off to an ominous start. For hardly had he finished reading the letter to me and scarcely had I time to express my joy and to begin telling him of my dreadful plight, before Moresquin came home. Knowing how vile a character he was, my father couldn't help feeling horrified to see him face to face and headed immediately for the door.

'I hope that you're not leaving because of me!' Moresquin stupidly asked.

'Excuse me!' my father replied, as he went out the door. 'Yes, it's precisely because of you that I'm leaving!' And not yet fully aware of Moresquin's true character, believing him to be simply an ordinary scoundrel, he came back to tell

---

[183] Henri Bachelin identifies Oiseaumont as historian and bibliographer Charles-Antoine Leclerc de Montlinot (1732–1801). Regarding the pseudonym used for him in the novel, Bachelin adds: 'On voit ici une des manières dont Restif forge ses pseudonymes: linot le fait penser à oiseau'. [We see here one of the ways Rétif devises pseudonyms: *linot* (finch) reminds him of *oiseau* (bird).] See *L'Œuvre de Restif de La Bretonne*, ed. by Henri Bachelin, 9 vols (Dijon & Paris: Éditions du Trianon, 1931), vol. 5, p. 496, note to p. 427. Testud confirms this identification and adds that Montlinot, 'doctor in medicine and theology, was also a writer; in 1784, he expressed the desire to meet Rétif and, since that date, the two men had stayed in touch' (*Journal*, vol. 2, p. 24, n. 7). Montlinot owed his position as head of the Church's alms house (Dépot de Mendicité) in Soissons to Le Pelletier.

[184] Le Pelletier de Morfontaine, prévôt des marchands. See note 182 above.

him: 'Monster! You're even worse than I anticipated!' As my father turned to leave, Moresquin rushed after him, brandishing his cane. If it hadn't been for a sentinel who arrived on horseback at that very moment to separate the two men, my father would undoubtedly have received one of those deadly blows that Moresquin knew how to deliver and that might well have killed him within a few months.[185]

Knowing how dangerous the situation was, I was trembling with fear and urged my father to leave quickly. I didn't dare restrain Moresquin, as women ordinarily do when their husbands start fighting. When my father was finally out of sight, I calmed down and faced Moresquin, who began to mistreat me. I'll admit that I was foolish enough to think that I would soon have more control over my situation thanks to the powerful protector my father was about to give me, a man who could restrain my husband's behavior. And so, undaunted by Moresquin's threats, I calmly told him:

'My father only came here to tell me that you are going to have a job. He read me a letter from his friend with the good news.'

Hearing these words, the coward stared at me with a surprised look on his face and said: 'But I didn't know that!' But then, after a moment's thought, he added that I must have made outlandish complaints to my father for him to treat me as he just had.

'I never said anything dishonorable about you. But to persuade my father to help find a job for you, I had to suggest to him that it would be better for me if you owed the job to him.'

This scene could have taken a turn for the worse if Moresquin, much the same as tigers and other ferocious beasts, had not been ravenous. If he acted more reasonably than usual on this occasion, it was simply because he wanted his dinner. He couldn't imagine that my father, who had just called him a monster, would be willing to help him. And only if he hadn't! But my father had no way of knowing that a vile secretary was going to ruin everything.

As soon as Moresquin was fairly certain that he would be hired, based on the information my mother sent him secretly, he took a trip to see his parents to tell them the news. Meanwhile, he resumed his habitual behavior, treating others with insolence and — what is both unbelievable and revolting — mistreating me as cruelly as before. But he took a different approach this time. He seemed to think that, by appearing jealous, people might overlook his abominable conduct.

---

[185] Rétif recalls this incident in his diary entry for 12 January 1785: '*Quaerla cum Augé.* [Quarrel with Augé.] He entered when I had come to read my daughter the Abbé de Montlinot's letter regarding Mr. Le Pelletier's offer to give the vile Augé a job. He said to me: "I hope that you're not leaving because of me!" and I replied: "Yes, it's precisely because of you that I'm leaving!" He was drunk; he ran after me. I called him a monster. He brandished his cane at me, calling me a scoundrel. A sentinel on horseback separated us' (*Journal*, ¶469, vol. 1, p. 168).

But he was at a loss whom to choose as a target for his jealousy until he thought of Fromentel and his quarrel with me about him at the Jardin du Roi. His accusations were of course completely unfounded, since I despised Fromentel almost as much as I did Moresquin! He was, after all, a clerk and shared their despicable morals.[186] How could people possibly imagine that, tormented and defamed by a husband who was a clerk that I would take another clerk as my lover! And how could I have, for heaven's sakes? A poor wretch — dressed in dingy clothes, her hands dirty from scraping mud off her husband's shoes, always looking like Cinderella or a charwoman — how could the thought of amorous adventures even cross her mind? In order to lead such an exuberant, dissolute life, one must have money and the freedom to enjoy good times and pleasure![187]

Before leaving to see his parents, Moresquin didn't speak to me of jealousy. He was gone for three days and came back very late on the third day. When he arrived home, he found me neatly dressed, looking refreshed from three days of calm and the promise of a job for him. He chided me for not going to meet him part way. I answered that it wasn't really necessary and that it made more sense for me to prepare dinner, to put his son to bed, and to get things ready for him. He grumbled a bit, but soon calmed down.

When we had finished dinner, the monster seemed eager to go to bed. He spoke to me in a friendly, gentle way. I would have been wary of him if it hadn't been for the job offer my father had secured for him and that I confirmed to Moresquin that evening. We talked together about it with a calmness that I had never felt with him except on our wedding day. When we went to bed, he caressed me in a decent and gentle way. I admit, to my shame, that my courage failed me. I forgot I was with a scoundrel; all I saw was my husband. I dared to hope that we were making a fresh start and that things would be different for us from then on. I imagined that the change in his behavior was due to his parents' advice. I

---

[186] In the notes to his edition of Rétif's diary, Cottin writes: 'Restif (probably because of Augé) detested clerks' and refers to the passage earlier in *Ingénue Saxancour* where Ingénue describes her first impressions of Fromentel: 'I felt I could trust this young man, who seemed decent and well-mannered to me. I didn't realize that, when it came to clerks, there wasn't a single honest man among them' (Cottin, *Mes Inscripcions*, p. 134, n. 2).

[187] One senses that the lady doth protest too much, given clear evidence in Blérie's letters to Agnès found among Rétif's papers that they were indeed romantically involved in the summer and fall of 1785. The originals of three of Blérie's letters to Agnès were found in the Archives de la Bastille at the Bibliothèque de l'Arsenal at the end of the manuscript of *Mes Inscripcions* (ms. 12.469); the others are in the Bibliothèque Nationale's collection (n.a.fr. 3300). See note 12 above for background on these letters and Rétif's reaction when he discovered them. Also see Appendix C, Excerpts 6–11, in MHRA's French edition of *Ingénue Saxancour* for extended excerpts from the letters and Appendix D, Excerpts 18 and 21, for Rétif's comments on them in his diary. Rétif's preoccupation with Agnès's relationship with Blérie is reflected in the fact that he published a short story based on their liaison titled 'L'Epouse aimant un autre homme' [The Wife in Love with Another Man]. See *Les Françaises* (Paris, 1786), vol. 3, pp. 17–83.

thought of my son, who bound me to Moresquin more strongly than any vow made at the altar. I was touched and even kissed him back, I think. Moresquin enjoyed his conjugal rights without profanation. I rejoiced inwardly and was filled with hope.

But the monster would soon reappear. He indulged in the pleasures of the flesh to the point of exhaustion. It was only then that he spoke to me of his jealousy, but using the most odious expressions that I'm going to tone down:

'You were treated to some nice feasts these past few days!'

'No, I ate at home.'

'What I mean is that you've been enjoying the kind of treat I just gave you, which seems to have left you cold!' These words were followed by a flood of revolting obscenities. He spoke of Fromentel and wanted me to confess the number of ….

'Is it possible,' I cried, 'that just when I thought you had become kind-hearted, after you had just covered me with caresses, that you could then speak to me in the harshest, cruelest manner?'

'You enticed me,' he replied, 'to hide what you've been up to! You're pregnant, and you want the stupid cuckold to cover for you.'

'You were free to abstain.'

'Ah, bitch! You didn't dress up all nicely for no reason! You know my weakness. But go ahead. He'll pay for it, or ….'

'I can't believe you'd think that of me! Have I ever given you a reason to have such suspicions?'

'Yes, you have! And I'm sorry not to have unmasked you! I should have abstained and instead forced you to do your duty.'

I won't explain here what Moresquin meant when he spoke of *my duty*.[188] Suffice it to say that he was referring to an unspeakably horrid act I was forced to perform out of fear of being brutally pinched, having my arms twisted, or even being jabbed in a hundred places with the tip of his sword. It made me nauseous, but I had no choice but to obey. Good God, such horrors women face married to certain scoundrels! How heartbreaking it is to raise daughters according to the strictest morals only to see them sacrificed to men like Moresquin who subject them to a stream of obscenities and filth!

My deep sadness returned after this cruel scene. Three days later, the same day where he was introduced to his new boss to discuss his new duties, he returned home in high spirits, that is to say drunk. At dinner, he used the crudest terms to promise me more of his detestable caresses. I didn't respond, convinced that, once in bed, the monster would fall asleep. That's in fact what happened. But he

---

[188] Baruch claims that Ingénue is referring here to fellatio. See Baruch, *Restif de La Bretonne* (2002), vol. 2, p. 572, n. 1. However, knowing Moresquin's sexual predilections, she might also be referring to anal sex.

woke up shortly before dawn when I was still sound asleep. A sharp pain interrupted my sleep. It was Moresquin who was pinching me. I blurted out before I was fully awake:

'Spare me, I beg of you! Don't mistreat me!'

'No, no,' he replied. 'I won't even make you do your duty. Since I have a job thanks to you, it's only right that you be treated as my lawful wife.'

I foolishly answered that I hadn't done anything wrong and had nothing to hide. At these words, Moresquin flew into a rage. Sensing the danger I had just exposed myself to, I wanted to flee, but it was impossible to escape. He placed me the way he wanted and, at the slightest movement, hit me hard. After subjecting me to the lewdest and crudest caprices, he soiled me in the most sinful way when I tried to resist.

'I'm going to put you to the test and find out if you're deceiving me. This is what I'll do every day; and if you become pregnant, I'll know you're a slut.'[189] I dared to remind him that he had not abstained the night he came home from visiting his parents. He denied it and flew into such a fury that I tried again to escape and succeeded this time.

Worn out from his vile exertions, Moresquin didn't try to stop me and instead simply hurled the chamber pot at me. I escaped to a neighbor's apartment, naked, with blood and urine streaming down my legs. He locked the door, expecting me to stay like that in the hallway where I'd either freeze to death or else be totally disgraced if people found me like that. An hour or two later, he went looking for me and found me at the neighbor's partially dressed in some old clothes she had given me. He ranted and raved against me in front of our neighbor, using the vilest expressions:

'You're absolutely good for nothing, not even for what whores do! What use are you to me? You don't work; you don't want to pleasure me because you're sated with what your gigolo gives you, you slut! And you don't give a damn about anything else!'

The neighbor was a narrow-minded woman and, believing what my husband had said, at least in part, she advised me to do my duty. Moresquin forced me to return home, shouting his usual vile insults at me as we went down the stairs.[190] With a violent kick, he pushed me into our apartment and then, since the neighbors were watching, he left abruptly.

---

[189] In other words, Moresquin plans to engage in anal intercourse, to abstain from vaginal intercourse, and force his wife to perform oral sex. That way, if she becomes pregnant, he can claim that the child is not his, but Fromentel's.

[190] In *La Femme infidelle*, in a note to a passage recounting the same events in similar terms, Rétif exclaims: 'What fate can a respectable woman expect when she is married to a murderer, to a man exiled in his youth for his violent behavior?' (*OC*, vol. 45, p. 820).

This all happened three days after Moresquin began the new position my father had secured for him. Once he was settled in his job, I no longer felt the need to hide anything. I gave my father a partial account of the horrors I had suffered. But there are many details I never had the strength to reveal to him and that can only be found here. Due to this reticence and because of my son, my father urged me to be patient. But also he promised me the protection of the influential man who had hired Moresquin and, to reassure me, he told me about his conversation with this man and how well he had been received.

When my father felt obliged by Monsieur d'Oiseaumont's letter to meet with Monsieur Le Pelletier, he went to see him and was received in the kindest, most flattering manner: 'I was delighted to hear that I could be of service to you!' said the director. One certainly could not speak with greater generosity and nobility of spirit or say anything that could inspire greater confidence.

Mr. Saxancour was deeply touched and seized the hand of this honorable man. 'I must admit to you,' he said, 'that I'm bringing you a scoundrel. He's a bad son, a bad husband.'

'He doesn't make his wife happy?'

'Ah, good heavens!'

'But is he honest?'

Unaware of any evidence to the contrary, my father replied: 'As far as probity is concerned, I believe him to be beyond reproach. But I beg of you, sir, to use your authority to restrain him.'[191]

'I promise you to do so and will speak to him accordingly.'

After calling Moresquin to his office, Monsieur Le Pelletier told him quite bluntly that as he was hiring him only as a favor to my father and to me, he expected him to make me happy and to show my father all the respect he deserved.

Moresquin replied: 'Your Eminence, I'll do all I can within my power.'

So that's how Moresquin began his new job and how my father sought to reassure me by promising strong protection for me. He went so far as to congratulate himself for placing Moresquin there, because he saw this good turn as a way to restrain him. On several occasions, he said to me: 'He now has a master

---

[191] Rétif notes in his journal that his conversation with Le Pelletier took place on 15 January 1785 and describes it in terms very similar to those in the novel: 'I went to see the prévôt des marchands on behalf of my daughter Agnès. He met with me privately and asked: "Is it true that I can be of help to you in some way? I'd be delighted to help in any way I can." I spoke to him about Augé and described him as a nasty fellow who was causing my daughter endless misery and that we needed to restrain by helping him. Mr. Le Pelletier promised to help. (We'll see what came of this promise!) Two weeks later, Augé began working for Mr. Legrand, Mr. Le Pelletier's head secretary' (*Journal*, ¶471, vol. 1, p. 169). Rétif also notes in his journal that he dined at the home of Mr. Pelletier a week later on January 22, which shows that he was on friendly terms with him (*Journal*, ¶475, vol. 1, p. 169).

to obey.' For the first time, a tranquil life suddenly seemed possible to me after years of despair. But how short-lived this illusory calm turned out to be!'

Scarcely had he begun his new job that Moresquin, conniving as ever, sought out Fromentel's company more than ever. For despite being the most dull-witted of men, he could be quite shrewd when it came to planning a villainous deed. Accustomed (as I later learned) to taking as his mistresses married women whose husbands pampered him and treated him to fine meals, Fromentel facilitated this scheme, unaware of Moresquin's ulterior motives. He often came to see us and joined us for outings. And since Fromentel was tight-fisted with his money, he often took us to the home of relatives in the countryside outside of Paris when it was his turn to entertain us. We were always warmly welcomed because of him, and the outings we did there made up for the meals we offered him in town. Perceptive people I've talked with since about this friendship so keenly desired with Fromentel suspected Moresquin's ulterior motives: that this vile monster wanted people to believe that his young colleague was my lover in order to use my alleged misconduct to justify his jealousy and the further mistreatment he planned to inflict on me. For Moresquin needed to be cruel. Indeed, viciousness was the very essence of his being, and he felt no pleasure until he saw a victim suffer from his barbarism.

One evening, as we were on our way to spend a three-day holiday[192] with Fromentel's relatives in the country, Moresquin kept commenting on the young man's good looks: 'My wife is even more aware than I am of how handsome you are,' he declared. 'She loves you, as you well know, and her fondest wish is that I'll die so she can marry you.' What possible response could one give to such comments! We remained silent. I knew there was no safe answer I could give. Moresquin pretended to feel sorry for himself and said, with tears in his eyes: 'Not to be loved by a woman I adore!'

---

[192] In *La Femme infidelle*, Rétif indicates that the excursion took place 'aux fêtes de Pentecôte' [Pentecost], a religious holiday that takes place seven weeks after Easter (in late May to late June depending on the date of Easter in a given year). See *La Femme infidelle*, OC, vol. 45, p. 830 and Appendix F, Excerpt 4, in MHRA's French edition of *Ingénue Saxancour*.

'Stop whining!' Fromentel replied. 'Do you think your tears make any impression on me? In any case, if Madam likes me, it's only because she has good taste; for you are damned ugly.'

Vexed by this response that he wasn't expecting, Moresquin thought about it for a moment and then replied: 'You're not the most dangerous one around!' Then, realizing he could spoil my reconciliation with my father and poison the rest of my life, he added: 'There's someone else I'm more jealous of than of you ....' I'll stop here. Simply to humiliate Fromentel, without believing a single word he was saying, Moresquin indulged in the pleasure he found so gratifying of making monstrously slanderous accusations.[193] When I ventured to ask him how he could even imagine the horrible things he was uttering, he insisted that he had heard it all from my aunt. Yet since then, in Madame Bitez's presence, he denied this and called me a liar. My aunt will sign these memoirs to guarantee their truthfulness.[194] I wanted to say something else, but a punch to my side, with a hard poke between two ribs, forced me to keep quiet.

Not believing the blow to be very severe, even though he saw me blanch, Fromentel smiled and said: 'You have a way of imposing your point of view! But I wouldn't advise you to use that method with just anyone!' Noticing that I was quite shaken by the blow, Fromentel offered me his arm, which I refused. A stern look from Moresquin forced me to take it. It was in this state, in pain and frightened to death, that I arrived at the home of the young man's brother.

The rest of the evening continued as it had begun. At supper, Moresquin — who is hardly sober and who has the insolent habit of treating his hosts like innkeepers — called for wine and brandy and soon became intoxicated. When we got up from the table, he refused to go to bed and, despite our hosts' pleas, insisted on sitting in front of the fireplace, drinking even more and spewing out

---

[193] This is a veiled allusion to Augé's accusation that Rétif had an incestuous relationship with Agnès — an allegation Augé later made public in a pamphlet he circulated among his father-in-law's friends and acquaintances, as well as in frequent verbal attacks against him. These claims, which Rétif indignantly denied, are nevertheless borne out by numerous entries in his diaries over an eight-year period, starting with expressions of incestuous desires toward Agnès in January 1785, followed by clear indications of sexual relations with her beginning in late April 1788, until she left her father's home in February 1794 to live with Louis Vignon following her divorce from Augé. As Testud remarks, 'the *Journal* leaves no doubt as to whether Rétif had incestuous relations with his two daughters [...]. The frequency of these entries varies over time, but over a period of eight years, they average one per month'. Regarding Augé's accusations, Testud adds: 'With this in mind, the reasons behind the fierce hatred that Rétif and his son-in-law felt for each other become much clearer: Augé, who accused his father-in-law of incest, knew the truth, and so Rétif did everything he could to discredit him' (Testud, 'Le *Journal* inédit de Restif', p. 1578). See the introduction for further discussion of Rétif's troubled relationship with his daughter.

[194] Here again, Ingénue names her aunt as a witness in support of her accusations against her husband.

horrible accusations against my father, who had just found a job for him! At two o'clock in the morning, our hosts, whose patience had run out, removed the wine, put out the fire, and went to bed. Moresquin fell asleep in his chair. At five o'clock, he woke up freezing cold, crawled into bed with me, and woke me up. He forced me to let him put his cold feet between my thighs and his two hands under my armpits. His body was so cold that I was soon shivering and coming down with a cold. It was one of the cruelest tortures I've suffered and shows most clearly Moresquin's tyranny, his brutal cruelty, and my servitude.[195]

Moresquin knew that Fromentel's room was next to ours and that he could hear us. Once he had warmed up, he wanted to satisfy his lust, and he used the most obscene expressions to make clear what he wanted. I didn't think it wise to resist, hoping that my docility would stop him from indulging in excessive debauchery or brutality, but I was mistaken. Moresquin outdid himself. Aroused by the thought that Fromentel could hear everything, he indulged in his brutal passion with unimaginable ardor, licentiousness, and frenzy. When I tried to moderate his behavior, he twisted my arms or pinched my thighs; and if I cried out, it was only an excuse to hurl horrible insults at me. Never was there a crueler night than this. For the wretched women who gave Moresquin sexual gratification never shared his pleasure. He raped his wives and mistresses, and it wasn't until his victims were crying in anguish that he reached his loathsome climax.

His furor lasted until seven in the morning, after which he fell asleep. I was tempted to get up, but as it was very cold in the room and still dark outside, I dozed off as well from sheer exhaustion. I woke up an hour or so later, chilled to the bone, without any covers. When I reached for the sheet and blankets, I realized that Moresquin was rolled up in them, snoring on the floor. Numb with cold, I dressed quickly and hurried to sit by the fire. I asked the two men of the house, Fromentel and his brother, to go wake up Moresquin.

'Certainly not! What a swine!' replied Fromentel's brother. 'I heard all the racket he was making this morning. That man's a sick degenerate, completely out of his mind! My wife couldn't stand listening to him and came downstairs to warm herself by the fire.' Fromentel said he was tempted to give him a good whipping since he suspected that Moresquin was acting that way because of him, but refrained out of respect for our hosts.

---

[195] Given all the other more violent and sordid forms of abuse Ingénue endured, some readers may find her claims here unpersuasive, even peculiar. Yet one could argue that this experience was more distressing to her than earlier incidents because it made her realize how completely she had become a thing in Moresquin's eyes, how every inch of her body was his to use and abuse at will. Her distress was compounded by the fact that she had just been wrenched from a few hours' sleep after an evening where her husband had humiliated her by his boorish, drunken behavior in front of their hosts. And it anticipates the equally humiliating scene that follows.

Since no one wanted to rouse Moresquin, we let him sleep until he finally woke up at two in the afternoon. Hearing him swearing and shouting, we went up to see him. Insisting that I should have stayed with him, he complained bitterly about being left on the floor and shouted cruel threats at me. Our hosts assured him that he had fallen out of bed after I left the room and that it would have been rude for me not to join the others downstairs. Reminding him that he was a guest in their home, they told him that he should learn to mind his manners and not disturb his hosts' tranquility and peace of mind. Then the mistress of the house scolded him so sharply for everything he had done and said since he arrived, that despite his usual shamelessness, Moresquin looked foolish and didn't say a word. He even tried to laugh about it, but Madame Fromentel wouldn't let him. She spoke to him sternly and forced him to apologize. He behaved himself until dinner, when he got drunk again, which led our hosts to ask us to leave and return to Paris. My heart began pounding with fear, dread, and horror at the thought of being alone with him again. For Moresquin's odious presence always filled me with every dark thought imaginable! But before we left, Madame Fromentel took me aside and spoke to me in private:

'You're far too indulgent! Bare your teeth to that cowardly brute, resist him, and you'll see the results! Trust me, show him your teeth!' There wasn't time for her to say anything more.

We arrived in Paris fairly early. On the way home, Fromentel reproached Moresquin in the harshest terms for his outrageous behavior, which had caused him such embarrassment. The two men nearly started to fight several times. Following the advice that Fromentel's sister-in-law had given me, I made no attempt to separate them, which infuriated Moresquin and left him spluttering with anger. I answered him firmly that if Fromentel gave him a good thrashing, he would only get what he deserved. At these words, he raised his arm, ready to strike me.

'If you dare strike me, you monster, I'll kill you, unless you kill me first!' I cried.

Instead of hitting me, the scoundrel began to laugh and said: 'Ah, I see the results of Madame Fromentel's advice! I recognize her tone, because she said much the same to me. Now look here, dearie,' he warned, 'don't ever talk to me like that again!'

I didn't answer. He tried to come closer to me, but I had my eye on him and pulled out my knife. He lunged at me to try to give me one of his vicious blows to the nape of the neck dealt with the side of his hand. I had just learned that it was a blow of this kind that had ruptured a vertebrae in his first wife's neck, leading to her death. I dodged the blow and, making a move as if to stab him, I cried:

'Monster! Today is your last day!' Moresquin was so frightened that he hid behind Fromentel, to whom I said: 'The wretch was about to strike me on the neck in the same way he killed his first wife!' This remark enraged Moresquin, who shouted insults at me, but dared not come closer.

Encouraged by his reaction, I really laid into him and told him what I thought of him. I reproached him for his scandalous, cruel, and despicable behavior. I was like a madwoman, a fury. 'Monster! My mind is made up! This night will be your last! I'm resolved kill you or to die, but die avenged! I married against my father's wishes. I have no one to blame but myself, and my only wish is to punish you — you scoundrel, who duped me so cruelly, hoodwinked my aunt, and took advantage of an unnatural mother's hatred. I swear to God I'll kill you! Or if you kill me, so much the better! You'll die on the scaffold on Place de la Grève.[196] But when you strike the first blow, either you'll kill me or I'll kill you. I won't stop until one of us is dead. You're the most contemptible and cowardly scoundrel in the world, slandering everyone — my father, your father, even your own mother who spoiled you! Vile, despicable man, your behavior this morning was the last straw! Your time is up!'

I fell silent, choking with anger and unable to say anything more. Fromentel was dumbfounded. He told a few lame jokes about women and then turned to Moresquin and said: 'You're just getting what was coming to you. And you'd better watch out! An angry woman is worse than a lioness. You're at the end of your rope! If you don't leave her alone, anything could happen!' Moresquin remained silent. As for me, I was trembling all over, but deep down inside, I was feeling only the courage I had just shown through my words.

As I hesitated, uncertain what course to follow, Moresquin approached me and said: 'If it's peace you want, that's what you'll have. All I ask is for your father to give me six hundred *livres* a year in addition to the job he obtained for me, and I'll be satisfied. From the beginning, the only reason I've mistreated you was to force you to convince your father to see me, to speak to me, to welcome me into his home. He has always heaped scorn on me, and I took it out on his beloved daughter. It's true that, in order to humiliate him, I would have liked to see you become a prostitute and for him to meet you out on the street. Nothing would have pleased me more. But I feel so little hatred for you yourself that I would have taken you back afterwards, and I would have shown your father that I'm capable of forgiveness.'

'Able to forgive a degradation you tried to inflict on me, you wretch!'

'That's true ....'

Hearing these words, Fromentel warned him: 'Be careful that others don't hear you. You'd be in big trouble!'

'Oh, what I'm saying is only meant to calm her down.'

I was surprised by Moresquin's restraint and conciliatory tone. I was deeply grateful to Madame Fromentel for her sound advice and for the persuasive way she had expressed it; for she was not the first to have given me this advice, but

---

[196] *La Grève*: Square adjacent to the Hôtel de Ville (the Paris city hall) where public executions took place. See notes 115 and 167 above.

she was the only one who had spoken to me forcefully enough to persuade me to take it seriously.

When we arrived home, I continued in the same manner, which I knew in my heart was the wisest course. How happy — or at least worthy of praise — I would have been, if my courage had not failed me. My father was ready to defend me; I made Moresquin aware of that fact and was gratified to see that he feared my defender. However, on one occasion, letting my guard down, I showed weakness and fear. There was a terrible scene; blows rained down on me like hail. I resorted to brandishing my knife. A good-for-nothing named Vaulda happened to witness this scene. Seeing my furor, Moresquin left me alone. I congratulated myself, believing I had found an infallible solution. But soon, other difficulties made it impossible for me to stay with Moresquin.

Even if the job my father had found for Moresquin had paid considerably more, it would not have sufficed, due to his spendthrift habits. He hounded me to persuade my father to give me an allowance. I was extremely reluctant to do this, after having foolhardily declared when I married that I wouldn't ask for help if we were ever in need. As I'm very proud and high-minded by nature, I suffered terribly from my situation. Had my honor not been at stake, had my troubles been ordinary and private, I would have borne them rather than reveal them. So I kept putting off speaking to my father. To force me to do it, Moresquin pretended to lack money for basic necessities. It's true that he often didn't need to pretend and that his poverty was only too real. After trying to speak to me in a more or less reasonable manner, Moresquin resorted to threats. I stood up to him and, as soon as he went out, I left for my father's with my son.[197] My mother

---

[197] Ingénue flees from her husband seven times in the novel: first to her aunt's home in mid-December 1782 and January 1783 and then to her parents' home in late January 1785, in late February of that year, and twice more before leaving him definitively in July 1785. Several of these dates match Rétif's accounts as in *Monsieur Nicolas* ('Neuvième Epoque', *OC*, vol. 69, pp. 3100–01) and in his diary (¶479, vol. 1, p. 172; ¶491, vol. 1, p. 177; and ¶521, vol. 1, p. 189). A key difference is that, according to these accounts, when Agnès fled the third time in late January (after the events reported here in the novel), she went to Blérie's apartment, not to her parents' home (as Rétif claims in the novel). This is made clear in *Monsieur Nicolas* (op. cit.) as well as in Rétif's diary entry for 31 January 1785: 'Agnès a fui, elle est chez Blérie, d'où je la tire le même soir' (¶479, vol. 1, p. 172).

shuddered at the thought that she and my father would have to provide for me. She arranged things in a way that led my father to insist that I return to Moresquin. He took me there himself and even stooped so low as to speak in a cordial manner to that wretch, thereby worsening my situation.

Moresquin thought my father was taking his side against me, and my mother assured him of this. Believing I no longer had any support from my family, he started to persecute me again, but in a different way. To try to persuade me to become a prostitute, he pretended to make only reasonable demands, spouting falsehoods and platitudes instead of his usual vile threats. He told me such stupid, revolting lies that I was outraged. Although I refused to go along with his schemes, he no longer dared to hit me or twist my arms. I no longer cleaned the mud off his boots and had this done by someone else, even in Moresquin's presence. This led him to hit me in some underhanded way, but that I returned blow for blow. What a life! How was I able to bear it! Moresquin made it even worse by coming home at midnight or at one or even two o'clock in the morning. Waiting up for him, I burned costly firewood; for Monsieur insisted on having a fire when he came home, even though money was short.

It was at night, after locking our doors, that Moresquin felt free to knock me around. But I forced him to stop with my cries and my calls for help to the watchman in the street below. He often threatened to smother me in bed. I dared him to do it, saying: 'Go ahead! That's all I ask.' That's one thing he wouldn't do, but he nearly caused me to freeze to death by maliciously pulling the covers off me at night. At the slightest murmur from his son, Moresquin pushed me out of bed to tend to the child, even though he needed nothing. On these occasions, he didn't let me to put on a robe or even slippers. I finally rebelled against this tyranny and, to punish the child for his capriciousness, I whipped him. Furious, Moresquin rushed at me in the darkness with his dagger. I threw open the windows and called to the night watchman for help in order to force Moresquin to calm down. But, as I said before, what a life! How could I continue to live this way with a scoundrel capable of anything? Whenever I pushed myself to the limit to fight back, I felt deathly ill from the distress it caused me.

Thus began a new chapter in the story of my marriage. Placed in his new job thanks to my father, Moresquin gloried in his new position, the importance of which he exaggerated when speaking to people unfamiliar with his office. He vaunted Mr. Saxancour's talents and influence, contradicting everything he had said about him earlier. People often pointed out this contradiction to him in my presence, to which he responded with stupid comments that only he could have come up with. For he troubled himself as little with decency as he did with truth or plausibility in speaking to old cronies like Vulda, Champdépines, and other worthy companions for a rogue like him.

From February to July that year,[198] I languished this way, with visits from my father, who consoled me and encouraged me to bear my situation as best I could, given that this was the path I had chosen. Moresquin continued to pretend to be jealous of Fromentel, but in a low-key sort of way, since he persisted in socializing with him. He even invited him out drinking one night when I happened to be along. The evening ended at a café, where Moresquin, capricious and moody by nature, unleashed a torrent of slander against my father and me.[199] When we pointed out that he was contradicting himself, he admitted that he was only speaking out of anger because Mr. Saxancour refused to welcome him into his home and circle of friends. Moresquin showed how truly deranged he was by speaking that night against his boss and benefactor, whose behavior he criticized in the most reprehensible manner, as well as against his immediate supervisor, the head secretary, whose secret affairs he revealed to us. This all was very painful to me, as he was speaking in a public place in front of several people who were listening to him who might know the secretary. I pointed this out to him several times, which led that wretch to shout all sorts of vile insults at me at the top of his lungs as we were leaving. I must admit that I was outraged and tempted several times to fight back. But spineless Fromentel warned me that he would take my husband's side if I did. When we got home, Moresquin tried to bully me, and I resisted at first. But I wound up getting a good thrashing anyway, laid out on the floor, unable to move.

---

[198] Entries in Rétif's journal confirm that the events described in this passage took place during the first half of 1785.

[199] Another allusion to Augé's accusations of incest against his wife and father-in-law. See notes 62 and 193 above. In *La Femme infidelle*, Ingénue's husband first makes these accusations during their visit with Blérie's brother and sister-in-law at their country house: 'That evening, after dinner, L'Echiné — who had drunk to excess — launched into a tirade in which he said the most dreadful things: he insisted that . . . ; and went on to make other remarks that were so revolting that our hosts asked him never to visit them again. I won't say anything more about this, except that these remarks alone made him odious to me forever; I would rather die than to have to endure his loathsome presence ever again' (*OC*, vol. 45, p. 832).

The following day, I went to my father's home, covered in bruises. He was very ill,[200] and my mother scolded me harshly, pointing out that, given his condition, I could cause his death. This convinced me to return to Moresquin.[201] I brought with me a letter my father had written in his sickbed that kept things quiet for a few days. But soon the mistreatment began again. Against all expectations, my father recovered, but his convalescence was slow and took until July. During that spring and early summer, I hid my troubles from him. For Moresquin gradually became as brutal as before, seeing that nothing happened if he mistreated or insulted me. As for me, my resistance had drained me, especially when I saw that my behavior was disapproved by people who didn't understand why I was acting that way. And so I cried and suffered silently, on the lookout nevertheless for a chance to leave the monster. Fortunately, the opportunity to escape eventually presented itself.

I'll explain how this separation finally came about, after recounting a few of the incidents that led up to it.

Despite what had happened at the home of Fromentel's brother, the young man continued to visit us, which led Moresquin to spout obscenities expressing his feigned jealousy. So a few days after our visit, I decided to write to ask him to end his visits to us and to break off all relations with Moresquin. Because I was so outraged against Moresquin, and since the man I was writing to and trying to get rid of was hardly any better, my letter was strongly worded. That evening, Moresquin came home earlier than usual as I was writing the letter. As soon as he appeared, I tried to hide it. He grabbed ahold of me to try to see what I was writing. At first, I refused to show it to him, but let him have it after he gnashed his teeth and punched me in the chest. After reading things that were as unflattering to him as to his friends, Moresquin pocketed the letter and, with a scornful laugh as ugly as he was and more ominous than his anger, he promised

---

[200] In his journal entry for 2 February 1785, Rétif notes that he was diagnosed with gonorrhea that day (¶481, vol. 1, p. 173). Subsequent entries that month indicate a worsening of urinary complications, pain, and fever due to his illness.

[201] In his journal entry for 10 March 1785, Rétif writes: 'Agnès leaves her husband; I send her back' (¶491, vol. 1, p. 177).

FIGURE 22.   'Moresquin came home earlier than usual as I was writing the letter. As soon as he appeared, I tried to hide it. He grabbed ahold of me to try to see what I was writing. At first, I refused to show it to him, but let him have it after he gnashed his teeth and punched me in the chest.' Illustration by Louis Binet, *Les Françaises* (Paris: Guillot, 1786), Estampe 25. (BnF)

to show everyone what I had written. Then, after binding my hands, he took sadistic pleasure in beating and slapping me and kicking me in the back. It was impossible for me to escape. But this turned out to be a good thing. Since he had not untied my hands, I couldn't get undressed and remained lying on the ground next to the cold fireplace. I tried for several hours to free my hands and finally succeeded, although my wrists were raw with rope burns as a result. As soon as my hands were freed, I ran to Moresquin as he was sleeping, took out the letter, and burned it. The cruel brute woke up in the middle of the night and, not finding me in bed, called out to me. I answered and, after slipping the rope back around my wrists, went to him. After a few more slaps, he untied me and told me to get into bed. I obeyed.

That night, I was spared having shameful acts inflicted on my body. But I was nevertheless forced to witness those that Moresquin performed on himself. He insisted that he had no need of a woman and that I was unworthy of receiving his embrace. Then he talked about the letter and tried to twist my arm when I answered in a firm and resolute manner. I jumped out of bed and climbed up into the attic, where I locked myself in.[202] There I was forced to listen to all the horrendous things that a depraved human being can express. But it was even worse the following morning when Moresquin couldn't find the letter when he went looking for it. He flew into a violent rage, the likes of which I had never seen before. He seized his sword and thrust it at me between the attic floorboards. But since it was daylight, the neighbors came running when they heard my cries, and the monster was forced to leave without killing me as he had intended. After he left, I fled to my parents' house, taking my son with me. But what had I done wrong? Nothing, except to have burned a letter that had offended him by its blunt truthfulness and that he wanted to read out loud in public places where everyone would have acknowledged the truth of what I was saying! Had he done this, people later assured me that Moresquin would have been the object of public scorn. He no doubt would have made a scene and been publicly chastised, as often happened in the cafés he frequented.

I arrived at my parents' home, wounded and distressed. My father was very angry. However, I only stayed there for two and a half days, because Moresquin promised to behave better in the future in order to keep his job. But it's hard to believe how short a time he actually managed to restrain himself.

---

[202] The French hear reads: 'Je sautai du lit et montai sur la soupente, où je m'enfermai'. In a note to the passage in *La Femme infidelle* describing this incident, Baruch maintains that a soupente in this context refers to 'un refuge sur le toit, auquel on accède par la fenêtre ou une lucarne et sans doute protégé par une rambarde' [a refuge on a rooftop to which one gains access through a window or skylight and which is no doubt protected by a guardrail] (*Restif de La Bretonne*, 2002, vol. 2, p. 407, n. 2). However, in the version given here, Moresquin thrusts his sword between the floorboards, suggesting that Ingénue took refuge in the attic to their apartment, not on the roof.

On Sunday, eight days later, we woke up late. This was quite normal for us, since we almost never went to sleep until two or three in the morning. Moreover, that particular night, Moresquin had outdone himself in his obscene mistreatment of me. Seeing how late it was when he awoke, he cried:

'What! My pot roast isn't cooking yet?'

He acted as if this were a terrible misfortune and went on and on about it. I got up to get dressed, but wasn't moving quickly enough for him, so he tried to hasten me by poking me with a stick. He in fact poked me so hard next to my eye that it caused blood to spurt out from my temple. I was soon ready and left quickly for the butcher's shop. But realizing that he would have to go to his office, I decided to go to mass so he would be gone by the time I returned home. But no such luck! He was waiting for me at home and doubly angry because I hadn't yet started cooking his lunch. He lifted a chair up in the air, ready to bring it crashing down on my head. The door was open, and I fled to my parents.

My father, still in poor health, was extremely annoyed to see me and forced me to go home before Moresquin returned from work. My mother told my sister to accompany me. For she was aware that my husband had little respect for her and often called her a double-dealing bitch for having tricked my father into agreeing to my marriage. Indeed, Moresquin was like the devils who blame the damned in hell for the crimes they persuaded them to commit. So not daring to accompany me herself, my mother sent my sister with me. And it was in front of this young lady — whose innocence and chastity he should have respected and whom he had no right to shock (a right he claimed to have with me) — that he launched into a tirade of obscene details about my supposed pleasures with Fromentel. He went so far as to claim that these details came from Fromentel himself. I was livid with rage and indignation. I was so furious that the monster was intimidated. I castigated both him and Fromentel so strongly that the abominable wretch, fearing a quarrel with his friend, acknowledged that Fromentel hadn't said anything about me and that it was he himself who had imagined everything. However, I wasn't satisfied and threatened to go looking for Fromentel and confront him. Moresquin began to gnash his teeth, a sure sign that he was about to beat me up as usual to try to stop me.

'I'm not afraid of you, you monster!' I cried. 'A person who doesn't fear death fears nothing. Come on, you brute! But take care to strike your blow carefully, because if you don't, I'll be sure to get you. I'm not full of bravado and bluster like you; I mean what I say!' And turning to my sister, I said: 'Return home; you don't belong here. I'm going to pit all the strength I can muster against this monster. And I'll do more: I'll use against him all the diabolical moves he's showed me so many times. Go on home! Before long, you'll see him hanging from the scaffold Place de la Grève.'[203]

---

[203] *Place de la Grève*: See notes 115, 167, and 196.

I said what I thought and felt; I was in despair after the frosty reception my father had given me when I arrived at my parents' home earlier that day. My sister refused to leave and found a way to get word to my mother for her to come. Madame Saxancour rushed over. However, by the time she arrived, the situation appeared calm. Moresquin had understood me; he sensed that my despair could very well push me to carry out what I had threatened to do. While my sister was out of earshot by the window, he had even asked me what I planned to do.

'Since no one can hear us, I don't mind telling you: I plan to kill myself so you'll be charged with the crime and be condemned to die a shameful death, just as you deserve. You need to understand, you scoundrel, that you can't inflict horrible abuse on a woman every day, reducing her to despair as you've done to me, and expect to get away with it! I swear that the fate I'm planning for you will be such that all the past crimes you've boasted about so often will receive the punishment they deserve. Go on, I have nothing more to say to you. Now it's your turn to be afraid.' When Moresquin tried to take my hand, I took him by the throat and threatened to strangle him. My mother arrived just as he was calling to my sister for help.[204]

Moresquin greeted her with a sardonic smile and invited us to a vaudeville show. My mother insisted that I join them. During the show, Moresquin took every opportunity to express the deep scorn he felt for my mother. In choosing seats and serving refreshments, he showed a mark preference for me over her. He made her give up her seat to me, after rudely saying: 'Can't she see that she's blocking my wife's view!' My mother smiled and changed seats with me. Later, speaking about my mother to someone in the box next to ours, he exclaimed: 'That w....'[205] Thinking he was referring to me, the other person asked him to explain. 'My wife is a respectable woman,' he exclaimed. 'I'm talking about her bitch of a mother.' I don't know if my mother heard him; she doesn't seem to have. In any case, those were two remarks he made, among many others, that afternoon.

That was just one incident among many that took place during my final days with Moresquin. If I told everything that happened, I would have to repeat over and over the same horrors I've candidly described so many times already.

Shall I recount another incident that, while it doesn't concern me at all, will nonetheless serve to better reveal Moresquin's evil character in all its horror? No,

---

[204] In *La Femme infidelle*, as in *Ingénue Saxancour*, Ingénue flees twice from her husband in March, 1785. However, the account of the second incident ends quite differently in the earlier novel, with no threat of murder, nor any mention of a trip to the theater with Ingénue's mother. In *La Femme infidelle*, Ingénue's father sends her home, accompanied by her sister and mother, with a stern letter to her husband that calms his behavior toward her for a while. See Appendix F, Excerpt 3, in MHRA's French edition of *Ingénue Saxancour*.

[205] The French here reads: 'Cette p...-là' which no doubt means 'Cette putain-là' [That whore].

I'll refrain from going into all the details and simply summarize. One night when Moresquin came back around midnight, he found a runaway child hiding in his courtyard and decided to take him home to his parents. The boy tried to trick him by telling him that his parents lived in faubourg Saint-Honoré. But when Moresquin learned from a friend of his family that they in fact lived on rue de la Verrerie, he thrashed the child with his cane and dragged him home to his parents, badly beaten. He claimed that he had caught him stealing, which was completely false. The following day, he had the effrontery to return to the parents' home for news of the child, who was near death. Outraged, the parents showed him the door, saying: 'Even if he were stealing from you, you had no right to kill him.' The truth later came out, and the parents considered pressing charges, given the sorry state their child was in. But, in the end, they decided not to, because Moresquin had in fact found the boy in our courtyard late at night.

I come now to the fateful day I finally left: July 22.[206] Moresquin, who was the primary lease-holder of our apartment building — and not the owner, as he had convinced my aunt before we married — had spent half the rent money he had received from the other tenants. He was missing 100 of the 200 *livres* he owed. Every day for a week, he had been telling me: 'Remember, stupid bitch, that I need money and that I'll beat you to a pulp if you don't find it for me.' I knew he was counting on my father to come up with the money. But stupid as he was, he didn't understand that a hard-working, orderly man like Mr. Saxancour would never give up the fruits of his labor to a scoundrel and miserable spendthrift who had the effrontery to joke about his benefactor's troubles, while greedily wasting what he had extorted from that man's kindness, hard work, and thrift. So my father made clear to me that he would give nothing to Moresquin. I was in despair since, on the other hand, Mr. Saxancour didn't want me to leave my husband, my son, my home.

When I asked Moresquin how he expected me to find that much money for him, he replied, raising his hand to strike me: 'It doesn't matter how you find it,

---

[206] July 22, 1785. In his journal, Rétif gives the actual date as July 21 (¶521, vol. 1, p. 189). See Appendix A in the present edition for a chonology of the real-life events on which the novel is based.

you scumbag, you good-for-nothing bitch!' Sometimes I dodged the blow; other times, I stood up to him. He threatened me again the night of July 21. But then, on Friday, July 22, he came home for dinner in what seemed like a good mood. I thought he had the money and that his supervisor,[207] whom he often praised and more often criticized, had generously helped him out of his predicament. But I was mistaken.

Moresquin ate dinner and then played with his son, without mentioning the money, which seemed to confirm what I had surmised. He fooled around with the child, whom he teased in a way that often made him insufferable, leading him to make mischief, play dirty tricks on people, poke them in the eye, and so on. After that, Moresquin fell asleep. For after work, the lazy bum, unlike most of his colleagues, refused to take on free-lance work to earn extra money. He stuck to his routine. In fact, he often found his job as a clerk so tiresome that he skipped work to go for a stroll, to gamble, or to engage in drunkenness and debauchery.

Moresquin slept for two hours, during which time I was busy doing piecework in a little alcove I used as a sewing room. Toward the end of his nap, a charwoman whom I paid to clean his boots, came by to drop them off. The noise she made when she arrived stirred the monster from his sleep, and he woke up in a bad mood, like a spoiled child. He complained a great deal about the fact that I no longer cleaned the mud from his boots like the lowliest slave. I calmly answered that, since I was working as a seamstress, I couldn't get my hands rough or dirty. How do you suppose this vilest, crudest, most despicable of all men replied? That I should take good care of my hands so that they were softer to ... Fromentel. This obscenity, uttered in front of a stranger, a woman of the lowest class of society, made me absolutely furious. I had endured crueler indignities than this, but I alone heard them. Despite my anger, I didn't say anything and left my workspace for a moment to get something. Moresquin went into the alcove, chasing after his son, with whom he had begun to play again. Fearing that all my work would be spoiled, I cried: 'Be careful! Stay away from my work!'

Even though he had no money to replace the ribbons I was cleaning, Moresquin pretended as though he was above it all and continued playing with his son. I begged him to leave my workspace, using the expression: *For the love of God!* Laughing scornfully, Moresquin punched me hard, right between the eyes. I fell over, momentarily blinded, unable to defend myself, but I cried out so loudly that all the neighbors came running. They hurled insults and threats at him. Among them was a woman, whose daughter he had falsely accused the night before of being a prostitute and of picking up clients on the boulevard. Moresquin angrily left the apartment, warning me as he stormed out the door:

---

[207] Rétif is referrng here to Legrand (called Megas in the novel), who was Augé's immediate supervisor and secretary to Le Pelletier de Morfontaine. See notes 182, 191, 216, 218, and 228.

'I'll take care of you tonight, you hussy, when no one else is around! I pawned your watch. But tomorrow, to make up the difference, I'll pawn everything you have, down to your last petticoat, and I'll throw you naked onto the street.'

After he left, I pondered what I should do, convinced that he would keep his word, at least in this case when it came to following through on his threats: 'Should I wait for him? Should I put an end to all my suffering tonight?' I asked myself. 'Or should I flee forever from a unscrupulous monster, a murderer, the scourge of his parents, and my tormentor?' After pondering these questions at length in my mind, I resolve to leave for good. But where would I go? My father was my only ally, and I didn't know how to reach him. I packed my bags nonetheless, putting what belonged to me into a trunk — at least what I could. I left what was at the laundress's, as well as my watch and jewelry, which had been pawned. So I ask my readers to take note of the fact that I was forced to leave behind many of my belongings!

While I was in this state of apprehension and anxiety, my father arrived. I spoke to him much more forcefully about my situation than I had ever dared to before. I told him that since I had witnesses to Moresquin's latest mistreatment, I wanted to take advantage of this opportunity and the scandal surrounding it to separate for ever from this man already condemned for past crimes; indeed, several sentences had been pronounced in absentia for the various homicides he had committed. Meanwhile, the clock had just struck seven, and we needed to hurry.

'Moresquin is a vile man, a despicable scoundrel,' declared my father. 'If paternal laws were still in force, he'd deserve to be beaten to death. Yet think carefully before you take this drastic step, which only should be a last resort. I'm neither forbidding you to do it, nor am I advising it, because of the possible consequences, which can be very serious either way. If you stay with him, something terrible might happen for which you could blame me. But if you leave Moresquin and his home, there could be extremely unpleasant consequences as well. I'll leave the choice up to you, but I promise to be ready to help you whatever you decide.'

I persevered in the decision to leave my tormentor and set out from the apartment at eight o'clock that night.

There are many details that have escaped my memory in recalling my disastrous marriage to Moresquin and the consequences of my disobedience, which I don't mean in any way to justify or excuse. I have recounted all this for the sole purpose of showing young women the terrible consequences of my transgression and the dangers of failing to make careful inquiries into the character and morals of one's suitor. Alas! For in taking a husband, we give ourselves a master and not only a master, but a major part of ourselves — someone who has control over our body, our soul, even our chastity, indeed over the happiness or sorrow of every moment of our life! So there I was, having finally escaped from the monster's clutches.

Young women, you believe I was free! Ah, you'll now see all the dangers I still faced! For the horrors that were to follow would equal, even surpass, those I've already described.

I had the support of an excellent father; but I still faced the hostility of an unnatural mother, my eternal, implacable enemy. It wasn't possible for me to stay with my parents; it would have caused too much trouble. So my father arranged for me to stay with the wife of an artist[208] he employed and to whom he paid room and board for me. I felt safe there. It had been more than four years since I had gone quietly to bed at an hour that was normal for respectable people of my class, without trembling with fear at the horrors that awaited me during the night and without wondering if I would be dead or maimed by morning. For the first time in four years, I went to bed in peace, feeling a deep tranquility that nothing could disturb. Oh, what a delicious pleasure it was to be mistress of myself after such a long servitude!

The following day, my hosts lavished kindness and attention on me — on me, who only the day before had been the lowliest of slaves. Breakfast was waiting for me when I woke up. Tears came to my eyes.

'You mustn't lavish all this attention on me!' I said to the wife and her husband. 'I'll be only too happy if I'm spoken to gently and with kindness!'

They looked at me with surprise: 'We can hardly do anything less for the daughter of a man whom we respect so greatly and who has been our employer now for six or seven years.'

I began to cry and couldn't eat. My hosts asked what was wrong. I remained silent for a moment and then explained: 'These are tears of joy that I'm shedding. I nevertheless feel a cruel torment to have left our four-year-old son in my husband's care. He'll spoil him with the poor upbringing he's bound to give him! I didn't want to leave my songbirds behind because he once amused himself by twisting the necks of my turtledoves. I didn't want to leave my little dog with him, and yet I left him my son! But I had no choice, since I never want to see Moresquin again. If I had taken his son with me, it would have given him a reason to come after me. So I chose to leave the child behind. My in-laws know what

---

[208] In his diary, Rétif indicates that Agnès was taken in by the wife of Louis Berthet, the artist who engraved many of Binet's illustrations for Rétif's publications, including *Les Contemporaines* (*Journal*, ¶521, vol. 1, p. 189).

FIGURE 23.   'The following day, my hosts lavished kindness and attention on me — on me, who only the day before had been the lowliest of slaves.' Illustration titled *Le Quarantecinquenaire guéri de sa passion* [The 45-year-old man cured of his passion] by Louis Binet, engraved by Pouquet, in *La Dernière Avanture d'un homme de quarante-cinq ans* (Genève: Regnault, 1783), Part II, p. 508. (BnF)

their son is like; if they think carefully about it, they'll take the child away from him!' That's all I felt comfortable saying.

I arranged for the dog to be given away that same day, and had already taken care of the turtledoves.[209] It may seem childish to be concerned about a dog and a few birds, as Moresquin later remarked more than once. But it wasn't a crime or even a error in judgment.

I left Moresquin's home — or rather his hellhole — the evening of July 22.[210] By noon the following day, my father had received a letter from him as stupid as those he usually wrote, but at the same time perfectly reassuring.[211] My father brought the letter to me as soon as it arrived.

'You see that you can rest easy,' he said. 'Far from wanting you back, Moresquin is delighted at the decision you've taken. I'm delighted as well. I much prefer for this odious man to leave us in peace! Fortunately, after the letter he's sent, he won't dare have the effrontery to ask you to return to him.'[212]

I agreed with my father. And who wouldn't have had the same impression — except, of course, for people who understood — even better than we did — Moresquin's vile character, capriciousness, and lunatic mind. And so, for a time, I felt safe, happy to be despised by someone I despised far more.

Until we received this letter, my mother had always blamed me for our quarrels with Moresquin. But after reading the letter, she sent my younger sister to reproach him for his treatment of me. My sister was a charming young woman of great merit and, above all, of angelic sweetness — a precious quality that I, too, had once possessed and that Moresquin had robbed me of, alas! And it was in front of this sister that Moresquin boasted about punching me in the face, which had left a nasty bruise on my forehead.

'Well, I gave her a good punch, anyhow!' Those were his very words.

My sister was outraged and left abruptly. When my mother heard what had happened, she cried out for vengeance against Moresquin, either because she really felt that way or else as a subterfuge that would enable her to help him secretly. We'll soon see the reasons why I suspected that she had the second plan in mind; for her behavior would otherwise be almost inexplicable.

---

[209] Ingénue later explains that she had entrusted her turtledoves to Fromentel, which roused the ire of both her husband and her father, who saw this as proof of their liaison.

[210] In his diary, Rétif gives 21 July 1785 as the date of Agnès's final escape from her husband (*Journal*, ¶521, vol. 1, p. 189). Although the dates given here match those in *La Femme infidelle* (*OC*, vol. 45, p. 833), the dates indicated in the diary are generally more accurate.

[211] This letter, in which Ingénue's husband seems to consent to their separation, is found in *La Femme infidelle*, *OC*, vol. 45, pp. 834–35, and is reprinted in MHRA's French edition of *Ingénue Saxancour* (Appendix C, Excerpt 5). However, there is no mention of this letter in Rétif's diary.

[212] According to French laws of the period, a wife could not leave her husband's domicile to reside elsewhere without his permission, and she could be forced by the courts to return to him if he refused permission to let her go.

I don't know whether it was a good idea or not, but my father decided not to tell his friend Olaüs Magnus, Moresquin's employer, about the separation. He did this out of consideration for Moresquin, but he should have unmasked the monster and worked against him. However, Moresquin had our son with him and needed to make a living. Besides, we thought he was content, even delighted, with our separation. How little did I know him! He was actually choking with rage. My father hadn't answered his letter, which he found insufferable, like everything Moresquin ever wrote. The style of this vile man, about whom he learned more every day from me, made him nauseous. And each time he learned further details of the horrific abuse to which his daughter, his own flesh and blood, had been exposed, he flew into a rage that was difficult to control.

While my father was trying to decide what to do, Moresquin was busy making mischief; for he was never idle when it came to hurting people or causing trouble. And what was he up to, that monster? He was slandering the unfortunate woman he could no longer mistreat, dragging her name through the mud. He spread the most far-fetched lies, the most outrageous slander about me![213] But why should he care? Did he ever try to justify his mistreatment of me? So why would he have bothered to make his calumnies plausible? Instead of taking care of his responsibilities, he spent his time talking to stable boys, spies, all sorts of riffraff, looking for witnesses to his wife's outings and her alleged rendezvous with Fromentel that never happened. He was crazy enough to presume that I would go to the home of that young man, with whom I was never on intimate terms and whom I didn't even like or respect.

Three days after I left, Moresquin went looking for me at Fromentel's apartment and found the birdcage and birds I had foolishly sent there. Not wanting to expose these poor little creatures to Moresquin's fury, I had planned to give them as a present to Fromentel's sister-in-law, in whose home Moresquin had behaved so badly. I knew that she was very fond of my birds, especially of a linnet she had given to me. I had written to her about them and, in the meantime, the neighbor with whom I had left them had taken them to Fromentel's apartment, where a messenger was supposed to come get them. I don't deny that it was unwise for me to take the birds and especially to have them sent to Fromentel. But people who are innocent don't foresee the consequences of an innocent action.[214]

---

[213] Moresquin (like Augé) accused his wife of adultery, incest, prostitution, and theft. Regarding theft, see note 217. Regarding the accusations of adultery, see notes 12, 165, 170, 187, 189, 209, 214, and the introduction. Regarding the accusations of prostitution, see notes 173, 220, 240, and 242. Regarding incest, see notes 62, 63, 69, 69, 193, 199, and 242, as well as the introduction.

[214] Here again, one senses that the lady doth protest too much. This convoluted explanation, whether true or not, reflects a compulsion to counter her husband's public accusations of adultery. In fact, a letter that Blérie sent to Agnès soon after she left her husband suggests that she gave the birds to Blérie, rather than to his sister-in-law, with the intention of reclaiming

As soon as Moresquin arrived at Fromentel's apartment, he caught sight of the birdcage, which his friend undoubtedly let him see, out of malice or sheer mischief, simply to vex him. The cage's presence in the home of the man he claimed was my lover provided useful evidence of my alleged affair.[215] The monster was then able to capitalize on the plot he had been hatching for nearly a year. Despite being ineptly villainous, as well as stupid to the point of idiocy, Moresquin had succeeded in gaining the support of his supervisor[216] by convincing him that I had a lover and that my father's hatred for his son-in-law was so intense that he (my father) would have been glad for me to have a lover in order to dishonor my husband. He claimed that my father had encouraged my ardent passion for Fromentel and that, to allow me to indulge that passion in complete safety, he had taken me from my husband's home and hidden me away in a room where no one could find me. To all this nonsense, he added other monstrous accusations concocted by his disordered imagination, among them that I had robbed him of property worth more than 15,000 *livres*. Yet this vile, unscrupulous man was penniless and had pawned everything down to my watch. I had taken only some sheets and my old, worn-out clothes, not even all of what I left behind, which was never returned to me.[217] It was an absurd web of lies, and yet Moresquin's supervisor believed it. My father had hoped this man would help keep my husband in line, but before Mr. Saxancour could explain the situation to him, he was already biased against me in favor of that scoundrel. I won't dwell on this inconceivable bias against my father and me, which no doubt has other, more private reasons behind it.[218] I felt it necessary to say a word about this in order to explain what happened later and why a man as respectable as my father and so deserving of the supervisor's esteem, was thwarted and betrayed by him.

---

them once she had settled into her new lodgings: 'Don't worry at all about your birds,' he wrote to her, 'I'll take good care of them until you're ready to reclaim them.' For the full text of Blérie's letter, see Appendix C, Excerpt 6, in MHRA's French edition of *Ingénue Saxancour*.

[215] This incident is confirmed in a letter that Blérie sent to Agnès, reprinted in MHRA's French edition of *Ingénue Saxancour* (Appendix C, Excerpt 7). Testud gives the date of this letter as 26 July 1785.

[216] Legrand, whom Rétif calls Megas in the novel. See notes 182, 191, 207, 218, and 228. What follows is a catalogue of the slanderous accusations against Agnès and Rétif that Augé circulated in his office and his neighborhood — accusations that deeply distressed Rétif and that he went to great lengths to contest.

[217] In *La Femme infidelle*, Ingénue stresses how little she took when she fled from her husband — and how little there was to take: 'I left the house at eight at night, carrying in an old trunk what belonged to me, along with a few household linens. After four years of drudgery [...], I deserved a far better salary than a few towels, a few handkerchiefs, and two pairs of sheets' (*OC*, vol. 45, p. 831). For the full text of the passage from which this passage is taken, see Appendix F, Excerpt 4, in MHRA's French edition of *Ingénue Saxancour*.

[218] Rétif suggests elsewhere that his son-in-law's supervisor Legrand was in league with Augé against him because he envied Rétif's friendship with Le Pelletier, his superior.

We were at peace, nevertheless. Certain of Moresquin's consent to our separation, based on the letter he had sent, my father's only concern was finding a means of support for me. It was out of a sense of discretion and propriety that I remained hidden in the home where he had placed me and that I avoided to go out for walks or meals with my hosts. In any case, I was in a state of grief and affliction that would last as long as I lived. Yet I no longer feared Moresquin, who insisted in his letter that he was delighted I had left because, he claimed, I was driving his household to rack and ruin. (It's true I had refused to earn money the way he wanted me to.) I didn't try to find out what he was saying or doing. Aside from my hosts and occasional visits from my father, I lived in complete isolation — only too happy to be left alone at last, to see evening come without trembling, to go to bed without having to endure vile abuse and horrible obscenities, and then to awake to a cloudless day without storms or strife. I hadn't yet written to my aunt, but when I learned that she was worried about me, I decided to write to her. Even though she had been the first cause of my misery, she had shown kindness to me afterwards, and I had forgiven her. She wrote back, and her answer shattered the illusion of peace I had enjoyed. Good God! Her letter relayed all the dreadful, mean-spirited lies that Moresquin had been spreading about me! The lies were so stupid, unimaginative, and absurd that intelligent people could only scoff at them. But fools are easily persuaded by such lies, and fools — alas! — make up three-quarters of the world!

My aunt began by advising me to avoid the area around Port Saint-Paul,[219] because Moresquin would use my presence there as a pretext for spreading terrible lies about my alleged affair with Fromentel, who lived in that neighborhood. He insisted that I was sleeping with that man, that we were served breakfast in bed by the woman in whose home I was staying, and that Fromentel's hairdresser had seen me in the young man's bed. He also claimed that a man who was getting into his carriage had seen me, as had some servants — through the

---

[219] Port Saint-Paul: River dock that used to be where the quai de l'Hôtel de Ville is located today on the right bank of the Seine, opposite the northeast tip of the Ile Saint-Louis. Blérie de Sérivillé [the person on whose character Fromentel is based], lived nearby, as did Augé, who spent much of his time drinking and gossiping in the cafés and bars of the neighborhood.

walls apparently, remarked my aunt — and that he had told me: 'Take heart, Madame Moresquin!' And, in addition to the man in the carriage, there were supposedly twenty-five witnesses at the Arsenal who had supposedly seen me in Fromentel's bed. It should be noted that, even if the carriage had doubled in height and been at the same level as the second floor of the building, Fromentel's lodging would have had to face the street. For it's not easy for someone in a carriage looking in from the street to see a woman in bed with a man. Yet Fromentel's apartment was in the back of the building and not at all visible from the street; one hardly needed to see his lodgings to understand that. According to my aunt, Moresquin further claimed that my name had been posted on a list of prostitutes at the entrance to the Jardin du Roi to prevent me from entering the garden.[220] He even claimed that Fromentel had been put in jail by the magistrate at the Arsenal, where he was awaiting trial. Such was the web of lies concocted by Moresquin's malicious mind! My aunt went on to say that Moresquin had fetched dresses of mine left behind at the dressmaker's, and that this woman had been spreading rumors about me as well:

'Unfortunately, all too many people are prepared to believe the worst without any proof and to accept these lies as the truth,' wrote my aunt. 'I sent someone to Moresquin's apartment to fetch your collection of Molière's plays, but he refused to give it back. He stopped by this morning and asked me, in his usual brutal manner, why I was sending people to his place. He accused me of spying on him and told me to stop it. He insisted that you had been Fromentel's mistress for a long time. I answered as tactfully as I could, but he flew into a rage and said that we were all …. That's the kind of the scenes I've been subjected to, often twice a day, since you left. You should go out as little as possible. He's like a madman, shaking and foaming with rage. He terrifies me. I wouldn't want to be alone with him as you've been. Above all, don't go out alone! If he finds you, you'll really be in trouble! He's sure to make a scene and to attract a crowd to humiliate you. He's been telling everyone that your Papa is your pimp. Such malice! I could fill a whole ream of paper with all the dreadful things he's been saying.'

---

[220] Among the flood of slanderous accusations he makes against his wife, Moresquin claims that her name had been posted on a list of prostitutes at the entrance to the Jardin du Roi to prevent her from entering. By the late eighteenth century, prostitution had become a problem in the Jardin du Roi, the present-day Jardin des Plantes.

I won't go into much further detail about Moresquin's behavior during that period and will focus instead on the main events.

After carrying on the way my aunt described to me, after spreading even more slanderous lies about us and setting my father at odds with Olaüs-Magnus's secretary, his supervisor, Moresquin happened one afternoon to be on the street outside where I was staying. It was the day of the last procession of the slaves ransomed from the Barbary pirates,[221] and I went to the window as they were passing by. Moresquin caught sight of me and came upstairs. He knocked softly at the unlocked door and, just as I ran to open it, he walked in. My legs started to shake and the color drained from my face; I didn't have the strength to utter a word.

'Ah, my dear,' said the monster, 'how delighted I am to see you again! Come back home with me! I forgive you for everything and want to make you happy.'

I should have cried out. But intimidated and beside myself with fear, I had only the strength to say: 'Not so loud! If my father comes ....' I didn't know what I was saying. Moresquin sat down and had me sit down as well. When the mistress of the household returned home, he was speaking to me with feigned gentleness. Her surprise at seeing me with a stranger increased greatly when he introduced himself as my husband. He seemed pleasant enough to her and as polite as a man of his sort could be. After all she had heard about his malicious slander against me, she couldn't believe her ears — or her eyes. However, since Moresquin pretended to be reasonable, she listened to what he had to say.

After awhile, we heard my father arrive, and Moresquin had the audacity to wait for him. Given all he had said against Mr. Saxancour and me, only a man like him would show such insolence, such shamelessness. But Moresquin was paradoxical and inconsistent by nature. It's impossible to describe my father's surprise and anger when he saw my tormentor, his slanderer and mine! He ordered him to leave. Shaking with anger, but conscious of my hosts' presence, the scoundrel went down on his knees. But Mr. Saxancour knew him too well to be touched by this charade. He pushed him away and forced him to leave, after venting all the scorn and revulsion he felt for him.

---

[221] Reference to the religious procession through the streets of Paris on 18 October 1785 of 315 Frenchmen (mainly sailors and merchants) who had been captured by Barbary pirates, held as slaves in North Africa, and eventually ransomed by the religious orders of the Sainte-Trinité and Merci. This was the last in a series of such processions through the streets of French towns and cities in which freed slaves gave thanks for their rescue. See Chantal de La Veronne, 'Quelques processions de captifs en France à leur retour du Maroc, d'Algérie ou de Tunis', *Revue de l'Occident musulman et de la Méditerranée*, 8 (1970), 131–42, especially p. 132. It was during this event that Agnès was spotted by Augé as she watched the procession from the window of the Berthets' apartment, rue Saint-Jacques.

The following day, Moresquin returned with our son. With a barbarism that was truly unthinkable, but worthy of him, the monster had coached him beforehand and told him what to say. So as soon as he saw me, the child cried out that I wasn't his mother, but another lady, and that he didn't want to see me. This was a cruel blow that hurt me deeply. When I tried to kiss my son, he pulled away and tried to scratch me. I left in tears, filled with even greater loathing for the wretch who was robbing me of everything he could!

* * *

I won't speak here of Moresquin's conduct at his office, of how he felt emboldened by his supervisor Mégas's petty jealousy of my father, because the secretary felt humiliated by his talents and by his friendship with their boss Olaüs-Magnus, or of the underhanded way he had taken advantage of this jealousy to torment such an estimable man as Mr. Saxancour. I'll come to this soon enough when I recount another black deed, worthy of its despicable perpetrator.

Moresquin had a woman write a love letter to Fromentel and had someone find it in the street outside the building where the young man lived.[222] He then went around showing the letter to everyone,[223] including his supervisor Mégas. Gloating over the success of his deceit with people who found the letter credible — his supervisor Mégas, that parasite Lapropre, the clerk Goupillon, and other people of that ilk — he had the audacity to write to my father that he had a damning piece of evidence against me. He added that he had already shown it to Mégas and to all his vile acquaintances in the cafés and bars of the capital. This was a terrible blow to my father, who hurried to Mégas's office. It was there that Mégas — to whom Moresquin had inappropriately entrusted the counterfeit letter — showed it to Mr. Saxancour. At first glance, my father acknowledged that the handwriting was that of a woman, but that it didn't look like mine. And after reading the letter, he insisted that I could not possibly have written it. Here are the contents of that letter, which Moresquin had dictated to some poor woman:

---

[222] In his diary, Rétif notes that he learned of the counterfeit letter on 18 December 1785, and that he and Agnès confronted Augé two days later at his office, where they persuaded him to burn it after discussing a possible reconciliation with him (*Journal*, ¶600, vol. 1, pp. 240). He suggests that Augé hoped to use the letter to pressure the Rétifs to drop their police complaint against him for assaulting Marion and to convince Agnès to return to him. However, Agnès wrote her husband a few days later to say that she would rather die than ever return to him. Rétif included the full text of her letter in *La Femme infidelle* (*OC*, vol. 45, pp. 924–27). See Appendix C, Excerpt 14, in MHRA's French edition of *Ingénue Saxancour*.

[223] In *La Femme infidelle*, in a footnote regarding the counterfeit letter, Rétif explains: 'The monster had read the forged letter aloud in several cafés and to all his acquaintances. It has now been burned' (*OC*, vol. 45, p. 441).

My dear friend,

I'm sending you a hair ribbon. I dedicated it to you just the way you wanted; you know what I mean … I've been distressed not to see you since the last time we slept together. Just imagine if I were to become pregnant and who would be blamed with a husband like mine, who has had only too many reasons to suspect us! After all, my friend, we haven't stopped having intimate relations since that first day early last October when we walked together to the Jardin du Roi. It was a memorable day indeed, and I bestowed my favors on you so easily that you were astonished. And you know that he realized what had happened. I told you all about it. Oh, all the accusations he made against you! But I'll hide everything from him; and then I'll try to get another man to ….[224]

The rest is unprintable. Mr. Saxancour pointed out to Mégas that a woman would never write such a letter. But the secretary was too obtuse to realize this. My father wanted to keep the letter, as was his right, but the secretary insisted on keeping it. Although he was outraged, my father gave it back to him, but only for safe-keeping. He played along with Moresquin and, through an honorable ruse, was able to convince him to burn the scandalous letter, to Mégas's great regret.

After burning the letter he himself had composed, Moresquin urged my father to work toward our reconciliation. Mr. Saxancour insisted that he couldn't force me to return to him and that it was up to him to gain my trust through good behavior toward me and at work in a way that would increase his chances of promotion. But incapable as he was of good behavior, Moresquin sensed that this would be impossible for him. All he was capable of was turpitude, obscenity, meanness, laziness, gluttony, love of gambling, and so forth. Yet he continued to press my father to arrange a reconciliation. Worn down by his importunity, my father finally agreed to draft an agreement, similar to the one in *La Femme infidelle*.[225] To make receiving the message more pleasant for Moresquin, he had my sister deliver it to him in person.[226]

Before telling what happened, I need to sketch my sister's portrait. She's a young woman who's quite pretty with a well-proportioned figure. But what

---

[224] The forged letter seems to imply that if Ingénue became pregnant following her relations with Fromentel, she would try to get another man to take the blame.

[225] Rétif reprinted the 'Acte Satisfactoire' (dated 5 December 1785) in *La Femme infidelle*, pp. 907–8. For the full text of the document, see Appendix C, Excerpt 17, in MHRA's French edition of *Ingénue Saxancour*. The reconciliation agreement that Rétif proposed never went into effect because Agnès refused to return to her husband after his brutal treatment of her sister Marion and his attacks on their family's reputation.

[226] This seems a rather lame justification for sending his younger daughter to deliver the agreement to Moresquin instead of going himself, especially given the warning Marion had received at the café to stay away from Moresquin and his brutal treatment of her when she returned the following day. This is yet another example of Rétif's attempts to excuse his questionable handling of events.

distinguishes her to an unparalleled degree is her air of touching candor and naiveté that matches the sweet sound of her voice and stirs the heart. Slender and fairly tall, she moves with grace and elegance. In short, everything about her is pleasing and apt to charm even the fiercest soul. This portrait is in no way exaggerated; it instead falls short of the truth — a fact that everyone who knows Marion Saxancour[227] can confirm.

My father first sent my sister to Moresquin's apartment at an hour at which he normally should have been home, but fortunately he wasn't there. On her way home, she stopped to ask for him at the café where he ordinarily goes in the evening. The owner told Marion's companion he wasn't there and, since Moresquin shared his business with everyone, he took the liberty of asking why she wanted to see him.

'I'm here with his sister-in-law who has a document for him to sign.'

Smiling, the owner warned: 'She shouldn't risk going to his apartment at night, nor even during the day.'

When my father heard what the café owner had said, it only made him laugh, even though he knew what Moresquin was like. The next morning at nine o'clock, he sent Marion and a woman servant to his apartment with the document. They arrived as he about to leave for his office, and Marion gave him the paper to sign. Moresquin read it and said he couldn't sign it without first consulting Mr. Mégas. Explaining that her father had specifically instructed her to bring back the document with or without a signature, Marion she took it from him. Furious, Moresquin grabbed the paper from her hands, knocked her over, and kicked her in the side as she lay helpless on the floor. Moresquin's housekeeper and Marion's companion pulled him away to stop him from hurting her more. The women helped Marion, who had fainted, and scolded Moresquin angrily for his inexcusable behavior. The wretch sensed how wrong he had been and asked Marion to forgive him. He invited her to have breakfast with him; she refused, but said that she forgave him. Yet as she was preparing to leave, he let out a sinister laugh and said that he would deny everything that had just happened. He

---

[227] Marion: Jean-Thomas-Marie-Anne Rétif (known as Marion) was born on 5 November 1764. She often served as her father's secretary and occasionally collaborated with him in writing articles, such as the sixty-page 'Supplément' to volume 1 of Jean-François de La Croix's two-volume *Dictionnaire historique portatif des femmes célèbres*, published in 1788. Found on pp. 741–808 of vol. 1, the 'Supplément' is signed Marion R.D.L.B. and ends with an article devoted to Louise Kéralio. The article closes with the following words: 'je suis charmée d'avoir été chargée de faire ce Supplément, parce qu'il me procure l'occasion de témoigner mon estime et ma reconnaissance à la jeune héroïne qui devient le chevalier du sexe qu'elle honore' [I'm delighted to have been asked to write this Supplément, because it gives me the opportunity to express my esteem and gratitude to the young heroine who is becoming the champion of the sex that she honors] (p. 808). That Marion and her father collaborated on the series of articles comprising the 'Supplément' is confirmed by the entry for 13 June 1787 in Rétif's diary: 'matin, fait trois art. Julien, Joli et Kéralio' [this morning, wrote three articles on Julien, Joli, and Kéralio].

Figure 24.   Portrait of Rétif's younger daughter Marion. Artist and date unknown.
Published in *Monsieur Nicolas, ou Le Coeur humain dévoilé*. Preface by Marc Chadourne
(Paris: Au Cercle du livre précieux, 1959), vol. 6, opposite p. 464. (BnF)

then uttered a stream of insults against Mr. Saxancour,[228] which he said he would deny as well. Horrified and still not fully recovered from the attack, Marion insisted on leaving the home of this abominable man and took refuge with one of his neighbors. As she and her companion were leaving, she overheard Moresquin's housekeeper say:

'You're completely out of your mind! It's as if you're trying to get yourself arrested! What! Mistreat your own sister-in-law! It's unheard of!'

Moresquin merely scoffed and replied with obscenities.

When she came home, my sister didn't say anything about her visit to Moresquin, except that he had kept the document to show to Mr. Mégas. It wasn't until the following day, when she needed to see a doctor, that she told us part of what had happened. Father was very irritated not to have known in time to file a complaint. And he was right! That complaint might well have averted other unpleasant scenes I'm about to relate. In any case, after Moresquin's violence toward my sister, reconciliation was out of the question, and that was the real advantage we gained from this incident. Moresquin's treatment of my sister exposed his secret intentions and confirmed the horrible rumors he was spreading: that he only wanted to have me back for three nights so that he could send me back to my father's with broken arms and ribs and infected with syphilis. Indeed, he had carefully prepared for the scene that was to follow; his recent activities and soiled linen, along with his words, had convinced his housekeeper that the monster had deliberately infected himself with venereal disease in order to have the barbaric and guilty pleasure of causing my death.[229]

---

[228] In his diary entry for 6 December 1785, Rétif noted: 'Sent Marianne to Augé's home for his signature on the agreement […]. He told Madame Normand [the woman who accompanied her] that I had sold my daughter to a nobleman, who was going to take her with him and keep her as his mistress. Marianne returned without the signature; the Monster wanted to show the agreement to Mr. Legrand' (*Journal*, ¶588, vol. 1, pp. 235–36).

[229] Despite claims by eighteenth-century medical practitioners and charlatans alike that venereal disease was fully curable, treatments — although widely available and often highly touted — remained largely ineffective. It was not an exaggeration to suggest that Moresquin's plot to infect his wife amounted to a murder plot. By the mid-eighteenth century, the French courts considered knowing infection of one's spouse with venereal disease as grounds for separation. See Trouille, 'For Better or Worse?: Venereal Disease as Grounds for Marital Separation (Reims, 1757 and Paris, 1771)', in *Wife-Abuse in Eighteenth-Century France* (Oxford, UK: Voltaire Foundation, 2009), pp. 59–93.

Let us now continue on to the twenty-first of February 1786. By then, I was living with my father, who had brought both my sister and me to live at his apartment after my mother's departure. I should explain that my mother, given her overly harsh attitude toward me and Moresquin's reprehensible behavior toward my father, had feared our well-justified criticisms. So she left for Burgundy, under the pretext of settling her mother's estate, but actually with the intention of remaining there, which she did. She left on November 27 and my father had come to take me home that very same day.[230]

Several months later, on February 21, I had a headache and went to get a breath of fresh air at the far end of the Ile Saint-Louis. I had walked the full length of the island and was about to head home when I felt a claw-like hand grip my shoulder. It was Moresquin, and I cried out when I realized who it was.

'You won't escape me,' he whispered ominously in my ear. 'I have you now and have been fasting long enough ....' What he said next cannot be repeated. He then said: 'You're coming home with me, after which I'll send you back to your father.' I had heard of his plan to infect me. Besides the horror that Moresquin naturally inspired in me, my suspicions gave me the strength to resist. I tried to flee. He dared not beat me in front of a group of working-class women standing nearby who would have torn him to pieces. But to affirm his rights over me, he had me arrested by the sentinel and ignominiously dragged to the district police station. There, he filed a ludicrous complaint that was so outrageous that the police commissioner's clerk advised me to file a counter-claim, which I did. As a result, we were referred to the local magistrate for an interim ruling. I had word sent to my father and sister to join us at the police station. When my father arrived, he didn't speak to Moresquin and simply glared at him scornfully.

The police commissioner accompanied us to the magistrate's office where he explained that I had requested a separation. Like many of his colleagues, this respectable judge found the prospect of separation troubling. Moresquin considered this heart-felt reaction an encouraging sign and gloated in anticipation of a ruling in his favor. But when the police commissioner recounted what had happened, the magistrate exclaimed:

'He had his own wife arrested by the sentinel! That's outrageous!'

Shameless as ever, Moresquin was in no way intimidated by these words and brazenly asked that I be ordered to return to him. But instead, the judge entrusted

---

[230] In his diary, Rétif gives 26 (not 27) November 1785, as the day he brought Agnès home to live with him and her sister Marion at his apartment rue des Bernardins after his wife left him that morning. The entry for that date reads: 'This morning, reproached my wife for her schemes and underhanded dealings with Augé [...]. She was so frightened by my criticisms [...] that she left the apartment, taking with her everything she owned down to the mattress off her bed. So here's this crazy old woman who, feeling guilty, runs away and, at her age, gives rise to the scandalous spectacle of a separation. This evening, I went to fetch my older daughter and brought her to live here with me and her younger sister' (*Journal*, ¶578, vol. 1, pp. 223–24).

me to my father's care and I returned home with him and my sister.[231] A few days later, we made the necessary arrangements through our lawyer so I could remain at my father's home permanently.[232]

Moresquin was furious and determined to retaliate. Every day, I heard of new lies and slander he was spreading about me and my family, but I refused to engage with him.

With the arrival of spring, a new chapter opened in my life that brought happier moments than those I've recounted until now.

We occasionally dined at the home of a retired field marshal and inspector general of artillery,[233] a friend of my father's who lived on the rue Saint-Maur on the outskirts of Paris. On May 5,[234] this esteemed officer asked us to stop on our

---

[231] These events are confirmed in *La Femme infidelle* (*OC*, vol. 45. pp. 929–30) and in Rétif's diary entry for 21 February 1785: 'Terrible day […] Agnès seized by that monster Augé and taken to the police station on the island. I've just come back from there to get the letter he sent on July 23. I went to the police station and then to the office of the local magistrate, where we were referred for an interim ruling. […] I pled my daughter's case in front of the magistrate, and she was sent home with me. Her case will be decided on Saturday' (¶657, vol. 1, p. 267). Rétif used the letter of July 23 as evidence that Augé approved the separation and had given Agnès permission to live apart from him.

[232] In his diary, Rétif indicates that there were actually two hearings held before the magistrate, the first on February 21 and the second on the 24th, at which she was given permission to reside at her father's home *temporarily* until a third hearing, set for March 7, when she was given permission to stay there permanently. According to the agreement signed that day, Augé would not be required to pay alimony if he agreed to a separation. See *Journal*, ¶660 & ¶667, vol. 1, pp. 268–69 & 273. The court did not issue a final separation decree until a year later on 18 March 1787. For a chronology of the long-drawn-out legal maneuvers leading up to Agnès's separation, see Appendix A in the present edition.

[233] Monsieur de Saint-Mars, chevalier de Saint-Louis, was a retired field marshal and inspector general of artillery, with whom Rétif had been friends since 1780. Testud notes that, 'it was in 1780 that Rétif became acquainted with him. At the age of 64, Saint-Mars was still a bachelor. He was enchanted by Marion Rétif's angelic face, which made her father think that his younger daughter might one day become Madame de Saint-Mars! But reality intervened to shatter this lovely dream: On 20 October 1787 was signed the marriage contract between François de Formanoir, chevalier de Saint-Mars […] and Mademoiselle Catherine Elisabeth de Stavayé'. (Testud, *Monsieur Nicolas*, vol. 2, p. 1353, n. 5 to p. 383.)

[234] In his diary, Rétif gives April 18 (1786) as the date of the dinner at which Rétif and his

way to pick up two of his friends, a brother and sister, and to come together to his house in the carriage of another officer, his older brother. The six of us arrived at the field marshal's beautiful house surrounded by gardens.[235] It was there that I could fully admire the charms of the lovely Félicité.[236] From that moment on, my heart was forever bound to her by the deepest, most tender friendship. My father and sister loved her as much as I did, and everything seemed to favor my attachment to her. After suffering a series of great misfortunes, the brother and sister were buying a small property in Normandy from our host where they planned to live in peace and quiet. Here, in brief, is Félicité's story.

She was the youngest of seven children. The ablest and most talented of her brothers had done very well professionally. After he was promoted to an important position as a tax agent, he decided to have his orphaned sister educated in a way that would prepare her to run his household one day. Félicité received a refined education and became an exceedingly charming, accomplished woman. At seventeen, she took charge of a large household. She was beautiful, with a stunning figure and dark, sparkling eyes. The sweet sound of her voice went straight to the heart. Loved and cherished by all her brother's acquaintances, she soon became the very soul of the household. Twenty suitors asked for her hand; but Félicité felt only one emotion: gratitude toward her brother, her benefactor. She made him the absolute master of her destiny and dedicated her life to him. And so the springtime of her life passed by, happy and carefree. Until then, she had gathered only roses without their thorns, but a cruel ordeal awaited her.

Her brother had always fulfilled his responsibilities as a director with diligence and integrity; and, as a result, he had made enemies among the auditors. He

---

daughters first met Félicité Mesnager, who was to become Agnès's close friend and Rétif's last great passion. It was at that dinner that Agnès's also first met Louis Vignon, who later became her lover, father of her second surviving child, and eventually her second husband.

[235] By the mid-1780s, Rétif had become a literary celebrity of sorts and was much sought after by Parisian high society. As the entries in his diary show, he was often invited to dine at the homes of aristocrats and high-ranking officials, despite his unkempt appearance and rather boorish behavior. His friend and biographer Palmézeau-Cubières points to the paradoxes in his character: 'Restif de La Bretonne did not bring to polite society the social graces of people who seek to please. By nature taciturn and sullen, he was rather boorish in conversation, as he was in his writings; in short, he sought favor with no one, but didn't mind if people courted favor with him; and he became especially eloquent when people got him talking about his work' ['Notice historique et critique sur la vie et les ouvrages de Nicolas-Edme Restif de La Bretonne', repr. in Paul Lacroix, *Bibliographie et iconographie de tous les ouvrages de Restif de La Bretonne* (Paris: Fontaine, 1875), p. 55].

[236] Born in 1751, Félicité Mesnager was thirty-five years old when Rétif and his daughters made her acquaintance through their mutual friend Saint-Mars. She married in 1796 and died in 1835. Rétif recalls their first meeting in Part XVI of *Les Nuits de Paris* in a story titled 'Félicité ou l'amour médecin', *OC*, vol. 86, pp. 155–59. In 'Mon Calendrier', he describes her as 'the last and most tenuous of my grand adventures.'

customarily sent the taxes his service had collected to Paris in a strongbox containing bills and notes payable. Unaware that his enemies were plotting his downfall, he continued this practice. His enemies sent the strongbox back to him and, before he could sort out what had happened, they arrested him and imprisoned him in his town's dungeon for embezzling royal funds.

It was in this situation that young Félicité — alone and abandoned by cold-hearted friends who believed her brother guilty — showed her deep affection for her brother and did everything she could to help him. She waited all day and night outside the door of his prison, asking only to see him and refusing to eat. When they finally let her see him, she rushed into his arms and fainted. Only he could convince her to leave him and, only then, by urging her to go to Paris to plead on his behalf. She hurried to the capital and boldly knocked at every door she could. There, they saw a delicate young woman — who, until then, had been so honored and welcomed into people's homes — besiege the residences of high officials and the offices of their chief clerks, deterred by nothing, putting up with crude remarks and unwanted advances.

She later explained: 'I was ready to do anything for my brother, to sacrifice body and soul to save him. And if I had been asked to do what the vilest women do, I think I would have agreed, providing I was promised that my brother would be freed and his reputation and fortune restored.'

One senses all the perils to which Félicité was exposed. There were no humiliations she did not face, no whim she did not have to satisfy. But what distressed her the most were the demands of a vulgar parvenu who had become her brother's immediate superior and who earlier had considered her far beyond his reach. This despicable man humiliated Félicité to the extreme and then betrayed her brother's interests. Outraged, she recovered her self-respect and, rising above this humiliation, she was able to gain more through her determination and defiance than through her favors. She returned to free her brother and then, with him, left a town that had been the scene both of her renown and her misfortune, but not of her shame.[237]

I didn't know Félicité's story at the time, but she had heard of my misfortunes before we met. As she dined with the Saxancour sisters, she didn't realize that I was the woman for whom she had felt such sympathy. But during dinner, our voluble host recounted my story to her, just as he would later tell me hers. So, as we left the table, this charming woman embraced me and said:

'Let us be friends, my dear Saxancour! There are a thousand reasons why we should be. Everyone is attracted to your sister, who is sweet and pretty. But I felt drawn to you even before I met you.'

---

[237] This recalls the episode in Voltaire's novel *L'Ingénu* in which Mlle de Saint-Yves sacrifices her virginity to obtain the release of the man she loves from an unjust imprisonment.

'Oh, she'll certainly become your friend!' exclaimed our host. And he took advantage of the first chance he had to tell me her story. Félicité and I soon grew closer, exchanging secrets and promising to help each other out. And so began our friendship, which would never end.

Félicité lived in Paris, very near Moresquin's apartment. She had heard of the abuse he had inflicted on me from her neighbors, as well as from her sister, brother-in-law, and their daughter. She had wanted to meet me without knowing who my father was. The reason why she was so intensely drawn to me was that I was both the woman for whom she had felt such strong compassion and daughter of a man for whom she felt such deep respect.

I won't conceal the fact that my friendship with Félicité was gratifying to me for yet another reason. My father, whose life was so precious to me, had been deeply distressed by my misfortune, and his health had suffered as a result. I noticed that his face lit up in the presence of Félicité's charms. I spoke highly to my friend of this man who was so dear to me, and she did not discourage him. In fact, she soon realized how attractive and engaging a man of great merit can be, even if he is no longer young, and I was delighted to see them fall passionately in love with each other. It was one of the happiest times in my life. My friend became like a mother to me. She and my father both confided in me; I told each of them what the other dared not say, and I saw them happy together.

My sister, that lovely young woman whom the monster Moresquin had so cruelly mistreated, was on the verge of making a fine marriage. The future looked bright to me, and my misfortunes seemed far behind me. But Moresquin was still lurking in the background.

The evening of May 18th, we had dined at our home with my friend, her brother, and a young magistrate.[238] After a delightful dinner with these six people

---

[238] Cottin identifies the young lawyer in question as Morel de Rosières, 'lieutenant-général au bailliage de Châtillon-sur-Seine' (chief magistrate of the royal court in northern Burgundy). His identity is confirmed by the entry in Rétif's diary for 18 May 1786: 'Dined at the doctor's home with Mr. Morel' (*Journal*, ¶728, vol. 1, pp. 201–2.) The doctor in question is Guillebert de Préval (see note 250). However, Testud maintains that Cottin confused Mr. Morel with his father and that the younger Morel was neither an *avocat général* (deputy magistrate), nor a *lieutenant-général*, although he was indeed a lawyer. In *Monsieur Nicolas*, Rétif explains that

who enjoyed each other's company and a few of whom adored each other, my father and our guests decided to take a walk around the Ile Saint-Louis. My sister and I stayed behind to tidy up, and the three men left with Félicité, whom they all adored, although for different reasons. As they crossed the bridge to the island, my father caught sight of Moresquin with his son. The monster was playing with the child, calling him little Saxancour. The two other men were baffled by this, but Félicité guessed who he was from his nasty appearance, even though she had never seen him before. She would have preferred to leave, but she continued on out of courtesy toward her brother. Moresquin tagged along, sometimes walking in front, sometimes behind them, stopping when they stopped and continuing on when they did. The two other men finally became quite annoyed with him, but Félicité calmed them down. He followed them all the way to my father's doorstep. We didn't understand why he did this, but it was a prologue to a terrible drama that would play out a week later in the Jardin du Roi.

I'll recount that incident now, so afterwards I'll be able to focus on more pleasant matters, if not in my own life, which will be tinged forever with unhappiness, then at least in the lives of my father and sister.

Félicité was dining at our home with the young magistrate. Moresquin, who had been spying on our every move since our friendship began with her, came to stand guard in the street where we lived.[239] He kept watch from a bar down the street where he drank to excess in order to bolster his insolence. At six in the evening, the five of us — my father, Félicité, the young magistrate, my sister, and I — walked over to the Jardin du Roi and entered through the new gate facing the Seine. We headed toward the labyrinth. My father was walking ahead with Félicité, while I stayed behind with my sister and our male companion, who was between us. For some reason, we stopped following my father and went up the central path. As we were walking toward the labyrinth, Moresquin came up to me and and slapped me twice. The young magistrate didn't realize what had happened until he saw the powder fall from my head as Moresquin was already running away.

'Who is that insolent fellow!' he cried out.

'It's my wife that I'm caressing,' shouted Moresquin as he fled.

Morel courted his younger daughter Marion, hoping to marry her, but that he discouraged Morel's suit, in the hope that the wealthier Saint-Mars, who had expressed interest in Marion, would ask for her hand. He further claims that Félicité, who hoped to marry Saint-Mars herself, succeeded in cooling Saint-Mars's friendship with the Rétifs by sending Augé to him to voice his well-rehearsed complaints against his wife and father-in-law (*Monsieur Nicolas*, 'Neuvième Epoque', *OC*, vol. 69, pp. 3114–25). Against her father's wishes, Marion later married her cousin Edmond, who worked with Rétif in his printshop. Left a widow at thirty with three small children, Marion kept house for her father from 1798 until his death in 1806.

[239] Numerous entries in Rétif's diary from 1786 mention Augé stalking his wife and father-in-law, insulting and threatening them and trying to excite bystanders against them.

Figure 25.   'As we were walking toward the labyrinth, Moresquin came up to me and and slapped me twice.' Illustration titled *Manon surprise par Monsieur Parangon* by Louis Binet, engraved by Louis-Sébastien Berthet, in *Le Paysan perverti* (Paris: Esprit, 1776), vol. 1, lettre 52, p. 249. (BnF)

My father had stopped to wait for us, without suspecting what had happened. When we reached him, he could tell from my pallor and look of distress that something disturbing had just taken place. Our male companion filled him in. My father was very angry, but masked his feelings. We walked to the top of the labyrinth, which people were beginning to ruin by doing I don't know what there in the bushes.[240] After that, we walked down to the formal flower gardens, where we encountered Moresquin again. The young magistrate had him arrested by the guard. My father, already outraged at Moresquin, became even angrier when he stepped on his foot. He pushed Moresquin away, a bit too aggressively perhaps. The wretch immediately cried out that Mr. Saxancour had struck him. The guard, one of those vile, mean-spirited fellows like Moresquin, took his side against my father. But the testimony of all the people who had witnessed the altercation — including that of the elder Mademoiselle Raguidon, a lovely person who has since become my friend — prevented the two rogues from being taken seriously.

The guard took us to the guard post at the entrance to the garden. There, in front of the guard and a large crowd of people, including the poet Mr. Robbé,[241] Moresquin — drunk and foaming with rage — spewed out a stream of the most outrageous insults at my father. He angrily accused him of incest and of prostituting me[242] and criticized him for all sorts of stupid, petty reasons. The director of the garden, a highly decorated retired military officer,[243] was summoned to deal with the dispute. As the plaintiff, Mr. Saxancour tried to speak first. But before he could utter a single word, Moresquin cut him off and erupted in a stream of vile abuse.

After listening to him for a few minutes, the director of the garden interrupted him and declared: 'Your own words condemn you. You're a scoundrel!' Then, turning to my father, he said: 'Monsieur, take the ladies home while I keep him here.'

'You're right to detain me.' Moresquin foolishly exclaimed. 'Because if I leave with him, I'll surely kill him!'

---

[240] In the late eighteenth century, the bushes of the labyrinth garden in the Jardin du Roi (present-day Jardin des Plantes) had become a notorious rendezvous for prostitutes and their clients, particularly at night. True to her name, Ingénue claims that she has no idea why the bushes had been trampled, despite the fact that Moresquin had, a few months earlier, accused her of prostitution and had her name posted at the entrance to the park to try to prevent her from entering. (See note 220 above.)

[241] Pierre-Honoré Robbé de Beauveset (1714–94), protégé of Madame du Barry and author of satires and licentious poetry.

[242] In his diary entry for that day, Rétif writes: 'He accused me of every kind of atrocity: incest, prostitution (he claimed that the home of my engraver Berthet was a brothel). He threatened to kill me, and so on. Taken to the police station, he said the most outrageous things against us' (*Journal*, ¶735 , vol. 1, pp. 308).

[243] Rétif notes that the director of the garden wore the cross of Saint-Louis, a high military honor established by Louis XIV for distinguished military service.

My father took my sister and me home and then went with Félicité and the young magistrate to file a formal complaint against Moresquin at the police station on the Ile Saint-Louis. They appeared before the same chief inspector who had heard Moresquin's complaint against me earlier that year on February 21.

As for Moresquin, he was detained at the Jardin du Roi until eight o'clock that evening. When they released him, they warned him that if he made another scene there, they would have him arrested and carted off to jail.

That's how the incident of May 25th ended.[244] The following day, Palais-Royal[245] echoed with gossip about what had happened. Moresquin himself went to boast about it to my aunt and his old friend Viellot, that contemptible scandalmonger, with whom Moresquin often played cards or checkers.

After the incident at the Jardin du Roi, Moresquin left us alone for a few days until he learned of the publication of a book written by a friend of my father titled *La Femme infidelle*,[246] in which he claimed to recognize himself in the character named L'Echiné. And it's true: L'Echiné was indeed Moresquin. The old gossip Viellot gave him his wife's copy. The two fools thought they could use the book to attack Mr. Saxancour and to triumph over him. But the scandalmonger's malevolence and Moresquin's rage were equally ineffective. By showing the book around town, Moresquin covered himself with shame and succeeded only in exposing the wickedness of his soul and the unprovoked malice of his friend.

All summer long, Moresquin came every evening to stand under our windows with the book in his hand, drawing a crowd of bystanders with his tirades against us. He brought his son with him, calling him 'little L'Echiné.' In short, frustrated by his loss of control over a weak and innocent victim, he pulled every dirty trick his twisted mind could contrive. His insolence would soon reach a climax! But

---

[244] An unusually long entry in Rétif's journal for 25 May 1786 recounts this incident in great detail and in terms very similar to his account here. See *Journal*, ¶735, vol. 1, p. 308, repr. in MHRA's French edition of *Ingénue Saxancour* (Appendix D, Excerpt 34). A similar account of this incident is found in the 'Supplément' that Rétif inserted at the end of vol. 23 of the second edition of *Les Contemporaines* [1788], also reprinted in MHRA's French edition of *Ingénue* (Appendix E, Excerpt 2).

[245] Located just north of the Louvre, the Palais-Royal originally served as a royal residence in the seventeenth century and then as the palace of the Duke d'Orléans, regent to Louis XV. In the 1770s, the d'Orléans family hired the prominent architect Victor Louis to transform their property into a vast complex of elegant boutiques, restaurants, cafés, gambling clubs, and public gardens, which soon became the commercial center of the capital and a favorite meeting place of fashionable Parisian society.

[246] *La Femme infidelle* was first published by Rétif in May 1786 under the penname Maribert-Courtenay (sometimes spelled Marivert). (See notes 28, 29, 118, and 278.) In one of two postscripts appended to the unabridged edition of *Ingénue Saxancour*, Maribert is again presented as a close friend of the narrator's family and as 'editor' of this equally controversial text, which the narrator is supposedly reluctant to publish. See the introductory section titled 'About the Text' for a discussion of Marivert-Courtenay's alleged role as editor of *Ingénue Saxancour*.

before explaining what happened, let us continue with the far happier story I interrupted concerning Mr. Saxancour's liaison with Félicité.

An older man in love is often ridiculous. So why is it that my father didn't appear that way? It's true that he was only fifty-two years old and was still young-looking. But, in my opinion, the real reason is that men of talent and distinction like him age better than others.[247] In any case, I believe that the appearance of ridicule is in the eye of the beholder, the person he loves. If she is tender-hearted and sincere, he will not appear ridiculous. It's only when she mocks him that he appears so; but, in that case, even a young man would look foolish. Félicité — whose affection for my father was based on esteem, even veneration — was both tender and passionate in her feelings for him. And, that being the case, her lover could adore her without appearing foolish. I witnessed their mutual tenderness, and it was a delight for me to see this attractive, refined, and widely admired young woman reject all her suitors and bring happiness to the most beloved of fathers.[248] I adored her as well, this lovely woman!

One day, I went to Félicité's apartment to invite her to dine with us, not realizing that my father had had the same idea. When I arrived, I found the door ajar, so I pushed it open. I caught sight of my father sitting in the next room with Félicité on his lap, wrapped in his arms. Surprised and a bit disconcerted, I stopped on the threshold, where I heard my father say:

---

[247] Another of Rétif's flattering self-portraits that, instead of expressing smug pride in himself, may reflect the insecurity of an aging womanizer.

[248] Félicité Mesnager was the last of Rétif's grand passions, but apparently she did not reciprocate his feelings for her — contrary to Rétif's claims and flattering self-portraits in *Ingénue Saxancour*. (See Cottin's preface to *Mes Inscripcions*, p. xxiii, and his note to ¶736, pp. 210–11.) Félicité actually had her sights on the older and wealthier Saint-Mars — a fact that Rétif himself recognizes in *Monsieur Nicolas*: 'When we arrived, I was impressed by Félicitette's warmth and charms! She frolicked with my daughters and the old chevalier [...]. At first, I greatly feared that the young lady would dash my fondest hopes by replacing Marion in the chevalier's affections. I was mistaken on this point, but not in the final outcome' (*Monsieur Nicolas*, 'Neuvième Epoque', *OC*, vol. 69, p. 3108). In the end, Saint-Mars chose to marry a 36-year-old woman of aristocratic Swiss origins — instead of either Mlle Mesnager or Marion. Despite the tensions caused by these rivalries, Agnès and Félicité remained close friends.

'My lovely, dearest Félicité! You've brought me such happiness, and I owe the recovery of my health to you! Yes, your divine caresses, your feelings for me that I would never have dared ask for or even dared hope for, have cured me of my malady. You're a celestial angel that I adore!'

And with these words, he clasped Félicité against his chest, and they exchanged the most tender kisses. Sinking into his arms, she said the sweetest, most passionate things to him, expressions I had never heard before or even imagined. As for me, I dared not speak and didn't know what to do. But their conduct remained strictly platonic, based as it was on the most affectionate esteem and mutual devotion. Félicité regained her composure, and the modesty of her expressions, the beauty of her feelings, and the delicacy of the compliments paid to her by Mr. Saxancour convinced me that it is not love so much as tenderness that heals an ailing heart.

What a difference between what I had just seen and Moresquin's behavior! Are he and my father alike in any way, even of the same species? I don't believe so. There are different kinds of men, perhaps as many as there are species of animals. Some, like Moresquin, resemble tigers or swine in their cruelty and nasty behavior. Others resemble donkeys, horses, or bulls; others are like sheep, and still others like goats, and so on. That's what the author suggests in an ingenious book I read titled *La Découverte australe*.[249] I heard someone declare that, in this enlightened age, no one in Paris had understood this book, except for two physicians, Dr. Guillelbert de Prévalet[250] and Dr. Lebègue de Prêle.[251]

* * *

But let us return to my dear friend Félicité. She was soon due to return to her country estate. And so she did all she could to strengthen Mr. Saxancour's health before her departure, giving him all the time she could take away from her business affairs. If she had to dine in town, it was he who accompanied her. She later told me that, as she went about her business, their conversation was always

---

[249] The book in question is *La Découverte australe par un homme volant, ou Le Dédale français* published by Rétif in 1781. In this curious work of science fiction, Rétif describes a futuristic travel odyssey in the vein of Etienne-Gabriel Morelly's *Naufrage des isles flottantes, ou Basiliade du célèbre Pilpaï* (1753) and Louis-Sébastien Mercier's *L'An 2440* (1771). It features a series of phantasmagoric illustrations picturing men and women with animal-like features reflecting their character, such as 'Les Hommes-cochons', 'Les Hommes-taureaux', and 'Les Hommes-ânes' [Pig-men, Bull-men, Donkey-men].

[250] *Guillebert de Prévalet*: Physician who treated Rétif for venereal disease. His controversial methods and publicity stunts eventually led the Faculté de Paris to revoke his license. On Guillebert's career and friendship with Rétif, see Baruch, *Restif de La Bretonne* (1996), p. 168.

[251] *Lebègue de Prêle*: Prominent eighteenth-century French physician who performed the autopsy on Jean-Jacques Rousseau in 1778.

delightful, based as it was on feelings that were never diminished by physical weakness.

It was decided that I would go with Félicité to the estate her brother had bought on the road to Normandy ten leagues from Paris. The estate was the ancestral home of a young writer who took Saint-Léger as her name.[252] We left on June 29th.

The first two and a half months of my stay in Montfort[253] (from late June until mid-September) were wonderful. Like my friend, I was warmly welcomed by everyone in the area. Her brother was extremely kind and attentive toward me. I made very pleasant acquaintances among the young people of the district. But my heart belonged entirely to Félicité. She spoke constantly to me of Mr. Saxancour. His portrait had recently been engraved[254] and, at her bedside, Félicité kept a copy, to which she sometime spoke and said the most touching things. One day when I witnessed this, I expressed my surprise to her, given the difference in age between them.[255]

'Ah! If you only knew how charming he is!' she exclaimed. 'He's one of those men who don't need to be young to be attractive and lovable. Even his preoccupation with his work has a certain charm, because people know it's genuine. Indeed, everything he says is heart-felt. If he pays a compliment, it's thoughtful and persuasive. He describes a woman's charms in a way that enhances

---

[252] Reference to the playwright and novelist Anne-Hyacinthe (Minette) de Saint-Léger (1761–1824), with whom Rétif became acquainted in April, 1782. Their correspondance continued until mid-1783, when the two friends had a falling out.

[253] Montfort-l'Amaury, 34 miles west of Paris. Elsewhere in the novel, the location of the Mesnagers' country house is given as Saint-Léger (Saint-Léger-en-Yvelines, 6 miles south of Montfort and about 38 miles southwest of Paris). Both villages are located in the forest of Rambouillet and correspond to the location described in the novel: 'à dix lieues de Paris, du côté de la Normandie' — about ten leagues from Paris on the way to Normandy. (In the eighteenth century, une lieue was roughly equivalent to four miles.) In Monsieur Nicolas, Rétif explains that Félicité's brother had recently bought a house and two farms in Montfort-l'Amaury from their mutual friend Saint-Mars. He also gives the reason for Agnès's extended visit with them: 'The brother, Prodiguer [Mesnager], [...] left with his sister on 29 June, taking with them my older daughter, whom they wanted to protect (they said) from the harassment inflicted on her by her despicable husband' (Monsieur Nicolas, 'Neuvième Epoque', OC, vol. 69, p. 3119). Regarding the Mesnagers' country house, Testud notes that Havard de La Montagne found the notarized bill of sale dated 19 May 1786, according to which Saint-Mars sold Félicité and her brother the house and two farms in Saint-Léger for 2,000 livres cash (roughly equivalent to €20,000 or $22,000) and 1,500 livres in annual rent (roughly equivalent to €15,000 or $16,000). See Monsieur Nicolas, ed. by Pierre Testud, vol. 2, p. 1354, n. 1 to p. 385.

[254] A new portrait of Rétif had recently been engraved — probably a reference to Binet's 1785 portrait of Rétif at age 51 engraved by Berthet (Figure 6 in this edition).

[255] In the summer of 1786, Rétif was in his early fifties and Félicité in her mid-thirties, so there was roughly a fifteen-year age difference between them.

her beauty and makes her feel deep affection for the man who fully appreciates those qualities.'[256]

That's the way the lovely Félicité spoke of my father. Alas, who would have thought that a man fifty-two years old would have left a woman with so many charms, grace, and the sparkle of youth. Yet that's what happened. Yet her only rival for my father's affections was preoccupation with his work.

I spent nearly five months[257] with my lovely friend. The first two months were, as I said, sheer delight. But in mid-September, I received a letter from Moresquin. It was only a page long and simply said that he knew about my stay in Saint-Léger. His letter poisoned the rest of my time there, since I expected to see him arrive at any moment and make a scene like the one at the Jardin du Roi. With every knock at the door, my heart began to pound. If I caught sight of someone when we left the house, I hid until I knew who it was. This constant anxiety made me ill, and I returned to Paris with a lingering fever.

Several times during my absence, Moresquin had made a scene with his son outside my father's apartment. In front of a crowd of onlookers, mainly working-class women of the neighborhood, he launched into another tirade against us. And, since he is the falsest of men, his version of events was no doubt the complete opposite of the truth. I heard about all the scandal he had caused when I returned. But I was under my father's protection and that of the law. We enjoyed a certain measure of peace and quiet until the 9th of February 1787.

That day marked the beginning of a new chapter in my story, but happily of short duration. It concerned Moresquin's last fit of rage and the one that proved the most disastrous for him.

---

[256] Another of Rétif's many smug self-portraits in the novel, which he amplifies further by claiming in the paragraph following that it was he (not Félicité) who broke off their relationship. He claims that he left her to devote himself to his work when, in fact, she left him for another man.

[257] According to Rétif's diary, Agnès spent four months (not five) with Félicité in Saint-Léger, from 29 June until 3 November 1786. (See *Journal*, ¶762 and ¶887, vol. 1, pp. 217, 260.) In his diary, Rétif also notes two other extended visits that Agnès paid to Félicité in Saint-Léger: a ten-week stay in 1787 (from 28 July to 8 October) and a three-month stay in 1788 (from 20 August to 1 December). See *Journal*, ¶1142, ¶1214, ¶1437, and 1541 (vol. 1, pp. 468, 493, 599, 632). Also see the chronology in Appendix A in the present edition.

The morning of February 9th, Moresquin rose very early to begin his operation. He went first to Montrouge to the home of Mr. Mercier,[258] author of *Tableau de Paris* and a close friend of my father's. But Mercier wasn't there; he was in Paris. Moresquin then went to the home of Mr. Letourneur[259] and had the temerity to ask to speak to him. He was shown into a room where five or six people had

FIGURE 26.   1797 Portrait of Louis-Sébastien Mercier by François de Bonneville. (BnF)

[258] Louis-Sébastien Mercier (1740–1814), French dramatist and writer, best known for his series *Le Tableau de Paris* (1781–1788). Rétif became friends with him in 1782, after Mercier published an enthusiastic review of Rétif's novel *Le Paysan perverti* in *Le Tableau de Paris*.

[259] Pierre Le Tourneur (1736–88), French author and translator, best known for his translations of Shakespeare and of the pre-Romantic English poets of the eighteenth century (the so-called Graveyard School). He was named secretary to the Count d'Artois and royal censor. It was perhaps in this latter role that Rétif made his acquaintance.

gathered; and, there, in the presence of people who all knew and greatly respected Mr. Saxancour, this madman spewed forth a torrent of dreadful calumnies. It seems likely that he had been planning this performance for a long time and that it was a final attack he wanted to make, without worrying much about the consequences. He seemed to feel that, however difficult his relationship with Mr. Saxancour might be, the fact of being his son-in-law was a social promotion for him and he was taking advantage of it in his own bizarre way. However, the things he said with the intention of causing a scandal didn't have the effect he expected. What he said was so outrageous that the people listening to him thought he was completely deranged. But Mr. Letourneur was nevertheless shaking with indignation and horror, and with good cause! Just imagine his shock and that of his guests to hear Moresquin accuse me, as well as my father, of every conceivable crime.[260] Word was spreading about his behavior. And after this latest incident, my father's friends all insisted on the need to stop him because a man capable of what he was doing was capable of anything.

On his way back to Paris from Montrouge, where he had left everyone at Mr. Letourneur's shocked and upset, Moresquin encountered the Viscount of T***,[261] the kindest, most honest of men. Moresquin let out a torrent of insults against Mr. Saxancour that was so outrageous that the usually mild-mannered viscount indignantly replied:

'Now I know what you're really like. Your own words have revealed your true character. You're only hurting yourself by speaking this way.'[262]

Mr. Saxancour heard about this exchange from the viscount himself that same evening. But both men were unaware of what had happened in Montrouge. It was only two days later that my father learned about that earlier incident from Mr. Mercier, first in a letter and afterwards in person.

Outraged, my father felt he should no longer show any consideration for a scoundrel whose behavior compelled us to unmask him. He drafted a judicial memoir[263] with an exact account of the facts that I delivered to my attorney. The

---

[260] This incident is confirmed by a brief note in 'Mes Ouvrages', where Rétif indicates that Augé 'went to say horrible things against us […] to Mercier, to that sly hypocrite Letourneur, etc.' (*Monsieur Nicolas*, vol. 2, p. 986).

[261] Charles Gaspard de Toustain, Viscount of Toustain-Richebourg, historian, author, and royal censor. He was Rétif's close friend and the last censor to whom Rétif's works were submitted for approval for publication, including *Ingénue Saxancour*. See Havard de La Montagne, 'Le vicomte de Toustain-Richebourg, ami et dernier censeur de Rétif de La Bretonne', *Etudes rétiviennes*, 14 (1991), 99–135.

[262] In his diary entry for 9 February 1787, Rétif notes: 'This evening, Toustain […] saw the monster Augé, who spoke to him in a fit of rage; the viscount is now completely against him' (*Journal*, ¶974).

[263] In this passage of *Ingénue Saxancour*, Rétif suggests that he began writing his 'Mémoire contre Augé' in mid-February (1787). However, entries in his diary indicate that he began drafting this summary account of his son-in-law's offenses on 8 August 1785. (See *Journal*,

account is shorter than what I've presented here because we omitted the most appalling incidents to minimize the scandal they would cause if they were revealed in court. My father then had Moresquin dismissed from his job, thanks to the intervention of someone in a position of authority.[264] The wretch was fired on February 19, ten days after his outrageous behavior on the 9th, the effects of which he had prolonged by repeating his calumnies in various houses in the days following.

Moresquin remained as despicable and mediocre as ever. However, now he was out of work and no longer backed by the stupid chatter of Mégas, Lapropre, Goupillon, and the other vile characters who worked for Mr. Olaüs-Magnus and who misled him out of envy toward my father. After he was fired, Moresquin left us alone, except for a written statement against us that he gave to Mégas, who later showed it to my father. This statement was so impertinent and inane that it inspired nothing but scorn. Nevertheless, my father was offended that Mégas brought it to him and so refused to ever see him again.[265]

Following Moresquin's latest offenses, we pushed ahead with separation proceedings. Through the testimony of two eyewitnesses, we were able to prove what happened at the Jardin du Roi — the slaps Moresquin gave me and his tirade at the guard station. Then thirty people bore witness to the scandalous remarks he made in Montrouge in front of Mr. Letourneur and his friends and later in Paris in front of a number of trustworthy people. Especially important was the testimony given by a lovely lady,[266] whose beauty, virtue, and charm have brought

---

¶527, vol. 1, p. 192.) Repeated references to the *mémoire* in Rétif's diary in late summer and fall of 1785 show that he devoted many hours to this document, a first version of which was completed in early December and inserted into his diary entry for 4 December 1785. This first version was given to Agnès's lawyer Cavagnac to counter the legal action Augé had taken on 2 December 1785 in a failed attempt to force his wife to return to him. In the months of court proceedings leading up to the final separation hearing in March 1787, Rétif continued to revise and expand his judicial memoir to include accounts of further incidents involving Augé and additional complaints against him. A final reference to the drafting of the *mémoire* is found in Rétif's diary entry for 25 February 1787: 'Went to see Madame Bleret [Blérie's sister-in-law] to talk about the monster; added material to the memoir against him [...]; finished the memoir' (*Journal*, ¶990, vol. 1, p. 426). See the chronology in Appendix A and the full text of the 4 December 1785 version of the 'Mémoire contre Augé' in Appendix D, Excerpt 25, in MHRA's French edition of *Ingénue Saxancour*.

[264] In his diary, Rétif indicates that his son-in-law was fired thanks to the intervention of Le Pelletier, director of the office where Augé worked, to whom he owed his job. (See *Journal*, ¶996, vol. 1, p. 428.)

[265] An alternate version of this passage adds the following sentence: 'I heard that Mégas kept Moresquin on as a clerk, which proves they're in league with each other' [cited by Baruch, *Restif de La Bretonne* (2002), p. 446, note a].

[266] Rétif is referring here to Countess Fanny de Beauharnais (1737–1813), salonnière, woman of letters, and godmother to the future Empress Joséphine, wife of Napoleon I. Her home in the Hôtel d'Entragues, rue de Tournon in Paris, was among the best-known salons in the years

Figure 27.   *Le Spectateur présentant à Fanny Marion R**. Illustration from *Les Nuits de Paris* (1788–94), vol. 7. Frontispiece to Part 14 picturing Rétif ('le Spectateur Nocturne') introducing his daughter Marion to Countess Fanny de Beauharnais (1737–1813), salonnière and woman of letters. Artist unknown. The original caption reads: 'Soyez la protectrice, femme digne de tous les hommages!' [Estimable lady, worthy of everyone's admiration and respect, deign to be a guardian angel to my daughters!] (BnF)

great happiness to her husband and to a son the same age as mine, but much happier. Our separation was finally granted,[267] based less on my attorney's judicial memoir than on the one my father and I presented.

I returned for another visit with Félicité, with whom I spent three and a half months in the summer and early fall of 1787.[268] I've been dividing my time this way between Félicité, my father, and my beloved sister, whose charms and endearing naïveté are rivaled only by those of my lovely friend. And it's in this blissful tranquility that I've undertaken to write these memoirs in which I've recalled cruel moments from my past only to better appreciate my present happiness.

Yet our happiness is only an illusion! How sad is our destiny! We are like birds perched on a branch, as the hunter lies in wait.

I'm finishing this memoir in Normandy during another visit with my friend and her brother.[269] They too have endured misfortunes, and that's what draws us together; but they at least now have nothing more to fear! ...[270]

---

leading up to the 1789 Revolution. It was a meeting place for literary figures such as the poet Dorat, Rétif de La Bretonne, Mercier, Cubières-Palmézeaux, and Olympe de Gouges. In the 1780s, Madame de Beauharnais became close friends with Rétif and his younger daughter Marion.

[267] After many months of legal suits, countersuits, complaints to the police, and court proceedings, Agnès finally obtained a legal separation from Augé in March 1787. In his diary entry for 18 March 1787, Rétif writes: 'The monster Augé said that [...] I won in civil court, but that I'll lose in criminal court' (*Journal*, ¶1010, vol. 1, p. 432). According to Marc Chadourne, the court ordered Agnès to reside with her in-laws outside Paris: 'After an investigation and hearing, the magistrate decreed in March that Agnès would not have to return to live with her grim husband, but would instead leave her father's to live in the home of her father-in-law!' [Chadourne, *Restif de La Bretonne, ou le siècle prophétique* (Paris: Hachette, 1958), p. 257.] However, entries in Rétif's diary make clear that Agnès continued to live with her father in Paris until her divorce was finalized in February 1794, except for several extended stays with friends outside the capital. See the chronology in Appendix A.

[268] Rétif's diary indicates that Agnès left for Saint-Léger on 28 July 1787 (*Journal*, ¶1142, vol. 1, p. 312) and that she returned to Paris on 8 October of that year (*Journal*, ¶1214, vol. 1, p. 493), after a two and a half-month stay.

[269] According to Rétif's diary, Agnès spent three months in Saint-Léger in the late summer and early fall of 1788. However, the diary also indicates that *Ingénue Saxancour* was completed in April of that year. (See *Journal*, ¶1437, vol. 2, p. 599 & ¶1410, vol. 2, p. 562.)

[270] These ellipses (and all those appearing in this edition without brackets) are found in the original text. Ellipses appearing *with* brackets indicate where material has been cut in the present edition.

1. *Postscript.* As Ingénue wrote these final words of her memoirs, she felt a sense of foreboding come over her. She didn't have the time to add anything more.

After returning from her last stay with Félicité, Ingénue found a semblance of happiness in her father's house. She took charge of assisting him in his work and serving as his secretary. She was delighted to see his business prosper, and her labors were rewarded with the satisfaction derived from a job well done. She was more beloved than ever by Mr. Saxancour and closer than ever to her lovely sister. As for Marion, she had the rare good fortune to become friends with a highly respected noblewoman[271] who showed her the warmest affection. And so the two sisters were each happy in their own right — a joy increased at the sight of their father's sweet satisfaction.

But Moresquin was still lurking in the background. The Saxancours had nearly forgotten about him, but that monster certainly had not forgotten about them! He kept a close watch on the family, waiting for a chance to taint or destroy their happiness! … And, sure enough, an outrageous incident occurred that showed how dishonest the human race can be! The servant of an attorney who was among their neighbors had reason to believe that her watch had been stolen.[272] Moresquin heard about it and had the gall to accuse his sister-in-law! He wrote two vile and stupid letters worthy of their author, one to Mr. Saxancour himself and the other to Madame Bitez, the same aunt mentioned in these memoirs […].[273]

Outraged by these despicable letters, Mr. Saxancour planned to seek redress from the courts and have their author punished. But then he fell ill and was unable to follow through on his plan. He died, leaving his daughters in a new predicament!

Although legally separated, Ingénue was accosted by the monster, who at first tried to win her over with sweet talk. Filled with horror, she pushed him away. He made a few more attempts to win her back. Realizing that his efforts were useless, he flew into a rage and, with the side of his hand, dealt her a blow to the neck that broke her vertebrae. She collapsed and survived for only a few hours. Carried dying to her sister, Ingénue summoned the strength to speak and to accuse her murderer.[274]

---

[271] Allusion to Countess Fanny de Beauharnais who, in 1787, became a close friend to the Rétif family and to Marion in particular.

[272] On 10 November 1788, a watch was indeed stolen from Poincloud, Rétif's neighbor and landlord of the building where Rétif had lived since 1781. According to Rétif, Poincloud wrongly accused Marion of stealing the watch and forced the Rétifs to move out. This incident is the focus of the short story titled 'Les Propriétaires de maison' published in 1788 in *Les Nuits de Paris*.

[273] Almost unintelligible due to spelling errors and lack of punctuation, these two letters are included in Baruch's 2003 edition of *Ingénue Saxancour*, pp. 608–9. They are supposedly the original letters sent by Augé in which he accuses Marion of stealing their neighbor's watch and insists that his wife should leave such a disreputable household and return to him and their son.

[274] In 'La Fillette reconnue', one of the stories included in *Le Drame de la vie*, Rétif imagines

As soon as Marion knew who was responsible for her sister's death, she hurried to denounce the crime and to seek revenge with the help of a respectable lady, the Countess of B*** who used her influence to have Moresquin punished quietly to avoid a scandal.[275] It was one of those occasions that show the efficacy of the king's ability to exercise his paternal powers to deal with crimes that might otherwise go unpunished.[276] The crime committed by Moresquin could have brought dishonor to a blameless son and compromised his future; although shame is a well-deserved punishment for scoundrels, it is unjustly inflicted on innocent family members. Rightly convicted for murdering his wife and for all his earlier crimes, Moresquin was sent to a penal colony in the Caribbean [...]. There, he is known under the pseudonym L'Echiné to avoid bringing dishonor to his family. His son is being raised by his aunt Marion whose pure heart and gentle nature are teaching him to love virtues and qualities unknown to his guilty father.

2. *Postscript.* In response to the two despicable letters he had received from Moresquin,[277] Mr. Saxancour wrote an angry letter expressing all the contempt he felt for that scoundrel. He reminded him of all his vile deeds, all the transgressions recounted in these memoirs. He underscored Moresquin's repeated threats to murder him, including those in front of the director of the

---

a death equally melodramatic for his wife Agnès Lebègue and for his son-in-law Augé (called Kugé in the story): On 30 June 1793, Kugé murders his mother-in-law, along with a passerby, before being shot and killed himself. See Appendix E, Excerpt 4, in MHRA's French edition of *Ingénue Saxancour.*

[275] Another allusion to Madame de Beauharnais, who did in fact intervene in the Rétif family's disputes with Augé.

[276] Allusion to *lettres de cachet*. Signed by the king of France, countersigned by one of his ministers, and sealed with the royal seal (*cachet*), *lettres de cachet* contained orders directly from the king, often to enforce arbitrary actions and judgments that could not be appealed. The majority of *lettres de cachet* were penal, by which a subject was sentenced without trial to imprisonment, confinement in a convent or a hospital, transportation to the colonies, or exile to another part of the realm or outside the realm altogether. Wealthy or powerful individuals sometimes obtained them to deal with troublesome relations. A prominent symbol of the abuses of the ancien régime, *lettres de cachet* were abolished by the revolutionary government.

[277] Allusion to the two letters mentioned in the first postscript.

Jardin des Plantes after striking Ingénue in the garden. He warned him of the severity of the courts toward reprobates like him and ended by calling down the wrath of God upon him with the kind of vehemence that Heaven could only approve.

The particular circumstances and motives behind the publication of these memoirs were then explained in these terms:

'It is I, *Marivert*,[278] who now take up the pen to complete this work that I'm publishing without the authorization either of my friend Mr. Saxancour or of his daughter Ingénue [...]. I solemnly declare that I have carefully recorded everything I heard; that I endeavored to obtain copies of all the documents and letters so I could include them in this conclusion. I feel that it is my duty as a friend. I sometimes shudder when I think that if Mr. Saxancour were to die, then two lovely and timid young women would be exposed to all the rage, wickedness, and zeal that villainy can produce. That is the reason why I'm publishing these memoirs, for this pilfering of sorts, for the artful discretion with which I'm hiding this publication from the people involved, who are unlikely to notice it among the flood of works appearing every day in Paris. Moreover, as I explain in the preface, it's the great, indeed immeasurable public good served by this work — that of edifying young women — that has compelled me to publish it. I realize that's saying a lot! But even though I'm betraying my friends' trust in a way, I feel that my decision is fully justified ... I shall now return to my chronicle of events, which I interrupted at the most crucial moment.'

Mr. Marivert then recounts the actions taken by Mr. Saxancour against the two female servants who slandered Marion and against Moresquin, whose crimes he denounced in his detailed memoir to two magistrates, the one who could be called the 'Avenger of Crimes' and the other magistrate who dealt with the vice squad. [...] He tells how the Countess de Beauville[279] met with the two magistrates and furnished them with the relevant details in a series of letters. Moresquin was summoned by the 'Avenger of Crimes' who had only to listen to him to know what kind of a man he was. After that, he was summoned by a police lieutenant from the vice squad, who treated him with the severity he deserved. But nothing could stop him. For not only is Moresquin a scoundrel, he's also a madman. And so, after trying to restrain him in every possible way, the situation seemed hopeless. That's when the efficacy of *lettres de cachet*[280] became clear, as

---

[278] For a discussion of the role attributed to Marivert-Courtenay (sometimes spelled Maribert) in Rétif's works, see the section titled 'About the Text' and notes 28, 29, 118, and 246 above.

[279] Another homage to the efforts that Madame de Beauharnais made on behalf of Rétif and his family.

[280] See note 276 above.

did the soundness of the king's response to the criticisms leveled against their use. The family was forced to have recourse to this means of detention. But, alas! it was too late, because the unfortunate Ingénue Saxancour had already been killed! ... There's no doubt that, in another era with more robust laws, this tragedy might well have been prevented ... So let us respect the laws and obey our head of State, our father and protector![281]

---

[281] For the original French text of the two postscripts, see Appendix E, Excerpts 1 and 2, in MHRA's French edition of *Ingénue Saxancour*.

APPENDIX A

~

Chronology of Agnès Rétif's Story

The following chronology concerning Agnès Rétif and her marriage is largely based on dates given in Rétif's journal.[282] These dates generally coincide with dates given for the same or similar events in Rétif's autobiographical works *La Femme infidelle*, *Ingénue Saxancour*, and *Monsieur Nicolas*. More complete chronologies of Rétif's life and works appear in Pierre Testud's critical edition of *Monsieur Nicolas* (Paris: Gallimard, 1998), vol. 1, pp. xxvii–liii, and in his edition of Rétif's diary *Mes Inscripcions (1779–1785); Journal (1785–1789)* (Paris: Editions Manucius, 2006), pp. 825–40.

1760

April 22: Marriage of Nicolas-Edme Rétif and Agnès Lebègue.

1761

March 10: Birth of Agnès Rétif, elder daughter and first child of Rétif de La Bretonne and his wife Agnès Lebègue.

---

[282] Rétif kept a secret diary in which he wrote brief entries each morning about his work and experiences the previous day: people encountered, anniversaries celebrated or mourned, manuscripts begun, continued, or completed. The handwritten diary for November 1779 through August 1787 was discovered in the 1880s in the Archives de la Bastille at the Bibliothèque de l'Arsenal and first published in a critical edition by Paul Cottin under the title *Mes Inscripcions. Journal Intime de Restif de La Bretonne* (Paris: Plon, 1889). An electronic version of Cottin's edition is available in vol. 56 of the 1988 Slatkine reprint edition of Rétif's complete works though the Bibliothèque Nationale's on-line catalogue. The continuation of Rétif's diary (from 20 August 1787 through 12 June 1796) was later discovered in the archives of the Bibliothèque Nationale of France. The entire handwritten manuscript has been re-transcribed and published in Testud's far more complete and accurate critical edition. Unless indicated otherwise, references to Rétif's diary are to Pierre Testud's two-volume edition: *Mes inscripcions, 1779–1785; Journal, 1785–1789* (Paris: Editions Manucius, 2006) and *Journal. Volume II, 1790–1796* (Paris: Editions Manucius, 2010). For more information about Rétif's diary and its publication history, see Appendix D in MHRA's French edition of *Ingénue Saxancour* and 'About the Author' in the present edition.

1776

June: Agnès Rétif is apprenticed at the age of 15 to a dressmaker, rue Saint-Denis in Paris.

1778

Agnès returns to live with her father.

1779

November 5: Rétif carves his first inscription into the stone embankment of the Ile Saint-Louis. This was the first in a long series of dates and memories he carved (often in abbreviated Latin) from November 1779 through the summer of 1785 during his daily walks on his beloved island. On September 1 of that year, Rétif began transcribing these entries into a notebook in order to preserve them. Thus were born *Mes Inscripcions*, the diary to which he added brief entries every morning concerning his work and experiences the previous day.

1780

March: While living at her aunt Bizet's home on quai de Gesvres in Paris, Agnès Rétif attracts the attention of Charles-Marie Augé, a 35-year-old childless widower living in the neighborhood.

August 9: In a letter to Rétif, Charles-Marie Augé asks for his daughter's hand in marriage.

September 30: Rétif's wife Agnès Lebègue leaves Paris to take care of her mother's succession in Burgundy and is absent for nearly four months.

November: Rétif makes the acquaintance of the chevalier de Saint-Mars, after having corresponded with him since July of that year.[283]

1781

January: Agnès receives a love letter from Augé.

January 21: Agnès Lebègue returns to Paris. With encouragement from her mother and her Aunt Bizet, Agnès Rétif agrees to marry Augé, despite her father's opposition.

---

[283] Monsieur de Saint-Mars, chevalier de Saint-Louis, field marshal and inspector general of artillery. Havard de La Montagne identifies him as François de Formanoir, born at Montfort-l'Amaury in 1716.

May 1: Marriage of Agnès and Augé.[284] Agnès moves into her husband's apartment rue de la Mortellerie (now rue de l'Hôtel de Ville), near the quai de Gesvres.

Late May: Three weeks after their wedding, Augé beats his parents' maid and begins to mistreat Agnès on a daily basis.

Mid-July: Augé beats his wife in front of his mother, who comes to her defense.

July 14: Rétif moves from his apartment rue de Bièvre to 10 rue des Bernardins, where his wife joins him.

October: Agnès, six months pregnant, is savagely kicked in the torso by her husband.

October 23: On her father's birthday, Agnès writes to him for the first time since her marriage asking for his forgiveness, announcing her pregnancy to him, and asking him to visit her.

December 28: Birth of Jean-Nicolas Augé, son of Agnès Rétif and her husband Charles-Marie.

1782

April: Agnès realizes she is pregnant again.

October: Rétif initiates a correspondence and friendship with the young playwright and novelist Anne-Hyacinthe (Minette) de Saint-Léger (1761–1824). Their correspondence continues until mid-1783 when the two friends have a falling out.

Mid-December: Agnès flees from Augé for the first time and takes refuge at the home of her Aunt Bizet, but returns to her husband the same night accompanied by her aunt's servant.

Late December: Premature birth of Agnès's second child, a daughter who dies in infancy?[285]

---

[284] Rétif did not attend his daughter's wedding, nor did he even record the date in his diary. He may have blotted out the event from his memory, either because it was too painful or because he was so caught up in his affair with Sara/Elise Debée — or perhaps for both reasons. In his diary entry for 18 February 1781, he wrote: 'Sara told me horrible things about her mother that I recounted in *La Dernière avanture d'un homme de 45 ans*. I comforted her; I promised to serve as her father and, since my real daughter was marrying against my wishes, that she would take her place in my heart' (*Journal*, ¶31, vol. 1, pp. 51–52). Rétif did not mention Agnès again in his diary until his first visit to her more than two years later in November 1783. Yet his entry for 1 January 1785 reflects the intense pain her marriage caused him and his obsessive hatred of Augé (see *Journal*, ¶460, vol. 1, pp. 165–66).

[285] In *Ingénue Saxancour*, we read: 'It was New Year's Day 178[3], four days after the birth of my daughter.' And in *La Femme infidelle*, after describing Ingénue's mistreatment following

1783

January 1: Augé threatens Agnès with his sword at home in front of witnesses; she flees to her aunt's for the second time, but returns to her husband soon after.

Late June or early July: Possible first visit of Rétif to his daughter.[286]

October 9 (Feast day of Saint-Denis): Agnès's first meeting with Blérie de Sériville (called Fromentel in *Ingénue Saxancour* and Rizblé in *La Femme infidelle*).

October [23?]: Agnès writes to her father a second time.

November 25: Rétif visits Agnès at her home.[287]

Late December: Possible birth of a third child to Agnès and Augé.[288]

---

the birth of her son, Rétif writes: 'A few months later, when I was pregnant for the second time with my daughter, who was born sickly and died in infancy, he punched me so violently in the head that I fainted' (*OC*, vol. 45, p. 799). He later attributes the child's death to the mistreatment she suffered during that pregnancy (*OC*, vol. 45, p. 831). Baruch points out that 'there is no documentary evidence of the birth of this second child, nor is it mentioned in Rétif's diary' [Baruch, *Restif de La Bretonne* (2002), vol. 2, p. 406, n. 1]. However, given that Rétif and his daughter remained estranged until November 1783, it would hardly be surprising that no mention of her daughter's birth or death is found in his diary.

[286] Among the letters appended to the end of *La Femme infidelle* is a letter from Ingénue to her father purportedly written two years after the first letter — hence in October 1783 (perhaps on his birthday, the 23rd). In this letter, she alludes to a visit with her father three and a half months earlier (hence in late June or early July 1783). In *Ingénue Saxancour*, Ingénue also receives a visit from her father in late June or early July, but in 1784 (not 1783) — eight months *after* his first visit in November 1783. Rétif may have confused or conflated the dates. Since there is no mention of either of these summer visits in Rétif's diary, perhaps neither visit actually occurred.

[287] Rétif's diary entry for for 25 November 1783 reads: '*Pax. Agnetem*. Peace is proclaimed. I go to visit Agnès' (*Journal*, ¶309, vol. 1, p. 130). Louis XVI had proclaimed this date a day of celebration for the signing of the Treaty of Versailles between France and Britain that ended hostilities between those two countries following the American Revolutionary War. This late November visit to Agnès is mentioned in both *Ingénue Saxancour* and *La Femme infidelle* (*OC*, vol. 45, p. 811).

[288] In *Ingénue Saxancour*, Ingénue's second child is born one year after her first child (hence in December 1782). In *La Femme infidelle*, in a letter purportedly written to her father the following fall, Ingénue claims to be seven and a half months pregnant. (See Appendix C, Excerpt 4, in MHRA's French edition of *Ingénue Saxancour*.) The hypothesis that Agnès was pregnant three times, three years in a row, is supported by the mention of *three* children born to Ingénue in *La Femme infidelle*: 'After four years of drudgery and three children, one of whom died because of the mistreatment I endured during my pregnancy, I deserve a far better salary than a few towels, a few handkerchiefs, and two pairs of sheets' (*OC*, vol. 45, p. 831). Given Augé's sexual proclivities and the lack of reliable birth control at that time, three pregnancies in a row would hardly have been surprising.

1784

April: Rétif becomes acquainted with Louis Le Pelletier de Morfontaine, director of Paris's municipal administration, who later hires Augé as a clerk at Rétif's request in the hope of restraining his behavior.

June 19: Augé arrives uninvited at the home of Rétif's friend Grimod de la Reynière in an unsuccessful attempt to speak to his father-in-law.

late June/early July: Rétif visits with Agnès?[289]

1785

January 2: Rétif's younger daughter Marion returns to live with her father, after living for five years with the Garnier sisters in Paris on the rue Mouffetard.

January 12: Rétif goes to Agnès's home to tell her that his friend abbé Montlinot has recommended Augé for a job with Le Pelletier de Morfontaine, prévôt des marchands (head of the municipal administration in Paris). Agnès begins to describe her husband's mistreatment to her father for the first time, but is interrupted when Augé returns home, quarrels with Rétif, and threatens him with his cane.

January 15: Rétif meets with Le Pelletier, who agrees to hire Augé as a way of restraining his behavior.

January 30: Augé begins his new position working as a clerk in the office of Legrand, secretary to Le Pelletier.

January 31: Agnès flees again from her husband and takes refuge at the home of their friend Blérie de Sérivillé. Dismayed to learn that Blérie is not married and fearing that Agnès's legal position and reputation might be compromised, Rétif takes her to his apartment for the night and then back to Augé the following day.[290]

---

[289] This visit is mentioned in *Ingénue Saxancour*, but not in Rétif's diary. Nor it is mentioned in the narrative of *La Femme infidelle*, where we read: 'Papa came to visit me twice: once at the end of 178*, and the second time in January of last year. He didn't visit again for a long time due to the distress my situation caused him' (*OC*, vol. 45, p. 811). The first visit mentioned here would have been on 25 November 1783 and the second on 12 January 1785 (both mentioned in Rétif's diary and in *Ingénue Saxancour*). It may be that the visit in June or July 1784 referred to in *Ingénue Saxancour* never actually occurred or that Rétif confused it with a visit with his daughter the summer before (alluded to in letter 36 at the end of *La Femme infidelle*, but not mentioned in his diary).

[290] This incident is recorded in Rétif's diary entry for 31 January 1785 (*Journal*, ¶479, vol. 1, p. 172) and described in greater detail in *Monsieur Nicolas* ('Neuvième Epoque', *OC*, vol. 69, pp. 3100–01). See Appendix B, Excerpt 4, in MHRA's French edition of *Ingénue Saxancour*.

February 20: Suffering from urinary complications from gonorrhea, Rétif falls gravely ill, but gradually recovers in the weeks following.

Late February: Agnès flees to her parents' home, but her mother forces her to return because of her father's illness.

March 10: Agnès flees to her parents' home again, but returns to her husband two days later under pressure from her mother because of her father's poor health.[291]

March 18: Agnès flees to her parents' home once again. Her father, still ailing, sends her back to her husband the same day, accompanied by her sister.

March 28: In his diary, Rétif notes that he dined with Agnès that evening, who told him of the escalation in Augé's violence against her.

March 30: In a conversation with his friend Toustain-Richebourg noted in his diary, Rétif expresses his concern for Agnès's safety and his hatred of Augé.

May 23: Rétif completes the manuscript of *La Femme infidelle*.

Late May or early June: The Augés are invited to stay with Blérie at his brother's house in the country for the three-day Pentecost holiday, but are asked to leave after one night because of Augé's outrageous behavior.

July 21: After a brutal beating, Agnès flees from her husband, this time definitively. Rétif accepts her decision to separate from Augé and takes her to the home of the engraver Louis Berthet and his wife rue Saint-Jacques, where she stays four months.

July 23: Rétif receives a letter for Agnès from Augé in which he appears to consent to her decision to leave him.[292]

July 26: Second letter from Blérie to Agnès in which he recounts an unpleasant visit from her jealous husband. A few days earlier, after Agnès left her husband, Blérie had sent a first letter thanking her for entrusting her songbirds to him and promising to take good care of them.[293]

---

[291] This incident is recorded in Rétif's diary entry for 10 March 1785 (*Journal*, ¶491, vol. 1, p. 177). However, the events in *Ingénue Saxancour* described as having taken place in late February and on 18 March 1785 are not mentioned in Rétif's diary.

[292] See Appendix C, Excerpt 5, in MHRA's French edition of *Ingénue Saxancour*. Subsequent letters from Augé are also found in Appendix C, Excerpts 13, 18, 24, and 27.

[293] In his entry for 30 October 1785, Rétif notes that he had discovered letters from Blérie to Agnès, addressed to her using the pseudonym Madame Dulis at the Berthets' apartment where she had been staying (*Journal*, ¶548, vol. 1, p. 204). Then in his diary entry for 20 November 1785, he refers to six letters Agnès received from Blérie in the summer of that year. The originals of three of the letters were found in the Archives de la Bastille at the Bibliothèque de l'Arsenal

July 29: Third letter from Blérie to Agnès inviting her to visit him. In a fourth letter, sent sometime in August, Blérie laments the scandal that Augé's accusations against him have caused, but still encourages her to come visit him.

August 8: Rétif begins drafting a summary account of his son-in-law's mistreatment of Agnès over the course of their four-year marriage and the deceptions leading up to it. Repeated references to this 'Mémoire contre Augé' in Rétif's diary in late summer and fall show that Rétif devoted many hours to this document, a first version of which was completed in early December and inserted into his diary entry for 4 December (1785). However, in the months leading up to the final separation hearing, Rétif continued to document further incidents involving Augé and his complaints against him. A final reference to the *mémoire* is found in Rétif's diary entry for 25 February 1787.

August 10: Rétif confronts Augé at his office and reproaches him for his mistreatment of Agnès in front of his superior Legrand. He sends a letter of explanation to Legrand the following day.

August 20: Rétif completes the eighth chapter ('VIIIe Epoque') of *Monsieur Nicolas* that summarizes his daughter's unhappy marriage.

August 28: In a cryptic note to Agnès, Blérie writes: 'J'ai de fortes raisons de garder le silence' [There are compelling reasons for me to remain silent]. The reason for his silence is explained in the sixth and final letter he sent her on September 3.

September 1: To preserve the dates and memories associated with them he had carved into the stone embankment of the Ile Saint-Louis, Rétif begins transcribing them into a notebook. Thus were born *Mes Inscripcions*, the diary to which he added brief entries every morning concerning his work and experiences.

September 3: In a final letter to Agnès, Blérie explains that he will no longer be able to see her or write to her for fear of losing his job due to the scandal caused by Augé's accusations over his involvement with her.

September 17: Rétif and Agnès meet with Augé's father, who agrees that Agnès should remain separated from Augé.

(manuscript 12.469, fols 64 to 66, microfilm R106396); the others are in the Bibliothèque Nationale's collection (N.A.F. 3300, fols 81 to 84). The letters are reprinted in the 'Annexes' to Ned Rival's biography *Rétif de La Bretonne, ou Les amours perverties* (Paris, 1982), pp. 303–06. The dates Rival provides for two of the letters (based on Cottin's notes) appear to be incorrect. According to Testud, only four of the letters are dated: 26 July, 29 July, 28 August, and 3 September (see *Journal*, vol. 2, pp. 217–18, n. 7). Relevant passages from Blérie's six letters are found in Appendix C, Excerpts 6 through 11, in MHRA's French edition of *Ingénue Saxancour*.

September 19: During a meeting at his office with his father and father-in-law, Augé agrees to send Agnès written permission to live apart from him.[294] They draw up a 'Projet de séparation,' which Augé later refuses to sign.[295]

September 21: In a letter to Agnès, Augé urges her to came back to him, to which she replies that she would rather die than ever return to him.[296]

October 18: During a religious procession through the streets of Paris, Augé catches sight of Agnès looking out the window of the Berthets' apartment and angrily confronts her.

October 20: Agnès moves her possessions out of her husband's home to the Berthets' where she had been staying since July 21. Aside from a two-week stay in Gentilly, she remains with the Berthets until late November.

October 23: During an evening stroll with friends on the Ile St-Louis, Rétif is angrily accosted by Augé.

October 30: Rétif discovers several letters Agnès had received from Blérie during the summer, addressed to her using the pseudonym Madame Dulis[297] at the Berthets' apartment where she had been staying. For the moment, he decides not to mention this correspondence.[298]

November 3: Agnès leaves the Berthet's home to spend two weeks at the country home of friends (probably Blérie's brother and sister-in-law) near Gentilly.[299]

---

[294] In his diary entry for 19 September 1785, Rétif notes: 'Verbal agreement in Le Pelletier's office [Augé's employer] between Augé's father, myself, and the *Monster*, who promised to give us written consent to my daughter's freedom' (*Journal*, ¶540, vol. 1, p. 198).

[295] Among the documents that Rétif appended to *La Femme infidelle* is a separation agreement that begins with the following article: 'I, the undersigned, declare that I give consent to my wife to remain separated from me until such time that we reach a mutual agreement to reunite' (*Femme infidelle*, *OC*, vol. 45, p. 862). See Appendix C, Excerpt 12, in MHRA's French edition of *Ingénue Saxancour*. However, this agreement was never put into place because Augé, on the advice of his attorneys, refused to sign it. It was not until March 1787 — a year and a half later — that Agnès finally obtained a legal separation from her husband.

[296] See copies of the letters in Appendix C, Excerpts 13 and 14, in MHRA's French edition of *Ingénue Saxancour*.

[297] In his notes to his edition of *Ingénue Saxancour*, Baruch points out that Dulis was one of Rétif's favorite pseudonyms. See Baruch, *Restif de La Bretonne* (2002), vol. 2, p. 587, n. 1.

[298] See diary entry ¶548 in Appendix D, Excerpt 3, in MHRA's French edition of *Ingénue Saxancour*. Commenting on this correspondence, Cottin writes: 'They leave no doubt concerning the tender feelings that Agnès and Blérie felt for each other' (Cottin, *Mes Inscripcions*, p. 134, n. 1).

[299] In his diary entry for that day, Rétif writes: 'I reluctantly agree to let Agnès go to Gentilly' (*Journal*, ¶550, vol. 1, p. 205). In *La Femme infidelle*, he notes that Blérie's brother and sister-in-law had a house there. This would explain his opposition to Agnès's trip; he no doubt feared that she would see Blérie there.

November 18: Agnès returns from Gentilly to Paris. In his diary, Rétif notes that he attempts to seduce her that evening and almost succeeds.[300]

November 20: After discovering another letter Agnès had received from Blérie during the summer, Rétif confronts her and expresses his strong disapproval of their liaison.

November 26: After a heated argument with Rétif over her alleged intrigues with Augé against their daughter, Agnès Lebègue moves out of their apartment rue des Bernardins. That evening, Rétif brings Agnès from the Berthets' home to live with him and his younger daughter Marion.

December 2: Agnès and Rétif receive a police summons (*citation judiciaire*) after Augé files a formal complaint accusing her of leaving their home without his permission and Rétif of refusing to return her to him, along with a number of slanderous accusations (accusing Agnès of prostitution and Rétif of being her pimp). Rétif and Agnès work late into the night responding to the police summons and to Augé's accusations. This is the first draft of what would become their 'Mémoire contre Augé.'

December 3: Accompanied by her sister, Agnès answers the police summons. During her meeting with a police inspector, she describes Augé's mistreatment of her and shows the letter he wrote to her on July 23 in which he appears to consent to her decision to leave him. Later that day, Rétif goes to Legrand's office, hoping to meet with him to contest his son-in-law's slanderous accusations. Legrand absent, Rétif finds himself alone with Augé, with whom he has a brief but pointed exchange.

December 4: During the night of December 3rd to 4th, aided by Agnès, Rétif completes a first version of his 'Mémoire contre Augé,' which he inserts into diary entry ¶ 586 for 4 December.[301] In the novel, Rétif claims to have written the *mémoire* in mid-February. However, the fact that a first reference to it appears in early August 1785 shows that it was begun not in February 1786, but some five months earlier.

December 5: Rétif intercepts a note from Agnès to Blérie and intimidates the messenger into agreeing to give him any further correspondence between them.

December 6: Rétif sends his daughter Marion to deliver a reconciliation agreement ('Acte Satisfactoire') to Augé, in which he was to acknowledge his past

---

[300] The diary entry for that day reads: '*Agnès redita sero pat. et ferè potta*' (*Journal*, ¶565, vol. 1, p. 216). Testud interprets this to mean: 'Agnès returned this evening, accommodating and almost seduced' (n. 5 to p. 216). This is the first overt seduction attempt recorded in Rétif's diary.

[301] See Appendix D, Excerpt 8, in MHRA's French edition of *Ingénue Saxancour*.

mistreatment of Agnès and promise to treat her better in the future if she agrees to return to him.[302] However, instead of signing it, Augé launches into a slanderous diatribe against his father-in-law and violently assaults his sister-in-law. Furious at his son-in-law, Rétif sends Marion to the lieutenant de police's office to deliver his 'Mémoire contre Augé,' along with a shorter account of events written by Marion.[303]

December 9: Agnès and Marion file a complaint with police inspector Henri against Augé for his assault on Marion a few days earlier.

December 12: Rétif scolds Agnès for remaining in contact with Blérie and for giving him his only copy of his novel *Nouveaux mémoires d'un homme de qualité*.

December 18: Rétif learns of a love letter allegedly sent by Agnès to Blérie that Augé had forged in an effort to pressure the Rétifs to drop their police complaint against him for assaulting Marion and to persuade Agnès to return to him.

December 20: Rétif and Agnès angrily confront Augé at his office, where they persuade him to burn the counterfeit letter after discussing a possible reconciliation with him. A few days later, Agnès writes to her husband to say that she would rather die than ever return to him and reiterating her complaints against him.[304]

December 21: Rétif dines at the home of Le Pelletier along with Le Pelletier's secretary, the lawyer Legrand, for whom Augé works as a clerk. Legrand reveals that Augé had committed '*un abus de confiance*,' but Rétif does not reveal in his diary entry what that breach of trust entailed.

1786

January or February: Agnès sends a third response to Augé in response to his repeated entreaties for her to return to him.[305]

February 21: Augé accosts Agnès in the street on the Ile Saint-Louis where, to humiliate her, he has her arrested as a prostitute. She is taken to the local police station, where she lodges a complaint against her estranged husband for battery. Rétif accompanies his daughter and the police to the office of the local magistrate, where she makes a formal request for a separation. The magistrate grants her request to stay with her father until the court decides her case.

---

[302] See Appendix C, Excerpt 17, in MHRA's French edition of *Ingénue Saxancour*.
[303] See Appendix D, Excerpt 10, in MHRA's French edition of *Ingénue Saxancour*.
[304] See Appendix C, Excerpt 19, in MHRA's French edition of *Ingénue Saxancour*.
[305] See Appendix C, Excerpt 20, in MHRA's French edition of *Ingénue Saxancour*.

February 22: Agnès is accosted near city hall by Augé, who has her arrested again. The police release her and reprimand Augé for his false accusations. Rétif adds a summary of these incidents to his 'Mémoire contre Augé,' which Agnès takes two days later to her lawyer maître Cavagnac to use as evidence in her separation suit.

February 24: During a preliminary hearing of Agnès's separation suit, Augé launches into a slanderous rant against Rétif and quarrels angrily with Agnès. Shocked and annoyed, the magistrate grants Agnès permission to remain with her father until the next hearing scheduled for March 7.

February 27: Rétif meets with Augé's superiors Legrand and Le Pelletier to discuss his son-in-law's slanders against both of them and against himself. Augé is fired.

March 7: Agnès signs a separation agreement drawn up by the lawyers according to which Augé would not be required to pay alimony if he agreed to a separation.

March 18: Rétif begins writing a short story about Agnès's marriage and separation titled 'L'Epouse séparée,' completed in eighteen days and published later that year in *Les Françaises*. This was first version of what would later be expanded into his novel *Ingénue Saxancour* (published in 1789).

April 5: Rétif completes 'L'Epouse séparée.'

April 18: Rétif and his daughters dine at the home of le chevalier de Saint-Mars. In a brief reference to this dinner in his diary, Rétif mentions for the first time two people who were to play key roles in their lives: Félicité Mesnager (who was to become Agnès's close friend and Rétif's last great passion) and Louis Vignon (who later became Agnès's lover and eventually her second husband). In *Ingénue Saxancour*, Rétif gives May 5 as the date they first met Félicité.

May 23: Rétif completes the manuscript of *La Femme infidelle*, published later that month.

June 24: Rétif completes *Les Françaises*, a short story collection that includes two stories about his daughter's unhappy marriage and her liaison with Blérie.

May 25: Angered by news of the publication of *La Femme infidelle*, Augé follows Agnès to the Jardin des Plantes, where he slaps her as she strolls in the garden with her father and sister, along with Félicité and Mr. de Rosières. After de Rosières has Augé arrested, Augé launches into another tirade against his father-in-law, threatening to kill him and accusing him of incest and of prostituting his daughter.[306] Rétif goes to the police station on Ile St-Louis to file a formal complaint against Augé for his harassment and death threats.

---

[306] An unusually long diary entry for that day recounts this incident in great detail. See *Journal*, ¶735, vol. 1, pp. 307–8 and Appendix D, Excerpt 17, in MHRA's French edition of *Ingénue Saxancour*.

May 26: Rétif meets with Agnès's lawyer to discuss the events of the previous day. In his diary entry, he notes: 'met with the lawyer to tell him what happened yesterday. He approved the draft of my complaint; it's certain that the separation will be granted; my *mémoire* is sure to be compelling!' (*Journal*, ¶736, vol. 1, p. 309).

May 30: First reference in Rétif's diary to Madame Laruelle.[307]

June 3: Augé, who continues to stalk Agnès, accosts her as she and her father accompany Félicité home that evening.

June 8: Rétif begins writing the definitive version of *Ingénue Saxancour* (referred to in his diary as 'Femme séparée').

June 10: Rétif continues work on his 'Mémoire contre Augé.' A final reference to the *mémoire* appears in his diary entry for 25 February 1787.

June 24: Rétif completes a short story titled 'L'Epouse aimant un autre homme' about Agnès's liaison with Blérie. It would be published in November that year in the short story collection *Les Françaises*.

June 29: Agnès leaves with Félicité Mesnager for a four-month stay at her country home in Montfort-l'Amaury near Rambouillet.[308] After nearly completing the core version of *Ingénue Saxancour* (108 manuscript pages), Rétif interrupts work on the novel for nearly two years. Testud suggests that Rétif feared retaliation from Augé, given his angry reaction to the publication of *La Femme infidelle*.

July 2 and 8: Rétif takes walks with Madame Laruelle.

August 21: Rétif learns that Augé is trying to block the sale of *La Femme infidelle*.

---

[307] In his diary entry for 30 May 1786, Rétif notes: 'Mlle Londo and Madame Laruelle met me and spoke about me' (*Journal*, ¶740, vol. 1, p. 312). Other brief references to Madame Laruelle are found in the entries for June 14, 15, 18, 19, 23, 28 and July 2 and 8 of that year. This is significant since it was during this same period that Rétif began writing the definitive version of *Ingénue Saxancour* (begun 8 June 1786). In his autobiography, Rétif recalls at length his first conversation with Madame Laruelle. See Appendix B, Excerpt 6, in MHRA's French edition of *Ingénue Saxancour*.

[308] In *Monsieur Nicolas*, Rétif explains that Félicité's brother had recently bought a house and two farms in Montfort-l'Amaury from their mutual friend Saint-Mars. He also gives the reason for Agnès's extended visit with them: 'Prodiguer [Mesnager] the brother [...] left with his sister on 29 June, taking with them my older daughter whom they wanted to shield from harassment by her vile husband' (*Monsieur Nicolas*, 'Neuvième Epoque', *OC*, vol. 69, p. 3119). In his diary, Rétif also notes two other extended visits that Agnès paid to Félicité in Montfort-l'Amaury: a six-week stay in 1787 (from 28 July 28 to 8 October) and a three-month stay in 1788 (from 20 August to 1 December). See *Journal*, ¶1142, ¶1214, ¶1437, and ¶1541 (vol. 1, pp. 468, 493, 599, 632).

Fall: In an angry letter, François Marlin breaks off his friendship with Rétif after reading *La Femme infidelle*.[309]

November 3: Agnès returns from her stay with Félicité in Montfort-l'Amaury.

November 6: Rétif gives Madame Laruelle the proofs of his short story 'L'Epouse séparée,' which he later expands into his novel *Ingénue Saxancour*.

November: Publication of Rétif's short story collection *Les Françaises*, which includes 'L'Epouse séparée' (about Agnès's marriage and separation) and 'L'Epouse aimant un autre homme' (about Agnès's affair with Blérie).

1787

February 9: Augé goes to Montrouge, where he hopes to see Rétif's friend Mercier. Not finding him at home, Augé goes to the home of Pierre Le Tourneur, royal censor and secretary to the Count d'Artois, where he scandalizes Le Tourneur and his guests with his violent denunciations of Rétif and his daughter. On his way back to Paris, Augé meets the Viscount de Toustain-Richebourg, another of Rétif's friends, and flies into another violent tirade. News of both incidents eventually reach Rétif, who vows to punish his son-in-law by publishing the 'Mémoire contre Augé' detailing his mistreatment of Agnès and responding to his slanderous attacks. This judicial memoir served the dual purpose of obtaining a separation for Agnès and causing Augé to be fired from the job Rétif had secured for him.

February 16: Augé goes to the home of Louis-Sébastien Mercier, where he flies into a tirade against Rétif, who files a complaint against him at the police station on the Ile Saint-Louis.

February 18: After meeting with their lawyer Cavagnac, Rétif and Agnès file a police complaint against Augé.

February 19: Denounced by Rétif, Augé is fired from his position with Legrand, secretary to Le Pelletier.

February 25: Rétif completes the final version of the 'Mémoire contre Augé.'

March: After many months of suits, countersuits, complaints to the police, and court proceedings, Agnès finally obtains a separation from Augé. In his diary entry for March 18, Rétif writes: 'The monster Augé says that [...] I won my civil case, but that I'll lose my case in criminal court' (*Journal*, ¶1010, vol. 1, p. 432).

---

[309] See Appendix C, Excerpt 21, in MHRA's French edition of *Ingénue Saxancour*.

July 28: Agnès leaves her father's home in Paris for a ten-week visit with Félicité in Montfort-l'Amaury.

August 17: Rétif begins writing the *Lettres du tombeau*, which include the story of a father's incest with his two daughters, who both become pregnant by him. Their names are anagrams of the names of Rétif's daughters. The collection was not published until 1802 — a delay apparently due to opposition by government censors.

October 8: Agnès returns from her stay with Félicité in Montfort-l'Amaury to her father's home in Paris.[310]

December 19: Rétif attempts to seduce Agnès, but she again resists, as the following diary entry indicates: 'Did not succeed with Ag^s' (*Journal*, ¶ 1285, vol. 1, p. 523).

December 31: Rétif again attempts to seduce Agnès. In his diary entry, Rétif writes: 'failed with A^s, quarrel, tears' (*Journal*, ¶1296, vol. 1, p. 528).

1788

April 17: Rétif resumes work on *Ingénue Saxancour*, interrupted since late June 1786; the manuscript is completed in six days.

April 22: Rétif completes the final version of *Ingénue Saxancour*.

April 28: Coded entries in Rétif's diary indicate that, on this date, he and Agnès (who was then 27) began incestuous relations,[311] which continued off and on for five years.

May 14: Rétif delivers the recently completed manuscript of *Ingénue Saxancour* to the printer Maradan.

August 20: Agnès leaves to stay with Félicité Mesnager in Montfort-l'Amaury for three months.

---

[310] Rétif's diary indicates that Agnès left for Montfort/Saint-Léger on 28 July 1787 and that she returned on 8 October. See *Journal*, ¶1142 and ¶1214, vol. 1, pp. 468 and 493.

[311] The French text of Rétif's diary entry for that day reads '28 Ap. matin: cares[sé] Senga [...] le soir [...] persuadé Senga' [28 April morning: caressed Senga [...] persuaded Senga in the evening' (*Journal*, ¶1416, vol. 1, p. 564). The entry on the following day makes clear what this meant: 'f^u Senga' [foutu Senga]' [fucked Senga] (¶1417, vol. 1, p. 565). In his note to a later entry, Testud explains that when the name Senga (anagram for Agnès) appears in the *Journal*, it ordinarily has a sexual connotation (vol. 1, p. 632, n. 5).

September 14: Rétif begins composing the 'Supplément à la *Femme séparée*',[312] which he completes on 29 September and publishes immediately in volume 27 of the second edition of *Les Contemporaines*.

November 10: Following a dispute with his landlord, who (according to Rétif) wrongly accused Marion of stealing a watch from his apartment,[313] Rétif and Marion move from 10 rue des Bernardins to rue de la Bûcherie nearby, both near place Maubert.

Late November: Publication of *Ingénue Saxancour*.

December 1: Agnès returns from Montfort-l'Amaury to visit her father and sister in their new apartment.

Late December: Rétif breaks off his friendship with Félicité Mesnager after learning that she had thwarted his plan to marry his daughter Marion to the chevalier de Saint-Mars in the hope of marrying the chevalier herself.[314]

1789

January 19: Agnès leaves for an extended stay at the home of Michel-Jérôme Baragot, curé of the village of Champs near Soissons.[315]

---

[312] For extended excerpts from the 'Supplément à la *Femme séparée*', see Appendix E, Excerpt 3, in MHRA's French edition of *Ingénue Saxancour*.

[313] This incident is recounted in the first postscript to *Ingénue Saxancour* (included in this translation) and in greater detail in the 'Supplément à la *Femme séparée*.'

[314] According to Testud, 'the *Journal* does not specify the date of Rétif's break-up with Félicité, which no doubt occurred in late December, 1788. In his entry for December 14, Rétif notes that he had dinner with her. There is no mention of her after that' (*Monsieur Nicolas*, vol. 2, p. 1365, note 4 to p. 395). Ironically, in the 'Supplément à la *Femme séparée*', published that fall, Rétif had written a euphoric ending to *Ingénue Saxancour* in which he marries Félicité, Agnès/Ingénue marries her brother, and Marion marries St. Mars. See Appendix E, Excerpt 3, in MHRA's French edition of *Ingénue Saxancour*.

[315] Daniel Baruch speculates that Agnès's sudden departure for Champs and her eight-month absence may have been due to a pregnancy with Rétif's child that she and her father wished to conceal. See *Restif de La Bretonne* (Paris: Fayard, 1996), pp. 216–17. Agnès's stay near Soissons may have been arranged through Rétif's friend the writer and bibliographer Barthélemy Mercier, abbé de Saint-Léger (1734–1799), to whom Louis XV had granted the living (*bénéfice*) of the abbey of Soissons in 1767. It is unclear how long Agnès actually stayed near Soissons, since an entry in Rétif's diary on 2 July 1789 suggests that she was forced to leave Champs for some unnamed reason (perhaps due to her pregnancy or to the publication of *Ingénue Saxancour* or both): 'Letter from Agnès who cannot stay at Champs any longer' (*Journal*, ¶1754, vol. 1, p. 689). Subsequent entries in Rétif's diary suggest that Agnès may have stayed in Paris with Madame Duchesne, who was Rétif's principal bookseller from 1774 until 1802. See, for example, the entry for 21 August 1789: matin *Agneti*, rep. à la lettre du 19 chez mad. *Duch.*', which Testud interprets to mean 'wrote to Agnès this morning at Madame

June 11: Rétif's estranged wife Agnès Lebègue is arrested, but then released without charges after Augé falsely accuses her of prostituting her elder daughter.

June 22: Rétif learns that Marion is pregnant with his nephew Edmond's child.

July 14: Rétif is arrested following an accusation by Augé.

August-September: Rétif writes a series of angry open letters in which he denounces Augé's mistreatment of Agnès and his continued harassment of her and her family after she left him. These letters were later published in the *Thesmographe*.[316]

September 12: Agnès returns from Soissons to her father's apartment in Paris.

September 16: Augé sends a letter of complaint to Toustain-Richebourg, the censor who had approved publication of *Ingénue Saxancour* the previous fall.[317]

September 28: Augé denounces Rétif to the authorities, but without success.

October 1: Augé and several accomplices wait outside Rétif's apartment late at night, allegedly in an attempt to assassinate him, but the plot fails because he had already returned home.[318]

October 26: Augé circulates a virulent pamphlet accusing his father-in-law of having published scabrous and libelous books (*La Femme infidelle* and *Ingénue Saxancour*, among others), as well as subversive political pamphlets.[319]

Duchesne's bookshop in response to a letter received on the 19th' (*Journal*, ¶1799, vol. 1, p. 703, n. 3). On 23 July 1789, Rétif writes: 'Duchesne: douleur' ['Duchesne: grief/pain?'] — a possible reference to the birth or death of a baby or putting the child up for adoption (*Journal*, ¶1772, vol. 1, p. 697). There are frequent references to Madame Duchesne in the diary entries for July 1789, but perhaps Rétif's visits to her were simply for business. Or perhaps her address served only as a conduit for his correspondence with Agnès during her absence, in order to avoid discovery by Augé?

[316] *Le Thesmographe ou Idées d'un honnête-homme sur un projet de réglement* [1789], repr. in *OC*, vol. 110, pp. 482–501. See Appendix C, Excerpts 25 and 26, in MHRA's French edition of *Ingénue Saxancour*.

[317] See Appendix C, Excerpt 24, in MHRA's French edition of *Ingénue Saxancour*.

[318] In a postscript to *Le Thesmographe* dated 2 October 1789, Rétif writes: 'I'm denouncing L'Echiné's latest offense. Yesterday at 11:00 at night, the scoundrel came to wait for me in my deserted street. But since I had already returned home, he grew impatient. A neighbor on the second floor was at his window. The monster asked him if I was home. — I don't know, he replied. — I'm here because I want him to return my wife to me. […] The neighbor went down to the street where he found a man with a dark complexion who said he was waiting for me so he could stab me or blow my brains out. He had several accomplices with him' (*Le Thesmographe*, p. 501).

[319] 'Dénonciation d'un beau-père par son gendre calomniateur', repr. in *Nuits de Paris*, *OC*, vol. 86, pp. 199–200, 202. Augé's text is preceded by Rétif's summary of his son-in-law's life and crimes (193–98) and followed by his denial of Augé's accusations (201, 203–237). David

October 28: Returning home at 10:30 PM, Rétif is arrested and held by the police until the morning of October 30, following Augé's accusation three days earlier. After Rétif succeeds in proving his innocence, Augé is charged with false accusations and detained for several days (November 1–3).

Early November: Following the events of October 29, Rétif writes and circulates the *Dénonciation contr'un beau-père par son gendre calomniateur*, which includes Augé's charges against him, followed by Rétif's responses to the charges and the official record of proceedings (reprinted the following February in *Nuits de Paris*).[320]

November 23: Agnès accompanies the ailing Madame Laruelle to her country home in Villabé, 23 miles (39 km) south of Paris.[321]

1790

February 17: Publication of Rétif's *Procès-verbal du district pour admettre la délation d'Augé*, the transcript of Augé's accusations and the hearing that followed.[322]

February 22: At her home in Villabé, Madame Laruelle dies of tuberculosis in Agnès's arms.

March 17: Agnès returns from Villabé to her father's apartment.

June 12: Agnès departs to stay with unnamed friends (perhaps the Nanteuils) until 3 July.

Late fall: Agnès leaves her father's home to stay with Madame Nanteuil, an old friend, in order to escape harassment from Augé.[323]

Coward convincingly argues that Augé's hatred of his father-in-law stemmed from jealousy and suspicions of less than innocent father-daughter relations — suspicions that intensified in 1788 after he appears to have learned through servants of Rétif's incestuous relations with Agnès. See Coward, *The Philosophy of Restif de La Bretonne* (Oxford, UK: Voltaire Foundation, 1991), p. 757, n. 36.

[320] See excerpts from Augé's denunciation and Rétif's response in Appendix C, Excerpts 27 and 28, in MHRA's French edition of *Ingénue Saxancour*.

[321] Baruch speculates that Agnès's stay served a double purpose: to help care for her friend during the final stages of tuberculosis, while at the same time rescuing her from Augé's importunities — and perhaps as well from her father's persistent sexual advances. See Baruch, *Restif de La Bretonne* (1996), p. 228.

[322] Rétif published the transcript of Augé's accusations and the hearing that followed in the 'Huitième Nuit' of *Nuits de Paris*, OC, vol. 86, pp. 207–33. Rétif no doubt did this in order to discredit Augé and to justify himself, as Testud has suggested (*Journal*, vol. 1, p. 729, n. 5).

[323] This according to David Coward, *Philosophy of Restif de La Bretonne*, p. 756.

1791

January 31: Rétif receives a letter from Agnès that Augé, informed perhaps by Madame Nanteuil, had discovered her hiding place at the Nanteuils' home and had come there with two friends to harass her.

February 1: Agnès leaves Madame Nanteuil's home and returns to her father's apartment in Paris.

May 21: Rétif's younger daughter Marion marries her first cousin Edme-Etienne Rétif, son of Nicolas's younger brother Pierre. They already have a daughter together and are expecting a second child. Rétif did not learn of their marriage until 16 June.[324]

May 29: Rétif receives a letter from Grimod de La Reynière in which he presents his aunt Beausset's criticisms of *Ingénue Saxancour*, criticisms with which he strongly agrees.[325]

July 7: Letter from La Reynière to Rétif in which, responding to his friend's attempts to justify publishing *Ingénue Saxancour*, he again criticizes the scandalous aspects of the novel and questions his friend's motives for publishing it.[326]

1792

September 20: The French legislature adopts its first divorce law, the most liberal in the world at the time. Rétif rejoices at the news.

October 12: Rétif sends a letter to La Reynière in which he breaks off their friendship, citing their political differences over the Revolution, which La Reynière vehemently opposes.

1793

February: Agnès begins a liaison with Louis-Claude Vignon, ten years her junior, whom she first met in April 1786 at the home of the chevalier de Saint-Mars.

---

[324] Testud speculates that Restif was as opposed to Marion's marriage as he was to Agnès's: 'The *Journal* does not mention anything about her marriage in the entry for May 21, but the entry for June 16 includes this exclamation: "Marion married!" From this, we may conclude that Marion, who was then about 27 years old, hid her marriage from her father and that he learned of it only two months later. This shows how strongly Rétif opposed the marriage' (Testud, 'Repères biographiques', in *Journal*, vol. 1, p. 836).

[325] See Appendix C, Excerpt 30, in MHRA's French edition of *Ingénue Saxancour*.

[326] See Appendix C, Excerpt 31, in MHRA's French edition of *Ingénue Saxancour*.

July 10: With her father's help, Agnès initiates a divorce suit against Augé.[327]

Mid-November: Agnès conceives a child with Vignon.

1794

January 16: The court grants a divorce to Rétif and his wife Agnès Lebègue. The couple had been separated more or less continuously since 1773.[328]

February 5: Agnès's divorce from Augé is finalized on the grounds of incompatibility.[329]

February 7: Agnès leaves her father's home to live with Vignon, who would later become her second husband.

July: Marion's 24-year-old husband Edme dies of tuberculosis, leaving her with three small children.

August 17: Birth of Frédéric-Victor Vignon, son of Agnès Rétif and Louis-Claude-Victor Vignon, whom she marries four years later in 1798.

1795

January 6: Augé marries his third wife, Jeanne Catherine Fournier.

1796

June 12: Rétif's diary ends abruptly, raising the question whether subsequent notebooks may have existed and been lost or else destroyed after his death by family, friends, or government censors.

---

[327] In *Monsieur Nicolas*, Rétif confuses the dates of Agnès's divorce petition in July 1793 with the granting of her divorce in February 1794: 'In 1793, my daughter Agnès R. left my home. She had asked for and obtained a divorce a few months earlier' (*Monsieur Nicolas*, 'Neuvième Epoque', *OC*, vol. 69, p. 3217). In his notes to his edition of Rétif's diary, Testud points to Rétif's error: 'Contrary to what Rétif wrote in *Monsieur Nicolas*, [...], we see here that he was confusing the suit for separation with its granting by the court' (*Journal*, ¶3372, vol. 2, p. 324, n. 9).

[328] In his diary entry for 13 January, Rétif notes: 'the paperwork for our divorce is nearly complete.' Then on 16 January, he reports: 'All the paperwork is signed' (*Journal*, ¶3349 and ¶3352, vol. 2, pp. 320–21).

[329] Rétif's diary entry for 4 February 1794 reads: 'divce prononcé' [divorce granted] and the following day, the entry reads: 'fini div^ce Agn^s son acte' [decree for Agnès's divorce issued] (*Journal*, ¶3371 and ¶3372, vol. 2, p. 324).

1797

Late September: The final volume of *Monsieur Nicolas* is printed. Printing of the first volume had begun four years earlier (in May 1793).

Late fall: *Monsieur Nicolas* is released to the public.

1798

November 10: Agnès marries Louis-Claude-Victor Vignon, her companion since February 1793 and father of her second surviving child (born August 1794).

1806

February 3: Death of Rétif at the age of 72.

1808

August 29: Death of Rétif's ex-wife Agnès Lebègue at her elder daughter's home in Paris.

Post-1810

Death of Charles-Marie Augé, Agnès Rétif's first husband. The exact date is unknown.[330]

1812

June 21: Death of Agnès Rétif at age 51, leaving two sons: Jean-Nicolas Augé, a printer, and Frédéric-Victor Vignon, a writer.

1856

August 20: Death of Frédéric-Victor Vignon, son of Agnès Rétif and Louis-Claude-Victor Vignon. Agnès's older son Jean-Nicolas Augé died sometime after 1855; the exact date is unknown.

---

[330] In the introduction to his 2002 edition of *Ingénue Saxancour*, Baruch notes that, in 1810, Augé was still employed as a tax-collector (contrôleur des Contributions) in Saint-Jean-de-Maurienne in Savoie. See Baruch, *Restif de La Bretonne* (2002), p. 468.

BIBLIOGRAPHY

∼

Selected Works by Rétif de La Bretonne

Note: The Slatkine reprint edition of Rétif's complete works (published in 1987–1988) comprises 117 volumes. Nearly the entire edition is available on-line through the Bibliothèque Nationale's catalogue (http://catalogue.bnf.fr), which lists the series title as *Oeuvres complètes* (instead of using the more common spelling *Œuvres*).

Les Contemporaines, 17 vols [1780–84], in *Œuvres complètes* (Geneva: Slatkine, 1988), vols 12–32

La Dernière Avanture d'un homme de quarante-cinq ans [1783], in *Œuvres complètes* (Geneva: Slatkine, 1988), vol. 35

Le Drame de la vie, 3 vols [1793], in *Œuvres complètes* (Geneva: Slatkine, 1988), vols 36–38

La Femme infidelle, 2 vols [1786], in *Œuvres complètes* (Geneva: Slatkine, 1988), vols 44–45

Ingénue Saxancour, ou La Femme séparée, 2 vols [1788], in *Œuvres complètes* (Geneva: Slatkine, 1988), vols 54–55

Journal: Volume II, 1790–1796, ed. by Pierre Testud (Paris: Editions Manucius, 2010)

Mes Inscripcions (1779–1785); Journal (1785–1789), ed. by Pierre Testud (Paris: Editions Manucius, 2006)

Mes Inscripcions: Journal Intime de Restif de La Bretonne, ed. by Paul Cottin (Paris: Plon, 1889; repr. in *Œuvres complètes*, Geneva: Slatkine Reprints, 1988), vol. 56

Monsieur Nicolas, ou le cœur humain dévoilé [1788–96], 2 vols, ed. by Pierre Testud (Paris: Gallimard, 1989) [Critical edition with extensive notes and background material on Rétif's life and works]

Monsieur Nicolas, ou le cœur humain dévoilé [1788–96], repr. in *Œuvres complètes*, 8 vols (Geneva: Slatkine Reprints, 1988), vols 64–71

Nuits de Paris, ou le Spectateur nocturne, 8 vols [1788–1794], in *Œuvres complètes* (Geneva: Slatkine, 1987), vols 79–86

Le Paysan perverti, ou les Dangers de la ville, 4 vols [1775], in *Œuvres complètes* (Geneva: Slatkine, 1987), vols 95–96

La Paysanne pervertie, ou les Dangers de la ville, 4 vols [1784], in Œuvres *complètes* (Geneva: Slatkine, 1988), vols 97–98

'Supplément à la *Femme séparée*', in *Les Contemporaines*, 2nd edn, vol. 27 [1788], in Œuvres *complètes* (Geneva: Slatkine, 1988), vol. 25, pp. 304–39

Le Thesmographe ou Idées d'un honnête-homme sur un projet de règlement proposé à toutes les nations de l'Europe pour opérer une réforme générale des loix, avec des notes historiques [1789], in Œuvres *complètes* (Geneva: Slatkine, 1988), vol. 110

La Vie de mon père [1779], in Œuvres *complètes* (Geneva: Slatkine, 1988), vol. 113

Suggestions for Further Reading

BARUCH, DANIEL, 'L'Indagateur et la marquise: Enquête sur l'activité policière de Restif', *Etudes rétiviennes*, 6 (Sept. 1987), 73–87

——, 'Introduction' and 'Postface' to Alexandre Dumas, *Ingénue: Un amour interdit de Restif de La Bretonne* [1853–54] (Paris: Editions François Bourin, 1990), pp. 7–17, 543–55

——, 'Notice' [Introduction to his 2002 edition of *La Femme infidelle*], in *Restif de La Bretonne*, 2 vols, ed. by Daniel Baruch and Pierre Testud (Paris: R. Laffont, 2002), vol. 2, pp. 175–82

——, 'Notice' [Introduction to his 2002 edition of *Ingénue Saxancour*], in *Restif de La Bretonne*, 2 vols, ed. by Daniel Baruch and Pierre Testud (Paris: R. Laffont, 2002), vol. 2, pp. 465–71

——, 'Postface: Histoire et Métamorphoses de la Véritable *Ingénue*', in Alexandre Dumas, *Ingénue: Un amour interdit de Restif de La Bretonne* [1853–54] (Paris: Editions François Bourin, 1990, pp. 543–55

——, *Restif de La Bretonne* (Paris: Fayard, 1996) [Biography]

——, 'Restif de La Bretonne et l'inceste' and 'Dossier' (Paris: Union générale des éditions, 1978), pp. 9–21, 431–43 [introduction and appendix to Baruch's 1978 edition of *Ingénue Saxancour*]

BLOOM, RORI, 'Privacy, Publicity, Pornography: Restif de La Bretonne's *Ingénue Saxancour, ou La Femme séparée*', *Eighteenth-Century Fiction*, 17.2 (January, 2005), 231–52

BRAHIMI, D., 'Restif féministe? Etude de quelques *Contemporaines*', *Etudes sur le XVIIIe siècle*, 3 (1976), 77–91

BRETONNIÈRE-FRAYSSE, ANNE et al., *De la Violence conjugale à la violence parentale: Femmes en détresse, enfants en souffrance* (Ramonville-Saint-Agne, France: Erès, 2001)

BRUIT, GUY, 'Rétif de La Bretonne et les femmes', *La Pensée*, 131 (1967), 125–37

CHILDS, JAMES RIVES, *Restif de La Bretonne: Témoignages et Jugements. Bibliographie* (Paris: Librairie Briffaut, 1949)

COTTIN, PAUL. 'Préface', *Mes Inscriptions. Journal Intime de Restif de La Bretonne* (Paris: Plon, 1889), pp. i–cxxv

COWARD, DAVID, *The Philosophy of Restif de La Bretonne* (Oxford, UK: Voltaire Foundation, 1991), in the series *Studies on Voltaire and the Eighteenth Century*, vol. 283

——, 'Rétif critique de Sade', *Etudes rétiviennes*, 10 (1989), 73–86

——, 'The Sublimations of a Fetishist: Restif de La Bretonne', in *'Tis Nature's Fault: Unauthorized Sexual Behavior during the Enlightenment*, ed. by R. P. Maccubbin (Cambridge University Press, 1988), pp. 98–108

CUBIÈRES-PALMÉZEAUX, MICHEL DE, 'Notice historique et critique sur la vie et les ouvrages de Nicolas-Edme Restif de La Bretonne', in *Histoire des Compagnes de Maria*, 3 vols, ed. by Cubières-Palmézeaux (Paris, 1811, vol. 1), pp. 1–200 [Posthumous collection of stories drawn from Restif's unpublished manuscripts]; abridged 'Notice' repr. in *Bibliographie et iconographie de tous les ouvrages de Restif de La Bretonne*, ed. by Paul Lacroix (Paris: Fontaine, 1875), pp. 1–75

DUMAS, ALEXANDRE, *Ingénue: Un amour interdit de Restif de La Bretonne* [1853–54], introduction and notes by Daniel Baruch (Paris: Editions François Bourin, 1990)

FLETCHER, DENNIS, 'Restif de La Bretonne and Woman's Estate', in *Woman and Society in Eighteenth-Century France*, ed. by Eva Jacobs and others (London: Athlone Press, 1979), pp. 96–109

GARBOUIJ, BÉCHIR, 'Rétif conteur: L'Utopie, l'inceste, l'histoire', in *Frontières du conte* (Paris: Editions du C.N.R.S., 1982), pp. 103–10

HERRERO, ISABEL, '*Ingénue Saxancour* de Restif de La Bretonne, ou l'ambiguité du point de vue', *Études rétiviennes*, 13 (December 1990), 21–40

HOURIEZ, FRANK, 'Collage et coherence dans *Ingénue Saxancour*', *Études rétiviennes*, 15 (December 1991), 15–30

HUE, GUSTAVE, 'La Famille de Restif de La Bretonne', *Mercure de France* (16 May 1910), 206–27

JOLY, RAYMOND, *Deux Etudes sur la préhistoire du réalisme: Diderot, Rétif de la Bretonnne* (Quebec: Presses de l'Université de Laval, 1969), esp. pp. 128–68

LACROIX, PAUL [pseudonym P. L. Jacob], *Bibliographie et iconographie de tous les ouvrages de Restif de La Bretonne* (Paris: Fontaine, 1875) [Includes a preface by Lacroix (pp. i–xv) and an abridged version of Cubières-Palmézeaux's 'Notice historique et critique sur la vie et les ouvrages de Nicolas-Edme Restif de La Bretonne,' pp. 1–75]

LAFARGE, CATHERINE, 'Exemples de violence dans *La Paysanne pervertie*,' *Etudes rétiviennes*, 31 (December 1999), 181–90 [On depictions of violence in Binet's illustrations for the novel]

LELY, GILBERT, 'Introduction', *Ingénue Saxancour ou La Femme séparée*, ed. by Gilbert Lely (Paris: Lattès, 1979), pp. 5–26

MONSELET, CHARLES, *Rétif de La Bretonne, sa vie et ses amours: Documents inédits, ses malheurs, sa vieillesse et sa vie* [1854] (Paris: Aubry, 1858)

NERVAL, GÉRARD DE, 'Les Confidences de Nicolas', in *Les Illuminés: Récits et portraits* (Paris: V. Lecou, 1852), pp. 77–242

PORTER, CHARLES, *Restif's Novels: Or, An Autobiography in Search of an Author* (New Haven: Yale University Press, 1967)

RIVAL, NED, *Rétif de La Bretonne ou Les amours perverties* (Paris: Librairie Académique Perrin, 1982)

RIZZIO, TRACEY, 'Sexual Violence in the Enlightenment: The State, the Bourgeoisie, and the Cult of the Victimized Woman', *Proceedings of the Western Society for French History*, 15 (1988), 122–29

TABARANT, ADOLPHE, *Le Vrai Visage de Restif de La Bretonne* (Paris: Eds. Montaigne, 1936)

TESTUD, PIERRE, 'Autobiographie et histoire dans l'œuvre de Restif de La Bretonne', in *Le Siècle de Voltaire: Hommage à Pené Pomeau*, ed. by Christiane Mervaud and Sylvain Menant, 2 vols (Oxford: Voltaire Foundation, 1987), vol. 2, pp. 893–903

——, 'Le *Journal* inédit de Restif de La Bretonne', *Studies on Voltaire and the Eighteenth Century*, 90 (1972), 1567–93

——, *Rétif de La Bretonne et la création littéraire* (Geneva: Droz, 1977)

——, 'Rétif et Sade', *Revue des sciences humaines* 212 (Oct.–Dec. 1988), 107–23 [Special issue on Rétif ed. by Jean M. Goulemot]

TROUILLE, MARY S., French edition of Rétif de La Bretonne's 1789 novel *Ingénue Saxancour*, accompanied by introductions to the text and author, footnotes, appendices, 27 period illustrations, and selected bibliography (London: Modern Humanities Research Association, Critical Texts Series, 2014)

——, 'La violence conjugale et la dysfonction familiale dans *Ingénue Saxancour* de Rétif de La Bretonne', *Etudes rétiviennes*, 43 (December 2012), 143–71

——, *Wife-Abuse in Eighteenth-Century France* (Oxford, UK: Voltaire Foundation, 2009), in the series *Studies on Voltaire and the Eighteenth Century*. See the following chapters:

'Introduction: Scorned, battered, and bruised: Marriage and wife-abuse in eighteenth-century French fiction and society', pp. 1–12

Chapter 1: 'Moderate correction, rule of thumb: The Norms of spousal abuse in eighteenth-century France', pp. 15–56

Chapter 9: 'Truth stranger than fiction: Wife-abuse in Rétif de La Bretonne's *Ingénue Saxancour*', pp. 273–307

WAGSTAFF, PETER, *Memory and Desire: Rétif de La Bretonne, Autobiography and Utopia* (Amsterdam and Atlanta: Rodopi, 1996)

WYNGAARD, AMY S., *Bad Books: Rétif de La Bretonne, Sexuality, and Pornography* (Newark, DE: University of Delaware Press, 2012)

——, 'Rétif, Sade, and the Origins of Pornography: *Le Pornographe* as Anti-Text of *La Philosophie dans le boudoir*', *Eighteenth-Century Fiction*, 25.2 (Winter 2012–13), 383–406

MHRA New Translations

The guiding principle of this series is to publish new translations into English of important works that have been hitherto imperfectly translated or that are entirely untranslated. The work to be translated or re-translated should be aesthetically or intellectually important. The proposal should cover such issues as copyright and, where relevant, an account of the faults of the previous translation/s; it should be accompanied by independent statements from two experts in the field attesting to the significance of the original work (in cases where this is not obvious) and to the desirability of a new or renewed translation.

Translations should be accompanied by a fairly substantial introduction and other, briefer, apparatus: a note on the translation; a select bibliography; a chronology of the author's life and works; and notes to the text.

Titles will be selected by members of the Editorial Board and edited by leading academics.

Andrew Counter
General Editor

Editorial Board

Professor Malcolm Cook (French)
Dr Andrew Counter (French)
Professor Ritchie Robertson (Germanic)
Dr Mark Davie (Italian)
Dr Stephen Parkinson (Portuguese)
Professor David Gillespie (Slavonic)
Dr Duncan Wheeler (Spanish)
Professor Jonathan Thacker (Spanish)

For details of how to order please visit our website at:
www.translations.mhra.org.uk

www.ingramcontent.com/pod-product-compliance
Lightning Source LLC
Chambersburg PA
CBHW072354030726
47505CB00014B/1813